CW01033336

Love, Sex & Frankenstein

'An enthralling read. Beautifully written, this story of a woman's
rage and her discovery of writing as an outlet is gripping'
Jennie Godfrey, author of *The List of Suspicious Things*

'Utterly compelling and immersive. I was hooked from the first page
and looked forward to every moment I could spend with this stunning
novel. Hauntingly beautiful, dangerous and magnificent, the isolated villa
on Lake Geneva and the wild storms which battered it held me captive,
as I witnessed Mary Shelley's transformation from lovesick teenager to
a fiercely feminist young. In short: I have been altered by this novel'
Anya Bergman, author of *The Witches of Vardo*

'A magnificent book – raw, rage-filled and wondrous.
A crackling, passionate story about Mary Shelley
and the monsters we suppress. I loved it'
Anna Mazzola, author of *The House of Whispers*

'Richly woven, gorgeously addictive, this is a *true* Gothic novel about
life, death, desire, fury and passion. Conjuring the transformation
that comes when we look into the dark shadows of the soul and
acknowledge the longing that resides there, I absolutely loved this novel'
Joanne Burn, author of *The Bone Hunters*

'Beautifully written and wonderfully intense, this is no glamorous
story of the rock star poets and their female muses but a
rendition of absolute powerlessness turned around through sheer
force of will. Lea throws light onto the true brilliance of Mary
Wollstonecraft Shelley, a girl raised to believe in freedom who
would live out her beliefs against all the odds. A thrilling read'
Elizabeth Fremantle, author of *Disobedient*

'An astonishing, spectacular masterpiece. Mary Shelley's battle to
find her own voice becomes, in Caroline's hands, about loving
the monster inside us all and the freedom that can bring'
Julie Owen-Moylan, author of *73 Dove Street*

'An exquisitely written Gothic thriller that captures the horror and romance of the life of Mary Shelley and the circumstances that gave birth to *Frankenstein*. Lea shows how Mary Shelley finds her strength and anger to create new life, bringing the past alive with sensitive insight. Wonderful'
Laura Shepperson, author of *The Heroines*

'An intoxicating tale about the monsters suppressed inside us. Fury and passion, obsession and revenge sizzle beneath the surface – what a firecracker of a story'
Fiza Saeed McLynn, author of *The Midnight Carousel*

'Nothing short of astonishing. A powerful, brutal and exquisitely crafted story of women's rage, will and passion. You will never think about *Frankenstein* the same way again'
Kim Curran, author of *The Morrigan*

'The best rendition of Mary Shelley to be found in a novel. Here is a glorious story of female awakening and rage. Brava'
Essie Fox, author of *The Fascination*

'A deliciously dark reimagining of the birth of literature's greatest monster, *Love, Sex & Frankenstein* is at once a heartbreaking Gothic love story and a chilling study of rage, betrayal and the mysterious origins of the creative impulse. A triumph'
Emma Stonex, author of *The Lamplighters*

'Lea creates a world that is so vividly realised, it is astonishing to read. All her characters are wonderfully nuanced, and you cannot help but fall in love with Mary, whose journey as an artist and as a woman is both absolutely heartbreaking and truly inspiring. This is a deeply moving, magical book from a consummate storyteller'
Elodie Harper, author of *The Wolf Den*

'A powerful examination of desire, and of an awakening – driven by the fury and resolve of one woman as she begins to understand how she must live. A passionate, propulsive read'
Sarah Marsh, author of *A Sign of Her Own*

Love, Sex & Frankenstein

CAROLINE LEA

MICHAEL  JOSEPH

PENGUIN BOOKS

UK | USA | Canada | Ireland | Australia
India | New Zealand | South Africa

Penguin Books is part of the Penguin Random House group of companies
whose addresses can be found at global.penguinrandomhouse.com

Penguin Random House UK,
One Embassy Gardens, 8 Viaduct Gardens, London SW11 7BW

penguin.co.uk

Penguin
Random House
UK

First published 2025
001
Copyright © Caroline Lea, 2025

The moral right of the author has been asserted

Set in Garamond MT
Typeset by Falcon Oast Graphic Art Ltd
Printed and bound in Great Britain by Clays Ltd, Elcograf S.p.A.

The authorized representative in the EEA is Penguin Random House Ireland,
Morrison Chambers, 32 Nassau Street, Dublin D02 YH68

A CIP catalogue record for this book is available from the British Library

HARDBACK ISBN: 978-0-241-49301-4
TRADE PAPERBACK ISBN: 978-0-241-49303-8

Penguin Random House is committed to a sustainable
future for our business, our readers and our planet. This book is
made from Forest Stewardship Council® certified paper

As always, for Arthur and Rupert and Roger,
with all of my love and a little of my rage.

Dear Reader,

You are eighteen years old. Cast out by your father, shunned by society, you have fled to Geneva with your lover and your sister. The closeness of their relationship makes you furious, but if you protest, your lover will abandon you. Confined by terrible storms, you find yourself in a house with your lover, your sister and Lord Byron, an infamous and magnetically attractive poet. You know he is dangerous, but you find yourself drawn to him. When he sets a challenge to write a ghost story, all the turmoil that has boiled within you finds a voice.

The anger pours from your pen in a roar of rage. Even as the monster that emerges terrifies you, you understand that it belongs to you. This creature that crawls across the page is the woman you were always meant to be. And in Byron, this furious beast that you have kept hidden for so long may have found a mate. You are eighteen years old. The creature you have created will howl its way onto page and stage and screen, burning its path across history in its desire to be seen, to be known, to be loved. The monster will never be silenced. Neither will you.

This story of Mary, her fury and her monster emerged from me in my own roar of rage. Who hasn't felt the pressure to be good and agreeable? Haven't you, too, been confined by the thought that only a certain part of you is lovable? The rest — the darkest, most monstrous part — must be hidden. Mary Shelley's rejected creature lives within all of us. This book unleashes it. Mary's story poured from me with a raw and urgent anger. Love, Sex & Frankenstein *is about love, longing, and the desperate desire to speak up, to speak out, and to have your heart heard.*

I hope your heart is heard.

Thank you for reading,

Caroline Lea
March 2025

Prologue

Geneva, 1816

At dusk, the sky over Lake Geneva is the colour of blood in a glass of water. The ash fragments falling over the city form a strange fog – a thickening of the air, which swirls through the deserted streets, past the spire of the old cathedral and over the walls of the new Protestant church. Inside, people are on their knees, praying for the uncanny cloud to lift. It is a judgement, they fear, a punishment from God, or else a curse.

This night, like so many before it, the choking dust has driven the residents of the city into the shelter of shuttered houses and places of prayer. Outside, there is no one to witness the way the ash gleams as it settles on the lake. The water flickers and shimmers, each tiny filament glowing like a candle, sinking into the silence, quickly snuffed out.

The lake is chill and dark and deep – not even the fishermen have fathomed its depths, or the small children who, on any other evening, would be taking turns to dive beneath the surface, competing to see who could swim down the furthest, stay under the longest.

No one is standing on the lake's stony shores to watch the water's surface glow, red as the strange sky above. No one is there to see the darkness beneath the water shift and stir and coalesce, parting for a breath, like two slick thighs, which fall back into the darkness with a gasp that is almost human.

*

Above, half masked by cloud, a thin slash of moon hangs hazy and indifferent. A lone figure stumbles down to the lake and scrambles into a small rowboat that one of the fishermen has left bobbing at the end of a long line. Looking right, then left, the man leans forward over the rope. Flash of steel from the blade in his hand. A quick tug and the boat is free. The man settles himself on the rocking boards, tugging the oars. No one will see him on this cloud-deadened, mist-muffled night. No one will stop him. Still, his breath stutters and stumbles. He must be quick. His hands ache, his chest burns. His eyes feel gritty as the mist parts before him, then closes around him, giving him the strange sensation of being swallowed.

He is a poor rower, the boat's progress weaving and uneven until, gasping, the man drops the oars and lies back, gazing up at the darkening sky, at the hazed half-smile of the moon. And beyond, the smothered light of the stars, like muted bells, calling to no one.

Later, they will say that Karl Vogel – who was young and handsome and had been popular once – was drunk and that was why he'd taken Matthieu Favre's boat, or that he'd intended to play a prank, then fallen asleep. They will say that he jumped into the water, that he tried to swim to shore and grew tired. They will whisper that perhaps he'd gone mad, at last, this lonely man who was only twenty-five but had borne enough grief for double that number of years. He'd lost his wife and two children to cholera the previous spring; perhaps he'd decided he couldn't go on. Grief takes some people that way.

All the same, they will say how strange it is, early the next morning, when his clothes are found in the beached boat, laid out exactly as he would have worn them – tattered shirt inside dirty sweater; the sweater inside the regimental red coat with the ragged yellow trim that he had worn proudly every day, though Napoleon's war has been over for more than a year. Karl Vogel's clothes are dry and unmarked – unremarkable, except that Karl Vogel is nowhere to be found.

Listen to the beat, the drumming of feet down the cobbled streets, through the forest paths, past the rust of last year's bracken, over the stones to the shore of the lake.

The body barely shifts in the shallows; no one moves to pull it from the water. The once-handsome face is pale-skinned and blue-lipped, as though carved from a rare and expensive marble, but this is not why the people have stopped, why they put their hands to their mouths, then turn away in confusion.

Certainly it is Karl Vogel – it must be him, for there are his muscular calves, see his narrow shoulders, note the shape of his hands, his fingers smooth from the past year spent indoors drowning his grief in bad wine – and, besides, who else could it be? And yet, where Karl Vogel's eyes had been a deep brown, this man's are marbled blue. Is it a reaction to the water? The eyes, which look nothing like Karl's, stare up at the sky, where that strange mist still lingers and where, every evening, the set- ting sun paints the sky an unholy red. The lake plays tricks on people – in certain lights, it is possible to see whole cities float- ing above the water. Spires and turrets, which have no place in Geneva, can be seen rising from the lake, but when fisher- men row out to investigate, the strange buildings vanish. Some believe it is the ghost of a drowned city that will one day emerge again from the water. Others think that the odd visions are glimpses of the future – a shadow of something still to come.

It is late May, the tail-end of spring. In any other year, warm wet days would give way to a stretch of sun-soaked evenings, but this year, the air is bitter, the sky shrouded in the strange mist no one can explain.

Beneath the funeral lace of leafless trees, three travellers wend their way across the hills overlooking the lake, cloaked and hooded against the griping cold and biting breeze. Skeins of smoke – or what looks like smoke – spiral through the air. Instead of the gleaming lake the travellers had expected, the water is almost obscured. They cannot yet see the group of people crowding around the body on the lakeshore. They can't hear the cries of shock and confusion.

Instead, the city seems entirely grey and silent, as though torn from an artist's sketchbook. Instead, as eighteen-year-old Mary Shelley squints through the stinging, gritty fog – at the beginning of summer – it starts to snow.

PART ONE
London

I

Nothing is so painful to the human mind as a great and sudden change.
Mary Wollstonecraft Shelley, *Frankenstein*

Three weeks earlier

Dawn in London. Low-hanging clouds, stained a strange pink. In this gauzy light, the streets are quiet as a held breath. Beggars doze in doorways or shelter under archways. Women wearing low-cut dresses and carefully assembled smiles retire to their rooms for a few hours of blissful solitude. The gentry and nobility are tucked into their beds in the new townhouses, which overlook the green squares of Mayfair. Dukes and duchesses snore while their scullery-maids light fires and their cooks load the oven with sweetened dough and dishes of lamb and capon for dinner.

Two bailiffs stride along Old Bethlem Street without turning their eyes to the oyster shops and butchers'. They step around beggars and over mounds of horse and pig muck, without once breaking their stride. The older man has spent the night at a tavern, drowning any doubts about what they are about to do; occasionally he staggers sideways. Once, he slips on a smear of manure and curses. The younger man is jumpy and red-eyed from lack of sleep. They carry wooden batons, the ends stained a dark ochre. The drunken man wears a belt; in it is a blade. He has told himself he will not touch it, that it's just for show.

The two men are accustomed to uncomfortable work: bashing skulls and smashing kneecaps at home is preferable to marching for days and risking death in a foreign field. They've been collecting debts since they were sent home injured from Waterloo last summer – it had been the younger man's first and last battle.

War-hardened though they might be, this particular task on this particular day is something both men tried to refuse. Harming women and children is a job for cowards and scoundrels.

But everything is more expensive in this dark year, when the ice of winter just will not pass – harvests have failed, meat is scarcer, and the price of bread has doubled. The men have families of their own to feed. So as first sunlight blushes above the sooty spires of the old city, they move with purpose, as if a thin thread is pulling them on towards the grubby rooms in Bishopsgate.

The knocking and hammering on the door jolts Mary upright in bed. Her eyes sting and her head is fuzzy, as if with too much wine. She tries to blink away the vestiges of another nightmare – this time, she had been lost on a wind-blasted hill, searching for her baby, who was somewhere nearby, screaming.

Her stepsister Claire is still asleep, curled into the grubby sofa, her dark curls fanned across the stained cushions.

'Open up!' the man growls, from behind the door.

Mary pulls her baby, William, close to her chest and huddles under the damp sheets – perhaps the covering of thin material might keep him asleep and quiet a little longer.

Claire wakes, sits up and tiptoes over to the broken rocking chair, picks up a water-warped copy of *Macbeth* and pretends to read, as though she can't hear the scuffing of boots and muttering from outside. Yesterday morning, when she did this, Mary had tried to laugh, but the men sound angrier today, their voices harsher.

'Just kick the fucking door in. It's half-rotten anyway.'

Mary clenches her jaw. She is not afraid. These men won't hurt her. She doesn't *think* they will hurt her. Her mouth is dry.

In the rocking chair, Claire makes a great performance of trying to focus, deliberately setting her face in a severe scowl, squinting at the pages and shaking her head, like an elderly accountant at his books. She's always been a great actress. Even on the coldest mornings, when their stomachs pinch with hunger and they shiver, staring longingly at the dead ash in the grate, waiting for the bailiffs to leave so they can light a meagre fire, Claire tries to make Mary smile. Sometimes, she feigns being hard of hearing, cupping her ear towards the cacophony outside the door. Or she pretends that her slice of dry bread is a feast – she blows out her cheeks and clutches her stomach, as though she couldn't manage another bite. Usually, the bailiffs give up after a quarter of an hour of hammering.

But this morning they start kicking the door almost at once. They've never done this before. When the first boot hits the wood and the door judders in its frame, Mary's heart jolts. Claire looks up in alarm, before returning to feigning deafness in the rocking chair.

'Who's there, in the name of Beelzebub?' she whispers to Mary.

Mary attempts a smile but her mouth trembles. She is so tired of being frightened all the time. She feels as if she has swigged from Shelley's opium flask – everything is slightly distant and unreal, as if it is happening to someone else.

'No use pretending,' a man shouts, his mouth pressed against the door, so the bass notes of his anger reverberate through the wood. 'We've been told you're in there.'

Mary glances towards the cracked wall. The family who live in the rooms next door won't be any help – they never come to see if the sisters are well, never respond to the baby's screams or the bickering, or the occasional howls of anguish and rage that they must be able to hear through the thin walls.

More hammering.

If only Shelley were here – but, no, that is a selfish thought. The bailiffs would drag him off to debtors' prison before breakfast. Then she would be truly alone. He is hiding somewhere in London. She can see him on Sundays, when the bailiffs aren't working. She must be happy with that.

Baby Willmouse grumbles and shifts in Mary's arms. She loosens her tight grip a little, then jiggles and hushes him, but it is too late: his eyelids flutter and he gives a wail.

The men boot the door harder and faster, slapping their palms against the wood.

'Come out, Shelley! No use hiding like a maid.'

Mary hasn't seen Shelley for five days. She has no idea where he goes between their weekly meetings, which he insists must be in a tree-shrouded corner of St Pancras Gardens or in the dark recesses of a busy coffee house. She longs to hear his voice, to hear him tell her where he has been or whom he has seen, while he holds their child or puts his arm around her waist. She would be content simply to lay her head upon his shoulder while he describes the books he has been reading, his warm hand resting on her thigh. But he insists it is safer if he stays away from her, if he keeps his distance while he is resolving his debts. The pain of his absence is an ache in her bones – like cold and hunger, those constant companions.

Occasionally, a flicker of irritation, which she quickly squashes by reminding herself of how brilliant Shelley is, how lucky she is to have him, how much she needs him. Now, she repeats it in time to the boots crashing against the wood.

You're lucky, Mary, you are. He loves you. He does. The words sound like foreign syllables, a meaningless blur.

Willmouse cries again. The men kick the door. The wood bends and cracks. Mary meets Claire's eyes, which are wide with panic.

The door splinters, revealing two pairs of the heavy military boots that so many men now wear, whether they fought alongside the Duke of Wellington or not. No way of knowing whether these two are battle-hardened soldiers. Most likely, they're just wearing the costume, like small boys who make themselves feel brave by pretending a sharpened stick is Excalibur.

One of the men shoves his shoulder into the door. A chunk of wood whistles across the room and clatters next to the grate.

The baby screams, outraged, and Mary feels the fear and fury travel through her too. She is standing before she knows she's made the decision to move. 'No!' she shouts at the door, at the same time as Claire calls, 'Stop!'

Is it Mary's imagination or is the house starting to shake too? How solid are the walls here? Last week, a house near Drury Lane collapsed without warning, crushing everyone inside. Perhaps she should open the door. She tries to envisage herself flinging it wide, roaring at the men to just go, to leave them alone, to pursue Shelley for his debts, rather than hounding Mary and Claire, day after day.

But to shout at the men she would have to put Willmouse down, when everything tells her she must keep him near. She clutches her baby close.

'Stop!' Claire calls again. She stands alongside her sister and grips Mary's arm tightly, then places the other hand over Willmouse's fragile form.

Claire's legs are shaking too; Mary can feel her sister's terror, her fierce resolve.

A final kick and the door bursts open. The two men stumble into the room with a blast of icy air, then stop at the sight of the two frightened, furious women and the bawling baby.

One of the men stumbles slightly, then rights himself with the loose movements of an inebriate. His eyes, when he stares at them, are bloodshot.

'Wheresh Shelley?' he slurs, then blinks, as if baffled by his own incoherence. He tries again, more slowly. 'Wheresh Shelley?'

His breath is ripe. Sour stench of old booze.

'I want you to leave.' She speaks clearly. She sounds unafraid.

The other man steps forward. His clothes are sharper and look newer. His cheeks are mottled with patchy stubble, the slight softness of youth in his jaw still.

'Your husband owes money everywhere, Mrs Shelley.' He sounds sober, weary, bored. 'If he doesn't pay up, it'll be Newgate Prison for him.'

'I'm not Mrs Shelley.' Mary lifts her chin in defiance.

The man frowns, turning to Claire. 'Mrs Shelley, just tell us where he is and we'll leave you in peace.'

'She isn't Mrs Shelley either,' Mary says.

Claire flashes small white teeth.

The man's face falls as he looks from one woman to another. 'Then which . . .?'

'Wheresh Shelley?' the other man slurs again. At his belt, a knife glints silver.

A tremor runs through Mary's legs; she tenses her muscles to conceal it. 'Get out of my house.'

'Iss not yer house. Iss rented roomss.'

'Leave.'

The younger man steps forward, his expression pugnacious. 'If Shelley can afford to rent rooms, he can afford to pay his debts.'

Willmouse starts to grizzle again; she kisses his damp fore-head. If either man moves to touch her child, she will . . .

What will she do? If she shoved her weight against the man's chest, it would feel as solid and pitiless as a wall.

'Get out *now*,' she whispers.

The men don't move.

Willmouse's cries rise in volume and pitch. The tempo of Mary's heart in her chest quickens too and she holds him closer, crushing him against her. He shrieks.

The men flinch and the drunken man lurches towards the women – by accident, perhaps, but his eyes are impenetrable and dark, like the Serpentine river in winter.

'No!' Mary shields her baby's body with her own.

At the same time Claire begins to scream.

When they were younger, Claire's screams were a thing of family legend. She would shriek with such raw rage – her eyes bulging, the tendons on her neck tight as wire – that she was given whatever sweet or trinket she wanted, much to Mary's confusion. Why was her stepsister rewarded for screeching like a street brat?

Mary's father had brought her up alone, after her mother died giving birth to her. William Godwin's parenting had been based around fostering a quiet, studious, thoughtful daughter. A daughter who, like her mother, would have the mind of a phil-osopher. She should spend her time reading or thinking. She should be grateful for what she was given and shouldn't ask for anything more. Mary would never have dared to raise her voice at all, let alone tantrum and shriek. But when William Godwin married Mary-Jane Clairmont, Claire roared into the house with all the fury of a feral animal. At first, Mary avoided her, as she might have skirted around a wild cat. Over time, she found that Claire was also full of fun and wit and fierce bursts of affection that made it hard to be angry with her for long. Mostly.

Now, Mary links her arm through Claire's as her sister screams and she screams along with her. The noise roars through her chest and she watches the men – these burly, brutish men – recoil.

When they fall silent, there is a hush that seems to extend into the streets outside and perhaps beyond. Mary visualizes the scream travelling like a wave through their priggish neighbours' houses, silencing them. She pictures it rushing like a torrent along the roads, all the way to the door of Shelley's stuffy father and grandfather, who have refused to give him a penny ever since they heard about his elopement with Mary. She wishes the fury-filled shriek into the dark alleys of whichever haunt Shelley is hiding in. She hopes the sound will draw him back to her.

In the quiet, the men look around the rooms, perhaps taking in, for the first time, the ragged sheets, the empty fireplace, the old sofa with horsehair spilling from the ripped cushions. Perhaps they notice the dark hollows under Mary's eyes or the way that Claire's dress hangs off her. Or perhaps it is Willmouse's shocked, tear-streaked face and his huge eyes that make them take a step back, towards the broken door – defeated troops quietly retreating.

In the doorway, the younger man pulls out a leather purse, takes a copper penny from it and jerks his head towards Willmouse. 'Child looks cold.'

Mary hesitates, wary, but Claire darts forward and plucks the coin from the bailiff's hand. He grabs her wrist; she wrenches free and tries to kick him.

'You shouldn't be here. That Percy bloody Shelley's a scoundrel. Everyone knows it. We'll return tomorrow. Make sure you're gone.'

He slams the rickety door behind him. An icy breeze gusts through the cracked wood.

Still trembling, the women turn to each other. In Claire's wide eyes, Mary's own terror is doubled. The wind whines and whistles through the broken door.

'We have to leave.' Mary's voice fractures. She forces herself to repeat it, as if this is what she truly wants. Her throat aches.

'We have to leave. Again.'

Two years earlier, July 1814

Sixteen-year-old Mary lies in her narrow bed at her father's house in Skinner Street, shivering. She hasn't slept, has kept herself awake by counting the tolling of the bells in St Sepulchre Church. Shelley has said he will come for her at four o'clock in the morning but the hours have stretched out so gelid and dark that Mary fears she might have fallen asleep after all, or foolishly miscounted the chimes. What if he has come and waited for her in the cold and then, what if – thinking she has lost her nerve – he has left?

She sits up and rubs her palm across the beads of condensation on the dank glass. No movement in the dimly moonlit street – even the lushes had staggered home from the taverns hours before. She can just make out the shadows of the carcasses hanging in the butcher's window across the street, pale flesh gleaming.

'Claire,' she whispers to her sister, who is lying still in the other small bed. 'Are you awake?'

'I am now. What o'clock is it?'

'Nearly four, I think.'

'Not long, then.'

'What if he's –?' What will she do if Shelley isn't coming after all? What if he's chosen to abandon her? Even to speak the words aloud would summon a terrifying, familiar shadow. It would creep into her lungs, into her limbs and make it impossible for her to speak or move. She exhales through pursed lips. 'What if he's late?'

'He won't be.' Claire is full of her usual certainty. Sometimes her sister's confidence is irritating. Tonight it is a comfort. 'Don't forget, I've read his letters too. He *wants* you. He *longs* for you.' Claire grins, a gleam of teeth in the dark.

Mary presses a hand to her chest, where the packet of Shelley's letters rustles and sighs. Claire has passed so many notes back and forth between them these past weeks, so many declarations of adoration, Mary should feel no doubt.

And yet that soft-voiced ghost waits always in the darkness, in the silence, in the pauses between her breaths.

What if he doesn't want me? What if he leaves me?

She has scribbled her fears into her journal, hoping to expunge them. Instead, they have grown. The journal feels heavy with the weight of all her questions.

What if . . . ? What if . . . ?

Clatter of hoofs. Scrape of wheels over cobbles.

Mary sits up, wiping her hand over the window again. In the street below, a coach and four horses. As she peers into the gloom, holding her breath, the coach door opens; a figure springs out. Slim, tall – even in the moon-dappled darkness, he is unmistakable.

'Shelley!' she breathes, heart jolting. It is hard to gather breath to speak.

Both girls climb from their beds and smooth down their skirts. They have been waiting fully dressed, so do not even have to pull on their boots. It will be hard to creep quietly down the stairs but there is less chance of knocking something over or being caught with one boot on by an enraged Mrs Godwin.

Claire holds up the key that she had earlier sneaked from Mrs Godwin's cabinet. The metal clunks as she turns it in the lock. Nobody stirs.

Mary's breath is tight in her chest as she tiptoes down the stairs, following Claire's dark curls. Her sister walks without hesitation but Mary pauses, glancing back at her father's closed door. His snores are steady and rhythmic as ever. Surely he must sense that she is leaving. He will open the door and call for her to stop, to get back into the attic room. He will lock her in, as he has every day for the past two weeks. His stern voice will rumble through the sturdy oak, sharp with disappointment. 'You must abandon this foolishness, Mary. It is beneath you.'

And Mary will stare at the dead wood of that closed door and say, 'Yes, Father. I'm sorry.' And she will gaze at the locked door while she scratches bloody welts across her arms, opening up the old scars that crosshatch her skin.

Claire tugs on her hand and whispers, 'Come *on*!'

Mary waits a moment longer, heart hammering. She is balanced on a cliff edge, transfixed by the churning waters below.

Claire pulls on her hand again. 'Shelley can't wait for long.'

Mary blinks, nods, then follows her sister out into the cold night air.

The moon is hidden by a scarf of cloud. In the darkness, the carriage looks black and forbidding. Inside, Shelley will be waiting with his warm arms and his open smile and his smell of cedar and tobacco from the coffee houses.

Her feet are fixed to the damp cobbles. If she climbs into the carriage, something terrible will happen.

She stands, frozen in a stream of moonlight, as if caught in a whirlpool that binds her legs, wraps around her arms, swirls its way into her throat, into her lungs. She cannot move, cannot even speak.

As Claire turns back to hiss at her to hurry up, the carriage door opens.

The *thunk* of the lock unfreezes Mary. Before she can see Shelley emerging from the carriage again, before she can hear him call out to her, she whirls around and runs back into the house, into the warmth of the family bookshop.

She inhales the sweetish, smoked-wood smell of paper. It is a scent that tells her to sit down, to stay still, to think, to reflect.

She crouches on the floor and closes her eyes. If she doesn't give up her relationship with Shelley, her father will not speak to her again, will not even look at her.

You will no longer be my daughter. It will be as if you had never been born.

She presses her palms against her closed eyes and tries to breathe through her rising panic. The books on the bottom shelves smell of trees, of soil, of rot. Mary pictures the silence and stillness of a grave – her mother's grave, in St Pancras churchyard. Her mother who had died before Mary ever knew her. Her mother, who had risked everything for love.

She stands, walks to her father's desk and takes up his quill.

My dear Father,

I write these few lines only to say how sorry I am for any pain I have caused you by my sudden flight. I fear your anger at what you may think of as my recklessness. I cannot reassure you that I repent my actions, for to do so, I would have to stay in this house. Father, I cannot. Love forbids me to remain with you and I can only hope that your love for me will cause your heart, in time, to soften into forgiveness.

I am, sir, your loving daughter,
Mary

She folds the note into his accounting ledger, where he will find it in the morning. With a final glance at his desk, she steps out into the biting night.

Now, it is not as though she is walking towards the carriage, but as though she is *being* walked, or swept along. The whirlpool, which fixed her in place before, is tugging her onwards. And although she is grounded by the wet cobbles, by the damp night air and the faint tang of blood from the butcher's shop, she is borne above it all. Some unseen dark current carries her towards the carriage, towards Shelley, towards some murky, half-sensed destiny.

When Shelley flings open the carriage door, her heart jolts and her final hesitation washes away. She runs the last two steps, holding out her hands so he can lift her into his arms. In the darkness, she can only half see his face but she feels him smile against her mouth as she kisses him again and again, clinging to him. After the chill and churning water, he is a warm shore.

He shuts the door and the carriage clatters onwards, into the night.

2

The companions of our childhood always possess a certain
power over our minds which hardly any later friend can obtain.

London, 1816

After the bailiffs have gone, Mary and Claire wedge the broken pieces of wood back into the doorway. When that doesn't work, Mary hangs a sheet over the gaping space, so they have a little privacy at least. The thin linen billows in the wind; a single candle on the nightstand flickers.

Willmouse grumbles in his sleep and sighs. Mary's jaw aches. When she tries to rub away the tension, it becomes a steady, piercing pulse.

'At least we have wood for the fire.' She throws a shard of shattered oak into the grate. 'We can take it with us when we move.'

'I'm so *tired* of moving around London.' Claire hurls a piece of wood towards the fireplace and misses. 'And they'll only find us again.'

A splinter stabs Mary's thumb and she hisses. 'There's one place we could go . . .'

'Home? Don't even think it.'

'I wasn't. Not really.' Her thumb is ink-stained as always, no sign of the splinter. When she presses the skin, there is a sharp stab of pain.

'Father won't have you. Not unless you promise never to see Shelley again.'

'I know.' She runs her teeth across the splinter, trying to draw it out.

'And probably not even then.' Claire nods towards the sleeping Willmouse, gives a sad smile.

'I *know*,' Mary says tightly. 'Although *you* can skip home whenever you please.'

'That's not fair!' Claire's tone is wounded. 'I stay here with you as much as I can manage. But sometimes I have to go home to Skinner Street. Mama misses me.' Is this said a little smugly, or is it Mary's imagination? Claire twirls a curl around her finger. 'She complains it is too quiet in the house without me.'

Well, she does like to complain. Mary forces a smile. 'I'm sure it is.'

Later, when Claire is sleeping, Mary will pull her journal from under the mattress and write, *How can Skinner Street be quiet when the walls must rattle with Mrs Godwin's spite and stupidity?*

Claire takes Mary's hand and sits next to her on the bed. Very gently, she presses on the skin around the splinter. 'We have another choice, Mary. Please consider it.'

'I *have* considered it. Willmouse is too young to travel.'

'That's not true. I *know* you want to leave London again – you love the Continent. We were so happy there two years ago.'

Mary nods wordlessly. When she thinks back to that time, she feels a fist of granite sitting in her chest. More than anything, she had wanted to run away with Shelley, just as she wants to escape now. Yet every time she has fled, it has cost her so much. And now she has so little.

'We all loved France,' Claire says. 'Remember those little farmhouses we sheltered in? It was so exciting!'

'I remember *vomiting* in lots of little farmhouses.' Mary tries to keep her tone light. 'Pregnancy is not a good travelling companion.'

Claire laughs. 'You were sick everywhere, you poor thing! But, truly, now *I* am so heartily sick of this dreadful weather. This dull light! We must go south for the summer – like swallows!'

Mary doesn't correct her to say that swallows fly north – her sister hates to be contradicted. The weather in London has been terrible for months. Not just cold but dark too, as if the sun itself has grown dimmer. The trees, which would usually be weighted with blossom, are almost leafless. *The Times* is full of reports of failed crops, along with bleak warnings of grain shortages.

Claire pulls out the splinter and gently kisses away the spot of blood. Why can't she be sweet all the time?

'Please, Mary. Byron has *begged* me to visit him and he is *desperate* to meet you.'

For weeks now, Claire has been talking about a grand escape to the Continent and, more specifically, to Switzerland, where Lord Byron will be summering by Lake Geneva. Claire has been obsessed with Byron since she first engineered a meeting with him at the Drury Lane theatre, pretending to be an actress to catch his attention. Mary is used to Claire's various infatuations and romantic fits, so had thought little of it, until Claire began insisting that they should follow Byron for the summer.

'Think of it!' Claire says. 'No more hiding from the bailiffs. You will be able to see Shelley all the time and there will be *sunlight* – see how you're smiling already!'

Mary does feel warmer, and as though she can take a full breath for the first time in weeks. Just think of sleeping next to Shelley every night! His long body stretched out next to hers. His weight on her when she wakes. When nightmares swarm behind her eyelids, he will put his strong arms around her, pulling her close.

Claire giggles. 'You look so pretty when you blush! And Byron will be so *good* for Shelley. He's an ardent devotee of his work. And of *you*! As you are a child of two geniuses, Byron supposes you must be a wonder – which you *are*, of course!'

Claire has always been able to shower people in compliments without a trace of irony. Most of the time, it is endearing.

She rushes on without pause. 'Byron will adore you. You and Shelley both! I shall accompany you, of course, but I expect I will be a silent witness to your lofty conversations. *Please* say you'll come, Mary! I know Shelley would be much happier. He would *hate* to leave you – he has said so to me a hundred times.'

Mary's stomach drops. 'Shelley has spoken of going without me? Of leaving me here alone?'

'Oh, *no*!' Claire clasps Mary's hands. 'He worships you! He could never leave you.' Claire pauses, perhaps realizing her mistake: Mary can see Shelley only on Sundays, when the bailiffs are not patrolling. 'He would *hate* to leave you, dear Mary, and would do so only under duress.' Her dark eyes are wide and earnest. Her manipulation is calculated, her expression full of sympathetic concern.

An owl calls into the quiet. Heavy boots thud outside their broken door. Mary's mouth dries; both women tense until the pounding footsteps pass.

Mary watches her sister fix her smile in place again. '*Please* say yes, Mary. Byron is so fascinating. I know you admire his poems and I'm sure you will esteem the man himself even more highly. He's so wonderful, truly.' Claire's voice catches.

Oh! How could Mary have missed it? How could she have been so blinkered?

This is no passing fancy. Claire's eyes are bright, her cheeks flushed when she says his name. Her palms, in Mary's, are hot and damp. Sitting cross-legged on the bed, facing Mary, her chestnut curls tumbling around her shoulders, she looks young and beautiful and full of hope.

She loves him.

'I've promised I will introduce you both to him. Say you'll come.'

Oh, but there are so many rumours about Byron: he is always drunk, always intoxicated with opium, which he foists on those around him. His sexual appetite is insatiable. He is notoriously unfaithful with men and women alike. He is recently divorced and has had a love affair with his half-sister. He travels with a menagerie of savage animals – when Cambridge University forbade him to keep a dog in his rooms, he'd kept a pet bear instead.

'I'm not sure he would be a *good* . . . influence on Shelley.'

'Nonsense! Shelley will adore him.'

Precisely.

'Please, Mary, dear. You'll adore him too. What a chance for you to spend time with such a great poet!'

The slight jibe at Shelley stings but Claire is right: they need to escape this place. Whatever dangers Byron might bring, whatever his reputation for chaos, Geneva will be safer than London. It must be. Mustn't it?

She nods, just once. Claire flings her arms around her, laughing, whispering, '*Thank you, thank you,*' into Mary's ear.

Mary smiles and holds her sister tightly, closing her eyes. How many months since they have both been happy?

'Let's tell Shelley!' Claire claps her hands. 'We'll leave tonight or early tomorrow morning, before those horrible men come back.'

'But how? I am to meet him in the cemetery behind St Pancras, but not for two days.'

This is where Mary's mother is buried, her gravestone shaded by oak and willow.

'We can't wait so long.' Claire frowns. 'We'll send a message to Portland Street now.'

'Portland Street? How do you know he's there?' Mary can hear the sharpness in her voice. She tries to soften it with a smile, but her face won't obey.

'Oh, he's mentioned it quite often,' Claire says airily.

He hasn't, Mary is sure of it. She would remember if Shelley had said even once, even in passing, where he lives. She can feel the corners of her mouth trembling and she stops trying to smile through the hollow feeling in her chest. 'Well. He hasn't mentioned it to me.'

'You've been so distracted.' Claire reaches out and strokes Mary's cheek with what feels like real tenderness. 'Willmouse is exhausting. You must have forgotten about Portland Street.' There is no telltale hitch in her voice; her eyes do not slide to the left or right.

She has always been an excellent liar.

Mary hears her teeth creak. She is clenching her jaw again. She scrubs roughly at her forehead, where the throbbing pain is starting to radiate outwards.

'Hush, be gentle with yourself.' Claire presses her cool fingers to Mary's temples. 'You're tired now, too – I can see it. Write the letter. Then rest.'

Mary swallows, nods, forces a small smile. Perhaps Shelley really had told her about Portland Street. Perhaps she really had forgotten. They've moved so often within the past few months and her mind is raw with exhaustion. When she does have the chance to see Shelley, she is so overcome with happiness and relief that it is hard to think of anything else.

Behind them, Willmouse grizzles.

'Write to Shelley now. You will feel such relief! I'll hold little

Willmouse. Come here, dear.' She picks him up and sways from side to side, kissing his forehead. He stops crying and smiles at her, then tangles his hand in one of her curls. She laughs.

They look like a dishevelled painting of the Madonna and Child. Mary is sure she doesn't seem so contented and look so beautiful when she is trying to soothe her baby.

Perhaps this, too, is a reason why Shelley stays away.

She squeezes the quill too tightly and ink splatters onto the paper. Before Claire can notice, Mary turns the paper over and hides it beneath another sheet. She draws a steadying breath – she must focus on the words she chooses in case the bailiffs intercept the letter. She must also take care not to sound angry or irritated, or even a little anxious. Shelley fell in love with her sweet disposition and fine mind; he can't stand to know that she is unhappy.

My Elfin Knight,

My sister and I keenly feel the chill of this country, its customs and its collectors of capital. I know that you, too, have long-since become weary of the distance that circumstance has placed between us. It gives me so much happiness, my dearest, to tell you that we all have an invitation to summer in warmer climes: the renowned peer, with whom my sister has recently become acquainted, has urged us to depart this place and join him as soon as we may. More can I not say here, but I will seek you this very evening and hope that we may exchange our thoughts on this, as well as the words and gestures of love which I long to shower upon you.

I am always your faithful and patient Pecksie

Pecksie is the pet name her lover uses for her. It is inspired by a children's book about a family of robins, in which Pecksie is the sweetest and kindest among a family of argumentative birds – Shelley has said, laughingly, that the similarities between Mary and her place in her own family are undeniable.

Mary's hand doesn't shake when she is writing; her voice is steady when she hails a messenger boy to run and deliver the sealed letter to Portland Street.

She would like to write in her journal but Claire is watching her, something smug in her expression. She *enjoys* knowing more about Shelley than Mary does.

Mary considers writing, *C reminds me of a satisfied cat. I must not forget her claws.*

Aware of Claire's eyes upon her, Mary forces the corners of her mouth upwards – she will not give her sister the enjoyment of seeing that she is hurt. She starts to fold her things into their battered trunks and valises. Black spots swim in her vision. She blinks them away and, to distract herself, she hums 'Frère Jacques'. Claire takes up the tune, her voice far overshadowing Mary's. She rocks Willmouse back and forth, singing loudly and sweetly, quite caught up in the beauty of her own music.

It grates on Mary's nerves but at least Claire is not studying her now. Mary can finally draw a full, shuddering breath, can finally relax the tight smile she has tried to hold ever since Claire mentioned Portland Street.

*

Mary's Journal, aged 6

30 August 1803
Today is my birthday. ~~Fahtr~~ Father gave me this journal and these words to copy. It took me only one hour. I am a good girl.

10 September
Today is my mother's death day. She ~~deid~~ died 6 years ago. We visited her grave. Her name is the same as ~~myne~~ mine. Thank

you Father for writing words for me to copy. I must practise
every day. I must write often to be like Mamma. This will make
you pruod.

15 September
I had my ~~nihgtmer~~ nightmare again. A creature was trying to
catch me. Father says I must write here very often when I have
bad dreams even if writing the dream makes me cry and be sick
down my new dress.

23 September
My nightmare creature again. I do not want to write it.

28 September
My nightmare again. Father says I do not have to write it
now because it makes it be more real for me. I must forget all
about it.

21 December
Today Father marryed a new wife. I said some bad words to her.
I will not say sorry. Now I must sit and copy these words until I
feel sorry.
    Dear Mrs Godwin Mamma,
    I am sincerely sorry for shouting. I do not hate you.
    I am yours,
    Mary Wollstonecraft Godwin

22 December
Mrs Godwin is not my Mamma. I hate her. These words are a
seycret. I am a bad girl for writing this.

23 December
Mrs Godwin has a duaghter called Claire and a son called

*Charles. He is loud and annoying. Claire screams all the time.
She always gets her own way. We are to be sisters. I wish she
was ded.*

2 January 1804
*Mrs Godwin took Mother's portrayt away. She said we must
not say Mother's name. I said it was my name also. I screamed
Mary Wollstonecraft Godwin two times and she smacked me. I
must say sorry. I do not care. This means I am very bad.*

5 January
*Claire cannot write at all. She wants a wooden doll and pretty
ribbons. She is very loud and very stupid.*

10 January
I am very alone.

*

It is almost sunset but the rooms are already filled with shifting
shadows. Mary huddles in the corner, warming her hands over
the stump of a candle, flexing her fingers. To her half-numb
touch, the pages of her journal feel soft and damp.

Like dead skin.

She thinks of baby Clara. Born two months early, she had
lived for just eleven days.

My fault, she writes, then crosses out the words. Shelley can
never know. The grief and guilt are like threadbare cloaks she
wraps around herself. She has grown so used to their prickly
discomfort that she doesn't know how to take them off.

Shaking, she sets down her quill, presses her palms against
her eyelids and pushes away the thought. Her head throbs still
and she rubs her temples again, then picks up the quill.

Inside most of the day. Weather dreary yet again. Read Milton. Practised Greek translation.

Over by the small fire, Claire puffs out her cheeks and sighs. When Mary pays no attention, she sighs again. 'He must have the letter by now.'

'Perhaps.'

'Why has he not rushed over?' Claire widens her eyes in affected dismay.

'I don't *know*, Claire.' Mary grips the quill more tightly. She can count the beats of her heart in the pulsing pain in her temple.

'Portland Street is not far.'

'Indeed.' Mary's voice is steady, but her shaking hand forms the words *Shut your mouth up*. She scrawls them in a spidery hand, the letters barely legible.

Then she crosses them out.

She pictures a hand clapped over Claire's mouth, a shiny seal of new skin stitched over her lips.

'Perhaps he is busy elsewhere.' Claire twirls her hair around a finger. 'Visiting friends, do you think?'

'I couldn't possibly say.' Mary swallows something sour; her throat burns.

She writes,

Why did she know and not I? When did he tell her that he was living so close? Why didn't she tell me? What else does she know that I don't? Sometimes I wish she would just — If she wasn't here, we could be content. I would be. I wish she was anywhere but here. I hate — I hate —

Her breath is loud in her ears. The pain is like a hammer, beating on the inside of her skull, as if something is trying to escape.

'Are you well? You look very pale.'

'Just a rheumatism in my head.' Mary hears her careful words as if someone else is speaking them – some calm, composed woman who keeps her face impassive and her voice measured, while her thoughts spin like shards of glass in a whirling wind.

The writing in her journal doesn't even look like hers, but like the scrawl of a small child. The letters are jagged, the ink smudged and blotchy.

Shelley loves to pick up her journal and read her thoughts; he loves to *immerse himself* in the beauty of her mind.

Her stomach drops. She rips out the page, screwing it into a ball.

'Mary! Dearest, what is wrong?' Claire rushes over and puts her arms around Mary's shoulders. 'Is your head very bad? Poor dear, let me rub your neck.'

'I'm well, truly. Leave me –'

'Nonsense!' Claire presses her fingers in firm circles along the back of Mary's neck. Her hands are strong and warm from the fire.

Mary feels as though something raw and spiked is squatting heavily in her chest. 'Thank you.' She crushes the paper inside her clenched fist. Her finger is bleeding where she has stabbed it with the quill. She hides the cut under the balled-up paper. It throbs within her screwed-up words, like a second heartbeat.

'I have written a letter to Byron,' Claire says. 'He doesn't answer me either. It is not the same as you and Shelley but I do know a *little* of what you feel.'

Mary squeezes the paper harder. Claire is always claiming she understands Mary. Each time she says it, Mary feels a little harder, a little hollower, a little angrier.

If only there were an illness that would render Claire silent.

Immediately, she feels guilty. Besides, Claire would only use her muteness to attract even more attention.

'Of course,' Claire says, '*I* am not a famous poet's object of adoration like you. I'm not his muse yet.' She gives an ironic little laugh.

To anyone else, she might sound truly amused by the idea, but there is a familiar breathy fragility behind her laughter. Claire pretends to care less than she truly does about important things, then feigns enthusiastic rhapsodies over minor events. It is so easy to see, behind her grand claims, the volatile child she was – eager to be heard, desperate to please, yearning for love.

Mary clasps her sister's hand. 'You'll be a wonderful muse.'

'Oh, I know! He'll compose sonnets about my eyes and write an epic about my beautiful –'

'Your beautiful behind!' Best to distract Claire with a joke and a compliment.

'*Mary!*' She looks delighted. 'I was going to say my beautiful singing.' Claire launches into another heartfelt rendition of 'Frère Jacques', without a single false note.

As she sings, Mary rips the torn page of her journal into tiny pieces. When Claire turns away, Mary stands and throws them into the fire, where they dissolve into spiralling ash.

'Do you think Byron will like this dress?' Claire picks up a blue gown that is at least two seasons out of date.

'It's very pretty.'

Claire presses the dress against herself. It has full skirts and a plunging neckline. 'Shelley says it brings out my . . . eyes.'

'Does he truly?'

'Oh, don't scowl – your face will wrinkle. You know he loves you and *only* you. He is free to say sweet things to me too. You mustn't be jealous. Now, what do you say to the dress?'

Mary pictures herself grabbing it and throwing it into the

fire. 'I think I'll go for a walk and catch the last of the light.' Her voice is falsely bright.

Claire reaches for her cloak. 'I'll come with you.'

'Oh, no, you stay here and pack. And Willmouse is asleep. You don't mind staying with him, do you?'

Claire opens her mouth, then shuts it and presses her lips into a thin line. 'Of course not.'

As soon as she is out of the dark claustrophobia of those grubby rooms, Mary can breathe more easily. Her head still throbs but, by inhaling the smoky air and falling in among the jostling crowds, she can almost ignore it.

She keeps her face down as she passes the windows of the family in the next room, who had been horrified when the sisters moved here, along with Mary's lover, the *married* poet Percy Shelley, who was well-known to be deeply in debt and, most shockingly, a revolutionary who wrote about atheism and . . . *unsavoury* relationships. And here he was, living with two women, neither of whom was his wife!

Every time the family passes Mary or Claire in the street, they avert their eyes. The oldest boy has taken to curling his lip and coughing '*Whores*' when he sees them.

The gossip has been harder to endure than Mary had expected. When she walks out, she often keeps her gaze on the cobbles so that she won't have to suffer the humiliation of locking eyes with someone she knows, then watching them turn away – as if they've never seen her before, as if she doesn't exist.

The hawkers' stalls and delivery wagons are bathed in the same uncanny glow that infuses the air almost every evening now. Although it is beautiful, although painters sit along the riverbanks, daubing their canvases with bright ochre and orange to capture the strange skies, the colour feels . . . *wrong*.

Ridiculous to believe the zealots, of course: they claim that the heavens are ablaze, that the end is near, that God, in His fury, has set the sky alight, that He has unshackled Earth from the sun, that in just a few years the world will be a blank, barren desert.

It is an odd pattern in the weather. That is all. Still, it is hard not to feel a sense of dread at the world growing slowly darker and bleaker. Sky the colour of dying embers and dead ash.

Mary is back in the dream that never leaves: she is huddled near a fire, trying to rub the colour back into lifeless flesh. She shudders.

The air, with its unseasonal bite, has the hawkers packing up their stalls in the gloaming light, blowing on their fingers and huddling into heavy winter cloaks.

Mary wraps her own thin cloak more closely around her shoulders and wishes she could return to her father's house on Skinner Street for some of her warmer clothes. But the door would be locked and they would pretend they couldn't hear her cries.

On the corner of Threadneedle Street, where the Bank of England is just closing, an iron-haired man with skin the colour of old ash shouts hoarse warnings: 'Turn away from your sinful ways. Mankind has been judged. We are condemned for our greed and our selfishness.' He points a bony finger at Mary. '*You* are being judged. You have been found wanting.'

Mary recoils and turns her face away.

'Aye, I see your shame,' the man says. 'And the Lord sees when you commit evil acts.' He is thin, with sunken cheeks and stooped shoulders. His voice cracks on *evil* and he doubles over, coughing.

Tears sting behind her eyelids. She blinks angrily. What does this ignorant man know of her?

'Your Father *sees* you,' the preacher rasps, and points at Mary again. 'Your Father sees your sin and has cast you out into the wilderness.'

'Imbecile,' Mary growls, though not loud enough for him to hear. She pulls the hood of her cloak over her head and hurries past. To drown the man's shouts, she mutters, 'Curse you,' under her breath, then says it again, in time to the beat of her boots on the cobbles. There is a grim satisfaction in hissing the words through her clenched jaw.

She bumps shoulders with a woman in a thick woollen cloak; still filled with fury, Mary glares at her. The woman flinches and Mary tries to force her mouth into a smile, but it must twist into a fixed rictus because the woman blanches. She takes two steps backwards, then rushes away, slipping on the damp cobbles.

Mary tries to steady her breathing and walks more slowly, back towards Spitalfields, with its stalls and sheds, its thunder and hum of vendors and customers.

Shelley always says how he loves to walk here in the evenings. *The place has such energy!*

She is not supposed to look for him between their meetings, in case she leads the bailiffs to him. She tries to summon his face, to feel his hand in hers, his lips on hers.

Her feet ache and it grows hard to make out faces in the gathering dark, but still she paces up and down the stalls, rehearsing what she might say if she finds him.

What a happy accident! She will widen her eyes, in the way Claire does when she is trying to seem innocent and surprised by something she has planned. *My love, I didn't expect to find you here.* She mouths the words, rehearses the expression – she will bring her fingers to her cheeks, or perhaps place her palm over her lips, shaped into an O of delight.

When she finally sees him standing by a bread stall, it is as though she has conjured him. The shock and pleasure of it thrums through her, down to her marrow then up through her chest, like a fierce bolt of light. Every time she sees him, it is the same. Every time like the first time.

April 1814

'Put that book down, you lazy girl!' Mrs Godwin cries, glaring at Mary where she has hidden herself in a corner of her father's bookshop.

Sixteen-year-old Mary slams down the copy of Charles Lamb's tales and stares up at her stepmother with the cool, unruffled expression she has been practising in the mirror. Eyebrows arched, mouth pressed into a thin line.

'Whatever is the matter, Mrs Godwin?' She makes her voice sugary, in case her father can hear.

Mrs Godwin scowls – she always insists on Mary calling her *Mamma*. 'As if you do not know! We've company coming for dinner and here *you* are, hiding away. I've asked you twice to polish the windows.'

'Betsy has already done it.' Mary has no idea if the serving girl has indeed polished the windows, but it's unlikely that Mrs Godwin will be able to prove otherwise.

'No doubt because you neglected it. Smug little madam, aren't you? I don't know where you got such idleness – it certainly wasn't from your father.'

Mary breathes through the anger she always feels when Mrs Godwin tries to slight her mother. Her eyes go to the blank oval above the fireplace where her mother's portrait used to hang. Mrs Godwin still sometimes remarks how glad she is not to have *that woman* staring at her daily.

Mary forces a tight smile. 'My mother wasn't idle. She was a teacher, a writer and a philosopher. Only last week, my father told me that my mother had the finest mind he'd ever encountered in a woman. Oh, you've turned quite pink, Mrs Godwin. Are you well?'

Later, Mary sits alone in her room, nibbling at the dry biscuit and wrinkled apple that Claire has managed to sneak up for her in place of dinner. Under her mattress is her journal. Tucked into its pages is a picture of a large bull seal, which she had found on her father's writing desk – possibly it is needed for one of the children's books her stepmother edits.

Good, Mary had thought, taking it. Now, in her journal, she writes, *The uncanny resemblance between the bull seal and Mrs G: 1) A luxurious moustache 2) No neck 3) Grunting.*

Footsteps on the stairs. She tucks the journal beneath the mattress.

Claire peers around the door, her face pinched with anxiety. 'Mamma is *so* cross – she's been shouting at *everyone*. Can't you just apologize?'

'I've done nothing wrong,' Mary says, with a calm that conceals the burning outrage she feels towards her father's wife. She daren't shout at her – she has done so only once, two years ago.

Leave me alone, you bloody old bitch!

She'd been banished to Scotland for months, with the story that she had a *bad arm* that would benefit from the sea air. Her arm had, indeed, been covered with lacerations. Even now, when she is anxious, Mary sometimes runs her fingers over the fine white scars where she'd raked her nails over the skin again and again for months. Every time she was anxious or angry or lonely, she'd drawn blood from the scabbed welts.

No more of that – a terrible habit, her father had said. Immoderate and foolhardy, not befitting an intelligent young woman. If she wanted to return home, she must be calm and obedient. Now the marks look like a message in some ancient script she cannot decipher.

'Just say sorry,' Claire sighs. 'It's only a word. You don't have to *mean* it. I say all sorts of things I don't mean and no one's any the wiser.'

'That's what *you* think.' Mary grins.

After Claire has gone, Mary listens to the hubbub of chatter and laughter from downstairs. The front door bangs open and shut, cries of greeting, glasses clinking. It is pleasant to be away from the dining room and the pressure of having to say something that will impress the guest and please her father. Far more comfortable to hide behind a book. She picks up *Thoughts on the Education of Daughters*, written by her mother. She keeps it under her mattress, away from Mrs Godwin.

She who submits, without conviction, to a parent or husband, will as unreasonably tyrannise over her servants.

Can she hear her mother's voice, if she concentrates? She shuts her eyes, puts her hand on her chest: she feels the steady ticking of her heart, but is there some other presence within her? As far back as she can remember, her father has told her that she resembles her mother.

You have her eyes, he will murmur suddenly, in the middle of a conversation about Napoleon's ambitions. Or he will come into her room, late at night, when sleep is dragging her into darkness, and he will place an ink-stained hand upon her chest, just beneath her throat.

'You have her heart,' he will whisper.

She will pretend not to hear him but will feel his eyes travelling over her face. Later, after he is gone, she will rise from her bed and, flesh goose-bumped, she will stand close to the tiny looking-glass on her dresser and gaze at her face, trying to see someone else beneath her skin. On her neck, just beneath her throat, the print of a finger and a thumb – like a painless bruise.

She sits up with a start – was she asleep? In her hand, the wrinkled apple is nibbled, its flesh soft and brown.

Silence from downstairs. She strains to listen but can hear nothing – no voices, no laughter, no scrape of cutlery on china. Has their guest left? How long has she slept?

Creeping to the top of the stairs, she still hears nothing. It's alarming – as if the house and everyone in it is holding their breath.

She pads down the stairs, easing each foot onto the creaky boards, as if, by being silent, by not disturbing anyone or anything, she can keep this stillness, this solitude.

Suppose they have all disappeared! Well, not *all*. But Mrs Godwin gone – oh, think of it! Mary would be able to read and write in peace. She'd be able to breathe without that brash, scolding voice, that screwed-up face, like an overbaked turnip. Picture the awful woman's eyes bulging in surprise as she vanishes in a puff of smoke. She'd leave a terrible stench, no doubt.

In Scotland, at least, Mary had been free of her. The banishment from her father had been dreadful, but in the wilds of Dundee, her imagination had been free to roam. Now, back in London, the house feels like a prison. If she wants to read in peace, she goes to St Pancras Cemetery and sits beside her mother's gravestone.

Still no noise, no movement from downstairs. Has she wished them all away?

Dim yellow glow of a light from the dining room. Mary holds her breath. She will find that the table is bare. Her father's chair will be deserted. It will be as though her family have been snuffed out, one by one, like flames pinched into darkness by unseen fingers. Or, worse, they will be dead at the table, felled by Mary's violent desire for freedom.

Along with her fear, there is a thrill that somehow *she* has done this. She has been liberated, but in the most terrible way.

Then she hears a man's voice – unfamiliar, deep, melodic. 'All things are recreated, and the flame of consentaneous love inspires all life.'

The hairs rise on the backs of her arms, on the nape of her neck. The voice, too, is something she has summoned. This man, unseen, is speaking to her alone, for her alone. She takes another step closer but can see only the corner of the mahogany table.

The man speaks again: 'The fertile bosom of the earth gives suck to myriads, who still grow beneath her care, rewarding her with their pure perfectness.'

Mary takes another step. Her heart is beating so loudly, she wonders that no one can hear it. She can see into the dining room now, but stands in the shadowed doorway, breathless, transfixed.

Her family are alive after all, seated around the dining table. Their whole attention is on the young man who is speaking. He is . . . *beautiful*: tall and slim, with full lips, strong cheekbones, clear blue eyes and sandy hair. There is an ease to his gestures, a fluidity to his movements. As he speaks, he closes his eyes: the words come from within him and from beyond him, as if he is invoking something elemental – syllables strange and familiar, which pull Mary closer, which steal the breath from her body so that she wants to gasp, not for air but for more of the poetry that pours from this man's soul straight into hers.

The man continues: 'The balmy breathings of the wind inhale her virtues, and diffuse them all abroad . . .'

As he speaks, he opens his eyes and sees Mary. He stops speaking mid-sentence, his mouth open. Then he smiles at her and, as though continuing with his poem, says, 'What fair

41

spirit is this, summoned from the earth to walk among us? Come closer, fair goddess.'

Mary opens her mouth but she cannot move, cannot speak. A blush floods her chest, her neck and cheeks and – *oh, mortifying!* One by one, her family turn to look at her. She stares at the wooden floor, then slowly raises her eyes to look at the man again.

Say something, Mary!

As if from a great distance, she hears her father's voice. 'This is my daughter, Mary Wollstonecraft Godwin. Mary, this is the poet Mr Percy Shelley.'

Say anything at all. How do you do? A pleasure to make your acquaintance.

His smile doesn't falter at her silence even though she must look a fool. As she steps into the light of the room and the beam of his gaze, Mary feels as though she is walking into sunlight for the first time, lifting her face to its warmth.

Leaning against the bread stall, Shelley has his back to Mary and she can take a moment to observe him, to collect herself.

Even standing on a London street there is something wild about him. His hair is rumpled, as always, his boots muddy, as if he has been walking in some windswept place, far from the city – as if he has been plucked from a brighter, fiercer world and placed here. He is, she thinks, like a spirit that has descended from the sky, or else, as she watches him throw back his head and laugh, like a demon that has risen at that moment from the ground.

Her breath catches in her throat and she is seized by the same feeling she'd had two years ago, in her father's house – that she dares not approach him.

*

He had insisted she come and sit next to him. She can barely recall what they spoke of – books and philosophy, he has since told her – but she remembers the reflected candlelight in his eyes. She remembers thinking how fitting it was that his blue eyes contained such fire when he seemed to light the whole room with his presence.

After he left, she went up to her dark little chamber and, lighting a single candle, wrote his name again and again in her journal. *Percy Bysshe Shelley.* She ran her fingers over the words, envisaged the face of the man. When she slept, she dreamed of the pale triangle of flesh at the base of his throat. As he spoke to her, she had watched it throb, had seen the tiny flutter of his pulse there. If she touched it, she wondered, would it be cool or warm, soft or rough?

The next morning, when she came downstairs, she sat in the chair where he'd been the night before and forced herself to eat her toast, though she wasn't hungry. Her father, immersed in a book as always, barely glanced at her. She wasn't supposed to interrupt his reading, but she couldn't help asking, 'Will Mr Shelley visit us again soon?'

'What?' William Godwin frowned, turned a page.

'Mr Shelley? When will he next visit? I so enjoyed hearing his ideas. And he is an excellent poet, do you not think?'

'Oh, he won't come back for some time. His wife dislikes him being away so much.'

'His . . .' Mary must have misheard. '. . . his *wife?*'

'Harriet. She is exhausted by their baby. Shelley has gone home while they find a new nursemaid.'

Mary felt cold insects crawling over her head, down her neck, along her spine. When they burrowed into her skin, she felt nothing. She tried to swallow. Her throat ached. 'Excuse me.' She ran upstairs and just reached the water jug in her room before she was violently sick.

Two years later, and seeing her lover is still like taking a head-swimming gulp of strong wine.

Why is he so handsome? Women slow their pace and turn to stare at him. Does he know the effect he has? He is always messy but that only adds to his dishevelled beauty.

Mary barely feels her feet on the cobbles. He is talking to the plump-armed bread-seller as she tries to offload the last of her loaves to the people rushing home from work. Mary is halfway across the street when a man knocks into the stall and a stack of loaves tumbles to the ground. 'Turd in your teeth!' shouts the woman at his retreating back.

'Yes, turd in your teeth!' Without hesitation, Shelley scoops up the bread, then pulls out his drawstring purse and empties all of the clinking coins into the woman's hands. Mary can hear the woman's protests – that it's too much, that he can't possibly want all the bread, it wasn't his fault – but Shelley refuses to take back the coins. Instead, he rips the doughy inside from one of the ruined loaves and, after brushing it off, he eats it, there in the street, ignoring the stares and tuts of passers-by.

The woman is laughing now. 'You're quite mad, sir! What will your family do with so much bread?'

His family won't have any of it. Or any of those coins he's rained upon you.

But Mary tries to quash her frustration because how very *Shelley-like* to raise a stranger's spirits by gallantly buying all her spoiled bread and eating it in front of her.

Mary plans to sidle up alongside her lover and surprise him but, at the last moment, he turns and sees her. Then, dropping the loaves back to the ground, he embraces her tightly. 'Mary! My love!'

'Shelley!'

A man in a heavy cloak glares at them and the woman on his arm sniffs in disdain. Mary closes her eyes and presses her lips to Shelley's, feeling him smile as he pulls her closer.

When she opens her eyes, the woman has stopped and is staring at them, her mouth twisted in distaste. Mary gives her a wide smile and kisses Shelley again. The exclamations of passers-by don't touch her. When she is so close to Shelley, there is a protective sheen over her world – he says all the gossip doesn't matter, she must ignore it. It makes Mary feel wild and elated.

It makes the void when he is not with her even colder, the darkness even bleaker.

Sometimes, when she hasn't seen Shelley for days, she wonders if she might have dreamed this closeness – whether she might have fantasized about the world where this man adores her, where his face lights up at the sight of her and he seems as breathless as she is. Sometimes, she has to reread her journal from two years ago, when they first met, those heady months, when he had wanted only her.

Mary's Journal, 1814

19 May

*Mr Shelley visited for lunch again today. Mrs Godwin
had seated him at the head of the table, next to Father,
but Mr Shelley moved places to sit next to me –
without asking. Mrs Godwin appeared very unhappy
but Mr Shelley paid her no mind. All his attention was
on me: though he talked to my father, he kept seeking
my gaze. Every time our eyes met, he gave me the
most luminous smile. Mrs Godwin had told me and*

Claire to sit silently and look pretty, so Claire ate very delicately and twirled her hair ribbon about her finger. When Mr Shelley and Father began talking about the importance of education, I said how vital it is that girls and young women be taught to think and reason for themselves.

Before I could say another word, Mrs G interrupted, in her most grating tone, and said, Now Mary, the men do not seek to know your opinion on serious matters.

I replied, very sweetly, But, dear Mamma, surely women must offer their opinions on serious matters. If they interrupt intelligent discussion only to scold other women about impropriety, they will appear dull and stupid.

Everyone was very quiet. Father and Mrs G looked furious and I thought I would be banished upstairs yet again. Then Mr Shelley said, Precisely! I have never heard a truer word.

He turned directly back to me, as if Mrs G had not interfered at all, and we talked about my mother's book. He thinks her the most admirable of women and dubbed himself a <u>Follower of Wollstonecraft</u>! As we spoke, the dull, dim world of Skinner Street seemed to recede. I have never felt so perfectly understood.

23 May
A letter arrived for me this morning. Happily I found it before Mrs G. She denies nosing through my mail but I know she is lying and have told her so. I did not dare to hope the letter might be from Mr Shelley and I found my fingers trembling as I opened it.

My dear Miss Godwin,

I hope that you will excuse my presumption in addressing this letter so familiarly. I have found my thoughts overwhelmed by memories of our conversation last week and my heart will not let me rest without begging for the chance to meet with you again. My request may be too forward but would you consider accompanying me on a walk so that we may continue and prolong the conversation that has so enlivened me? If the impropriety of our meeting alone concerns you, then perhaps your sister could accompany you near the Charterhouse School, tomorrow at noon.

I am your faithful servant,
Percy Bysshe Shelley

10 June
I have walked with dear Shelley four times now. I call him <u>dear</u> only in these pages. I dare not risk telling him how <u>very</u> dear he has become to me, over these last weeks, for what if he does not return these feelings of affection? Affection! It is such a weak word for the thunder of my heart at the thought of him, for the thrill that runs through me at the sight of him. I try to remind myself that he is a married man. I try to tell myself that this longing I feel cannot be returned. Yet his gaze is so tender when he looks at me and there is such passion in his eyes when we speak.

 Claire has always been captivated by romance and excitement, so her willingness to accompany me on our walks and to conceal their true purpose from our parents gives me no surprise. She is content to stay some distance away from us, so that we might talk more freely. When I ask if she thinks Shelley might feel an attachment to me, she says she does not know, which is most unlike her:

47

usually, Claire professes absolute confidence in all her opinions.

16 June
It is hard to express how he enlivens my mind. I confessed to him my secret hope: that I might one day write a great work of philosophy, like my father and mother. Shelley believes I can write <u>anything</u> I desire. He says I have the soul of a poet, as well as the mind of a philosopher. When he talks, I see myself reflected and magnified in his eyes: all that I might be.

19 June
He finds my thoughts captivating. Never before has he found a mind so in agreement with his own. He confessed that his wife does not understand him <u>at all</u>; he has been separated from her, body and spirit, for many months.

I, too, find myself so perfectly understood that it is impossible to convey my happiness and sense of liberation. With him, my thoughts blaze. The small, cramped rooms of Skinner Street fade and I dare to dream of a future that is larger and more thrilling than anything I have ever envisaged.

The first time they make love, they are lying on her mother's grave. Late evening, the sun a bright halo behind his head as he kisses her and rolls on top of her, his face cast in shadow. She is aware of the weight of him, the closeness of their bodies, the fabric of their clothes – a thin barrier between his skin and hers.

'I love you, sweet Pecksie.' There is a question in his words, which might be, *Are you sure?*

And in the dizzying breathless rush of her senses, she is

not sure of anything except her need to feel him touch her, to feel him close to her.

'I love you too,' she says, which means, she realizes, *Yes, I am sure.* Even though part of her is terrified, another part is watching, as if from above, as a girl, who looks like her, lies down across her mother's grave with a married man, lets him hitch up her skirt, reaches out to tug the material to one side.

His lips are soft against hers, then firmer, more urgent, his breath hot as he presses against her. Between her legs, an urgent pulse, an ache and then – suddenly – him. The shock of his flesh against her and, as the pressure increases, as he pushes into her, a sharp pain, which is also a relief, which is also the knowledge that she has made a choice. She is choosing to draw him closer, to push her hips against him, to kiss his neck and cheeks and mouth as he moves inside her.

Everything will be different now.

When she returns home, she creeps into the house unseen, tiptoes up the stairs unheard and pulls out her journal from beneath her mattress. She wants to write about the day but how – *how* – can she possibly mark the way in which it has transformed her?

In the end, she writes only, *The beginning is always today.*

It feels like a pledge to what she has done and a promise to all she might be – the bright future of freedom that she will have with Shelley.

The next day, standing outside her father's study, Mary mouths *He loves me*, and cannot help the smile that curves the corners of her mouth. Will her father be surprised? Although she and Shelley have kept their walks a secret, he must suspect something, must have noticed that, when Shelley comes for dinner, he stares at Mary and hangs upon her every word.

Her grin widens as she rehearses telling Mrs Godwin that Shelley loves her, that she is leaving Skinner Street for ever. She pictures waking next to him in the rooms he plans to rent for them – *a bower of love, where we will read and write and take delight in one another.*

She raps lightly on the study door, hears a growl from within. 'I'm *not* to be disturbed.'

'It's me, Father. It is important.'

A weary sigh. 'Come.'

The study is dark and dusty. It smells of candle wax and damp paper.

Her father is bent over his desk, writing, and doesn't look up as he says, 'What is so urgent? If somebody is bleeding, you should send for the doctor.'

'No one is hurt.' Even her father's irritation feels amusing today. 'I have happy news.'

'Can it not wait?'

She takes a breath. 'I am in love. And the gentleman loves me in return. I came to seek your blessing.'

Her father's face softens; he puts down his quill. 'In love, eh? Why isn't the gentleman here himself?'

'He would be, but I wanted to speak to you. I insisted.'

'You *insisted*?' He gives a dry chuckle. 'You are your mother's daughter, certainly. Who is this brave and fortunate fellow?'

'It is Mr Shelley.'

His smile vanishes. 'Shelley? *Percy Shelley?*'

He must be feigning surprise, for who else could she mean? But, no, by the severity of his expression, his shock is genuine. He truly hadn't suspected and he is, *oh, God,* he is angry and disappointed and shocked and – *oh, God.*

A humming sensation in her fingers and toes. Her body urges her to leave the room.

'We love each other . . . and it is a true sympathy of our

minds and our ideals, as well as of our hearts, just like you and Mamma – my *true* Mamma, I mean, not Mrs Godwin.'

She is gabbling and she should not have mentioned *that woman*'s name so dismissively because her father's expression darkens further, but now she cannot stop talking. 'I understand this seems sudden, Father, but I thought you would be happy to know I am upholding my mother's ideals – and yours. I have fallen in love with a poet and philosopher and we are so very happy –'

'He. Is. *Married*.'

'But . . . You do not believe marriage to be an essential institution.' Mary knows that when she was conceived her parents had not been married: they had wed only to protect her from scandal and gossip. 'Marriage is certainly not a prerequisite for love. You have said so yourself –'

'He has a *child*, Mary. His wife is pregnant with another.'

'I am aware,' she says acidly, then takes a breath, tries to steady her tone. If she can only lay out her argument clearly, her father will understand – she knows it. 'Shelley will support them, as any man should support his children. But nothing should keep man or woman in a loveless union, except foolish adherence to social convention – convention *you* have raised me to challenge and ignore.'

'I will not permit this.' Her father has paled. He is staring at her as though seeing her for the first time. His mouth twists in something like revulsion. She flinches from his contempt, but she is angry too, now. She lifts her chin and glares back at him.

'*All the sacred rights of humanity are violated by insisting on blind obedience*.' She feels a thrill at hearing words from her mother's most famous book in her own steady voice. 'My mother, whom you have told me I should emulate, saw no reason to marry before she had a child –'

'You have lain with this man? Mary, tell me you have not –'

'There is no reason for women to subscribe to chastity –'

'Have you lain with him?'

'Forcing modesty is simply a way of making women subject to men –'

'*Have you lain with him?*' He thunders the words, his face puce, his eyes boring into her. The last time he shouted at her, she was banished to Scotland and didn't see her family for months.

She grips her skirt, forces herself to speak. Her voice quivers. 'I do not belong to you. I am not your possession that you may dictate my actions.'

Her father has taught her to argue like a philosopher, even when her whole body is seething with shock and fury. He will concede to her logic – which has been the logic he has taught her all her life. He will apologize, will beg forgiveness. He will take her hands in his and tell her that he is proud of her fierce, independent spirit.

His face is stone. 'You disgust me. The shame – that a daughter of mine would be so reckless. You are a selfish, foolish child and I cannot bear to look at you. Go up to the schoolroom and wait while I think what to do with you.'

Each of his words is like a slap. She can feel her legs trembling.

'What to *do* with me? I have done nothing wrong, have done *nothing* except follow your ideals. I am not a child. You cannot banish me to the schoolroom –'

'Go! Get out,' he roars. 'Leave my sight before I do something I will regret.' He lurches forward, as if to grab her – does he mean to beat her?

She bolts from the study, pushing past Claire and Mrs Godwin, who have been listening outside the door.

As she paces the schoolroom, her breath comes in ragged, rage-filled sobs. She is supposed to meet Shelley in St Pancras

Cemetery at six o'clock. She must tell him what her father has said. But then . . . will he reconsider his promises towards her? Might he think that offending her father, whom he so respects and admires, is too great a cost?

Her arm stings. Without realizing, she has been scraping her nails over her scars, the raised shiny scratch marks that had been red and raw for so many years. It is an old habit. A child's habit and she is a woman now.

She balls her hands into fists, digs her nails into her palms.

Shelley will *not* forsake her. This will not change anything. She will leave Skinner Street to be with her lover. Over time, her father will realize how he has wronged them.

A heavy tread on the stairs.

She turns, ready to hear her father's apology.

His face is stern and pale. He says nothing.

He slams the door. The key rasps in the lock.

For a moment, her mind is a white blank and she cannot comprehend what has happened. It must be a mistake – her father would not lock her away. She tugs the handle. The door doesn't open. She slaps the wood. 'Father! Father, open the door. Let me out!'

No reply.

'Father, *please*! Don't leave me here. Please, *please*, Father!'

He is there, on the other side of the door, she is sure of it, but as she calls for him again and again, the only answer is silence.

Her palms sting as she slaps the door, throws her body against the heavy oak, beating it with her fists, kicking it until it judders, until the noise must travel through the whole house.

She sits on the floor and screams and screams until she tastes blood on each breath.

The door remains shut. No one comes.

The church bells chime five o'clock. What will Shelley think when she fails to meet him? Will he suppose she has changed her mind, or that something terrible has happened to her?

She goes to the window – she will climb out if she must. But it is too high – she will slip and fall and hit the cobbles below. Her legs will break, her skull will smash. She hears the crack of her bones against unforgiving stone.

It grows dark outside; she has no candle. She sits and waits by the door, trying to quell her rising panic. Soon, she knows, Claire or Mrs Godwin will bring her food.

She will shove past them and escape.

Shadows swarm in the corners of the room like the long-fingered creatures that lurk in her nightmares. She will not look at them. She will not listen to the voice in her mind, the voice she has heard since she was a child, which tells her that she is all alone in this world, that everybody will leave her in the end, that it is all her fault –

'Quiet,' she hisses to herself. 'Quiet!'

The sound of her voice makes the shadows shift. In the silence, shattered only by her panicked breaths, they reach for her. Each gulp of air is hot and tight, the shadows wrapping around her neck, like damp rags. The heaviness of them. Their rancid, wet weight. There is a fleshy hand rooting inside her ribcage, clutching her lungs, grasping her throat and crushing, crushing.

She can hear her own breaths, as if they belong to someone else, as if the rasping panic is happening to some other girl locked in a dusty attic, on her hands and knees, wheezing, coughing, crying. It is the same feeling that haunts her dreams, the sensation she has always had: everyone has left her. Everyone will always leave her. And something terrible is reaching up from the black pit that always squats on the edge of every breath.

The darkness has found her. The darkness is around her and inside her, and she will have to face it alone.

'No,' she growls, as her vision narrows to a single, pulsing pinpoint of black.

'No!' She will *not* slump on this floor and let the darkness drag her down. She will *not* let this feeling take her. She will rise to her feet and find a way to leave this place.

Slowly, painfully, she manages to stand, to steady her breath. Then she stares at the door, waiting. Someone will have to come for her soon. When they do, she will be ready.

Church bells toll the hours as evening deepens into night. Seven o'clock, eight o'clock. Still no one.

Nine o'clock. She is sure she can hear voices outside, can hear a man shouting her name. She leans out of the window but she can't see the front of the house, only the side-streets with the shut-up butchers' shops, the metallic bite of blood heavy in the night air.

'Shelley!' she calls. And she is certain she hears noises below – the slamming of a door, an angry cry, a woman's shriek.

Feet on the stairs. The rasp of the key.

The door flies open and Shelley bursts into the room.

He pulls Mary into his arms, clasping her tightly. She can feel the hammering of his heart against her chest, can hear the anger in his voice as he says, 'Are you hurt?'

She shakes her head, so relieved to see him that she can't gather breath to speak.

More footsteps on the stairs and light from a candle in the doorway. Claire's face is pale, her eyes filled with terrified excitement. 'I fetched him as soon as I could. Father won't speak to either of you but Mother is coming up. She won't let you leave.'

'She can't stop us.' Shelley's voice is hard, his jaw set. It is the demeanour of a man who is used to getting whatever he wants – a man who shapes the world around his own desires.

'Indeed I can.' Mrs Godwin reaches the top of the stairs, wheezing, and glares at the two girls. 'Mary, you will not cause your father more grief by running away like a silly, spoiled child. You have always been over-indulged. This latest selfishness comes as no surprise to me but I will not permit you to bring more public shame and private sorrow on this family. Your departed mother caused enough grief to last your father a lifetime.'

'And yet he chose to add to his grief by marrying *you*,' Mary snaps. She can feel Shelley staring at her and she is suddenly aware that he has rarely heard her use anything except the sweetest and most measured tones.

Mrs Godwin must notice his surprise because her expression turns cunning. 'You see, Mr Shelley, the girl is all sugar in her voice and roses in her cheeks, as long as she gets her own way. I suppose you've not seen her angry before? Pure poison, it is. You be warned.'

Mary imagines pushing past Mrs Godwin, imagines shoving into her on the stairs. She pictures her stepmother's smug smile turning to shock as she begins to fall.

Shelley's voice is flat and hard. 'I love Mary beyond all reason, and you cannot keep her here. So I pray, let us past.'

'She's a child. A girl of sixteen. And you, a married man of twenty-two with children.'

'That matters not.'

'It matters not *to you*, but I dare say it will matter to the officers who pursue you for abducting a young lady from her home. I dare say it will matter to the judge when he decides whether you may see your children or not.'

A pained expression crosses Shelley's face. Mary's heart plummets. He will choose his children before her – of course he must.

He presses his forehead to hers. 'We shall be united for ever, sweet Pecksie. I will not let them part us.'

From his pocket, he pulls something cold and heavy. She hears Mrs Godwin gasp as he presses it into Mary's palm, wraps her fingers around it.

Claire cries, 'Stop, Mary!'

She looks at the pistol, her mind struggling to catch up.

Surely he can't mean for her to use it against Mrs Godwin. It is one thing to picture pushing her down the stairs, but *this* . . .

'I don't –' Mary tries to drop it but he won't let her. Instead, he takes her right hand, holding the gun, in his left hand, presses his thumb over her finger on the trigger and pushes the barrel into the skin beneath his jaw. With his other hand, he takes a small bottle from his pocket and shoves it towards her.

Unthinkingly, she takes the bottle. Cold, like the gun.

'Enough laudanum to kill a man.' His words throb down the metal barrel, into her shaking hand. She will drop the gun, let the bottle fall to the floor, – but *no*! She is terrified to let go, terrified that the gun will go off or that Shelley will pick it up in anger and despair and then – and then she doesn't know what he will do.

There is a fierce exhilaration in his eyes. He looks like a stranger.

'You will drink the laudanum and I shall stay with you while you fall asleep, sweet love. Then I shall use this.' His voice becomes a strangled whisper as he jabs the gun hard into his own throat. 'I shall follow you into eternity. We shall be together for ever.'

Claire and Mrs Godwin are sobbing. Mary finds it hard to breathe. This man loves her enough to die for her – he cannot bear to live without her. It is like a spell he has cast: shoot, drink and sleep. She need only do as he says and nothing will be able to separate them. She dares not move, so she stands, staring into the love and despair in his eyes.

'Don't you want to be with me for ever?' he whispers. 'Don't you long for me?'

She nods, shaking.

But even as she is agreeing with him, her body trembling, she flinches from the idea of death, from the thought of the dark hand in her dreams, which is always reaching for her. The part of her mind that knows she must live tells her she must remain rational and detached to survive. *Argue like a philosopher.*

'I long for you,' she says. 'I want to be with you, more than anything. But I want to *live* with you. True love may demand sacrifice but it does not ask that we kill ourselves. If it be true, surely our love will find a way beyond this, a way to rise above whatever impediments are put before us.'

She can see his expression softening, can see the strange, half-crazed fire in his eyes fading. Gently, carefully, she kisses the knuckles of his hand, still clasped around the gun. 'Shelley, I do not want to die.'

In the candlelight, his eyes are huge; he looks frightened and relieved as he lets the gun drop. Mary puts her arms around him, pulling him close. He is shaking too. He whispers, 'I cannot live without you.'

'You won't have to.' In a low voice, so Mrs Godwin cannot hear, she says, 'We'll find a way. I promise. We'll find a way to escape together.'

Troyes, France, August 1814

The tiny fire splutters in the bare room of a deserted farm-house. Like many of the villages they have travelled through, this place has been ransacked by Napoleon's retreating army.

In the corner, a mud-encrusted jacket has been discarded next to a brownish stain on the bare floor, which may or may not be blood. No bed, just a broken pile of boards and straw and horsehair, where a bed might once have been. Everything smells of black rot. The floorboards are damp under Mary's fingers.

Claire is curled up asleep in a broken armchair, while Shelley sits on the floor, leaning against the wall, Mary's head pillowed on his shoulder. He has folded one of his coats and a cloak to make her a bed – *a nest for my sweet Pecksie*. Occasionally, he pauses in writing to kiss her forehead.

Are you warm enough, my love? Are you hungry? Do you want for anything? Sometimes, he passes her a bottle of cheap wine. They take turns swigging from it, laughing at the acidic burn.

She is cold and exhausted and uncomfortable, and she has never been happier.

Watching the play of orange light over his cheekbones, over his lips as he writes, she lets her thoughts drift, closes her eyes and sees a hand reaching for her face – she jolts awake with a cry.

Shelley's arms are strong around her. 'Pecksie, what's wrong?'

She shakes her head, not wanting to summon the image from the dream, its dark menace.

As he kisses her and strokes her hair, her eye falls on the paper where he has been writing.

My dearest Harriet,
I write to you from this detestable French town; I write to show that I do not forget you; I write to urge you to come to Switzerland, where you will find me waiting for you, my heart full of love and friendship for you, as ever it has been. Send a letter to Neufchâtel, where we shall travel next, and let me know if I might soon delight in your company and welcome you to some sweet retreat

'What is this?' Mary pushes Shelley away, clutching the paper in fingers that feel suddenly numb, as if they have been touched by some vast, bleak portent that her mind cannot comprehend. 'Are you writing to your *wife*?'

'Oh, it is nothing at all! Only a little note to comfort her.'

'This is not *comfort*.' Mary spits the word, shoves the letter into his chest. 'Are you *inviting her* to join us?'

'As a friend only –'

'She is your *wife!* When did you plan to tell me of this? Or did you think you might avoid telling me? That you could wait until she *appeared* somewhere on our travels and I would be unable to protest? How *could* you?' She jabs her finger into his chest again.

This time, he catches it, holds it. His gaze is shuttered, as if something within him has closed off. 'Do you believe I own you, Mary? Do you believe you are my possession, that you should do my bidding and I yours?'

'You *know* I do not!' The unfairness of his words only stokes her rage – he is using her mother's arguments against her. 'But this is different.' She pushes the piece of paper into his chest again. She would like to shred it, or burn it, as she sometimes does with her secret, fury-filled journal entries.

'Is it different?' he asks calmly. 'How?'

She cannot give an answer, only an incoherent roar. Clenching her teeth around the sound, she tries to swallow it, tries to shake her head. She needs a moment to breathe. She holds up her hand and knocks into the wine bottle, sending it spinning into the wall. It shatters, splashing the dark remnants of the wine over Shelley's letter.

Mary stares at him, appalled, as Claire jolts awake. 'What is it? What's wrong?'

'Nothing, dear Clairie, go back to sleep.' Shelley doesn't shift his gaze from Mary's. His expression is narrow now, calculating. She has seen the same look when he is trying to rent a room for the night and has found the price is too high.

Very quietly, so Claire cannot hear, Shelley murmurs, 'They warned me about your temper. Your father and Mrs Godwin. They told me you could be . . . *impossible*. They said I would not want to remain with you, once I had seen it for myself. Perhaps I should have believed them.'

Mary's mouth feels full of choking dirt, as if she has swallowed the darkness and rot in the room, as if it is pressing on her tongue, sliding down her throat, dampening the rage in her chest, turning it to terror. Weeping, she throws her arms around her lover, begs him to forgive her, begs him to love her still. And while she is entreating and begging and weeping, it is as though part of her is observing from above. Something inside her watches with faint disgust as Mary makes herself small and weak and pathetic so that Shelley will scoop her into his arms and comfort her.

After he has fallen asleep, she lies curled up on her side in the nest he has made for her. Cradling her hands around her stomach, she tries to breathe through the nausea that pulses there, tries to envisage the tiny creature growing, the small speck of life that she will keep safe, no matter the cost.

Now, on the London street, Shelley wraps his arms around her. 'My sweet Pecksie, I came as soon as I read your note.' He kisses her again, long and hard. Mary leans into him, her whole body humming.

The bread-seller hoots. 'You can take your front-door work away from my stall.'

Shelley laughs and bows to the woman, then links his arm through Mary's; her face is hot and she can't meet the other woman's gaze.

'Spare your blushes, my love.' Shelley kisses her flushed cheek. This draws more raucous laughter from the bread-seller, a tut and a sigh from a woman who has to step around them.

'Fancy *tutting* at strangers to show your distress.' Shelley grins. 'Fancy *sighing* to express your disapproval. Fancy living with a discontented woman who sighs and tuts!' He kisses her again and pulls her closer as they walk.

Mary smiles. 'She had a mouth that looked like snarled darning.'

'I was going to say she had a face that would sour fresh grapes – that's Shakespeare. Where's yours from?'

'Me.'

'Your genius bewitches me at every turn.'

'I have this for you.' She holds out a little packet of the rosemary soap she uses. He has always said he loves its smell, that it makes him think of her.

'I hope you're not giving me rosemary for remembrance.'

'Not at all,' she says lightly. That is exactly why she has given it to him.

'I think of you every moment we're apart. You believe me, don't you?'

'I do.' As she looks into his eyes, holding his hand, this feels like the truth.

'I long to be with you and little Willmouse. But I wish these damned bailiffs would leave me be! Poets should remain un-acquainted with mundane matters.'

'But surely you are very well acquainted with the bailiffs by now – enough to hide when you see them.'

It is a teasing barb but she knows she has gone too far. Shelley's expression sharpens. Quickly, she adds, 'I am glad you have evaded them, of course.'

In fact, Shelley likely hasn't seen a bailiff in months – it is

Mary and Claire who are woken by them pounding on the door, who are terrified by their threats. But he is still scowling, so she makes her tone teasing. 'I'm giving you rosemary so you *remember* to wash your face.'

He laughs and leans close to her ear. 'You're a wonder, Mary Godwin.' The relief she feels is worth all the hurt and anger she must swallow daily while he is away.

'You have missed me, then?' he asks.

'Not too much,' she lies, 'although I have missed the wine you used to bring for us.'

He chuckles, as she knew he would. She loves this about him too: all her life she has been told she is too sharp, too abrasive. She has grown used to checking her speech and editing her conversation so she will not be considered rude. She must wear a sort of . . . façade to be acceptable or likeable. When she is with Shelley, the mask shifts. When she is with him, she is a livelier, funnier, prettier version of herself. He finds her quick wit and sharp mind captivating – as long as she shows no irritation towards him.

'Your letter today gave me such joy,' Shelley says. 'I can hardly wait to travel south with you again, to leave all this behind us. Well, we won't leave *everything* behind us.' He runs his hand down the back of her skirt and gently cups her behind.

She jumps and laughs, then looks over her shoulder in case someone is watching them together. The fear of the bailiffs following her is impossible to escape. But there is only the moon, hanging small and low, like a clouded jewel, above the black silhouettes of the rooftops.

They walk quickly together to St Pancras Cemetery, deserted now in the dull evening light, which is bluish and raw.

Mary doesn't hesitate in lying down on the ground when Shelley spreads out his cloak and kisses her again and again.

Like the first time, the fear that there might be eyes on her, the feeling that she doesn't care. There is danger in the openness of their act. In the brazenness of the risk, there is freedom. He pulls her on top of him, his lips insistent on her neck, on her breasts; her hair falls around their faces and they are alone together, only his lips on her skin, his body beneath hers, his hands on her hips.

She moves above him, he moves within her, and she has already left this place, has already been transported to another world, which exists only in the shared space of their bodies.

Afterwards, she lies next to him on the cold ground, his arms wrapped around her, her cloak across them. The darkness itself feels like a comfort, hiding them from prying eyes.

'I can't wait to see Geneva with you, my love,' he murmurs. 'A new beginning. You'll see.'

From somewhere in the trees, a nightingale's song unfurls into the navy sky. Mary's spirits rise. As if this moment, with all its music and darkness, could lift them upwards and carry them somewhere new and unknown. It will be the two of them, together, just as she has always wanted. They can leave London, with its bleak memories, its shadows and ghosts.

The grubby, misty streets dissolve, the dull English weather fades into the ether, along with its sour-faced people. Once she has Shelley to herself, the darkness will fade – she is sure of it. The nightmares will vanish and she will know – she will *truly* know – that he cannot leave her, that he will not desert her again. She will stop worrying that, somehow, he has found out her secrets and is quietly repulsed by her.

'What are you thinking?' he asks.

How long has he been watching her? She smooths her expression.

'I'm looking at the stars.'

'Yes, but what are you *thinking*?'

'Nothing at all,' she lies, and kisses his forehead. 'I'm just so happy.'

3

The world to me was a secret, which I desired to discover.

Morez, France, 1816

'So, you're telling us it's not safe to travel now?' Mary asks the *voiturier*.

Outside the tiny boarding-house in Morez, the man shakes his head and scowls. Stoop-shouldered and hatchet-faced, he has frowned or glowered every time Mary has spoken to him over the past week, as they have travelled south through France in biting wind, rain and even sleet.

Willmouse has been red-cheeked and screaming for days. Her exhaustion is bone-deep. She turns to Shelley. 'Perhaps we should stay here until the weather improves.'

'Perhaps.' He kisses her distractedly, but she can sense the way his thoughts are in the mountains already, slipping and sliding down the treacherous slopes.

She puts her fingers on his wrist and presses lightly to bring his attention back to her.

Look at me. For God's sake, look at me.

He glances at her, brushes his lips over hers, then gazes out again at the clouds massing on the mountains.

'I want to wait,' she says softly. '*Please*, Shelley.' The thought of putting Willmouse in danger opens a hollow space within her, an empty chamber, which echoes with baby Clara's last cries.

Of course you don't know how to be a good mother – your own mother died.

'We *can't* wait,' Claire says. Her eyes are red-rimmed, her lips chapped and raw where she has been chewing them. 'We have to go *now.*'

'I worry about Willmouse.'

'You're always worried about *everything.* Remember, you nearly didn't come to France with us two years ago.'

And you never think of anyone except yourself. No point in saying it.

Claire used to kick Mary in the shins under the table at Skinner Street, then look smug when Mary was scolded for cursing at her sister. *Sorry,* Mary would have to say, forcing her expression into sweetness, her voice into lightness. *Sorry, Claire, sorry, Father.* Then she would turn to Mrs Godwin and say, with heavy sarcasm, *So sorry, Mamma. Forgive me, I beg you.*

Such interactions were followed by the usual banishment to her room, where Mary would scrawl in her journal and scratch bloody welts on her arms.

Now, Mary shoots a savage glare at her sister and says, through a gritted smile, 'Claire's memory fails her. And I see no benefit in risking ourselves in this weather.'

But she can sense Shelley wavering, can see him remembering how she delayed leaving Skinner Street, how she fretted about deserting her father. Her father, who will not even look at her now. Her father who, last time she tried to see him, left her weeping on the doorstep in the rain, longing to launch a rock through his shuttered window.

It wouldn't make him see her, wouldn't quiet the furious, animal rage within her.

Shelley takes her hands. 'Pecksie, you mustn't be so fearful – think of the adventure!'

The snow-peaked mountains look like jagged teeth in the smashed black mouth of the yawning sky. The thought of travelling through them in the stormy darkness sends spiked flickers of terror through her chest. She has to force herself to breathe slowly, to speak calmly. 'I don't think it's safe.'

'*Beaucoup de neige et glace,*' the *voiturier* mutters.

'Lots of snow and ice,' Mary says. 'So, we should wait?'

The driver shakes his head again.

'He just wants to be paid more,' Claire says. 'Offer him more money, Shelley.'

At the word *money*, the driver's expression brightens, but now Shelley seems hesitant.

'Please let's stay here, Shelley,' Mary says. She is torn between wanting to beg him and knowing he will be more impressed with her – that he may even love her more – if she is brave, if she chooses to go in spite of the danger.

He sighs. 'I can pay a *small* supplement . . .'

Claire frowns. 'I thought you had more money now.'

'I have,' Shelley says, 'but not enough to be wasteful. Now quiet a moment – let me think.'

The sharpness in his voice freezes Mary instantly. The moment he shows any displeasure, she feels petrified and alone. Before she ran away with him, before she bore his children, she'd never felt he completely belonged to her. She'd hoped that the passing of the years would make her feel closer to him, happier with him, safer with him. But holding on to Shelley is like trying to clutch sunlight: you might think you have it, might feel it gilding your palm, then look down to discover that the clouds have shifted, the light has moved onwards.

Now you are alone, waiting in the shadows, hoping for its return.

'Shelley, please!' Claire says. 'I can't bear to wait –'

He holds up a hand to quiet her. Claire pushes it aside and flings her arms around his neck, sobbing. Mary shoots her a furious glare. Claire shuts her eyes, presses her cheek to Shelley's.

'Please, Shelley, dear! We *must* leave now! If we wait, Byron will think we are not coming. He will believe I have forgotten him.'

Claire pulls away, gazing up at Shelley, her cheeks tear-streaked, soft mouth trembling.

Mary would like to slap her hard across her face. Claire's head would whip around – oh, the sound would be so satisfying! She can almost feel the sting in her palm.

She pictures Shelley's disappointment, sees the stiff set of his shoulders as he turns away.

She knits her fingers together and squeezes until her joints ache.

'Please, sweet Shelley,' Claire croons, her face inches from his. 'I will be lost without Byron, but only you can help me now.'

Shelley loves rescuing young women. He has told Mary, proudly, of how he'd saved his wife, Harriet, from her dreadful family. Before Harriet, he'd liberated a young schoolteacher from her awful sister. And Mary. He freed Mary from her father's expectations, released her from society's shackles. This is what he tells her.

'Please say you'll help me,' Claire begs.

When he nods, she gives a squeal of delight and hugs him tightly.

'You are so generous! You have made me the happiest of women.'

Mary has to turn away. When she looks back, Claire is staring at her over Shelley's shoulder. Her chewed lip splits; a trickle of blood seeps from it. Claire licks it and grins, her teeth pinkish.

'Perhaps Willmouse and I should stay,' Mary says stiffly.

'Nonsense!' Shelley laughs. 'I'll pay for ten strong men to follow in another carriage. If we become stuck, they can dig us out.'

Don't be ridiculous, Shelley. She doesn't say it, of course.

He reminds her of the boys in Skinner Street who would beg the butcher to give them a pig's bladder, which they'd fill with air. They would kick it around, whooping and laughing, for hours. Long after it had deflated, Mary would see them chasing it, bellowing, pretending to each other and to themselves that the ragged, flaccid organ was still a ball of sorts.

'Do we have enough money for ten men?' Mary tries to keep her voice light.

'I have a little more money of late.' He smiles and strokes her cheek. 'You need not worry about anything, sweet Pecksie.'

A humming in her ears, like a fly. 'Where is the money from?'

'Doesn't she know about your allowance?' Claire asks.

The humming grows louder. 'Your allowance? They've given it to you again?'

Shelley's father and grandfather had cut off his allowance two years ago; he has been borrowing from the bank ever since.

'Why are they giving you back your allowance?'

Stillness shutters Shelley's expression. Hostility creeps into his gaze. From the corner of her eye, Mary sees Claire shake her head.

Stop talking, Mary. Stop asking questions.

'That is not your concern, Mary.'

The humming grows to a buzz. Mary speaks over it, her voice too loud. 'It is my concern! If you have money, I should know something of how you came by it.'

'Stop this.'

'We are equals in love and –'

71

'*Enough!*' Shelley snaps.

'But –'

'Stop with all your *questions*, Mary. You do not need to *know* everything. Is it not enough that I provide for you and for our child?'

He waits for her to respond but she can't speak, can't gather breath into the yawning hollow in her chest. The humming settles into her skull.

Nod. Smile. Nod again.

'If I tell you I have enough money, you must trust me. You *do* trust me, don't you?'

She bites the inside of her cheek, tastes metal, blinks. Her eyes burn. She knows – she *knows* what he must have told his relatives to persuade them to restore his allowance.

'And so it is settled.' He gives a broad smile, which stretches too widely across his face, not touching his eyes. 'We will leave tonight. By tomorrow we will be in Geneva, the weather be damned. Such an adventure, isn't it, Mary?'

He has told his family he is still in love with Harriet. That he plans to return to his wife. That Mary is a mistake, that their child is an unfortunate by-product: he doesn't intend to stay with her, with the other woman, who cannot take the name of Mrs Shelley.

'It will be wonderful, won't it?' he asks again, more brightly, gripping her fingers.

She feels as if some frozen breath from the mountains has forced its way into her lungs and lodged there. Her hand lies like a dead animal between his palms.

'Forgive me for snapping, Pecksie. We are all tired and you are scared of this journey when there is no need to be. We will feel differently by tomorrow.'

She doesn't reply as he leads her upstairs. She lies down on the bed, lets him place her limbs where he wants them, lets him turn her onto her stomach, like a jointed doll. When he presses his lips to the back of her neck, she closes her eyes. When he puts his mouth between her legs and asks if she forgives him, she gasps, protesting that it's not fair to hold her hostage with his tongue.

'But do you forgive me?' The words vibrate against her, hum through her.

Yes, she says. Yes. Yes, of course she does.

London, November 1814. Eighteen months previously

Mary retches again into the basin, wipes her mouth with a rag and slumps back on the sofa, exhausted. She has never known tiredness like this: every joint is weighted, every breath laboured – even her eyelids seem made of lead.

Shelley has been away for three days, trying to *resolve his finances*. This means begging money from friends or visiting his grandfather, demanding he restore Shelley's allowance.

Maybe he will return today with money – at least enough for a comb, she will say, as she tries to untangle her hair with her fingers. Perhaps that will amuse him. She mustn't demand the money or start to cry. Last time she'd wept, he'd put his arms around her and apologized, then quickly left, promising to return the next day with money. She hadn't seen him for two weeks.

She loves to gaze out of the window at the clustered houses, the line of trees leading up to St Pancras Church and somewhere, just out of sight, her mother's gravestone. It is a comfort to feel her so close by. Mary doesn't believe in an afterlife, not really, but sometimes she can almost *hear* her mother's voice.

Mary watches people rush past – to and from St Pancras

Church, or off to the market or who knows where? These other lives, so full of hopes and fears and dreams, are as real to the strangers as Mary's expectation that, any moment now, her lover will open the door.

She stares at the knots and cracks in the wood. *Come back, Shelley. Now.* On the back of the door hangs the navy-blue wool coat he wears to the theatre – when they *used* to go to the theatre. When he asks for money, he wears his old brown coat with the ragged hem and the missing button.

Mary lifts it from its hook and puts it on over her cotton house dress. She presses her face to it and inhales. It smells of wood and wool, paper and smoke. It smells of him. The sleeves are comically long on her – he will laugh when he arrives. She will take it off slowly, provocatively, as though it is a silk nightgown.

She rests her hand on the small mound of her stomach – will he still find her beautiful? He says he finds her more ravishing than ever. Last week, he'd kissed her aching breasts and whispered that he loved her even more because she was fecund.

'*Fecund!*' She'd laughed. 'That's a *terrible* word. It makes me think of mushrooms.'

He'd chuckled. 'Fruitful, then.'

'Better.'

'Flowering.' Another kiss.

'Better still.'

The church bell tolls ten, eleven in the morning and he doesn't come. Midday and the door stays shut.

Usually, Claire would go out to find him, but she is trying to make peace with her mother at Skinner Street.

Mary puts her cold hands deep into the pockets of his coat. In the left side pocket, she feels soft leather and pulls out a single glove. How like Shelley, she thinks, smiling, to have only one glove. She pulls it on, enjoying the thought of her hand in the space that his hand has made. It fits perfectly. She frowns and stares at the glove, examining the fine grain of the leather, the elegant stitching, the tiny buttons at the wrist.

A woman's glove.

Her stomach plummets. She rushes to the basin, retching again and again, bringing up thin streams of bitter, yellowish bile.

The clock has struck three before the door opens and in he comes, beaming, arms flung wide. 'I have a surprise, sweet Pecksie!' He whirls her around, pressing his rough cheek against hers.

Usually, she would laugh and kiss him, pulling off his coat, his shirt, her dress . . . Today, she stays rigid and doesn't make a sound. She feels as though she is made of the same dead, lumpy stuff as the scuffed horsehair sofa.

'What's wrong?' He examines her. 'My coat looks excellent on you!'

She fixes her gaze on the grubby floor. It is hard to take a full breath. In her clenched fist, in the pocket of his best coat, she holds the glove, which belongs to another woman. She clamps her fingers around it, as if crushing the life from some small, dark-toothed creature.

'Are you well, Pecksie? Have you missed me? You're so pale, my love! But I have a surprise – my university chum, Thomas Hogg, has loaned me one hundred pounds. My father may repay Hogg, even if he won't give *me* the money, because he knows Hogg's family, so the shame of the debt will madden him . . . Why aren't you smiling? This is such good news, don't you see?'

She steps away from him. It is impossible to think with him so close, impossible to find the words she needs.

Drawing her hand out of the coat pocket she opens her fist. The glove is screwed into a tight ball and lies on her palm, like an injured animal.

His face turns stony, his gaze remote. Something in her shrinks from his anger. She feels, already, like the small girl who used to be scolded for sneaking into her father's study and searching through his desk. She'd only been trying to find something that belonged to her mother, something she could keep, but her father had dragged her to her room and refused to speak to her for a week.

Words stick in her throat. Both of them stare at the glove.

'What?' Shelley finally says; his voice is flint.

'It's a glove, a – a *woman's* glove.' Her throat aches.

Her father's voice in her head, *You must argue your point like a philosopher, Mary.*

'Ye-e-e-s.' Shelley draws out the word, as if she has said something stupid.

Through gritted teeth, she manages to say, 'It's not mine.'

'And?' He folds his arms. When she risks looking up at him, his expression is still flat, his mouth pressed into a bloodless line.

'Well . . . whose is it?' *Logic is the thing, Mary. Logic and rationality.*

'Does it matter?'

'It matters to me.'

'I think you should calm down, Mary. The glove is insignificant. It means nothing.'

A surge of anger. It *is* significant and it means *something*. How can he treat her like this – as if she is stupid and an irritation, as if she is making a fuss over a triviality?

'Whose glove is it, Shelley?'

'Think of the baby. Calm down.'

'I *am* calm.' Her voice wobbles. 'Tell me.'

'I'm not going to tell you about something that doesn't concern you.'

The anger burns inside her now. 'It *does* concern me! How can you say it doesn't?' He tries to speak but she talks over him, raising her voice. 'I'm carrying your child. I'm nauseated and exhausted and all alone here. No one talks to me. I have no money, no friends, *nothing*. You disappear for *days* and I trust you to return. I *trust* you.'

She is breathless now, her thoughts like knotted wool, her argument garbled and irrational, illogical, but it feels good to raise her voice at him, good to let the words pour from her. 'How can you tell me that it doesn't concern me? How *dare* you tell me that –'

'That's enough,' he says. His voice is flat, his expression bored. 'I'm not going to explain myself to a woman who shouts at me.' In spite of his tone, she sees that his hands are shaking.

'But –'

'No, Mary. You don't own me and I don't own you. Do I ask for an account of every second of your day while I'm gone? Well, do I?'

'That's not fair! I have no choice.'

'You have a choice, Mary. The choice is very clear. You can stay here and I will look after you and love you, as I have been doing.'

He waits, looking at her. His face is all hard angles and tight muscles – the face of a stranger. She can feel the next words hanging over her, like the blade of a sword above her naked neck.

'You can let me love you, as I want to, Mary. Or you can leave.'

Her legs tingle, grow frigid, grow numb. She sits on the

sofa. There is a loud pulsing in her ears, like a drum warning her of some barely sensed danger.

'But –' Her voice cracks; she swallows, tries again. 'But where would I go?'

Shelley gives a little shrug, as if shifting the weight of something uneven across his shoulders – something like a woollen coat with one pocket a tiny bit heavier with the weight of a woman's glove. Not a weight he would ever really notice. Certainly not a weight he would ever need to put down.

'I don't know, Mary,' he says levelly. 'Where would you go?'

Morez to Geneva, 1816

Mary is trying to doze with her head on Shelley's shoulder. Willmouse is asleep in her arms; every time the carriage jerks forward, the baby startles, flinging up his little hands in surrender.

Shelley chuckles. 'Don't know how he stays asleep.'

'He can sleep through anything. You'll see.' Mary's cheeks ache from forcing a smile. How will she keep him safe if Shelley leaves them? How will she keep him alive? She pictures herself going back to her father's house; she would fling herself at his feet on bended knees.

She sees him turning away.

If she is going to survive – if she is going to keep her child alive – she will need money. She has none of her own. Even the five silver thaler coins in her little purse are Shelley's.

'You won't mind giving these to the driver, will you? I've already paid him but he seems to want more. I can't stand to be fiddling about with money.'

Mary had taken them, feeling their weight and warmth in her palm. Then she'd tucked them into her purse. They feel too heavy. They feel too light.

'Stop *fidgeting*, Mary!' Claire sighs. 'You can't still be nervous, surely?'

Mary is about to reply when the carriage skids and lurches to one side. Her stomach plummets and she clutches Willmouse closer. 'Please slow down!' she calls. 'Please.' The carriage slides again. She closes her eyes.

This is what love is like, she thinks. A careering slide along an ice-rimed path. A single false step, a stumble: annihilation.

'*Ralentissez maintenant!*,' Claire calls to the driver. When he doesn't slow, she bangs on the side of the carriage with her fist. '*Trop vite! Ralentissez!* For Heaven's sake! Does he want to kill us?'

The driver has already been slowing the horses at every turn, saying, '*Doucement, doucement*,' in such a soothing tone that Claire's bad temper – when *she* had insisted on travelling in these conditions – feels even more unreasonable.

Shelley opens one eye sleepily. 'Christ! How much longer will this take?'

Mary apologizes to the driver and asks him to slow down but he ignores her, chewing his moustache, muttering something that sounds very much like '*Bâtarde anglaise.*'

Perhaps she should tell him to stop, should give him one of the coins. She closes her hand more tightly around the little purse. When they reach Geneva safely, she will pay him.

'Byron has his own driver,' Claire says. 'And a valet, even his own doctor. I wish I was with them now, instead of here!' She chews her lip. 'I wish he'd reply to my letters.'

'He's travelling,' Mary says. 'Perhaps he's distracted.'

'Do you mean he's ignoring me?'

'I mean only that he must be busy.'

'You're suggesting he'll have forgotten who I am! Why are you so spiteful, Mary?'

Mary bites down on her frustration. She closes her eyes,

and sees the words form behind the lids, as if she is writing them in her journal: *Perhaps, Claire, he doesn't remember who you are with your clothes on. Perhaps he would only recognize you with your legs apart . . .*

A breath. Mary opens her eyes, fixes a smile. 'Perhaps he doesn't recognize your writing so hasn't opened the letters.' This seems to pacify her sister, who returns to staring gloomily out of the window.

Mary tries to imagine what Byron will be like. She sees a giant of a man, with a book in one hand and a flagon of wine in the other. She has always tried not to be intimidated by famous men – when she was as young as ten, her father had encouraged her to debate philosophical ideas with his friends, even great poets like Coleridge.

But what can one say to a man with a reputation as scandalous as Byron's? How does one make conversation with the most famous poet in all of England, who has had affairs with the wives of at least two lords, who is besotted with his half-sister? Did she *really* have his child?

One can hardly talk about the weather with such a man. One can hardly enquire as to the health of his family.

How are your sister and your niece? Or should I say your lover and your daughter?

Shelley, still with one eye open, murmurs, 'Doesn't Byron also travel with a harem of women to service his every need?'

'You're a beast!' Claire growls. 'And a hypocrite.'

'I was only jesting.' Shelley's tone is mild but, with her head on his shoulder, Mary feels the sudden tension run through him.

'It wasn't funny.' A tear rolls down Claire's cheek.

'Forgive me, Clairie.' Shelley pats her arm. To Mary, he murmurs, 'And I didn't even *mention* Byron's relationship with his sister.'

'Why did you call Shelley a hypocrite?' Mary asks, staring at Claire, willing her to answer.

Claire narrows her eyes, says nothing.

Mary refuses to drop her gaze. She feels a tiny thrill of victory when Claire turns away and looks out at the bleak, monochrome mountains.

For a moment, Mary has the wild urge to ask Shelley the same question, but she knows that if she does, he will look her in the eye and lie to her. And Mary will sense the lie, will hear it in his voice and see it in his face, but she will have to pretend that she believes him.

She feels an urge to write in her journal: *When C is sad, she looks like a spaniel.*

Instead, she grips the reassuring shape of her journal through her skirt. She looks out of the window at the snow-swept mountainside, at the houses that cluster along it, like snail shells clinging tightly to a rock.

'Think of living so far from everything. How do they survive being trapped in the winter?'

'I'd go mad if I was shut in. Perhaps the beauty keeps them sane.'

'Do you think they notice the beauty, when they see it so often?' Mary tries to envisage scratching out a life on this steep slope. What would she do if her baby was ill? Would she go to her neighbour? Perhaps they would build a fire together and take turns to watch the child through the night, while someone else braved the darkness and the wind to fetch the doctor.

'I'd far rather live in a city,' Shelley says. 'Less lonely.'

Mary hears door after door slamming in her face in London; she sees friend after friend pretending not to know her. She draws a shaky breath, tries to place herself inside one of these houses. Frozen and lonely, yet she feels a thread of longing for these people who have clustered their lives so closely. What would it be like to live alongside those who had known and loved you all your days – whose lives fitted into yours, like the knitted bones and muscles of a breathing body?

The scars on her arms throb. She scratches at them absently.

Shelley takes her hand, kisses her knuckles. Sometimes she wonders if he can read her thoughts, or perhaps it is just that something in him senses her sadness. He leans across and presses his lips to her cheek. 'It will be wonderful here, I promise,' he whispers. He smells of the rosemary soap she'd given him. She leans against his shoulder. Of course it will be better now they have escaped London – of *course* it will. No bailiffs, no scraping together pennies for food, no freezing nights huddled beneath a blanket, wondering where her lover is, whom he is with. In London, he was always hiding something, but no more of that.

In Geneva, she will be with Shelley, and Claire will be with Byron. They will read books and drink wine and Mary will feel at last that she has the space to think, the freedom to write.

The carriage slides again. The driver growls at the horses as one of the animals slips. The carriage skids and Mary's stomach keels.

'Perhaps we should walk this part,' Shelley says, his focus still firmly on his book. 'I thought you'd paid him to travel carefully.'

'I'm sure he's doing his best.' She clutches the five coins in her purse. 'But perhaps walking would be safer.'

Shelley doesn't like shouting orders and, though Mary's French is inferior to her sister's – Claire speaks like a native – Mary calls, '*Monsieur? Monsieur? Arrêtez un moment, s'il vous plaît.*'

Mary's terrible accent draws a smile from Claire and she accepts Shelley's hand to help her down from the carriage.

The road gleams with ice; their breath ghosts the air in

front of them. Shivering, Mary holds Willmouse closer under her cloak and kisses the top of his head.

Without waiting for her, Shelley sets off towards a promontory overlooking the valley. Mary imagines the city as perfect – as if the foul weather has rinsed it clean. Unlike the bitter grime and grind of London, Geneva will be nestled safely in the midst of these mountains. In her mind, somehow, it is sun-dappled.

'Oh!' Shelley stands on the promontory, gazing down at the city.

There is no city.

The roiling mass of fog has scrubbed out Geneva altogether. Mary can see nothing – not the spires of the churches she'd envisaged, or the buildings of the famous university, or the lake. Instead, a thick pall of cloud conceals the city in a grim shroud. It is hard, in fact, to believe that a city is hiding there – the whole place and all the people in it might have been smothered beneath the weight of this swirling haze.

Claire, still red-eyed and puffy-cheeked, groans. 'Has the stupid *voiturier* got lost?'

Mary looks back at the gloomy driver, who is slumped, barely glancing at the mist-cloaked city below. His face is thin, his cheekbones sharp. Does he have a family, back over the border, whom he must feed?

She digs a silver coin from her purse and walks carefully across the icy path to the carriage. 'Here.' She holds out the coin. 'For you.'

He takes it without looking at her, offering no thanks. She feels snubbed but keeps her voice bright. 'This is Geneva?'

He nods, morosely. '*Le temps est mal.*'

'Is it always so bad? It seems very . . . dark.' What Mary wants to say is that the city makes her think of the dank, clouded air that haunts a graveyard.

He gives a Gallic shrug. She turns to walk back to the promontory, where Claire is leaning against Shelley's shoulder, her arms wrapped around him. For once, Mary doesn't mind. Holding Willmouse with one arm, she puts the other around both of them. As awkward as it is, there is some comfort in their solidity.

She squints at the grey cloud and can make out a darker shape within it, which might be the blackness of the lake below; it is hard to tell.

A drop of moisture hits the back of her neck and crawls down her spine.

Mary swallows hard against the nausea in the back of her throat – she thought she'd left her dreads and terrors in London. But here they are still. She feels as if she is standing alone in a strange, weighted silence, waiting for something terrible. This is nothing like the freedom she had hoped for. She visualizes travelling back to London, back to the bailiffs, back to Shelley's absence and distance.

She forces calm into her voice. 'The driver says it's just bad weather. He thinks it will pass soon.'

It is worth the lie to see the slight lift in Shelley's expression, to feel him reach across and hold her hand. He compresses her fingers, kisses them. His lips are dry. She closes her eyes. When she opens them, he is staring at her. Hard to tell if the distance in his gaze is the reflection of the snow, or if she has glimpsed his longing to be somewhere else, with someone else.

Then it begins to snow.

PART TWO
Geneva

4

Everywhere I see bliss, from which I alone am
irrevocably excluded.

They clatter through sleepy, fog-muffled streets, where close-crammed houses silently overlook the mist-shrouded lake. Shelley whoops as they pass shuttered shops and bolted churches; he puts his head out of the carriage window and shouts, '*Vite!*' at the driver, who urges the horses into a faster trot, then an uneven canter.

The carriage skids and lurches; Willmouse bawls; Claire and Shelley's shouts of laughter pierce the muffled air. Mary grips the edge of the seat, white-knuckled. She sees them as if from above: these awful loud English guests, sweeping chaos into the sleepy city.

They grate to a stop outside the Hôtel d'Angleterre, where Byron is supposed to be staying.

Claire claps her hands. 'He will be so pleased to see me – I know it! He is probably waiting for me in his rooms.' She looks feverish, her eyes bright with a hot sheen, her cheeks too pink, her hands clenched as if she is trying to cling hard to something.

'Should you rest, before you go to find him?' Mary ventures. 'Perhaps you will feel better after you've slept.'

'You're saying I look terrible?'

A flare of irritation. 'For God's *sake*, Claire!'

'Oh! I look dreadful, I know it.'

'You look . . .' Mary takes a steadying breath, '. . . you look *beautiful.*'

Not quite true but not a lie either. She gently brushes a smudge of travel dirt from her sister's cheek. 'Perfect.' Her head pulses.

Claire tries to smooth her curls, brushes off her dress, and while Shelley pays the taciturn driver, who is still chewing his moustache moodily, she rushes into the hotel, singing out, '*Attention, s'il vous plaît!* Fetch Lord Byron *maintenant*! Tell him that Claire Clairmont has arrived.'

Her blue gown is travel-creased; her hair is a windswept, tangled mess. Almost, Mary calls her back, but from what Claire has told her, Byron won't even notice her clothes as he rips them off.

'I have a surprise for you,' Shelley murmurs, close to Mary's ear.

'Oh!' She jumps and turns, ready with the usual apology he expects her to give for snapping at Claire. But his expression is bright again, all the scowls and glares of the journey melted away.

'What surprise?' She is so used to shifting the temperature of her moods in response to his that she barely notices the strain of smiling.

'Give me Willmouse.'

She hesitates before passing over their sleeping baby. Shelley takes him awkwardly, his arms rigid; Willmouse's head lolls. Mary supports it, under the guise of smoothing his wispy hair.

'Now close your eyes,' Shelley says.

'Why?'

'Don't be so suspicious, Pecksie! You trust me, remember?'

Mary shuts her eyes.

Shelley's feet crunch on the path around her; a brush of air as he passes close by, then sudden cold as he moves further away. Is he fetching something from the hotel? A gift of some sort – something he has sent ahead for her? She shivers. Perhaps a thicker cloak to replace this old thin one she has worn since they ran away to France. But, no, her lover is not so practical: it will be a book – to help with her Greek translation, or some other way to stimulate her mind.

She tries not to hope for the gold ring, heated by the palm of his hand, which he will push onto her finger. He doesn't believe in marriage – she *knows* that. Yet how would it feel, that perfect gleaming sign of his devotion encircling her finger?

Harriet, his wife in London, wears a gold band studded with tiny turquoise stones and diamonds. Mary had followed her once, creeping alongside market stalls, her eyes greedy for the glint of gold. Staring at it was like poking an open wound again and again, unable to stop, in spite of the pain.

Enough! Don't think about it. He cannot marry you.

He married her. If he doesn't care for public approval, why doesn't he divorce her?

The fastest way to become unbearable to another person is to marry them.

She knits her bare fingers together, grips until her knuckles throb.

Footsteps again; Mary readies a smile for whatever gift her lover brings.

'Open your eyes.' Shelley's breath is soft against her cheeks. 'Look!'

He grins, nodding towards a pretty young woman on the path. Is she carrying the gift . . . ? But no, her hands are empty.

'*This* is Élise,' Shelley says. 'Isn't she perfect?'

'Perfect?' The word dies in her throat. Shelley can't mean . . . This *can't* be his surprise.

The girl is smooth-skinned and dark-eyed, with a fresh-air flush to her cheeks. 'Madame,' she says, dropping into a tiny curtsy. 'My pleasure is meeting you.'

Mary swallows. 'Shelley . . . who – *in God's name* – is *this*?' She can hear the sharpness in her voice that he so hates, can hear the tone that made Mrs Godwin send her to her room and made her father banish her to Scotland for months. She pulls on her left sleeve, even though her arm isn't visible. Her scars are hidden.

'This is Élise, my love.'

'Who *is* she?' Mary knows she should stop but she can't help growling, '*Why* is she here?'

'I thought she could help you with Willmouse.'

'With Willmouse?'

'So you can spend more time with me.'

Shelley walks across to Élise and, before Mary can stop him, her lover puts her sleeping baby into this strange woman's arms. Willmouse stirs a little but Élise rocks him until he settles. Then she looks up at Mary and Shelley, rosy-cheeked and beautiful.

'What do you think, my love?' Shelley's eyes are bright with anticipation. 'Is she not the most wonderful surprise?'

'I don't . . . I don't know her,' Mary says, faintly. Everything is distant, as though she has inhaled a lungful of opium smoke, or has only just woken from one of her nightmares and is still half dreaming. She can't unpick her confusion from the anger that threatens to spill over.

'I asked the hotel owner to find a nursemaid. I didn't expect him to choose so perfectly.' His eyes search her face; his expression hardens. 'What is wrong? You said you were tired.'

'Of course I'm *tired*.' She can't conceal the savagery in her tone. She is glaring at him, can see his cheeks reddening, his gaze narrowing.

Calm yourself, Mary.

'Did you not tell me that you long to be able to read again? To write?'

Not like this. How can you believe I wanted this? How can you be so oblivious?

The words die in her throat. In his stern gaze and scolding tone, she hears the echo of her father's disapproval – of his abandonment, of her own loneliness.

'Yes, I long to read, but –'

'And you long to spend more time with me?'

'Of course, but . . .' The girl is so beautiful, so fresh and vibrant. She looks like an ideal mother, a perfect companion. Next to her, Mary feels like a ragged, beige-coloured moth. And she didn't *ask* for this. It's yet another thing that he's decided for her. *Oh, God.* She swallows, exhales. She sees the closed door of Skinner Street. Her father's face had slammed shut when he saw her.

Shelley waits. His gaze presses down on her, like a weight. There is only one way to lift it. 'Thank you, Shelley.' She puts her arms around him. 'Forgive me . . . I'm tired, as you said.'

His expression softens. 'My love, then you must admit that Élise is the perfect gift. Besides, she is in desperate need of employment. When I heard about her, I knew I had to get her away from her home.'

Another young woman to rescue. Mary tastes something sour, forces herself to swallow, to breathe. The last three times he has helped women, he has run away with them or married them or replaced his wife with them. 'She will be *living* with us?' Mary feels queasy.

'Yes. Her father is an awful brute, so I have done wonderfully, freeing her from that house.'

Mary cringes inwardly. 'But . . . where will she sleep?' She pictures a bed with herself and Shelley lying in it, then Élise on his other side, next to Willmouse's crib.

All the while she is asking these measured, practical questions, in a measured, practical voice, she wants to demand,

How could you? She wants to growl, *How dare you?* She wants to take his beautiful, smiling face in her dry, chapped hands and pinch it into some expression of sympathy, some look that shows he understands how she feels. She wants to shape him into the man she thought she'd known two years ago. But every day with Shelley, she is the one being shaped. She contorts herself into whatever position he demands – no matter the pain, careless of the cost.

'She will have her own room, with Willmouse,' he says blithely. 'Think of all the time we will have together.'

'I don't want to give him to another woman . . .' As Shelley's expression sharpens again, she adds, 'Perhaps I will become used to it, in time.'

'You go after Claire now, into the hotel. Leave Willmouse with Élise.'

'But . . .' She looks longingly at her child.

'Go on.'

Élise nods encouragingly.

As Mary walks away from her baby, her arms feel too light without his anchoring weight. When she has left him before, it has always been with Claire. Now she is stepping away from her child, stepping into the part of a different woman. She is not sure how to do it or who she is meant to be.

She feels unmoored and, beneath her anger and confusion, a surge of guilty relief in leaving him with someone else. Some snare around her heart has tightened and loosened.

She follows where her sister went, into a cavernous entrance hall, which is almost windowless and lit by the dim glow from a dusty crystal chandelier.

Claire, in her faded, travel-creased dress, is sitting very still and very upright on an elegant, threadbare sofa, beneath a huge mirror, the gilding flaking from the frame.

'Claire?'

She doesn't respond, doesn't move at all. Mary wonders what can have happened to her sister in such a short time – her face is pale, as if this shabby, glamorous hotel has sapped some essential energy from her.

'Claire, dearest, what's the matter?' Mary reaches out to stroke her hair.

Claire slaps her hand away. 'What do *you* think? *Byron*'s not *here*,' she snaps. She is trying to hold back tears. 'Something terrible must have happened to him.'

'Perhaps the weather has kept him in France.'

'What will I do if he's been hurt?'

Mary keeps her voice calm – it's the same steady tone she almost always uses with her sister nowadays. 'I'm sure he's well. He'll arrive soon – perhaps this very day.'

'You don't know that!'

Mary chews her lip. She can't say what she's really thinking – that Byron may have moved on to some other woman or man, and Claire cannot be sure that the fickle poet is coming to Geneva at all. What words would Claire use to comfort her in a similar situation?

'Perhaps he has been delayed and is, at this very moment, frustrated and thinking of you.' Mary tries to sound confident.

Claire nods morosely.

What Mary really wants to ask is whether Claire had known about the pretty nursemaid and, if so, why she hadn't mentioned her.

Claire sniffs. Her eyes are red-rimmed, so Mary adds, 'He will be longing to see you, sweet Clairie.'

'Yes. Yes, he will.' Claire sniffs again and lets Mary blot the tears from her cheeks. 'It's just that I have – and you will think me foolish – but I have an awful fear that something is terribly wrong.'

Mary considers telling her about the sinking dread she'd

had when it had started to snow; she nearly asks her about Élise, nearly tells her of the fears she has about spending so much time with Shelley – that he will become bored with her, bored with the baby, tired of the everyday sameness of it all, when what Shelley craves is excitement and new things. New books, new ideas, new lovers.

She shakes her head to clear her thoughts, takes Claire's hands and looks directly into her sister's eyes. 'All will be well. You will see. Byron will arrive and he will adore you, just as he did before. We will drink wine together and we will eat and talk and laugh. And then Shelley and I will go to our room and you won't have to worry about being woken by Willmouse crying in the night because *you* will be in *Byron's* room. And then you really *will* be tired.'

Claire nods hesitantly, then more enthusiastically at Mary's words. 'I will take him straight to bed!'

'See! You look happier already!'

'Don't *mock* me! You have Shelley and Willmouse. Your life is blissful.'

Blissful? Mary would like to remind Claire of the sleepless nights with the baby screaming and Shelley nowhere to be found. But she can't *remind* her sister of those nights, because Claire had so often escaped back to Skinner Street, sleeping behind the safety and quiet of the door that will always remain locked to Mary now.

'I'm not *mocking* you.' Her voice is tight. 'I hope you will be happy soon.'

This, at least, is true. Perhaps, when Byron arrives, Claire will direct her hysteria towards him.

'Thank you,' Claire says. 'I almost forgot – I have these.' She reaches into her coin purse, draws out two little paper wraps of sugar and passes one to Mary. 'Here.'

Mary thinks it likely that Claire has saved the sugar for

Shelley, or even for Byron – she likes to present men with little gifts. Mary opens the packet, pressing her finger to the grains, then letting them dissolve on her tongue. It seems incongruous, such sweetness in this grim, forbidding place. Then she sees the words on the torn scrap of paper in her hand. It is Shelley's handwriting – she would recognize his scrawl anywhere: *trust, my darling, and she will come to understand, in time*

'What's this?' Mary swallows a sudden nausea. 'Where did you get it?'

'Oh!' Claire's cheeks flush. 'That's just something from the wastepaper basket at the last inn. It could belong to anyone.'

'It's Shelley's writing.' A pulse presses at her throat – Mary has to force the words past it.

Claire snatches the piece of paper. 'No, it's nothing like it.' Before Mary can protest, Claire balls up the paper and throws it into the dying embers of the fireplace.

'*Claire!*' Mary gasps. 'How could you –?'

'Stop it!' Claire whirls around, her expression vicious. The reception hall falls silent. Mary becomes aware of the eyes on them, the susurrating whispers.

'*Stop* trying to create a scene, Mary. That letter was nothing to do with you.'

Mary glares, her blood beating in her ears. She imagines grabbing Claire, shouting at her, demanding to know what had been written on that note. But even as she feels anger flaming through her chest, tightening her throat, her fists, her breath, she hears her father's voice in her head: *No shouting. You're a philosopher, Mary, not a street urchin.* She feels ten years old again, alone and misunderstood. As if part of her is unseen or hiding – or both.

A shout from the door. Both women turn.

At first, all Mary sees is Shelley and the stricken expression on his face.

Oh, God. He knows. He knows what I've done. He's read my journal and now everything will fall apart. She curses herself for leaving her journal in her case. A moment ago she'd felt invisible: now she is raw, exposed, ashamed. She readies an explanation for her rage-scrawled words, the cruel jibes, the dark confessions.

But, no, that's nonsense – an old fear. Her journal is tucked into the pocket she has sewn to the inside of her skirt. It is always safely there, or stowed under her mattress, where no one else can read it.

A wild-haired man rushes in – a stranger in a shabby brown cloak and hat. He gabbles something in French, too quickly and urgently for Mary to understand.

Shelley blinks and shakes his head, as though he has just emerged from icy water. Claire inhales sharply and stands, her hand over her mouth.

'What is it?' Mary asks.

'They've found a man's body by the lake.'

5

How mutable are our feelings, and how strange is that clinging love we have of life even in the excess of misery!

Outside the hotel, people are rushing towards the lake, calling in rapid French, to hurry, to go faster, to run. Mary reaches for Shelley's hand but he surges forward, joining the crowd without a backward glance.

Mary stops on the hotel steps, itchy anxiety crawling over her skin at the sight of the strange crowd, whose faces are half hidden by hats and bonnets but who wear bright shirts and aprons over their black skirts and trousers. The atmosphere seems incongruously festive, almost celebratory, as the men and women run towards the lake, shouting about the body. *Le corps!*

'Shelley!' He pauses, but doesn't turn back.

'Where is Willmouse?' Mary looks around wildly. Has Shelley left their child with the stranger? Where is the girl? 'Willmouse!' she shouts. The fear is instant, a knee to the gut, a fist to the throat.

She is back in London, alone in a dark, damp room in the middle of the night. Her baby's skin is cold. The little face pale and blank and unmoving.

She shakes her head, tries to blink away the image, but the terror twists, sharp-clawed. *What if it happens again? Your mother died. Your baby daughter died. It's a curse you carry . . .*

She grasps the stone gatepost. 'Willmouse!' She looks for Claire. Her sister, too, is gone.

'William!' she calls helplessly – ridiculously, because her baby can't reply. 'William!'

People in the crowd turn to stare, their faces curious, but they quickly move on. To Mary, they are all versions of the same uncaring stranger. She is entirely alone.

'Madame?' A soft voice behind her.

She turns to see the girl – Élise – holding Willmouse, sleeping peacefully in her arms. Mary grabs her child, presses her lips to his soft skin, inhales the yeasty scent of his scalp, the milkiness of his breath. 'Thank you!' Her vision shimmers with tears. 'I was so frightened. I thought he was . . .' She is back in that dark room, her body aching, the weight of a secret heavy in her arms.

She blinks, forces a smile and the mountains return, the frosty air returns, her living child returns.

'I keep him safe, Madame. You find your husband.' The girl holds out her hands for Willmouse. Mary fights the urge to turn away, to shield her child with her body.

Élise waits, hands outstretched. 'He is safe with me, Madame,' she repeats patiently. 'If he is hungry, I feed him or I find you.'

'No – don't feed him.'

Some emotion flickers across the girl's face – anger, perhaps? She blinks back tears as she nods. 'Yes, Madame.'

Without being told, Mary understands that this girl has lost her own child – perhaps it was taken from her, or perhaps it died, but Mary recognizes the grief that tightens the girl's features, that makes her voice tremble. Élise swallows – Mary watches the muscles in her throat constrict.

They are a similar age, she thinks. She tries to see herself standing in front of a foreign stranger, holding out her arms to take the woman's baby. She cannot. It is too horrible.

She passes Willmouse into Élise's embrace and kisses his head. 'I'm sorry.'

Without waiting for the girl to respond, she joins the crowd moving towards the lake. It is like stepping into a flood. She cranes her neck, searching for Claire or Shelley, but can't see them amid the sea of red aprons, green dirndls and white shirts.

The crowd has gathered near the lakeshore, their voices quieter now, almost reverent. Clouds hang thick and low, the sky like the nailed lid of a coffin. Mary doesn't believe in God, but if she did, if she tried to pray, all her wishes would fall back to earth.

Mary can hear Shelley's voice, though she can't see him through the wall of backs and hats, cotton and wool.

'Please excuse me.' No one moves. Smell of sweat, with something dark and acrid beneath it. Rusty and earthy, like a birthing chamber.

Everyone is too close now, penning her in. She is trapped, breathless – the people behind her crowding and shoving, crushing her against those in front.

Mary fights down the urge to scream, swallows her nausea and shouts, 'Shelley!'

The woman in front of her turns, stares, doesn't move.

'Shelley!' Mary shouts again.

Then, from near the lake, 'Here!'

As if his voice and hers are threads winding towards each other, the crowd slowly shuffles aside and allows Mary through.

When she sees him by the lakeshore, she gives a cry of relief, but his attention is on the thing at his feet.

Mary follows his gaze. The man is lying on the dry stones, away from the water's edge. His skin is white and waterlogged, like an outer casing which might peel off. Someone has laid a black cloak over his torso, but Mary wishes it covered his face too – the man's lips are horribly swollen and protrude away from his teeth in an uncanny leer.

Mary tastes bile. She wants to turn away, wants to look anywhere else, but she can't. Her gaze is pulled back, again and again, to the pale skin, the dark hair, still wet from the lake. On a living man, it would look thick and beautiful. Here, on this corpse, the lustre of those locks only creates a more horrible contrast to his pale skin and blank eyes.

Shelley crouches, peers directly into the dead man's open eyes.

Nearby, separate from the large crowd, three older women stand, their faces ashen and tear-streaked. The man's mother and aunts, perhaps? One of the women stumbles towards Shelley, plucks at his sleeve and asks a question. Shelley waves towards the lake but gives no reply. He doesn't take his gaze from the man.

Mary pitches her voice low. 'Come away, Shelley, please.'

He still doesn't look up. 'Not a mark on him. They say his eyes have changed colour – could the water do that, do you think? His eyes were brown before.'

The eyes are blue, like Shelley's own, but strangely opaque. They stare blankly at the cloudy haze in the sky above.

Mary fights down her frustration and her growing feeling that something is wrong with this lake, with this body.

'These people are *grieving*, Shelley. We shouldn't stay.'

'They think I'm a doctor.'

'A *doctor*. Why?'

'Only way I could get close to the body.' He takes out the little notepad from his coat pocket, starts scrawling on it.

'Are you writing a *poem*?' Mary can't keep the disgust from her voice.

Shelley's gaze is flinty. 'Well, Mary, I am a *poet*.'

'You can hardly think me oblivious to that,' she snaps. 'But composing a verse while standing next to a corpse seems a little callous.' *Even for you*, she wants to add.

Shelley scowls.

When they had first met, he'd adored their debates. Her mind was *captivating*, her thoughts *intoxicating*. She'd felt dazed and elated to have found a man who loved her for her intelligence.

Slowly, she'd realized that Shelley wanted her to dispute his concepts – his hypotheses, his theories – but only so he could explain why she was wrong. What he did *not* want was for Mary to object to his behaviour. What he did *not* like was for his lover to criticize his actions.

Still frowning, Shelley tucks his notebook back into his pocket. 'It's the poet's duty to describe the melancholy, as well as the sublime,' he says piously. 'See here, how his hands look like gloves – as though he has drawn on someone else's skin?'

'For goodness' sake, Shelley, his family can *hear* you.' Mary averts her gaze from where he is pointing, though she knows it is too late – the image will be there waiting in the darkness, behind her closed eyes.

'Is it Byron?' Claire calls, high-pitched, from behind the crowd. 'I can't bear to look.'

She rushes towards them, but stops some distance away, hands clapped to her cheeks. From somewhere, Mary notes drily, she has found a black silk ribbon, which she has looped loosely around her neck.

'If it's Byron, I shall *die*,' Claire calls. 'I shall take my own life, I swear it.'

Not everyone in the crowd understands English, but some of the men, dressed in what look like scholars' robes, glare disapprovingly at Claire. Though Mary tries not to care about propriety, it seems in poor taste to be threatening death while standing near a body.

'It's not Byron.' Mary keeps her voice low, mindful that the man's family are nearby. 'I like your widow's weeds but they're a little premature.'

Claire ignores the jibe, pushing past Mary to the edge of the lake where she stops next to the body.

She claps her hands to her mouth. 'Thank heavens! Oh, thank heavens.'

And much as Mary wants to hush her, she too is relieved that the drowned man is a stranger, that it is not Byron, lying still as marble on the bank of the lake.

As they walk back to the hotel, Shelley's gaze is distant, his mood morose, his handsome face set in a frown. She puts her hand on his, but he ignores it. Her fingers grow numb – the blue-tinged skin reminds her of the dead man's. She winces, tucks her hand back beneath her cloak.

Shelley makes no comment, seems not to notice.

Claire rushes to catch up and links her arm through Shelley's.

'That was horribly *grisly*! And no one knows what happened to the man – I'm sure Byron will find it fascinating. He'll probably write an epic about it.' She has always been cavalier about death. When they used to visit Mary's mother's grave, Claire would scuff the weeds with her boot and complain that she was bored.

'At least feign respect, Claire. His family might hear you.'

'It's excellent inspiration!' Shelley's face brightens. 'I've made notes for a poem.'

Mary has always been the person he talks to about his work. Now he angles his body away from her. Claire raises her eyebrows at Mary and puts out her tongue, as if it is all a huge joke, as if she has scored a point in a silly contest between sisters.

Mary clamps her jaws shut.

The space between herself and Shelley is no more than the

thickness of their clothes, yet she feels as though he is standing on the other side of a thinly frozen lake. Even if she were to shout across to him, even if he cared enough to listen, her voice would be lost in darkness and distance.

Claire tilts her face up to gaze at Shelley as they walk. 'Tell me all about this poem – you and Byron can exchange ideas. How exciting!'

There is something watchful and calculating in her eyes. As Shelley talks about the man's body and the images he will write, Claire leans her head against his shoulder.

He takes Claire's hand and rubs her fingers between his strong palms. When she closes her eyes, Mary can almost feel the callus on his forefinger, where his quill has hardened the skin. Underneath her cloak, Mary clenches her cold fists.

'You're freezing,' Shelley says to Claire. 'Let's go back in.'

They walk hand in hand, seeming not to notice that she is two paces behind. Looking at them, you would never guess them to be anything other than blissfully in love.

Mary's eyes sting; she has to blink and breathe, blink and breathe until the tight fist of pain in her chest passes. Shelley craves adoration – he wants her to feel his absence like a slicing blade, wants her to be consumed by the desire to win back his attention, to charm him and flatter him.

She straightens her shoulders, anger crackling through her muscles.

I'm not a plaything! And I won't play your damned games.

The rebellion feels new and loud, furious and powerful.

Mary turns her gaze from Shelley and Claire's intertwined fingers and looks up at the sky, where the carrion crows circle and caw. Beyond them, clouds, heavy and grey, like balled-up paper. Mary sees the words scrawled across them in Shelley's hand.

My darling.

Mary thinks, *If I'm not that woman any more, if I'm not playing Shelley's games, who am I? Whose game am I playing?*

The answer appears, as if she has scrawled it across the centre of her journal: *Your own.*

Inside the hotel, the air is hot and close with bodies and gossip. The reception room buzzes with guests, who have returned from the lake and are talking about the dead man. The word *corpse* buzzes around in French, in German, in English.

A fire blazes in the corner and someone has placed candles along the mantel and on the tables. Perhaps this is supposed to conjure cosiness and cheer, but it emphasizes the gnawing dread outside the hotel, deepening the darkness – everything is muffled in a strange twilight. Looking through the window towards the lake, Mary sees only her ghostly reflection, pale-skinned and large-eyed. Her double is surrounded by people – Shelley and Claire are just next to her, talking animatedly. Mary feels separate and alone, as if she is made of glass, or of whatever silvery substance casts her reflection so brightly. *Light*, she thinks. *It is only the light in here and the darkness outside, so early in the day, that make me look strange.*

Still, she can't shake the sensation that she is a different person in this place, in this room. That she has peeled away from herself: one Mary is standing close to the fire, trying to thaw her hands, while another observes the creature that looks like her. The other woman is detached, amused, coldly content. There is something knowing in her gaze: she understands things that Mary herself is only beginning to grasp.

Behind her reflection, gazing at her, is the figure of a man. Who is he? She recognizes him from somewhere, but where? When she turns to find him within the room, she can't make him out from the other dark-suited men.

She shivers and tries to rub some heat into her arms, but her fingers are numb.

'Pecksie!' Shelley says next to her ear, and she startles. 'I'm talking to the little hotel man about the rooms. Élise has already taken Willmouse up to hers. Claire can share a room with us until Byron arrives, can't she?'

'No.' The answer comes out before Mary can stop it. The word feels so good that she says it again. 'No, she can't.'

Shelley blinks. 'What do you mean?'

'I mean *no*.' Mary's heart strikes a frantic drumbeat in her chest, her throat. Her face feels as if it's been roughly hewn from stiff wood. In the window, her reflection, smooth-skinned, gives a wide grin. 'She can't stay with us.'

'Are you unwell?' He takes a step backwards, confusion in his large blue eyes.

'Quite well.'

'All right.' Shaking his head, he returns to the manager.

Mary looks up at her reflection again. There is hardness in her gaze, a grim set around her mouth, judgement in her raised eyebrows.

Good, she thinks.

Claire's arm is hooked through Shelley's, so Mary pushes herself between them. From the corner of her eye, she can see Claire's indignant expression, but she ignores it and, looping her own arm through Shelley's, she smiles at the hotel manager.

He is a well-fed, shiny-skinned man, who looks from Mary to Shelley to Claire with something like excitement in his eyes. The engraved gold plaque on his desk declares, rather grandly, that he is: *Monsieur Favre. Directeur. Manager. Maître d'hôtel.*

'You have a change for your rooms, Madame?' he asks, with a slight hitch of his eyebrows and a slyly knowing expression. With so many English guests in the hotel, is it possible that this man recognizes the name *Shelley* and associates it with scandal?

'Two rooms,' she says firmly. She takes Shelley's hand in hers and grips it hard. Her skin still seems numb but, when he squeezes back, the sensation travels through her – an electric thrill, like the crackle of rage-filled energy she had felt by the lake. It reminds her of a feeling she'd had two years ago, when the handsomest man she'd ever seen had sat at her father's dinner table and hung on her every word and movement, rapt. Once they were alone, he'd whispered to her that she was perfect, that she was surely a genius, that she would write wonderful works, that he desired her, wanted her, longed for her.

She'd felt huge with the power of his regard. Now, she catches a quiver of a similar sensation – the freeing potential of something new unfolding. It doesn't come from Shelley's admiration, his longing or desire. It flickers within her, a tiny luminous flame, burning just beneath her skin.

Their room is more luxurious than any in the dusty boarding-houses and inns where they'd stayed in France. In the corner, a mahogany writing desk gleams alongside two intricately carved chairs. There is a strong smell of beeswax polish and the faint scent of smoke from the lit fire, though the grate is clean and the chimney breast looks freshly painted. Thick red velvet drapes hang over the windows and around the large bed – someone has already been into the room to pull them over the windows, despite the early hour, so the artificial darkness feels intimate, rather than filled with the strange foreboding Mary had felt downstairs.

Do they go to such trouble for every guest?

'This looks very expensive. How will we afford it?'

But *of course* – Shelley has been given more of his family

money and she is not supposed to have guessed how, is not supposed to ask why.

For a moment, the spectre of Shelley's wife, Harriet, enters the room.

Mary meets his gaze in the mirror; his expression is a shuttered blank.

A beat of silence, heavy with his expectation: she must apologize or explain why she had insisted on a separate room. Part of her wants to gabble an excuse; another won't let her speak. Words sit in her throat like swallowed stones, but she doesn't choke: she breathes easily. There is strength in holding herself still and silent.

In the mirror, Shelley's gaze shifts into something darker, more intense. He's so beautiful – his dark-lashed blue eyes, his cheekbones, his high forehead, his full mouth.

He walks up behind her, brushes her hair to one side and presses his lips to her throat.

She leans back into him, letting him take her weight. Her skin rises in goose-bumps, and she closes her eyes as he kisses along her collarbone. He pushes the neckline of her dress to one side. She shivers.

'To bed, Pecksie,' he murmurs. 'I'm ravenous.' His words vibrate against her skin, and she shivers again – she feels raw, somehow, and exposed.

Still kissing her neck, Shelley pushes her towards the bed. Mary closes her eyes and tries to forget everything except his touch. When he pulls her close, everything else disappears. Her thoughts, her worries, her arguments. All scorched away by the need that flickers between them.

It is a different nightmare from the usual one. Mary is watching her mother twist and writhe in the grip of a fever. Her eyes are dark with pain and deeply socketed. When she throws off the sweat-soaked sheets and screams, her dry lips crack like overripe plums.

Mary watches, not as the baby she had been, restless and squalling in the wooden crib, but as the young woman she is now: terrified in the knowledge that this poor woman will die, unable to stop the fever's spread.

In the corner of the room stands the doctor who has been attending her mother – he dips his filthy hands into a bowl of grubby water, then dries them on his trousers before moving forward to prod at the infected wound between her mother's legs.

Mary shouts at him to stop but no sound emerges. In any case, it is too late: the damage is done. The first time he examined her mother, a week ago, he'd poked at the tender, torn flesh and left a smear of the blackened dirt from under his nails.

In her dream, Mary swallows her nausea and turns to the screaming baby in the crib. Puce-faced little monster, it shrieks and shudders because no one will feed it or even hold it. Its blanket has come untucked, and it must be freezing – its fingers have a bluish hue. Mary wonders if she should cover the pitiful little creature. She doesn't try. Something in the baby repulses her – its desperate, selfish need, its greedy hunger for life when its mother is dying. This horrible little demon has killed its mother, yet it screams for comfort.

Finally able to move, Mary sits on the floor and watches through the bars of the crib as the child bawls its selfish rage and loneliness. When the pitch of its cries rises, Mary shuts her eyes and places her hands over her ears. Then, leaving the baby in the crib, alone and screaming, Mary walks from the room.

She jolts awake, her heart thundering, the desperate shrieks of the baby – of herself: they were her own cries – still echoing in her ears. The room is dark and silent, the curtains still blocking out the grainy early-morning light. In the distance, a church bell rings out six chimes.

She reaches for Shelley, but his side of the bed is empty. The slight indent left by his body is cold.

'Shelley?' She sits up, a faint hum of fear in her stomach. He can't have gone anywhere at this hour, surely. She calls his name again.

No reply.

The hallway, too, is dim and quiet – each door firmly shut, no sign that anyone else is stirring. The quiet feels oppressive, as if it carries a physical weight. Mary pictures some noiseless creature creeping through the gloom, spreading a slick of heavy silence.

She returns to her room, shuts the door, presses her fingers to her closed eyes, then opens them again.

No reason to be disturbed by Shelley's absence. The dream has upset her, that's all.

Perhaps he has left a note. She searches the desk, bed, behind the curtains, in the wardrobe. Nothing, except a faint film of dust and ash from the fire.

She pulls on her clothes, pads along the hushed hallway. On a whim, she pauses outside Claire's room. She tells herself she is trying to hear the soft snores Claire sometimes makes, but, even as she presses her ear against the door, she knows that, really, she is listening for her lover.

No sound at all. She knocks and whispers Claire's name. No response.

What if everyone has left you? The thought comes unbidden, as clearly as if someone has hissed it in her ear.

She swallows her nausea and says aloud to herself, 'I have to see Willmouse.'

Unease ices her skin as she taps on the door where Élise is sleeping with her child. Again, no reply. She raps louder.

A rustling from within. Shuffling feet: the door opens.

Élise's pale face, puffy and soft with sleep. She stares at Mary, wide-eyed. 'Madame! It is morning? I should be awake! I did not know –'

'It is very early – just six o'clock. I wanted to see him.'

'You want to feed him? I feed him in the night, four times. He is a hungry boy.'

Mary flinches. 'I told you *not* to feed him.'

'Yes, but your husband tells me to feed him. He says this is better and you can rest, no?'

Realization hits her: Shelley has made these decisions without asking her because he thinks she is a poor mother.

Oh, God. All the incompetence she thinks she has hidden, all the confusion, the exhaustion, the occasional resentment she feels have made Shelley decide, within a week of watching Mary with his son, that his child needs a new mother, a *better* mother.

'Oh, God,' she says aloud. That other shadowy version of herself nods in agreement and whispers, *He knows what you did.*

Mary backs away, shaking her head. When Élise starts to speak, Mary holds up her hand. 'Please. Go back to sleep. I shouldn't have woken you.' Cheeks blazing, she rushes along the landing – not sure where she is going, but filled with a desperate desire to be away from Élise's expression of surprise and the judgement Mary feels in it.

At first the front door will not open. Is she locked inside, trapped in the hotel? She pulls hard and it shifts. Oh, not locked, then – only heavy and swollen from the rain and the biting mist that rises from the lake. She tugs hard with both hands. To her relief, the door opens without creaking.

The air is brighter than yesterday, and it is no longer snowing. Still, her breath fogs the air and she wraps the shawl more closely around her shoulders.

Down by the lake, the ground is white with thawing snow, apart from the patch of rocky soil where the slush has been trampled by milling feet. Are her eyes playing tricks, or is there a darker space still in the outline of a body? She shudders.

She'd intended to walk along the lakeside, hoping to catch sight of Shelley and Claire, but something about the water repels her: not just the cold, but the way it seems to radiate darkness when everything around it is dusted with white and muffled with a muted beauty.

Instead of looking for him by the lake, she takes the path that leads between the houses and the darkness of the forest beyond. There is no sign of anyone, anywhere – Mary might be the only soul stealing through this strange place.

'Shelley!' she calls. The forest flings her voice back at her. She waits in the echo, listening.

Nothing, except a faint flapping of wings flaring high in the trees.

A bitter breeze touches the back of her neck. When she turns, there is nothing except the shadowy sketch of trees and hills and, in the distance, the fragmented silhouettes of houses where people are muffled still by sleep.

'Shelley?' she whispers, more to hear a human voice than because she expects him to reply.

The valley lies like a cupped hand, water cradled in the hollow of the palm, while trees interlaced with paths fringe the bony fingers, and snow-capped mountains stretch beyond the bare knuckle of the thumb. On the forest floor, life breeds in the decay. Moss smoulders on fallen stumps, dissolves wood, tree, leaf and branch to the same mulch, but out of that decay, fungus blossoms. Lichen blooms golden on old wood, tiny ears of mushrooms creep across the forest floor, casting out tendrils from the spoil, the promise of life lifting from the rot.

Her boot brushes something soft. As if her thoughts have summoned it, the body of a baby owl – half bald and livid-skinned in the leaves. It reminds her of her nightmare – the baby in the cot, the baby that had been her – blue and screaming. It reminds her of another baby.

As soon as she thinks of Clara, the guilt is back, a squeezing hand at her throat.

No, don't. Look up at the branches, listen.

Her breath steadies. Birdcalls float through the branches, the sound muted by the strange mist – but not so quiet that she can't make out their music, both foreign and familiar. She used to sit in the cemetery by her mother's stone, listening to the birds, watching their flight, naming them aloud, one by one, as if telling a story, reciting a poem to a dead woman.

Song-thrush, sparrow, linnet, jay. Blackbird, goldfinch, blue tit, lark.

Whisper of wings now through the branches, flame-flicker in the dead leaves or distant shadow in the air high above.

Ahead, a movement in the trees, like the shadow of an animal – or someone walking.

Shelley! Relief floods her and she is about to call him when something stops her. The figure can't be her lover: though it is wearing his dark cloak, it is hunched and lumpen. It lurches away from her with a lop-sided, staggering gait, as if it is injured.

What is this . . . *thing?* It reminds her, so much, of the creature from her dreams. The clawing hand that reaches for her nightly is here.

She should call for Shelley but her voice clogs in her throat. Besides, if she shouts, she will draw the attention of the creature. She needs to move, needs to make herself search for him, but her muscles are frozen. When she tries to stand upright, her legs buckle and her head swims. She leans back against the tree, her breath a panicked wheeze.

The ancient oak is huge, with a deep cleft at the base of its trunk, large enough to conceal a body. Mary pushes herself back into the gap.

You're a coward, she thinks.

She is behaving like a child, scared of the ogres of her dreams. Her exhausted mind must have conjured this strange beast, yet she can't shake the terror she has of it, the feeling that, if she pursues it, the creature will finish the task of the nightmare beast.

It will press a heavy hand over her mouth; it will crush and smother the air from her lungs.

She forces herself to stand, to move, to put one shaking foot in front of the other, to count her breaths and clench her jaw and follow the grotesque thing, which might lead her to Shelley.

She should have stayed there, eyes clamped shut, imagining the ravaging monster, imagining Shelley lying injured and alone somewhere. She should not have gathered all the ragged seams of her strength together and forced herself to walk after the limping beast. She shouldn't have followed it through the winding paths of the woods and watched it go nearly to the lakeshore, to the spot where the man's body had lain yesterday, his waterlogged skin like pale lilies, his brown-blue eyes fixed on the sky.

If she had stayed hiding behind the tree, she wouldn't have seen the hunchbacked thing cast off its cloak and separate into two figures, leaning against each other. If she hadn't followed them, Mary wouldn't have seen Shelley lay his cloak on top of a rock, sit Claire on it, reach down and begin unlacing her boots.

Even from a distance she recognizes the expression on his face – tender, attentive, focused.

She hears the chimes of Claire's laughter, sees her close her eyes, her expression blissful.

It is suddenly hard to breathe, hard to think over the roaring in her ears – the noise that must be her own blood but sounds like the thunder of a crowd, baying at Mary to act, to shout, to howl her rage and her grief. She can't do it. The force of her wrath is terrifying, filled with the images from her nightmares: flayed muscles and skinless hands. Her anger is too huge to unleash.

She turns away, her body numb, her mind a white blank, taking no care to tiptoe over the rattling stones or to silence the cracking of branches.

Behind, she hears Shelley and Claire calling her name. She doesn't stop, doesn't turn. She blunders on, heedless of the brambles scratching and stinging her legs, ignoring their pleas for her to come back, to wait. Choking, she runs until she reaches the cleft in the old oak.

She crawls inside it and clasps her arms around her knees, closing her eyes and trying to ignore the shouts of her lover and her sister, calling her name again and again into the dark forest.

6

*The natural phenomena that take place every day before
our eyes did not escape my examinations.*

For a long time after Claire and Shelley have left, after their
calls for her have stopped, after she's heard them walking back
in the direction of the hotel, Mary stays crouched in the cleft
at the foot of the old oak. The bark digs into her legs; her
hands ache from gripping the tree, as if she is hanging from
a narrow ledge and only the strength in her cramping fingers
can keep her from smashing onto the rocks below.

The church bells chime seven in the morning, then eight.
Light rises, mist settles.

She can't go back to the hotel. But what is the alternative?
She has no money to flee to London. Even if she could reach
England, she has no friends there now and her family won't
see her. Worst of all, worse than anything else imaginable, she
would have to leave Willmouse.

She forces herself to uncurl her limbs, tries to begin back
along the path, but her legs are mutinous, and she can do
no more than stand, frozen, in the middle of the wood, her
mind a scoured void, her body filled with a wild, uncontrol-
lable panic. Sinking to her knees, she claws at the soil, as if
she could somehow dig her way into the dark peacefulness
of the earth, its steady rhythm of rise and rot.

A church bell tolls the half-hour. Half past eight. She must
return.

The sun is rising properly now, but it is a muted white beyond the thick layer of cloud and the light it emits is dull and powdery. Iced wind lashes Mary's hair across her face. When she brushes it away, she finds her cheeks are wet.

What would her mother do? She closes her eyes, tries to sense her way into the mind of a woman who feels as absent and distant as one of the Catholic saints – like Mary the mother of Jesus. Perfect and holy and wholly untouchable.

What should I do? Mary presses her flattened palms against her closed lids until everything is a screaming and painful purple. Still there is no answer. When she takes her hands from her face, her fingers are smeared with soil and blood. For a lurching moment, she thinks she must have clawed at her face without realizing. Then she sees that her fingers are cut from scrabbling at the soil.

The sight of the blood shocks her back to herself. When she and Claire were young – perhaps ten years old – they would challenge each other to see who could hold her breath until her vision darkened, who could keep her palm above a candle flame until the skin pinked and blistered, who could dig Mrs Godwin's darning needle deepest into her arm without flinching. Before they started, Claire had always been sure she would win: Mary was a cry-baby and a coward. Mary, too, had been half afraid that she'd lose to her loud, stubborn sister.

But she discovered that if she closed her eyes and let her thoughts drift, she could make the pain belong somewhere else. In those moments, she looked inside herself, beyond her still-beating heart and still-breathing lungs, and found hardness, an emotionless obstinacy. Some dark inner part of her knew the very worst things that could happen – some of them had already happened – but she could survive them, could outlast them, while watching the skin on her palm rise and separate from her body.

Now she takes a deep, shaky breath, stands upright, brushes her bloodied hands on her filthy skirt and sets off towards the hotel.

In the large mirror of the hotel atrium, Mary catches sight of her face – pink-cheeked from walking in the frigid air, hair teased into an untidy mass by the wind and damp. She practises the cool expression she will turn on Shelley and Claire. It looks rigid, but the corner of her mouth trembles. She will not give them the satisfaction of seeing her grief. While she decides what she must do, she will not let them see her devastation. They will only try to soothe and smooth and allay her fears. They will console and cajole and flatter until she forgets the outrage that makes her want to leave – the fury that makes her determined to stretch beyond the cramped prison of her biddable, agreeable mask.

They will ask why she ran from them, or why she hid. Can she say she thought it was a game of sorts? They won't believe her, of course, but perhaps they will pretend to, as she used to pretend to trust Shelley in London when he said he was visiting his friend Thomas Hogg. She would watch him in the mirror, combing his hair, smirking at his reflection, and she would feel as if something was closing in her throat. She would count her breaths and, when he asked if she was well, she would show her teeth and say, 'Very well. Give my regards to Thomas Hogg.'

And he would say, 'I will do.'

In the mirror, they would lock eyes and give the same carefully smoothed smile, as if neither could sense the snarling nest of unspoken words that writhed beneath the surface.

If she turns that same expression on Shelley when she goes up to their hotel room, she is sure he will pretend to believe whatever she tells him. She will do the same.

She is at the bottom of the stairs when Monsieur Favre steps out of his office. She jumps.

'Forgive me, Madame!' He smooths his hair. As he shuts the door to his office, she catches a glimpse of towering piles of paper and a long, narrow chaise covered with blankets and pushed against the back wall.

'Forgive me,' he says again. 'I am unquiet that you have been walking alone.' His eyes travel over her wind-whipped hair, her dirty skirt.

'I don't think it's your concern where I walk or if I am alone.' Mary knows she sounds haughty – rude, even – but she is weary of being expected to behave in a certain way, to *be* a certain person.

'I do not mean politeness. This is not my concern. *Mais* I am unquiet – it is not safe.' He looks at her intently, as if willing her to understand something more than he is saying. His brow is creased with worry, not disapproval.

'Do you mean . . . because of the body?'

'The body, *exactement*! Poor man, so young!' Monsieur Favre's small hands flutter protectively over his chest, his heart. He looks endearingly like one of the chubby-cheeked cherubs that float on the ceilings of French Catholic churches. 'Such tragedy.' He sighs.

Mary can't help asking: 'Perhaps he had been drinking?'

'These are the things they are saying, yes. Or *suicide*. But . . .' his eyes dart left and right and he leans forward a little, so Mary is obliged to lean away from him, '. . . but he is not a man who drinks. I know this. And he swims very strong.'

Despite her attempts to stay calm, to be rational, the hairs rise on Mary's arms; her scalp ices.

'There are strange things on this lake, Madame. People drown here, sometimes. This is expected, yes, when living near water?'

Mary thinks of the Thames and nods, silently.

'But this lake is more strange. Very deep – we do not know what is under the water. Sometimes, when there are clouds and then the sun, things are floating and moving above it.'

Has she misheard, or has Monsieur Favre misspoken, confusing his English prepositions? 'You mean things floating *on* the lake?'

'*Above* the lake, Madame. I have seen this. Houses, castles, people walking – all above the water! This sounds *fou . . . folle*, I don't know how you say, like folly?'

'Like madness.'

'*Oui*, Madame. Like I am madness. But I feel there is something dangerous. *Alors* I am unquiet you walk alone. And I am unquiet, Madame, that you go on the boat on the lake.'

'I haven't been on a boat. I only walked.'

'Madame, your husband. He is saying you must go on the lake. Rowing! He loves it! He tells me this. He wants to take the boat. He pays. I must agree, but it is not safe. There are strange things here. You must warn him.'

Just then, Shelley appears at the top of the stairs, a book in one hand; in the other, he holds his boating hat, which he has dubbed his *eccentric*. A sort of squashed topper, it is hardly fashionable, yet it somehow makes Shelley *more* handsome.

She can't meet his gaze. When she tries the composed expression she has prepared, her face feels rigid and awkward, as though she has pressed her features into one of the blank wooden masks that rich women wear to hide their faces at the theatre.

'Good morning.' She waits for him to rush to her and ask where she has been, demand to know why she had run away from him and Claire. She waits to hear the excuses he will give for what she saw.

Instead, her lover grins and holds his arms wide. 'My Mary,

my Mae, my sweet spring in winter! Let's flee this dark place and go out on the water!'

It is as though he is at the theatre, standing in the centre of the stage, playing the role of the doting lover, delighted to see his beloved.

He puts on the hat and tilts it a little, winks rakishly.

She widens her wooden smile, heart pounding. Surely he can't pretend that nothing has happened.

'Shelley, I –'

'We'll take humour and wine – in wit we'll delight! A watery adventure in the sun's pale light.'

He has always loved chanting such doggerel to cheer Mary, or placate her or, occasionally, to seduce her. He has never used it to blank out another conversation so brazenly.

She can't meet his gaze. If she does, she'll say something terrible in front of Monsieur Favre and two of the guests – older ladies, who are openly staring at her and Shelley, taking in every word and glance.

'What do you say, sweet Mae?' A little more urgency in his voice, a little more strain.

She remembers his threat in London: *You can let me love you, as I want to. Or you can leave.*

'I don't want –' The words feel like stones. She is barely aware of what she's saying – anything, *anything* to fill the strained silence. 'Are you sure the lake is safe?' Her voice high-pitched, breathless. It belongs to another woman – the sort of woman who hangs off her lover's arm, asking him to tell her what to think and how to feel.

Stop deceiving me, Shelley.

But no. He will throw her out. He will cut her off.

Where would you go, Mary?

The thought of her world without Shelley is like a blade of ice through her battered heart.

She must plan what she will do, where she will go.

To do that, she must find a way to accumulate enough money.

And she must find a way to cut off her love for him.

In the meantime, she must smile until her face throbs.

'Of course it's safe, sweet Mae!' His voice is bright with relief. 'You are in excellent hands. In another life, I might have been in the navy.'

'More likely you'd have turned pirate.'

'And shared my bounty like good Robin of Sherwood. Pirate ships are wonderfully democratic.'

'But wouldn't you rather have breakfast here and spend the day reading in the drawing room? We could walk up to the cathedral.'

'The cathedral, yes.' Monsieur Favre nods. 'Churches too. On Sunday, people are going to the church, not on the lake.'

Shelley hesitates – he is a fierce atheist, but he loves the grandeur of religious buildings. Then he shakes his head and brandishes his book. 'I can read on the lake – we'll take a picnic breakfast. Claire will come too, and I have asked Élise to dress Willmouse.'

'I'm *not* taking Willmouse on the lake.' She expects him to meet her flinty tone with his own; she braces herself.

'All right,' he says softly. 'Whatever you want, my love.'

She swallows, lifts her gaze to meet her lover's eyes at last. She can see the strain on his face, the desperation in his expression. She wishes she didn't feel so drawn to him, even as he disappoints her, hurts her, betrays her.

It is not just that he is beautiful. There is some understanding that sparks between them, a filament of connection that she'd felt from the first moment she saw him. He'd felt it too, she knows. And when she looks at him now, she senses it still, the luminous thread that pulls her back to him, time and again.

I'm sorry, he mouths, holding out his hand.

'Mary!' Claire gasps, from the top of the stairs. She comes rushing down and flings her arms around her sister. 'I was so worried! I thought –'

Shelley coughs. '*I* thought we could go out on the lake. Mary has agreed. She is quite taken with the idea, Claire. No need to discuss anything further.'

He places a heavy emphasis on the last words. Claire's eyes widen as she turns to Shelley. A moment of silent communication between them. They must have decided already that they won't talk about what happened in the forest, what Mary might have seen.

Each private glance, each shared thought between her lover and her sister feels like a slap.

In the fireplace, the logs are still glowing. Whoever had heard of a log fire on a summer's morning? Everything is distorted here; nothing makes sense. Mary is viewing her life played out by performers while she sits in the audience, her face unreadable behind her mask.

'Byron still hasn't arrived.' Claire pouts. 'I am quite weak with worry.'

'Oh dear,' Mary says flatly. 'You'll have to fling yourself at a different man.' Instant relief, as if she has lanced a boil.

'Mary! That's not fair!' Claire's mouth trembles.

'How brave of *you* to tell *me* what is fair.'

'I don't understand why my own sister would speak to me so.'

Mary gives a harsh bark of humourless laughter. 'You don't understand? Let me enlighten you, *dear sister* –'

'Pecksie!' Shelley snaps. And though she is still staring at Claire, Mary hears his warning, can almost hear his thoughts. *Don't make a scene, Pecksie. Be reasonable.* And behind that demand is the reminder of everything she will risk if she speaks her mind. 'Poor Pecksie is simply tired,' Shelley says. 'And you mustn't fret so, Clairie.'

Claire chews her lip. 'But what if Byron's fallen ill? What if it's typhoid? Isn't there an outbreak in France? What if he's sickening somewhere, longing for me?'

Mary digs her nails into her palms.

Please, Shelley mouths.

There are glove-puppet shows in Covent Garden in which husband and wife enact the same arguments again and again, while the audience guffaws, comforted by the farce and the familiarity. She sighs, puts her hands on Claire's shoulders. 'Byron will be well,' she says woodenly. 'He must be delayed but he will be longing to see you. I'm sure of it.'

A glacial breeze blasts across the water, turning it the mottled grey of tarnished pewter. Next to a wooden platform at the lake's edge bobs a small rowboat. Mary has changed her skirt, rinsed the mud and blood from her hands, but her fingers still throb. The earlier sour feeling lingers, though Shelley and Claire are full of forced cheer.

Shelley whoops and steps down into the boat, then mimes flailing and nearly falling into the water. Claire simpers and climbs down next to him. Mary considers letting them go alone – boats often make her vomit. She could claim that just looking at the water makes her nauseated.

But they would know, really, why she wasn't coming out on the lake.

Again, she hears the conversation, the confrontation.

Her sister and her lover gaze at her expectantly, smiling. Claire beckons and Shelley waves one of the bottles of wine he'd bought from Monsieur Favre.

She forces herself to seem calm as she takes Shelley's hand to step down into the boat.

'Are you worried about sickness, Pecksie?'

'A little.'

'For sickness, I prescribe a good captain and bad wine.'

'Wine before breakfast?'

'Wine *for* breakfast.' He grins, reminding her of the days they had spent in France together, heedless of the time, of any demands or responsibilities. Drunk on wine and each other's bodies, they had lain for hours, passing a bottle back and forth, saying whatever silly or serious thought came into their heads. Mary had believed they shared a single mind, that the shape of their love and the direction of their desire were reflected in each other's eyes.

How can they recapture that time, find that seamless joy again?

Shelley uncorks the wine, takes a swig, passes it to Mary. It tastes like vinegar. She coughs, swallows another mouthful and gives it to Claire, who gulps and wrinkles her nose.

'Is this wine terrible or does the boat stink of fish?'

'Both, I think.' The inside of the boat shimmers with a fine patina of scales. Mary's palm, which has been resting on one of the ribs, glistens silver.

'Do they have mermaids in lakes?' Shelley asks, pulling on the oars.

'Perhaps.' *How can he pretend so easily?* 'Monsieur Favre says it's very deep – no one knows what's at the bottom. Something strange.'

'Surely stories don't scare *you*, Mary,' Claire sneers, still annoyed by Mary's comments in the hotel. 'You're too *sensible*.'

Mary shoots her a dark look but clamps her teeth around her retort. Claire wants only to cause a scene. It gives Mary some satisfaction to say nothing. She turns her face away from her sister and stares out across the lake.

A shadow in the distance catches her eye – a boat, perhaps, only it is too small. It almost looks like a person standing *on* the water, in the middle of the lake . . . but that can't be right. She thinks of the man yesterday, the strangeness of his body on the shore, all the questions about him that can never be answered.

The hairs stand up on her arms. She squints and shades her eyes but the figure – or whatever it was – has gone. If it was ever there at all . . .

A shout from the shore startles her. A dark-cloaked figure stands on the wooden dock, waving them back in.

Shelley squints. 'Is that Monsieur Favre? The man's a menace.'

Mary shades her eyes: though the sun isn't bright, the hazy air means it is difficult to make out anything clearly. 'Too tall to be Monsieur Favre.'

Two women join the man now, all beckoning the boat back in.

'Whatever's the matter? What do they want?' Shelley asks.

'Perhaps Byron has come!' Claire claps excitedly. 'Row closer, Shelley, quickly!'

Mary rolls her eyes – the first unguarded reaction she has allowed herself to show all morning. Her sister's childlike conviction that everything revolves around her own desires is endearingly naïve and infuriating.

'*Que s'est-il passé?*' Claire calls.

The replies are too rapid for Mary to fully understand, though she hears the word *retour* repeated angrily, along with more frantic waving. 'Are they saying it's dangerous?' she asks, remembering Monsieur Favre's warnings, the man's body, the strange figure she'd seen.

'Not at all!' Claire frowns. 'Apparently, we shouldn't be rowing on a *Sunday*. They haven't said anything about Byron.'

She cups her hands around her mouth and calls Byron's name in a question. The people shake their heads and shout a reply. 'Oh, for goodness' sake! They want us to come to their *church* service.'

'Tell them I would burst into flames if I tried to pray,' Shelley calls.

He opens another bottle of wine, which he passes to Claire. Then he rows away from the platform, away from the people, who are still calling, waving frantically, as if crying out for rescue.

Mary settles back into the boat, leaning her head against the wood. The slap and hush of the water are soothing. She dozes and dreams of a woman who looks just like herself, although she is dressed in dark rags. She is sitting on the floor of a grand room, staring at her grubby reflection and stuffing something into her mouth. Behind her, the shadow of a man. Though Mary cannot see his features, she knows it is Shelley.

Slowly, Mary realizes that the woman is eating her own tongue. When she cries out and attempts to stop her, the woman explains, in a garbled mess of bloodied lisps and hisses, that it doesn't hurt at all.

She jerks awake. When she opens her eyes, weak sunlight is gilding the water. Through her lashes, in the distance, she sees the outline of a figure – and, yes, it's definitely a man, walking, except . . . He appears to be *floating above* the water. Is he on some sort of platform? Is he stranded? Oh, God – is he planning to jump in, so far away from land?

She sits up and calls out, pointing. The man fades, then reappears. 'Over there!' she says.

Is the man real? He seems to flicker, as she points at him. As he turns to face her, she thinks not of the dead man yesterday on the lakeshore but of her father.

She hears his voice in her head. *Come now, Mary. Be rational.*

Shelley drops his book. 'What is it? Are you well? Mary, answer me.'

The man is gone. The skyline is empty of everything except the shifting mist. Mary frowns and squints again at the hazy horizon. 'Nothing. It's . . . nothing.'

The sun has gone behind a cloud again. The air returns to the strange powdery light, as if nothing has changed from yesterday, even though it feels as if something has been ripped away or torn apart. Mary shudders. 'Let's go back in.'

Monsieur Favre is waiting to greet them at the hotel door. Before they can protest, he bustles them through the reception hall and along an oak-panelled hallway, which is lined with more of the thick-stemmed lilies that Mary had noticed in their room. Beneath their heavy, floral scent lurks something old and tired. She pictures damp corners and ancient rot.

'You must have breakfast now, yes,' Monsieur Favre says. 'Good food is very important. It is late.'

Shelley yawns. 'Not sure I'm hungry. After that wine on the lake, I could do with a nap.'

'But no!' Monsieur Favre stops and turns. Behind his glasses, his eyes are large, his expression wounded. 'You must eat. I have everything waiting.'

Mary notices then how quiet the hotel is. All the people who had crowded the reception hall the day before are gone. Surely he hasn't cleared the hotel for them.

Then Mary steps into the large dining room. She stops, panic rising in her chest. Almost every seat is full and, as they walk in, every single person turns to stare at them. Above their heads, a huge dusty chandelier reflects the light from the candles on the walls. The air is humid, weighted and sour, as if it has been exhaled from some large animal's mouth.

Each wall holds a long line of ancient mirrors, their surfaces dim in some places, crazed with cracks in others. They create the impression of a much larger room, enclosed by hundreds of people.

A woman in a fur-trimmed dress whispers something to the man sitting next to her; they smile. It reminds Mary of London, where she couldn't walk down the street without knowing she'd been seen by one of her father's old friends or Shelley's acquaintances, who all knew that she was the woman who'd stolen him from his wife and family.

Sweat beads the back of her neck. In a room so crowded, she will feel all their actions are observed. She will be even more aware of having to say the right thing, of having to appear calm and blissfully contented.

Do these people truly know who they are? Why do they care?

Mary has her answer when she sees Monsieur Favre's expression, which is both delighted and embarrassed. This is the main hotel for English guests in Geneva: Monsieur Favre must be peddling the shameful gossip of his notorious guests, using them as some sort of attraction.

He leads them towards a small table in the centre of the room. It will be like sitting on stage. Can she leave? Refuse to eat?

Shelley puts his hand over hers and she realizes that she has been rubbing at the scarred and thickened skin on her left arm. Before she sits, Mary notices that there is another empty table, tucked away in the corner.

'Can we sit there instead?'

'*Désolé non.*' Monsieur Favre doesn't even glance at it. 'It is reserved.'

Throughout the meal, which Mary barely tastes, the table in the corner remains empty. The food is ashy in her mouth and she has to force herself to swallow. All the time, she is aware of the eyes on her, the hushed whispers. She tries to calm herself. None of this gossip matters, none of these people matter. Still, the scrape of knives and forks across plates grates on her nerves, as if something sharp and metallic is being dragged over her skin.

'*That* woman . . .' someone whispers, the rest of their words lost in the rustle of fabric and the clatter of cutlery.

'Which one – that one?'

'No, the *other* one.'

The voices are behind her, but when she turns to see, everyone is absorbed in their food, or gazing out of the window, or studying the heavy-bodied lilies, which shroud the room in dense perfume.

Mary bites the inside of her cheek. Wherever she goes, she is *the other one.* The other woman. Meanwhile, her lover eats on, unconcernedly shovelling food into his mouth, studying her as he chews. Is he considering her anew? Perhaps he is looking right through her; perhaps he has never truly seen her at all.

She'd thought she was escaping everything by coming to Geneva, that she was leaving their past, that they could start afresh – that she could be the carefree woman she had glimpsed two years ago in France.

But the past will not stay buried. It beats in Mary's blood, in her breath, like the anger she tries so hard to conceal. It simmers beneath the surface of everything, threatening to break free and scorch her world to cinders.

7

There is something at work in my soul, which
I do not understand.

Days of relentless rain spent cooped up in the hotel. Time dissolves into a blur of wine-soaked afternoons in bed, or early mornings spent reading by the window in the gritty light, or dark nights of thunder when the noise of the storm rouses Mary and Shelley from sleep and they reach for each other.

She tries to lose herself in his touch, in the feel of his mouth on hers, but it is hard to ignore the storms. She has never liked thunder and lightning: in London, storms spelled flooded streets, a scramble for cover and a distraction for the cutpurses and pickpockets. But more than that: storms made her father clench-jawed and brooding.

You were born, Mary, on the night Herschel's comet blazed across the sky. Ten days later, there was a terrible storm and your mother died.

Mary's father had never called either the comet or the storm *portents* – he was far too logical and rational to give voice to such superstitions. He would have been disappointed in Mary if she'd suggested that they were ill omens. Still, every time he told her about the strange lightning across the sky, she couldn't help but think that he secretly believed in a whole unknown world of blessings and curses and omens.

She doesn't mention that morning in the forest and neither does Shelley. Sometimes, when she is nearly asleep, she senses him studying her face. After the church bells toll one or two, she feels him ease his weight up from the mattress, one inch at a time, pausing every so often to see that she is still asleep. She puts her arms around him, pulling him close.

'Where are you going?'

'Nowhere. Just to walk.'

'Stay.'

He laughs, kisses her. 'It's like being dragged underwater by an octopus. A kraken.'

She stares up at him in the half-darkness. 'Should I let you go?'

'Never!' He kisses her mouth, cheeks, throat, then works down her body. 'Never, never.'

His lips stoke a fever in her: she is the one being dragged under. In those brief moments, she embraces it.

Afterwards, they fall asleep with their limbs entwined.

She wakes, hours later, to an empty space where his body should be.

She counts the clock chimes while he is gone. Four o'clock, five. Her heart beats hollowly; she feels small and furious and hateful. If she dozes, she dreams of landscapes carved from ice. A vicious wind sings through the glaciers. In that blue-white world, she is entirely alone.

It is past six when he sneaks back into bed almost noise-lessly, burrowing into her. His hands feel like marble. Perhaps he really has been walking.

He presses cold lips to her cheek, whispers, 'I love you.'

I hate this, she thinks. *I loathe you.*

Except she doesn't. If she did, everything would be easier. She could howl her indignation and rejection; she could watch his face shutter, his love and admiration for her guttering with every savage word she spat.

The third night he leaves her, tears burn behind her closed

eyelids. She lies very still, shaking with rage, with terror that he will not return. Once he is back lying next to her, she stays awake, watching the grainy dawn light seep behind the curtains, trying to formulate a plan.

In London, she has seen women in the street who feel wronged or aggrieved hawk phlegm into the face of the person who insulted them. She watched a thin woman with scabbed skin punch a man who tried to grope her. Another woman – large, with muscled arms that Mary could almost envy – smacked her forehead into the skull of the weaselly fellow who was harassing her.

All these things Mary has observed in the curious way she might watch dogs scrapping and snarling, or angry cats clawing each other. Now she wishes she could summon the bravery of those spitting, punching, skull-slamming women.

By the time he leaves her the next night, she is ready. She waits for him to shut the door, then creeps from the bed.

His coin purse is on the chair next to his jacket. It clinks when she picks it up, weighing it in her hand. Perhaps she could remove one or two thaler coins without him being able to tell. Any more would risk him noticing. What if he accuses Monsieur Favre of stealing his money? She pictures the uproar, the whispering of the other hotel guests, the stares, the speculation.

She falls asleep with a coin clutched in her hand. In her dream, she is sitting in a small, sunlit room, Willmouse on her knee. She doesn't know where she is, doesn't know how she came to be here, but she knows somehow that the door is locked. And she knows she has to leave. On the table next to her, a journal, which will tell her how to escape. When she tries to read the words, the book dissolves. All that remains is a single scrap of paper. On it, Shelley's words: *my darling.*

She wakes, sweating, her head swimming with the need to leave, spinning with the knowledge that she cannot. Shelley's place in the bed is empty again, the sheets cold.

Clenched in her hand, still, the coin. She drops it into her purse, then takes her journal from under the mattress. Faint moonlight casts a pallid glow on the desk by the window.

She will write about a woman who lives alone, serenely, in a state of complete contentment.

The woman was a saintly soul, Mary begins, *whose gentle presence shone like a lamp throughout her peaceful home.*

Her hand moves across the page, almost without her thought.

Her husband was often absent, and she longed for him to return, though she could never say so, for he wanted only for her to be a pretty present, a delicate mirror that he could seem to gaze at in adoration, while delighting in his own reflection. At times, he quite forgot her, so busy was he with the secret tasks he undertook. Lonelier and lonelier, she grew furious with her husband. Longing to escape her life with him, where she felt she must cram herself into a tiny cage they had built between them, especially for her —

Mary scores through the words, ink splattering the page. Growling in frustration, she slams the journal shut and stuffs it back beneath the mattress.

She takes three more thaler coins from Shelley's purse. Hands shaking, she buries them in the bottom of her travelling trunk, inside the sleeve of a yellowing chemise that she rarely wears. Her heart clamps, a frantic fist battering her ribs. As she hurries back to bed, she tries to steady it, tries to slow her breathing.

Then she realizes she has forgotten to return Shelley's coin purse to his case. It sits, half open, on the desk. Before she can move it, the door clicks and Shelley pads back into the room. The mattress dips; she lies very still, eyes squeezed shut.

A storm rumbles outside and he stirs, pressing against her, pretending that the thunder has woken him. She pretend-wakes too, and so that he won't speak, so he won't catch sight of the silhouette of the purse, she kisses him, pulls him on top of her, pushes her hips up to meet him.

Thunder again. White flickers of lightning over Shelley's body make him look waxen, uncanny. She imagines the wind slapping the water outside. How terrifying it must be in the storm, how lonely. What would Shelley do, if he knew she'd taken money from him? Would he tell her to leave, cast her out into the cold?

The windows rattle, as if something from outside is battering at the glass.

She tries to shut out the drumming rain, the moaning wind, tries to close off the image of the body by the lake, of the figure she'd seen above the water. If she can just block out everything but her lover, perhaps she can chase away the feeling that the world has slipped out of joint, that the life she is living is skewed and twisted. Closing her eyes, she presses her lips to the pulse at Shelley's throat. She listens to the thud of his heart, tastes the warm salt of his skin.

As he collapses on top of her, she arches her back and holds him close while his breathing lengthens and deepens. When she is sure he is asleep, she tries to ease herself from under him. He pulls her back, wrapping his arms around her.

The next morning, she watches him pick up his coin purse. He pauses and looks inside it but says nothing. He stares at her reflection in the mirror. She meets his gaze and gives her wooden smile. He returns it with one of his own.

*

By the tenth day, she has twelve thalers in the bottom of her case. She doesn't know the price of things or the value of the money in this unfamiliar country, but it doesn't seem enough to pay for her journey back to London. And what will she do when she is there? She tries to imagine herself begging her father to forgive her. She can't. The words won't come. In her mind, the door to Skinner Street is locked and silent. She is frozen and furious and alone.

Still, each morning when she wakes and stares at the sliver of grainy light that slices through the curtains and falls on her case, she pictures the coins resting within it. They are grains of sand on a set of scales, slowly tipping in her favour, or they are knotted threads in a silver net that might one day be strong enough to hold her.

She has grown to dread the dining room, with its tables of staring, giggling, whispering guests. Goodness knows what gossip Monsieur Favre has spread about them.

Each morning, she tries to distract herself by finding the person wearing the strangest item of clothing or jewellery: a little hat made from the splayed body of a tiny green bird, which a woman with black hair wears just above her ear. Every so often, she reaches up to stroke its gleaming feathers, as if it is alive. Another woman, with pink, fleshy features that remind Mary of the butchers' windows in Skinner Street, has a little purse, made from the orange and black striped skin of a tiger. It dangles from a gold chain on her shoulder. When the woman walks behind Mary's chair, her nostrils sting at the strong scent of the cured skin, which is like soured pickling vinegar.

Usually, Mary would share this with Claire – they might laugh together, or Claire's nose would wrinkle in disgust – but her sister has been carefully avoiding her. At the table, she sits closer to Shelley than to Mary and any conversation she makes is murmured privately to Shelley or directed loudly at both of them.

By the tenth day, Mary's jaw aches from clenching her teeth but when Shelley announces he is hungry, they follow the hum of voices to the fuggy dining room, with its gleaming mirrors and its thousand eyes.

No one is looking really, she tells herself, even though she is sure that Monsieur Favre has been spreading more talk about them. Every time they pass him at the desk, he watches them with an expression of delight.

'You have passed a quiet night, Monsieur and Mesdames? No disturbances for you? I think I have heard some noises. I hope these did not wake you.'

In his eyes, a knowing glint tells Mary that he has seen or heard Shelley going into Claire's room.

Before she enters the dining room, Mary braces herself, as if she is about to step into some dark liquid. Each person's gaze is like black ink staining her skin.

When Claire and Mary enter, arm in arm, the noise dies down. Shelley wanders in behind them, reading as he walks. The chatter stops. Mary forces herself to pass the staring guests without looking at them or acknowledging their curious glances. As if they have already discussed where to sit, they make towards a table set apart from the others, in front of a window.

'This will do very well.' Claire shoots a cool gaze at the other guests, who are still staring. As Claire stares back, they return to their quiet chatter and scraping cutlery across their plates. Where does her confidence come from? Is this the same brashness that allows her to walk by the lake with her sister's lover? The same self-regard that lets her take Shelley into her room, then sit beside Mary the next morning, her brow smooth, her expression untroubled?

Mary clenches her jaw so hard her teeth creak.

'What shall we eat, Shelley dear?' Claire asks. When he reads on, oblivious, she catches Mary's eye. They exchange the ghost of a smile – half a breath and the past two years dissolve. For three heartbeats they are, once again, just sisters, sharing unspoken frustration with a glance, no need for words.

At the same moment, they remember: Mary feels the grim visor slam across her expression even as she sees the steel in her sister's gaze.

Monsieur Favre appears at Shelley's elbow. 'Ah, you are tired of bread and sugar and have brought Mrs Shelley for a *bon dîner*.'

Without looking up from his book, Shelley says, 'Bread and sugar is the food of the gods and that's not Mrs Shelley.'

A hush falls over the room again. Mary can feel the other guests straining to hear.

She tries to swallow her frustration and embarrassment – she and Shelley have argued about this before. He claims there is no need for him to prove his love for her by pretending that she is his wife. They care nothing for respectability, after all. He will sign their names as *Mr & Mrs Shelley* in hotel guest books, simply for ease, but if he is asked, he will not pretend they are married. It is a matter of principle, he says. Why should he sacrifice his ideals for the sake of respectability? He simply doesn't *believe* in marriage.

And yet you believed in it enough to marry once before.

She feels a surge of dislike. How can he pretend he doesn't care about other people's opinions when, really, he cares so deeply? Last year, when reviewers ignored his poetry collection, *Alastor*, Shelley had drunk a flagon of wine, flung it at the wall, then wept.

Of course, that was *his* reputation, not hers.

'Selfish,' she hisses, through gritted teeth, but Shelley

doesn't hear – no one hears. She might as well have been talking to herself.

'Mrs Shelley,' he says, still not looking up from his book, 'is safely in London looking after my children. My *oldest* children. My youngest son is upstairs, as you know, with the pretty nursemaid.'

It is hard for Mary to breathe. Her hand is rigid, bloodless. When she looks down at her clenched fist, she is holding a small silver fork. She doesn't remember picking it up.

She imagines stabbing it into Shelley's thigh.

'Now.' He snaps his book shut and drums on the table. 'What's to eat? I'm famished.'

The fork glints in the candlelight; each of the tines holds her blurred reflection, in miniature. Her featureless face could belong to any woman – reduced, enclosed in the echo of her own image.

'Mary?' She hears Claire's voice, but it is at a distance, beyond the laboured sound of her breath and the unsteady thud of her blood in her ears. She sees it now, the truth about her lover.

'You don't truly want *me*. You just want someone to adore you.' Her voice is low and fierce.

Shelley picks up his book again, frowning. 'What's that?'

Mary's heart is beating hard. She could stay silent now, could let her lover settle back into his fictional world. She could continue to pretend that she isn't hurting, that she doesn't feel lost and frightened and alone – as if he has taken her by the wrist and led her into a twisting labyrinth, promising to walk alongside her, then abandoned her in the dark.

But saying the words had felt good, like stepping into sunlight and feeling it thaw your skin, your blood, your bones. She takes a breath, forces out the words. 'You just want a woman to adore you. That's all you want from me.'

139

'Mary,' Claire says, softly, urgently.

Shelley blinks, amused. 'It's not *all* I want, Pecksie. I am happy you adore me, of course, but I need other things too.'

'What *other* things?' Her voice is a growl; she barely recognizes it as her own.

'Are you quite well, Mary?' He makes her name sound like an admonishment.

'What other things do you *need*?' She spits the last word.

'Mary, *please*!' Claire puts her hand on Mary's wrist. 'Stop this.'

Mary shakes her off. '*You!*' she snarls. 'Don't *you* tell me what to do.'

Claire recoils, rubbing her skin as if Mary has struck her. 'What have I done?'

Shelley stares, open-mouthed. The dining room has fallen silent as, one by one, people turn to watch.

Mary thinks of all the awful insults that are levelled at women in the street. *You bitch, you slut, you slattern, you whore.* The words stack like bullets on the tip of her tongue.

But to say them? It would be like jumping off the edge of an icy crevasse into a black abyss. It would mean being truly abandoned in the wilderness, in the darkness, with nothing but twelve silver thaler coins to keep her warm.

Still, she has to say *something*.

'I know,' she whispers, so quietly that only Claire hears her.

'What's that?' Shelley says, leaning forward.

'I *know*!' Mary repeats, glaring at her sister.

Claire's eyes roll back. She crashes from her chair to the floor, as if she has been slammed about the head with a brick. Someone nearby screams. Crash of glass shattering, clatter of metal –

'Claire!' Mary cries, kneeling next to her. Shelley crouches too, leans close to her face, calls her name. He strokes her sister's cheek.

She lies very still, apart from her eyelids, which flicker.

'Claire, get *up*!' Mary's words sound empty. Other people crowd around her sister, pushing Mary out of the way. Through their jostling bodies, she watches Claire trying to sit up. Shelley cradles her head and shoulders in his lap.

Mary has seen this before. It's a performance. She will *not* play along.

All through their childhood, whenever Claire was upset, she would throw herself to the floor in pretend fits. Sometimes she would bite her tongue and a thin trail of blood would snake its way down her chin. Always, she would be taken into the drawing room and laid on the good velvet sofa, where her mother would bring her sweet biscuits and little cakes and hot milk with sugar stirred into it. Mary would be called to read her sister a story. Claire would nibble and sip and dab at her forehead, while Mary gripped the book of stories so hard that her hands shook.

In the dining room, Mary can hear Shelley comforting Claire. Her sister gives a weak cough and asks if she might have a little hot milk and sugar. *Un petit gâteau*, perhaps.

Monsieur Favre rushes off in the direction of the kitchens.

Out of the window, the strange fog roils on the surface of the lake. Beyond, Mary can see the houses and villas across the water, their pale stone glowing with the faintest whisper of sunlight. She tries to conjure up a Swiss wife in one of those villas, cosy and content, eating pastries while staring out across the lake. That happy woman, homely and rounded, fingers heavy with gold from her adoring husband, would be unable to conceive of a creature like Mary. Too thin, too weak. Torn between her longing to be with her lover, her need to please him, and her desperate desire to say what she thinks, to do what she wants. In the Swiss wife's comfortable view of the beautiful world, Mary simply wouldn't exist.

A sudden rattle on the balcony window makes the diners jump. One of the older ladies cries out. Mary peers into the swirling mist that never fully lifts. Is a darker shape moving out there? She thinks of the strange figure she had seen on the lake before, the man who had looked as though he was walking *on* the water. Squeezing her eyes shut, she takes a breath, then opens them again.

No one is there.

Just hail. It sounds like knuckles beating on the glass. The clattering intensifies, the air turning darker, hail blocking the pale sunlight. Mary has never seen anything like it. Heavier and heavier, until even Claire struggles to her feet and turns to the window, where the hail is piling up, ankle deep already. Frozen stones the size of babies' fists.

'*Mon Dieu. La fin du monde*,' Monsieur Favre whispers, crossing himself.

'Foolish man – he's beyond tedious,' Shelley mutters.

And yet Mary feels it too. *The end of the world.*

For the rest of the day, they stay in their rooms. Claire needs to rest, so Shelley goes to read to her. Mary doesn't stop him. She paces the confines of their room, runs her fingers over the plush curtains, the gleaming wood – it feels like a glossy prison.

She keeps going over the moment in the dining room when she'd found the courage to speak up; she tries to summon it again, to dredge up that hot, white rage.

Nothing. Nothing. Nothing.

She clutches the purse of thaler coins to her chest. It is too small and too light. Anger is expensive. Rage and escape are costly. Mary doesn't know how she will ever afford them.

Sometime in the middle of the night, she is dragged from a dream of waves breaking over her head and water slapping her face. When she opens her eyes, the sensation stops but the sound continues – a loud drumming and shouting.

She sits up with a gasp. Shelley is fast asleep next to her. When had he returned? In sleep, his face looks peaceful. The drumming continues and Mary thinks of Willmouse – perhaps something has happened, and Élise is calling for help. But there is no sound from along the landing. The noise, she realizes, is coming from outside.

Part of her doesn't want to pull back the curtain, doesn't want to look out of the window and see, perhaps, the ghostly shape of a man moving in the fog.

She grasps a tiny piece of flesh on the inside of her arm and pinches it between her nails until the pain makes her draw a sharp breath. In the morning, there will be a bruise among the crosshatching of old scars.

Outside the window, rain is sheeting down. The darkness is absolute, apart from the orange glow of two lamps moving below, near the front door of the hotel.

As she watches, another lamp moves towards the door, then another and another. In the growing light, she can make out the shape of two men. Behind them, a coach driver is standing beside a horse – or perhaps a team of horses.

She presses her nose to the damp window, holding her breath so that she won't mist the glass. In the faint light, she can just see the shape of an enormous coach, a monstrous thing, large enough to carry ten men. More shouting and hammering. And a name echoing through the night air.

'Open up! Open up for Lord Byron!'

8

When falsehood can look so like the truth, who can
assure themselves of certain happiness?

Morning, and the sky has cleared to a bright and lidless blue, though a sharp wind still gusts down from the mountains. It feels strange to be overlooked by ice-capped giants, rather than the close crush of buildings that had enclosed Mary in London. Away from the dark looks and whispers and scrabbling streets, she knows she should feel free, but she cannot escape the feeling that she is trapped. Perhaps, now Byron is here, people in the hotel will gossip about him instead. Perhaps Claire will leave Shelley alone.

She dresses quietly, promising herself she will wake Shelley, will wake Claire, will tell them that Byron has arrived. But when she imagines them meeting him, she can only see herself on the edge of everything. She pictures the great poet embracing Shelley, kissing Claire. Meanwhile, Mary stands away from the group, invisible to everyone – even, after a while, invisible to herself – her longings and desires buried under the weight of louder, more demanding voices.

So, she leaves her lover to sleep and creeps from their room. As she tiptoes down the stairs, she feels a tingle of anxiety: what will she say to a man who had published poems aged only seventeen, then had the books recalled and burned because they were too scandalous, too full of violent passions?

'I am Mary Wollstonecraft Godwin,' she rehearses, under her breath, 'and I admire your work very much.' But, no, that sounds foolish.

'I would like to ask how long it took you to write *Childe Harold*,' she tries. 'I hope, one day, to have my own work published.'

Saying it aloud makes her inhale and stand taller.

Movement from the reception room. Loud laughter from a deep voice that is filled with confidence, which knows no hesitation. She pauses. Her feet and skirt must already be visible from below. The next step will allow her to see him but might also let him see her.

She eases herself onto the step and freezes. Byron makes her think of a figure in a painting, who has turned to gaze out of the frame, then stepped from it. She recognizes the angular face, the full lips, the dark curls and vivid eyes, but everything about Byron is brighter and bolder than she'd thought possible. He is signing Monsieur Favre's guest book; she watches him scrawl something with a flourish, hears him laugh again.

'Perhaps that will keep the tiresome little man quiet,' he says, to someone Mary can't see.

His voice is a bass growl. He is used to commanding a room, an audience. People must drink in his every word, his every breath and movement. He has a sheen about him, an assuredness, which makes him seem untouchable and a little unreal.

Mary feels as she did when she was a girl: when famous poets visited her father, she used to sneak into his study and hide behind the curtains or under the sofa, just to hear them read, the thrill of their words sending a chill over her skin.

Pull yourself together, Mary. She is not a sighing girl now, not a child who must creep unheard, unseen.

When she meets Byron, she will look him in the eye. He must be used to women gazing at him adoringly. Mary will *not* feel intimidated by his brilliant mind; she will *not* be flustered by his handsome face. When she is ready, she will speak to him calmly. She will not simper and blush.

And for now she will return to her room. She will not greet him from the stairs, as if she cannot wait to speak to him.

She retreats, backing up the steps, nearly tripping over her skirt. She tugs it free of her shoe and holds her breath, trying not to make a sound, then steps up again.

The stair creaks. From the corner of her eye, she sees Byron turn.

'Hello!' he calls.

She bolts, half running up the stairs and along the landing until she is safe in the confinement of her room, where Shelley is still asleep.

She leans her head back against the door and shuts her eyes. She is sure she can still sense the new guest in the hotel – can hear the movement and breathless bustle to accommodate him, can hear the faint scraping of something that sounds like claws scratching against wood. Behind her eyelids, a pulsing of light, like a drumbeat, red and orange, orange and red.

They breakfast late, the dining room empty and still.

Mary says nothing of Byron, says nothing at all, but watches Claire and Shelley. They seem smaller, somehow, than yesterday – their conversations about the food and jokes about the weather are childish and petty.

Watching them, she realizes they have been living in a carefully preserved carapace, all three of them, confined in comfortable disquiet. She keeps to herself the news of Byron's arrival, eating slowly, holding the words back. The unspoken syllables sit, like pieces of carefully cut glass, just beneath her tongue, or in her chest perhaps, gleaming and beautiful and sharp.

Monsieur Favre's eyes are on them, bright as wet pebbles. After the plates have been cleared, he brings over the guest book, which he lays on the table in front of them, next to the smear of egg yolk on the starched cloth.

With one pudgy finger, he points to the most recent entry. Byron has written his name with a flourish. Underneath *Age*, he has scrawled, *one hundred years.*

'Byron!' Claire gasps, and her hand flies to her mouth, as if she is a stage actress.

'He has excellent handwriting for a centenarian,' Mary says, 'although I fear he may tire too quickly for you, Claire.'

Claire's giggle is shaky, as though her bright expression will collapse at any moment. She glances towards Shelley, who is staring out of the window, paying no attention to her. But Mary sees the blankness in his gaze, sees the set of his jaw, recognizes his expression as disappointment.

It feels like a blade jabbing between her ribs: *he doesn't want to share Claire's affection.*

'But who's this?' Claire points to the guest book.

Beneath Byron's signature, there is another name: *Dr J. Polidori.*

Mary had ignored the rumours that Byron took his doctor everywhere with him to sustain a steady supply of intoxicants; she'd always thought it to be just another overblown myth, like the tales of him drinking from skulls and keeping a menagerie of animals, or the stories of his volatile temper and the rumours that he has bedded more than five hundred men and women.

Claire stands. 'Which room is he in?'

'I cannot share this, Mademoiselle,' Monsieur Favre says smugly.

'Oh, but he will want me to know!'

'I want to meet him too,' Mary says. Shelley gives the tiniest flinch – no more than a flickering of his eyelids but Mary feels a surge of satisfaction.

'Please, Monsieur Favre,' she says. 'Lord Byron will want to see us, and we are desperate to meet such a celebrated poet. He invited us here.' She doesn't look at Shelley but hears each of her words as a small, sharp stone. She hopes they hurt.

'Ah, he is on the lake since early this morning, Mademoiselle,' Monsieur Favre says, then leans forward conspiratorially. 'He is drunk already but he takes *three* bottles of wine. Three! For two men!' His eyes are round with delighted horror.

'Sounds like my sort of chap.' Shelley's tone is distracted, as if he has just remembered something.

'I'm going to the lake!' Claire declares breathlessly. 'He will be *aching* to see me.' She leaves her breakfast half eaten and rushes to the door, without bonnet or shawl.

Mary doesn't move. The thought of running to Byron alongside her sister, showering him with simpering adoration, makes her feel a little nauseated.

'Come with me.' Claire turns, chews on her bottom lip. 'Byron is longing to meet you too.'

'I'll be out shortly. I have to . . . feed Willmouse.'

'Don't be so *dull*!' There's an edge to her teasing tone. 'Willmouse is a dear thing but surely he can wait.'

'You're right, Claire. Far better I should leave my baby to scream.'

'You needn't be so snappish. I'm not telling you to *starve* Willmouse. I'm simply asking –'

'You're asking me to put your whims before my child's needs.'

Claire's cheeks are pink. Mary feels the wearisome instinct to apologize, to soothe and placate. Beneath it seethes the fierce, vicious energy that has been building since before they left London.

'Don't –' She breaks off. She can feel Shelley staring at her.

'Mary,' he says warningly, and the voice she hears is not his but her father's. When she was a child, emotional outbursts meant solitary confinement in the nursery.

The old scars on her arm throb to the beat of her furious heart.

She stands, mutely gazing at her lover and her sister, who are side by side now, facing her, their expressions disapproving, disappointed.

All the words she wants to say die in her throat. It is a struggle, suddenly, to breathe.

'I'll go ahead with Claire,' Shelley says. 'Pecksie, you can follow – after you've fed Willmouse.'

He takes Claire's arm in his. As they walk out together, Mary leans against the cool marble pillar, breathing hard. She can't decide if Shelley used her nickname as a way of thanking her for being so dutiful and devoted to their son, or if he was trying to remind her that Pecksie is supposed to be the most agreeable and least quarrelsome of birds.

Up in Willmouse's room, Élise is singing to him quietly while he sleeps and she knits tiny woollen boots. She looks delighted when Mary comes in, puts her finger to her lips and then carries on singing. The sweetness of the scene sets an ache in Mary's chest that she can't quite identify.

This, she thinks, *is what motherhood should look like.*

She feels a longing to lie down on the bed with her baby and doze, listening to the soft lilt of Élise's voice, the click of her needles.

Willmouse is fast asleep. She could leave him here, but it occurs to her that, if she takes him, she will be carrying an explanation for why she hasn't written more, why she hasn't already produced a great work.

'*Je prends il dehors*,' she says to Élise. When the girl frowns, Mary thinks her French must be wrong, so points to Willmouse. 'Outside.'

Élise shakes her head. Perhaps she really doesn't understand. Most of their conversations have been about Willmouse's feeding patterns and sleep.

She reaches for her sleeping son, but Élise lays a hand gently on Mary's arm and shakes her head again. 'Too cold for baby.' She mimes shivering, then returns to her knitting, her expression calm but resolute.

'Only for a short while. *Un moment.*'

Willmouse doesn't stir but burrows into her neck. Mary kisses his head, inhaling the sweet, bready scent of him, averting her eyes from Élise's.

'*Un moment*,' she says again, then leaves the room, feeling as though she is stealing her own child. The strange sensation mixes with the other dark, nameless stirrings from this morning, which make her chest burn and her throat ache. All the words she cannot say are fluttering there, battering frayed wings.

Outside, the wind slaps their faces and Willmouse wakes. He grizzles, taking gasping breaths, as if preparing to dive deep underwater.

Mary is trying to wrap her billowing cloak around him when Monsieur Favre comes to the door. Why is he always interfering? She turns her back on him. *Leave me alone*, she thinks.

'Here, Mademoiselle.' He holds out a green woollen shawl, much heavier than her cloak; when she hesitates, he wraps it around Willmouse. His hands are gentle.

'Thank you.' Mary is too surprised to say anything more.

'This wind is very bad for the children.' Monsieur Favre tucks the blanket more closely around Willmouse's shoulders. 'You must not let him to be cold.'

'I know.' Her throat still aches – perhaps more so at this unexpected kindness.

Monsieur Favre gazes fondly at the baby and gives her a small nod. He looks like a different person, Mary thinks guiltily. She has thought of him as someone exaggerated and unreal, like the depictions of villainous men she used to see in the fairy stories Mrs Godwin published for small children. But the man before her is kind-eyed and concerned.

'I have a small hat also. I will find it.'

It is a strange feeling, being cared for by a stranger. She is so used to finding that people's concern for her is just a way of making her behave properly or speak more politely.

'You shiver?' He mimes her chattering teeth. 'You will wait here. Inside, *alors*, the wind will not bite you.'

She smiles at the poetic turn of phrase as he bustles back to his desk and rummages through the drawers, pulling out papers and what she guesses must be old guest books. 'You don't need to give him a hat,' she says. 'I don't want to trouble you.'

'This is not trouble.'

But it is to her. She can hear her father's voice, as if he is standing right next to her. *Always making such a fuss, Mary.*

'Please. I don't want to make a fuss.'

He ignores her, unloading yet more paperwork from the drawers. Finally, he produces an intricately carved wooden box and opens it to reveal a lock of light hair and a pencil sketch of a baby, placed on top of a red knitted hat. With slow reverence, he takes out the hat and pulls it gently over Willmouse's sleeping head. It is too big and falls comically over his eyes, but he sleeps on, angelic.

Monsieur Favre grins at Mary. Again, his face is transformed. 'A beautiful child. He is safe now.'

Mary stares at the lock of hair. 'How old are your children?'

His eyes shine. 'My son, he died. He was six months only.' His voice is flat, emotionless. 'My wife too. The cholera. Very quick. Very terrible.'

It is as though something hard and heavy is squatting on her chest, squeezing the air from her throat. She tries to speak. Fails, tries again. 'I'm so sorry.' The words are inadequate. They are all she can manage.

'This was long time past. For many years I am very angry. All the people talk about me here always. I am the man with the story of the bad luck, you see.'

She nods, because she does see, now – the way he hoards stories and secrets, the way he stokes scandal. Mary had thought him a malicious man, greedy for gossip when, really, he is searching for somewhere to place his pain. She feels it with him – the rawness, the agony, which swirls inside her always, like a black mist. It is an effort to push it away, an effort to breathe. It is impossible to ignore the memories.

Grief marks a person as fire marks a house. You can paint over the soot and repair the boards, but the rooms will be haunted always by the scent of ashes.

'I'm sorry,' she says again, trying to make her voice kind. 'Thank you for the hat. And the blanket.'

He inclines his head, then turns back to his guest book, flicking through the pages, his eyes small and round and eager once more, as if he has resettled a mask in place. She feels abandoned, somehow. An uncomfortable sensation, like stepping into a worn-out pair of boots, which will leak and rub blisters into her skin but the discomfort is so familiar, the fit so exact, that she barely notices the pain.

Just as she is about to step outside with Willmouse, Élise is at her shoulder, her expression grim.

'Too cold,' she says scoldingly. 'I take him.'

Mary holds him for a moment, kissing the top of his head. She has a sudden swooping feeling that she has been here before, that she has made this decision before, and that by walking away from her child, she is setting some terrible pendulum in motion.

And yet, when she contemplates going down to meet Byron, it is as though she is noticing, for the first time, some thread that is tightly knotted around her wrist – a thin, invisible line that has always been there and is leading her inexorably towards the famous poet, towards the dark water of the lake. And afterwards nothing will be the same.

Stop making a fuss, Mary.

Mary gives Élise her baby and walks away, her arms suddenly light. She has the sensation that she is abandoning her child, but also, that she can still feel him, nestled close to her in the icy, empty air. The exposure fills her with dread. She is the daughter of two great thinkers and writers: Byron will be expecting a genius. She must be Mary Wollstonecraft Godwin, proud of the name she bears, the inheritance she carries. Today she is aware of its weight, of the terrible burden of her name and all that it should represent.

She steps out into the cold.

9

I ought to be thy Adam; but I am rather the fallen angel.

Shelley and Claire are near the lake. To Mary's relief and disappointment, there is no sign of Byron and his doctor. In spite of the sunlight, an icy wind whips through the branches of birch and ash, which are yellow rather than green in this strange summer. Their leaves give a muted rattle, like the bleached ivory keys on a gutted pianoforte, all song leached from their veins by lack of light.

The end of the world. Mary thinks of all the talk of farmers' crops failing, of wheat withering in the fields and frost-blasted blossoms falling from the trees. She'd hoped that things further south would be better, but every stark shape spells hunger. It's hard, in this dismal, grey country, not to be crushed by a feeling of foreboding.

Only the mountain-tops are full and luxurious, their craggy pinnacles crowned with white. Skeins of snow unwind from them today with every blast of frozen air. If Mary were inside by a fire, she would admire the way their softly peaked surfaces look like rich cream. She shudders and wonders how someone would survive at the top of one of those mountains. And what would happen to someone who died up there, among all that snow? A strange burial.

The darkness is filling her thoughts with shadows. She forces herself to gaze back at the lake, which has the forbidding appearance of rumpled steel.

Only a madman would row out in this wind surely. But Claire and Shelley are waving towards a speck on the water and, as Mary watches, a figure on the far-off boat lifts a hand and waves back.

Byron.

Her stomach pitches. Perhaps he hadn't seen her this morning, after all. Or perhaps he won't mention it. Still, she remembers the dizziness she had felt observing him from a distance. How will she manage to look him in the eye, to speak to him without stammering?

'He's seen us!' Claire waves both hands above her head. 'He's seen *me*! Oh, look, he's coming this way. He's rowing back to shore for me!'

Claire's face glows with excitement and Mary sees again how very beautiful she is – not just her daily, preening, self-conscious beauty, in the way she angles her jaw and her mouth to flatter her features, the way she pitches her voice and flirtatious titters just so. It is something more than that – some nearly concealed and neglected inner loveliness that lies beneath the carefully constructed sheen.

Mary had seen Byron only once before, from a great distance, three years ago in London, when her father had taken her to listen to the famous poet. They'd been seated at the back of a huge hall, packed with bodies. Mary, only fifteen, had barely been able to glimpse Byron through the crowd. His voice, though, had filled the room, his words rebounding from the walls until Mary had felt her own head humming with his thoughts. She had grown up with the idea that great poets and thinkers must be serious and rational and reasoned, like Coleridge or Wordsworth – indeed, like her own mother and father. Byron drank wine as he strode up and down the stage; he called out his poems like an actor on the boards. Even though he walked with a slight limp, his calves were strong, his legs muscular.

Between cantos, he paused to slosh more wine into his glass, eventually putting it to one side and drinking straight from the flagon to a smattering of aghast, delighted applause.

Mary's father had shaken his head and pursed his thin lips throughout the performance. On the way home, he'd listed Byron's faults and wrongdoings: he was a debauched peacock, living off his family's estate and drinking himself into an early grave. A shame because the scoundrel clearly had some talent.

'But *that*, Mary, is not the way for a man of letters – or especially not a woman – to behave. Your mother would have heartily loathed him.'

Now, as the boat approaches, Mary's excitement at meeting him is tinged with the same stirring of unease that had made her glad to leave Byron's reading.

Her father's approval doesn't matter to her. *It doesn't.*

Still, she feels her heart beating in her throat. She clasps her fingers together and squeezes until her hands ache. Under her heavy skirt, her legs shake. Her body hums with anticipation.

She thinks of the metal pitch-pipes musicians blow so that they know the right note to play.

'Percy Bysshe Shelley!' Byron booms, standing up in the boat and spreading his arms wide. The boat wobbles and he lurches to one side. He gives a wild whoop and steadies himself against the man who is rowing. That must be the doctor, the man who supplies Byron's opium. London gossip says he sleeps at the foot of Byron's bed to make sure he doesn't stop breathing in the night, or choke to death on his vomit.

Byron whoops again, stretching his arms above his head. His shirt is half unbuttoned; the sleeves are rolled back past his elbows.

Mary is transfixed. She glances sideways at Shelley, whose eyes are wide. His mouth is open, as if he wants to speak. No words emerge.

Byron jumps from the boat into the water, disappearing, then emerging, swimming towards them with strong strokes. He stands when the water is still knee-deep and splashes over to the shore, grinning. 'Christ, that's cold!' His shirt clings to his muscled chest, the material stretched across his broad shoulders.

Next to him, Shelley looks almost gaunt.

'Albe, my love!' Claire gasps and rushes into the water towards him. He walks straight past her, his gaze fixed on Mary and Shelley.

Has he not seen her? Is he playing some strange game by ignoring her? Mary watches as Claire follows him slowly out of the water, her soaked skirt dragging around her legs.

Mixed with the pity Mary feels for her sister, there is a tiny flicker of . . . what? Satisfaction? Smugness at seeing Claire rejected.

An ugly feeling, yet Mary can't quite squash it. She doesn't try for long.

'Lord Byron!' Shelley calls. 'I am Percy –'

'Percy Shelley! Such a gifted poet needs no introduction!' Byron is still showing no sign of having seen Claire.

As he walks from the lake, Mary can't help noticing the way his dark, curled hair frames his forehead. Are his eyes blue or hazel? Claire had described him as handsome, but Byron is breath-stoppingly beautiful. Mary tries to distract herself by looking out at the lake, but her gaze is drawn back to the strength of his jaw, the expanse of his shoulders through the thin material of his shirt. She swallows.

Even his limp, which is rumoured to be due to some slight disfigurement of his foot that he's had since birth, is barely noticeable as he strides across the uneven stones. The slight hitch in his step is endearing. He gives the impression of being very tall, though she sees, now, that he is a little shorter than Shelley, but broader and more assured – more imposing.

This is a man who would fill a whole room with his presence, even if he was just sitting quietly in the corner. Are such men born or made – and if made, how? What force creates such magnetism? She tries to collect herself. As a child, she'd met many great poets: there is no reason to be overawed by this one.

'I'd offer you wine, but I fear we've drunk it.'

'Was your journey –?' Shelley begins, but Byron speaks over him.

'I see you've brought your selection of women.' He grabs Shelley's hand and shakes it vigorously. 'No wonder you look exhausted.'

Mary feels a little pulse of revulsion. She is glad of it, glad of the way it steadies her breathing and straightens her spine. Byron turns to her and his eyebrows lift.

'Ah! The great Godwin-Wollstonecraft progeny!'

'Ah! The great . . . poet.' She hadn't intended to pause quite so tellingly. Her implied insult hangs in the misty air, with the cloud of her breath.

To her relief, he grins, then looks her up and down. She braces, half expecting to feel her skin crawl – so many people have spoken of his appetites and perversions. But his gaze is amused, detached, assessing. She stares back at him, refusing to shrink or hide. There is a thrum of fear in her stomach still, but her legs no longer tremble; her hands are steady.

'Intriguing,' he says. 'Is she usually so . . . rude?'

'Are you?' The words come before she can stop them. What on earth is happening? She wants to clap her hands over her mouth, has to fight the urge to apologize.

She can sense Shelley staring at her. She keeps her own gaze on Byron, just as she would continue to watch an enormous hound that had fixed her in its sights.

Still looking at Mary, Byron gestures to the rower, who has

climbed from the boat and is tethering it to the jetty. 'Allow me to introduce Dr John Polidori. He is my level-headed companion. This means, I am afraid, that his conversation is quite dull. Happily, his intoxicants are *delicious*.'

'P-p-pleased to meet you.' Polidori reddens, drops the rope and wipes his oily hands on his trousers, holding out one blackened palm, then thinking better of it and nodding at Shelley.

'Unfortunate stutter.' Byron grins. 'But he's p-practising p-persistently, aren't you, P-Polly? He's a p-perfect p-purveyor of pills. One day, he'll be a p-proper person too, won't you, Polly?'

Shelley looks amused. Mary feels sorry for the poor doctor, whose face and neck turn a deeper red. He peers at the battered leather of his boots. How like a bullied schoolboy he seems, shuffling his feet, desperate for approval from the big boys.

Byron nudges Polidori in the ribs. 'No need to look so glum, Polly. It's all in jest.'

Perhaps he doesn't notice the doctor's discomfort; perhaps he doesn't care. How could Byron understand feeling utterly dwarfed by the people around you? Mary knows it well, the sensation of being unable to speak up, being unheard. Byron, she would guess, does not.

Polidori seems quietly shy – the sort of awkward, clever man who remains silent to avoid being tormented. He busies himself now with straightening the oars in the boat, running his hands over the paintwork.

Another man, in dark clothing with a bored expression, walks down the path from the hotel, proffering a thick cloak.

'Away, Fletcher!' Byron shouts. To Shelley, he says, 'My valet. I call him Nanny. I've threatened to get him a pinny and apron. If I wanted to be pestered constantly, I'd find a wife to bother me again.'

But how would you finance the divorce? Mary wonders. She wishes she had the bravery to say it and has to turn away to hide her smile.

When she looks up, Dr Polidori is staring at her with an expression of knowing amusement, as if Mary has spoken aloud. She quickly makes her face blank and impassive.

Claire has been waiting breathlessly, almost wringing her hands with excitement, her wet skirt still clinging to her legs. Byron's gaze passes over her as if she is a pebble on the shore.

'My lord Byron,' she finally says, stepping forward and sinking into a deep curtsy in front of him. It is flirtatious and amusing. Mary expects Byron to reach out and raise Claire to her feet, to embrace her. Claire's expression is so doe-eyed and hopeful that Mary *wants* to see him gather her up: for the first time in weeks, she wants to see her sister have what she desires.

Byron doesn't look at Claire as he steps around her. 'Such strange weather, Shelley – all across France, too. Have you found it inspirational? I've started a new canto of *Childe Harold . . .*'

Mary doesn't listen to the rest, doesn't hear Shelley's response as the two men begin walking along the lakeshore. All she can hear is the rasp of Claire's breathing as she tries to hold back tears. Claire wobbles, then falls back to sit on the wet mud and sharp rocks. She makes no attempt to get up.

Mary feels a flash of anger towards Byron – not just at his callousness but at his indifference, as though Claire is less than the dirt, as if her heart is less important than one of the stones he picks up to fling into the lake.

When Mary rushes to help her sister to her feet, Claire takes her hand but doesn't shift her eyes from Byron's broad retreating back.

He is walking beside Shelley, both talking animatedly about the body of the man who had washed up – had it been an accident or suicide? Something to do with the strange weather, perhaps.

'Don't mind him, Claire,' Mary says, as gently as she can. 'We can go back to the hotel. Here, lean on me.' It's the soothing voice she used with Claire when they were children and her sister had scraped her knee.

'I don't understand,' Claire murmurs. There are tears in her eyes. 'He must be pretending – to tease me.'

Before Mary can stop her, she picks up her filthy, sodden skirt and runs after Byron, shouting his name.

Mary watches hopelessly. She wants to call her back, but the stubborn set of her sister's jaw tells her there will be no distracting Claire from this.

And why should there be? Why should Claire have to be calmed and placated? Why shouldn't she be angry? Why shouldn't she be allowed to scream?

Mary remembers how, when Claire first came into their house, she'd been appalled whenever her sister shrieked in rage. Yet some small part of her had been captivated by the small girl who howled her feelings, who demanded to be seen and heard.

Now, she wills it.

'Albe!' Claire calls.

He continues walking.

'Albe!' she shouts. 'Albe, *look* at me!'

Finally, he halts and turns, his expression remote. 'Yes?' It's the impatient sigh one might direct at a quarrelsome child. 'What do *you* want?'

Claire gives a shaky smile. 'You can't have forgotten about *us*, Albe.'

'Sadly, I remember you all too vividly.'

Mary flinches, as if he has directed that flat tone, that sardonic expression at her.

'Well, then. Will you not greet me? You invited me here and –'

'I did not.'

Mary feels a stirring of dread, but Claire is still smiling, as though she thinks Byron is playing a trick on her.

'Albe, you *did*! I said I longed to spend more time with you, and *you* told me you would be in Geneva this summer. You meant me to follow you –'

'I *meant* to escape you. I hoped to forget about you, along with all my other tiresome obligations and debts.'

Claire whitens, as if he has struck her. Horrified, Mary moves to pull her away. Shelley reaches out to take Claire's arm. She brushes them off.

'You can't mean that! In London, we shared such – So many times, you lay with me and – you looked at me as if . . .'

'As if what?'

'You were so passionate and –' Claire's chest heaves. A sob fractures her voice. Mary longs to put her arms around her. No matter how furious Claire has made her, she doesn't deserve this.

She reaches out again. Again, Claire pushes her away. Mary can see a muscle pulsing in her jaw, can see her trying to express her thoughts clearly. Mary wonders if Claire, too, hears William Godwin's voice telling her to speak calmly.

Her voice shakes but it is clear. 'Albe, you must know I'm devoted to you. You must feel something for me to have kept on –'

'I shall tell you how I *feel* about you, Miss Clairmont.'

Claire gazes at him, her expression hopeful. Mary grips her skirt, willing him to be gentle.

Byron holds up his hands, addressing all of them, as if

reciting to one of his audiences. 'How do I feel about Claire Clairmont? Now. Have you ever had an ulcer in your mouth? It irritates you beyond all measure, but you just can't stop yourself *poking* at it with your tongue. Or have you had an inconvenient boil on your face that keeps returning and you just wish you could scrape it off with a nail or a knife, or anything at all?'

Claire's eyes are wide. She says nothing. Mary tries to swallow but her mouth is dry. This is too much, too brutal. Surely Shelley will say something. But Shelley gazes at Byron with the same dumbstruck awe as when he'd leaped from the boat and swum through the icy water.

Byron's voice is acid. 'In case the metaphor is too much of a challenge for you, Miss Clairmont, *you* are the ulcer. *You* are the boil. And I would like you gone.'

Claire's mouth trembles. As Byron turns to walk away, she reaches out to catch hold of his sleeve. He brushes her off, wipes his fingers on his cloak and stalks away.

'Come on, Shelley.'

Mary feels fury boiling in her chest. She waits for Shelley to challenge Byron, to rebuke him. Instead, Shelley whispers to Claire, 'Don't cry, Clairie – I'll persuade him.'

And, to Mary's disbelief, her lover follows Byron. She can hear them talking about Petrarchan sonnets. Polidori goes after them, hanging back a little.

'Oh, Claire!' Mary whispers. 'Come here.' Her anger has turned into a solid ache now, like a rock in her chest, heavy on every heartbeat.

When Mary puts her arms around Claire, her sister doesn't move. Then, slowly, she sinks down again onto the wet stones and the freezing mud, the stinking sludge from the lake.

Mary sits next to her and takes her hand. Claire's fingers feel like marble. Mary puts them to her cheek, then kisses her palm. She wants to offer some comfort – to say that perhaps

Byron is tired or teasing her. Hadn't Monsieur Favre mentioned *three* bottles of wine? Though he'd looked and sounded coherent enough.

Even as Mary conjures useless excuses for his cruelty, she knows they are hollow. Claire would know it too. From her sister's throat, from deep in her chest, comes an animal groan. The raw noise drags Mary back to her own most desperate moments. It takes her back to the arms that reach for her in her nightmares, to the tiny body resting against her chest in a dark and lonely room. She wants to put her hands over her ears and block out the noise.

Claire draws a shuddering breath and groans again and again. Mary rubs her back and whispers empty platitudes until, finally, Claire leans her head on Mary's shoulder and weeps. Mary's own eyes fill with tears as she clasps Claire tightly.

Here it is, still: the closeness that bound them together when they were young – running together from Claire's mother's hard hand, whispering outside Mary's father's quiet study, hushing each other while they hid under the sofa to listen to Mr Coleridge read a poem that had transported them to an ocean, a murdered albatross and a ship full of dead men, while a living man burned with the need to tell his tale: *Alone, alone, all, all alone, Alone on a wide wide sea!*

'I'm here with you,' Mary says. It's the only thing she can think of that is absolutely true. 'I'll help you. I promise.'

Claire shudders and raises her eyes to watch the men. They are walking back to the hotel, as if they've forgotten about the women altogether – as if the women don't exist.

'What can I do, Mary?' Claire whispers. 'What am I going to do?'

10

I am malicious because I am miserable.

When Byron and Polidori go into the dining room, Claire tries to follow but Mary takes her arm gently. 'Let's go upstairs. We can eat in my room. Monsieur Favre will send something up.' She looks across at the hotelier, whose expression is a little pained as he nods.

'Yes, Madame. But you are sure you are not easier eating with the gentlemen?'

From the dining room they hear a clang and a loud burst of male amusement. Monsieur Favre looks longingly towards the commotion, then shoots Mary a pleading glance.

'Quite sure.' Her voice sounds too harsh, so she forces a smile and adds, 'Thank you.' She is tired of the performance. She is so furious at Byron's cruelty and Shelley's weakness that she cannot risk facing them.

'Why are you so good to me?' Claire asks, as they walk up the stairs to Mary's room. Then she starts to sob again.

Mary helps her to undress, giving her sister her own nightgown and tucking her into bed, stroking the hair back from her face, as if Claire is a child again. She has a strange feeling of standing outside herself, watching herself being calm and kind, her movements light and gentle, while all the time rage burns through her. She wants to slap and claw and spit. Some wild animal has woken within her, and it is harder and harder to conceal it.

'You're angry with me,' Claire whispers from the bed. Her eyes are red, her cheeks puffy – she looks as she did when she was a girl and had a fever. Mary used to nurse her then too, without ever complaining.

'No,' Mary says – it is a habit, as instinctual as breathing, to deny her fury, to crush even the slightest stirring of irritation. And she isn't just angry with Claire – she's furious with all of them.

'I've been terrible to you.'

Mary's throat is dry. The words of denial and comfort stick there.

'I didn't mean to be,' Claire says. 'But I promise that Shelley has been nothing closer than a brother to me here.'

'Ha!' The cynical laugh Mary gives surprises them both. She swallows, then says tightly, 'I don't want to hear more . . . fabrications.'

'I'm telling the truth! I only needed his comfort. He listens to me and –'

'Comfort? You needed his *comfort*?,' Mary growls. She can feel a scream building in her chest – or something more animal than that: a roar. She pictures it filling the room, drowning her sister's voice, smothering her lies.

'I *promise*, Mary, there was nothing untoward or improper. When you saw us in the forest, I had gone out to look for Byron. I asked Shelley to come with me for safety. Then I hurt my ankle. I know how it must have seemed but . . .' She trails off.

'But you didn't *say* anything,' Mary says, fighting to keep her voice level. 'And you let him come to your room at night and –'

'Nothing happened between us, Mary. Please believe me.'

'*How?*' It's a guttural roar that comes from deep within her. It feels so good to release it that she demands again, '*How,*

Claire? And even if I could believe you, *why* didn't you try to reassure me? You must have known what I believed.'

'I . . .' Claire's face is wet with tears again. 'I'm sorry.'

And Mary knows she can't explain, that perhaps Claire doesn't even know herself why she has been content to flirt and giggle with Mary's lover, to take his time and to draw him away from her sister. Perhaps she really doesn't understand why she would allow Mary to believe the very worst, why she needed that power.

Mary takes a deep, shuddering breath. Her sister can be shallow and vain, yes, but she is also desperate for love, desperate to be seen and heard and adored. And, after all, isn't that what Mary wants too, really?

She sits on the sofa and covers her face with her hands.

She wants to embrace Claire, to comfort her.

She wants to scream at her – to claw the dark, glossy curls from her sister's scalp.

Her shaking hands are freezing, blanched and bloodless, as if they belong to someone else. She tucks them beneath her thighs and waits until the prickling urge to hurt her sister has faded. This isn't her fault – or, at least, not *entirely* her fault.

'How can I face Byron?' Claire rasps. 'I can't bear it. If he looks at me like that again – did you see? As if I was no one to him, *nothing* –' Her voice fractures and Mary feels a surge of pity.

She can't make herself embrace Claire – she is too angry, too empty – but she manages to say, 'It will be all right, I promise. I will think of something.'

And, lying sleepless next to Claire in the suffocating darkness, waiting for Shelley to return, listening to the mournful bells, tolling out the empty hours, she does.

When the first grey light edges beneath the curtain, Mary

creeps from the bed. Shelley has spent the night elsewhere, but she will not allow him to overtake her thoughts. She needs to be clear this morning, and calm. The worst thing would be to appear panicked.

In the corner of her chest, underneath her old chemise, the pile of silver thaler coins glints in the grainy light. Only twelve, but it must be enough for a start.

They clink as she puts them into her purse, with three of the coins Shelley had given her for the *voiturier* when they first came here. For a second, she feels a stirring of guilt – but *no*!

There is no room for guilt today, no space for sadness. There is only a list of tasks that she will complete, one after another, like threading glass beads onto a piece of string.

At the clattering of the coins, Claire stirs and sits up. 'Where are you going?' Her voice is still hoarse from yesterday's tears.

'I'll be back soon, I promise.' Mary presses a kiss to her sister's damp forehead. The coins jingle in her purse.

'Mary, you're scaring me. This isn't like you.'

Mary can't stop herself smiling. 'I know.'

The beginning is always today. It sounds like an old voice, long forgotten, but also a new idea: she might make a beginning for herself somehow.

As Mary walks from the room, she feels a new clarity. There is purpose in her stride. For the first time she is not following Shelley's plans or her father's edicts. It is her own breath drawing her onwards, her own fire burning through her limbs.

Instead of going past the lake and into the forest, she walks in the other direction, towards the houses and what must be the outskirts of the city. The streets are cobbled here and cleaner than in London, where the stench of rot and rubbish clouds everything. The air, though, is thick with the same silty grit she had noticed in the weeks before – a fine dusting of sediment even coats the ferns and grasses, although no one she passes stops to look at it or squints out over the clouded lake as she does.

Once or twice, she senses someone watching her – that she is being observed from a distance and judged. She shakes her head, trying to rid herself of the feeling, which must be her guilt – the familiar voice in her head, which is so like her father's: *What are you doing, Mary? Is this wise?*

The Swiss women look happier than people back in England, or perhaps they are just more used to smiling at others in the street. They nod as they pass her, long sticks of bread under one arm, their baskets containing butter, cheese and meat, despite the shortages in England and France.

A carriage clatters past. Mary raises her hand to stop it. The driver ignores her, and she has to press her back to the wall while it thunders by.

Perhaps this is a bad idea – she doesn't know what she is doing. Shelley has always planned their journeys. She'd hoped to see more carriages but maybe it is too early. She pauses – should she return to the hotel? Then she remembers Byron's hostile expression and Claire's sobs. She recalls the distance in Shelley's eyes.

He has happily spent nights away from her, without ever trying to explain. He, too, must have known what she would assume. Has he let her think the worst because he knew she would never leave him? Or does some part of him want to crush her, keep her small, weak and longing for him?

Angry tears form behind her eyes.

Stop it! She clenches her fists and walks on without paying attention to where she is going. Dimly she is aware of the cries of hawkers, of the bustle of grain being unloaded and weighed at the corn market. None of these people can give her what she wants, so she ignores them, just as she ignores the sensation, at every turn, of eyes on the back of her neck, cruel and assessing.

She isn't sure where she is going but doesn't want to appear lost, so she stays close to the city wall. It zigzags back and forth, past three churches and a public water pump, where there is a queue, despite the early hour. She trails her fingers along the wall. On a map she'd looked at before they arrived, the city was shaped like a child's unfinished drawing of a many-spiked star. Now, the repetitive accordion-like structure makes her feel as if she is walking in an endless cycle of points and depressions.

She passes another church, a pronged iron city gate, which is closed, and a foundry, with its thick smoke and sharp smell of burning metal.

As last, she sees what looks like a large barn containing three carriages. A group of men laugh as they harness the horses. Her heart lifts, but when she calls to them, they don't respond.

She calls again and they ignore her. Perhaps they don't speak English.

'*Bonjour!*'

One of the men pauses in adjusting the reins on a chestnut horse and turns to her with a bored '*Quoi?*'

'*Je voudrais voyager* – I want to travel today. Away from Geneva.'

The man scratches his beard. His face is grubby, his eyes pouched with tiredness. 'Day journey?' His accent is thick. 'To mountains? Not today – bad weather.'

'Not an excursion. I want to go . . .' It is an effort to get the words out, as if by saying them she will have broken something, will have cracked some bond with Shelley that can never be repaired.

Again, she remembers his amusement at Byron's cruel

jokes. His awed expression as Byron had mocked Claire, had called her a boil, a sore.

All the nights he has spent away without any attempt at explanation.

Damn him!

'I want to leave – to go to Calais.'

'Calais.' The man guffaws. 'You know Calais – in France, yes? One week in carriage. Very expensive.' He eyes the purse in Mary's hand. His eyes light up at the clink of coins.

She goes to empty it in front of him, then thinks better of it. 'I have fifteen thaler.'

'Fifteen thaler?' His face is ruddy with amusement as he shakes his head. He calls something to the other two men, who burst into laughter too. The sound knits them together and shuts her out, like a door slammed in her face. It reminds her of the wall of male jocularity from the dining room yesterday. She backs away.

As she walks hurriedly from the barn, she is sure she can feel eyes following her again. She turns. She can see only the men, still chuckling and slapping each other on the back.

The mocking sound of their mirth chases her, and she is so intent on escaping it that she nearly trips over a heap of rags that someone has dumped near the wall. As she side-steps, the bundle of clothing stirs and sits up.

Mary's blood jolts and she is poised to run from whatever creature is lurking there.

It's a woman, wearing a black handkerchief tied around her head and a ragged blanket around her shoulders. Her expression is dazed, and she smells strongly of stale liquor.

'*S'il vous plaît. S'il vous plaît.*'

She has a young face, but her skin is deeply lined and smudged with dirt. She lifts a grubby hand, reaching for Mary's cloak. Mary recoils, stepping back. But the woman is only lifting the blanket to reveal, huddled next to her, a small child, who can't be more than two years old. A boy, Mary sees, as he holds out his tiny hand, palm up.

Oh, God.

Mary wants to leave, wants to walk away, wants to pretend she hasn't seen the pair.

Looking at them is like glancing into a quivering dark pool and glimpsing another life, which always lurks behind her wavering reflection. One false step, and this might be her. One different decision made, one different word spoken, and this could be Mary with Willmouse, skinny-limbed and cowering under a blanket.

If Shelley leaves them, or if she leaves him, this is their future.

She presses a thaler coin into the child's hand. As she hurries away, she is once again sure she senses someone watching her from the shadows near the wall. When she turns, there is no one.

Mary can smell a bakery ahead. The warm scent of fresh-baked bread pulls her onwards. She will buy something and eat it where she stands – she will be able to plan her escape more clearly without hunger clawing at her belly.

Then she sees the butcher's shop and stops. The sudden twist of homesickness is overwhelming. As a child, Mary was used to looking out of her window and seeing animal corpses strung up, dripping pinkly onto the stained stones. It is all familiar: the metallic smell of blood, the iron tang of meat and viscera laid bare in summer and winter alike, stippled with flies or solid with ice.

Even after she met Shelley and they mostly stopped eating meat, she didn't find the carcasses repulsive. There was beauty in the delicately strung harps of the ribcage, the once-tight drum of skin over the abdomen, slack and split where the butcher had made his clean cut.

Willmouse has been looking too pale and should have some meat, although Shelley says this is nonsense. Vegetables sustain many animals, from monkeys to elephants. Surely she doesn't plan for their son to grow larger than an elephant. *You worry too much*, he says. *You care too much about these things.*

But how is it possible to worry less about her child? How can she stop caring so much about him?

She heaps these thoughts onto the glowing coals of her anger towards Shelley – she has to stay furious with him to continue with her plan.

Perhaps the butcher will be able to help her: he must take deliveries of meat. She tries to imagine herself, Claire and Willmouse leaving Geneva on the back of a butcher's cart. She sees her child sitting in the puddled blood and gore. The image is so sickening that she leans against the wall and presses her fingers to her temples, trying to rub away the pulsing pain that has been building all morning.

How has she become so trapped? How is it possible, after leaving the locked attic in her father's house two years ago, that she now finds herself standing in the wide-open space of a foreign city but *still* she is hemmed in at every side?

Every choice she has made has bound her more tightly to Shelley. Every time she has stayed quiet or refused to protest or has done as he wanted – out of love or fear or both – she has wound a knotted net of chains between them. And now she will never be free.

That feeling, again, of eyes on her. She drops her hands from her temples and glances around but sees only unfamiliar faces, strangers bustling about their business. She turns to go into the butcher's shop then stops: is a figure moving in the shadows on the other side of the street?

It is the man from the lake – she sees the fixed expression on his face, the blank stare of his blue eyes, just as she'd seen his reflection in the mirrors in the hotel. Her throat constricts. She is about to bolt when the figure steps from the shadows and the face resolves itself.

Byron.

He is the last person she wants to see. But he raises his hand: it is too late to avoid him. As he crosses the street, she tries to look pleased; her face won't obey.

'Well met, Mrs Shelley.' He *knows* Shelley's wife is in London – is he trying to be polite, or attempting to provoke her? 'Did you sleep well?'

'Not at all.' Then she can't stop herself: 'Have you been *following* me?'

'Why would you ask that?' His voice is amused, but his eyes are flint. And he hasn't denied it. What has he seen her do? Did he watch her talking to the men by the carriages? Did he see her take out her purse? Perhaps he heard their laughter and went to speak to them.

'I wanted to . . . walk, to meet people in the city.' She can feel her face reddening, but she continues: 'I've walked halfway around the walls, and I stopped to talk to some people, but I thought I felt . . .'

She trails off – it sounds ridiculous, as though she is being hysterical. Her father's voice in her head. *Be sensible, Mary.*

She makes her voice stronger, more matter of fact. 'You surprised me, just now. How long have you been watching me?'

'I wasn't watching you.'

'I'm not a fool. Your denial is insulting,' she snaps. Several passers-by glance over.

Byron takes half a step back, his eyes travelling up and down her, his expression thoughtful. 'You are very different from your sister.'

'We are stepsisters. We share no blood.'

'I mean it as a compliment to you.'

He gives a slow smile and, though she looks down at the damp cobbles, she can feel his gaze on her face. 'Save your compliments for my sister. I have no use for them.' The words are out before she can stop them. What is it about this man that makes her so rude?

'You are unusual, then.' He raises an eyebrow. 'Most people enjoy my words.'

'I admire your words on *paper*.'

His smile widens. 'Ah, but you object to the words from my mouth?'

'Precisely.'

For goodness' sake, Mary. Apologize!

She turns towards the door of the butcher's shop.

'I must go, Lord Byron.'

'Please, call me Albe.' He reaches out, as if he means to put a hand on her arm, then lets it fall.

Claire calls him Albe – an affectionate blurring of the initials LB. When she'd used the name yesterday, he'd behaved as though she hadn't spoken, then verbally savaged her. There is a sour taste in Mary's mouth; she won't use that name.

He is still smiling expectantly; her stomach lurches. If only he wasn't so handsome. If only his gaze on her didn't feel so . . . *intimate*.

'Lord Byron. Excuse me. I must go . . .' Flustered, she gestures towards the butcher's shop.

'I'm not sure I can stomach the smell of blood so early.' He folds his arms across his chest and leans against the wall. 'I shall wait outside for you.' He looks entirely at ease, as if he often spends his mornings waiting outside shops for ladies he has only just met.

'I don't require an escort.'

'I wouldn't dare to suggest you do. But I would like to be on friendlier terms with you.'

'I don't require more friends, either.'

'A pity.' He holds her gaze for a moment too long. 'You're a figure of some intrigue.'

His voice, too, is intimate. He steps closer. She hadn't noticed before, but his blue eyes are flecked with gold – a bright corona around the pupil. He blinks slowly, his lashes long and dark.

'I would imagine, Lord Byron, you might be sick of intrigue, given how it follows you.' She is relieved that her voice sounds level as she turns unhurriedly to the butcher's shop. She can feel him watching her, can feel his gaze, like a touch. She doesn't let herself look back.

A bell above the door jangles as she steps inside the shop. A woman stands behind the counter. Her hands are stained red, but her expression is serene as she calls, '*Bonjour, bonjour,*' and something else, which must be '*What do you want?*'

Mary mutters '*Bonjour,*' then falls silent because, well, what does she want?

She wants to be away from this place, these people. She wants this stranger to help her.

The shop smells of iron, of copper and of something sweeter. Is it the familiarity that has brought her here? Perhaps it is the reminder of her father's house and the people who work on his street, who used to call a cheery hello when they saw her, who used to deliver packages of free off-cuts, sometimes, wrapped in brown paper. The butchers had always looked so strong and capable – trustworthy even, as if working with death had rendered them purer and more honest.

Foolish to feel this connection but, still, here she is.

The woman doesn't pause in her bloody work but stares intently at Mary's face. '*Vous avez besoin d'aide?*'

What can she answer? *I want to know how you can get in and out of this city. I want to give you money. I want you to help me leave.* The butcher returns her attention to the small birds laid out in front of her, raises her knife.

The wooden block is an altar, bloodied and stained with years of precise and gentle violence. The air thickens with the spatter and crack of flesh sliced from flesh, bone cut from bone.

'Can you help . . .? I want to leave.' Mary's voice cracks on the final, crucial, word.

The butcher lays down her knife and stares at Mary's face, a small frown creasing between her eyes. 'You want *sortir?*' She gestures at the door.

'No. Yes. I want to *sortir* Geneva. I need . . .' *Escape* sounds foolish, surely. She digs into her purse, empties out the silver thaler coins. They glint in her palm, tiny glimmers of hope.

'I tried to pay for a carriage, to *voyager*, but I can't afford it. *Pas d'argent.* Do you have *un* cart *ou* you can tell me where I can *chercher* . . . I need to *voyager à Calais.*'

She can feel herself reddening. She might as well be describing a dream in a language she can barely speak. It made perfect sense in her head. Aloud, in her broken French, it sounds ridiculous.

A breeze brushes the back of her neck; again, she senses she is being watched. Even as she tells herself it is all in her mind, her cloak stirs in the draught from the open door.

She turns. Byron is standing behind her, his head cocked to one side. His mouth lifts in a wolfish grin. 'Planning to cook a lump of beef in your hotel room?'

'No, I . . .' Her heart hammers in her ribcage.

She has to say *something*, to invent a reason for asking the woman about Calais, but there is no point because he has overheard, and he knows. *Of course* he knows.

And now he will tell Shelley. And everything will be over. Her life will be over.

If she is lucky, her lover will take Willmouse from her so that her child, at least, will survive. She will die alone, in the darkness, on these foreign streets.

She tries to breathe but it is as if there is a stone in her throat.

She feels another breeze. Byron is standing very close to her, the same watchful expression on his face as before. As he exhales, his breath brushes her skin.

'Please, continue,' he says. 'Don't let me stop you.' He turns away to look at the shelves of mustards and pickles, humming to himself as he inspects the jars, one by one.

Mary's cheeks flame: she stares at the butcher, wide-eyed, hoping she can communicate that the woman shouldn't speak.

'You want leave?' the butcher says again.

'No, I – I want to stay here. It is pleasant, much warmer in here.' The shop is as cold as it is outside and smells of meat, but it is too late to call back the stupid words.

'You want stay?' the butcher says. 'I work. You think what is the thing you want.' She indicates, with one bloodied hand, the pile of plucked chickens on the counter.

Dry-mouthed, Mary nods.

She watches the woman's tender hands, as she slips quick clever fingers into each carcass, like a cutpurse drawing out riches. She can feel Byron looking too – he has stopped humming, though he still stands just behind her, his breath stirring the hair at the nape of her neck.

There is something calming in watching the butcher's action. As she loots the carcasses, she doesn't look greedy or desperate: the calm focus on her face reminds Mary of the expression of people lost in worship. Her hands, delicate and purposeful, entering, pausing, leaving each body, like a priest entering church after church, in pursuit of peace.

Mary tries to exhale, tries to tell herself that if she can find calm here, in the midst of all this death, she can find the strength to go back to Shelley. She will love him when she can; when she can't, she will play along and pretend.

But what will she do with all her pain? Now she has acknowledged the rage, it simmers in her constantly: she cannot ignore its fierce heat and light, any more than she could pretend not to see a fire that was eating through a house, one room at a time.

'I will wait for you outside,' Byron murmurs, close to her ear. She takes a step away from him, then nods. Perhaps this is a trap. Does he know that she is trying to escape and wants to watch her pay the butcher for the journey so that he can tell Shelley? As he turns to leave, his expression is shuttered and unreadable.

She can feel him watching her through the window. Through his eyes, she can feel Shelley's gaze, measuring her actions; and she can feel her father inspecting her, judging her. Beyond all of these, she is watching herself, as she always does – she feels some part of herself, like a critical witness, observing her actions, measuring them, telling her how to behave, how to be.

A hand on her elbow. She opens her eyes – she hadn't realized she'd shut them again, hadn't realized, until the butcher passes her a handkerchief, that she must be crying. Pain in her throat again, a hard bolus of all the feelings she can't put into words, all the words she cannot say.

'*Vous avez besoin d'aide.*' The woman's brow is creased with concern.

Her first instinct is to shake her head, even as something inside her says yes, yes, she *does* need help. But what can this woman do? Mary is so confused, so angry, so full of *feeling* that she doesn't know what to say – to Byron, to Claire, to Shelley. What can anyone give her?

'You are with the English poet,' the butcher says.

Mary nods, remembering Byron outside, waiting for her, but when she looks, he isn't there. Panic, sharp and sour.

'Things are hard for you,' the woman says.

Mary nods again, takes a shaky breath. 'Is it so plain to see?'

'It is small, this place.' The woman shrugs. 'People talk always.'

'London is big but the same.'

'In all places, I think. People tell the stories, some true, some false.'

'Yes.' Mary thinks of how people in the hotel must talk of her, as part of Shelley's story, or as a new part of Byron's story, or both. Whichever tale she is in, she will be a minor character – just one of the women in the great poets' lives.

Mary wants to ask about the cart again, but she cannot risk being caught leaving. The thought of Shelley discovering her plan feels like gazing into a dark abyss.

She thinks of the woman she had seen earlier on the street – her face too young and too old, her eyes full of brief hope and deep despair.

'You buy something,' the butcher says.

'No. My . . . He doesn't eat meat often, so . . .'

'Ah!' the woman says. She disappears behind a thin, cotton curtain into a room beyond. When she emerges with something in her hands, her eyes are bright. She indicates for Mary to hold out her own hands, then presses two warm eggs into her palms.

'For you. I am cooking these today. You hold. *Bon confort*. Then eat.'

Not wanting to be rude, Mary thanks her and gives her one of the silver thaler coins. The butcher pockets it and makes no move to give Mary any change. Feeling slightly stupid, Mary doesn't know how to protest, though she is sure the coin should have paid for far more than two eggs. Her cheeks blaze with embarrassment but the woman seems unruffled. She taps one of the eggs on the edge of the counter, carefully peels the shell and pulls off the thin pale skin beneath it, translucent as wet paper. When she has finished, she gives the egg to Mary again. It feels soft and alive in her palm; it feels, somehow, like a benediction.

'Thank you,' Mary whispers, and realizes she means it.

Emerging from the butcher's shop feels like leaving the hush inside a chapel and being submerged in clashing light and noise. Thank goodness Byron hasn't waited for her. She wipes her cheeks dry and inhales. The sun is higher but still ghostly in the strange fog. Behind her, the church bells toll ten. How has she been away so long? She must hurry back so that Shelley will not miss her, will not suspect anything, and she must return to Willmouse. If she can gather more coins over the coming days – Claire too – they may be able to find a way to leave.

She walks as fast as she can, then hears boots behind her. Looking over her shoulder, she sees a man striding along, trying to catch up, a hat pulled low over his head. Her heart jolts and she has a breathless moment of panic before she sees it is Byron again.

'Running away, Mrs Shelley?'

'No! I didn't recognize . . .' She indicates the hat.

'Oh, I returned to the hotel to plan our departure.' His eyes slide from hers and she feels sure he has said something to Shelley, has told him she has been asking about routes out of the city. She tries to conceal her dismay.

'You're leaving so soon?' Claire will be devastated but Mary feels a flash of relief. Everything about him makes her uncomfortable: the intensity of his eyes, the breadth of his shoulders, the shape of his mouth –

Stop!

He smiles lazily, as if he can hear her thoughts, and his gaze lingers on her face. 'Just to a house across the lake. I believe your husband plans to move too. There is a smaller house he wants, near the Villa Diodati, where Polly and I will stay.'

For a moment, Mary cannot speak. The idea of moving to be nearer to Byron, to spend more time around his cynicism, his magnetism and his constant watchful gaze makes it suddenly hard to draw a steady breath.

Breathe. Blink. Swallow. Feign calmness.

'When did Shelley decide this?'

'We settled on it last night. Polly found out about the houses straight away. He might seem a bit pathetic but he's a useful chap.'

Mary doesn't think Polidori seems pathetic, only – like the rest of them – in awe of the famous poet and defenceless against his quick charm and savage wit.

'We had talked about staying in my villa together, but then I'd be at the mercy of your sister's moods.'

Mary bristles. Claire's moods can be difficult, but Byron has caused this upset. He has no right to be so constantly cruel. 'She only wants to be noticed for you to see her.'

'I can hardly miss her. The woman spends most of her time weeping and wailing.' He grins when Mary glares at him. 'Ah, I have offended you.'

'It is my sister you have offended,' Mary says tightly.

'You're *defending* her!' He stares at her, incredulous.

'Why is it so hard to believe that I would defend my *sister* against the cruelties of a stranger?'

'I simply thought – It's widely believed that she is a . . . competitor for your husband's love.'

Mary's breath stops in her chest and she feels shame colour her cheeks. When she can speak, she tries to sound dismissive. 'Idle gossip. And Shelley is not my *husband*, as well you know.'

'Ah, yes, falling in love is a wonderful thing but, as far as I can tell, the fastest way to fall out of it is marriage.'

When she glances sideways at him, he is watching her face – pleased at having needled her.

'I would have thought,' she says, 'that *you* of all people would know how little value there is in cheap gossip about sisters.'

When he frowns, she feels her own spiteful surge of satisfaction, quickly followed by irritation that he has made her so petty.

'Touché,' he says, a little sadly.

Good, she thinks, trying to push away her humiliation, trying to be wholly glad that Byron really does have a weakness.

They walk up the hill in tense silence. The houses here are spaced more widely than those in the London side-streets, where buildings are crammed together, like dirty overcrowded teeth.

'It would cost a lot of money,' Byron says. 'To reach Calais.'

Mary's stomach drops. She can't speak, can't even gather the breath to deny anything.

'And then there is the matter of how you would pay for passage across the Channel. And where you would stay in London.'

'I don't know what you mean.' Her voice sounds too high, too quiet.

What has he said to Shelley? Will she find that he has packed her bags for her? Will he banish her? She will never see Willmouse again. Even if Shelley allows her to take Willmouse, how will they live? She cannot beg with him on the streets. She cannot return to her father. She needs a better plan. She needs to find a way to survive.

Her head spins. She thinks she might vomit.

'Steady.' Byron takes her arm and gently guides her to a

wall. His hand is strong and solid. She sits, closing her eyes against the sensation that the world is whirling around her.

'Have you eaten?'

She shakes her head. To her surprise, he turns her hand over and places two fingers on the inside of her wrist. His touch is deft and certain – too intimate against her skin. She wants to pull away but can't move.

Everything feels very distant, as if it is happening to another woman.

'Polly taught me this,' he says, in response to her wondering gaze. 'Ah! You have a pulse. I'm told that's usually a good sign.'

She still can't speak. What would she say? The only word she can think of is *please*. Please don't tell him. Please pretend you saw nothing, that you know nothing. Please help me.

'I haven't said anything,' Byron says, as if he can sense her fear. 'I haven't told him.'

Is it her own dread, or does 'yet' hover in the silence between them? She is very aware of his firm fingers on her wrist, of the strength of his hands. There is a dark shadow of faint stubble along his jaw.

'I . . . Thank you,' she manages to rasp, pulling her wrist free. She loathes herself for thanking him and she loathes him for making her feel grateful that he hasn't set her whole life ablaze. She can still feel the pressure of his fingers against her skin.

His gaze is steady, unruffled. 'I don't have any food with me, but I can fetch something from the hotel while you wait. Or I could go to the bakery?'

Her mind is still reeling and the idea of being left alone sits in her stomach like a shard of ice. She presses her arms against her middle and that is when she becomes aware, again, of two warm, ovular shapes in the pocket she has had sewn into her skirt.

She draws out the eggs and begins to eat the one that the butcher had peeled for her, the one she'd meant to give to Shelley.

Byron gives an amused snort. 'Sorry, I'm not mocking . . . It just seemed like a conjuring trick.' He scrubs his hand through his hair. 'You're not as I expected.'

'You're exactly as I expected.' This isn't true. She doesn't know why she said it. He blinks, as if she has wounded him. She feels the urge to apologize, squashes it.

There is an awkward silence.

As she swallows the last of the egg, Byron's blue eyes crinkle at the corners. 'You look better already. Brighter.'

He reaches out. Before she can move away, he brushes a finger over her chin. 'Yolk.'

'Oh.' Her cheeks heat. She wants to wipe the feel of his fingers from her skin. She wants him to touch her again.

When she looks up at him, his expression is intense, something fierce and focused in his eyes. He leans closer.

She steps back, holding her hands up to ward him off, palms out.

He stays very still but his expression is the same. She reads it clearly now – greed, want, hunger.

'*Don't,*' she says, her voice clear and low. The strength in it surprises her, steels her. She says it again, with more vehemence: 'Don't . . . touch me.'

He flinches and his face shifts into surprise, then hurt. She wonders if anyone has refused him before – if any woman has ever said, *Don't touch me.*

'Forgive me.' His neck reddens. He looks much younger suddenly. 'I don't know what I was thinking. Say you forgive me.'

'If I say it, will you leave me be?'

'Possibly.'

'Then I forgive you.' She knows her face is rigid and

that her voice sounds strained but, when she sets off back towards the hotel, Byron walks alongside her without pressing her to say anything more. She tries to pretend he isn't there, tries to breathe slowly, to calm every nerve in her body – how close to her he is, the sound of his breath, the strength in his fingers when he puts out his hand to steady her, then, remembering her reprimand, withdraws it.

Mary is climbing the steps to the hotel and Byron is just behind her, when the door opens and a woman emerges, sees them and stops.

It takes Mary a moment to recognize her sister: Claire has changed her hair, pulling more ringlets down to frame her face and pinning the rest into a high pile of curls, the style from a painting of Byron's half-sister, Augusta.

Claire looks back and forth between Mary and Byron, her eyes round. She looks as though she might give a peal of wild laughter. Then her lips tighten and something slams shut in her face. She turns to go back into the hotel and Mary reaches out to grab her arm.

'Claire! It's nothing for you to – Stop! Please –'

'Leave me alone,' Claire growls. She steps back into the hotel and shuts the door, then stands, leaning against the glass.

Mary watches her readjust the pins in her hair and walk away, without looking back.

I I

My heart was fashioned to be susceptible of love and sympathy.

Inside the hotel, there is a buzzing chaotic energy as men shoulder past each other, heaving loaded bags and heavy trunks.

'I should follow my sister,' Mary says distractedly. If Claire finds Shelley first, goodness knows what she will say.

'It seems unwise to spoil one of her hysterical fits,' Byron says drily. His cynical mask is firmly back in place – no trace of his hurt from earlier. 'Leave her,' he continues. 'She so enjoys her performances.'

Mary glares at him; he gives another of his unruffled grins.

She turns away – she hasn't time for this arrogant, cynical man. She must find her sister and explain that Byron means nothing at all to her; she must tell Claire she really had tried to help her, had tried to find them a way out of Geneva.

At the bottom of the sweeping staircase, Monsieur Favre appears, his expression frantic. 'Ah, Mademoiselle, you are not going also? And, Lord Byron, you must stay, please.'

'You're leaving the hotel *now*?' Mary asks.

'Sooner than now, if possible. Which appears to be *this* ferrety little man's objection.' Byron indicates Monsieur Favre, who is puce-faced, talking in rapid French to a porter.

Favre turns to Byron. 'You have these rooms for one week. You sign the book.'

'I might have *signed* for a week, but I've only *stayed* for two nights. And you've been rifling through my cases. Rent the rooms to someone else.'

'I have not touch your cases!' Monsieur Favre seems genuinely outraged. 'And I cannot rent these rooms to any person. They are full of your animal shit.'

Mary feels nauseated. Byron looks gleeful. 'You seemed happy enough to host me, my animals *and* their shit when you thought you could sell tickets to see us, as though we're a travelling circus.'

'I have not selled tickets!' Sweat glimmers on Monsieur Favre's upper lip.

'There are people at the windows watching us right now.'

Sure enough, Mary can see that the garden furniture, which had been stacked next to a hedge, has been dragged out onto the patio. A crowd of fifteen or so people are peering through the windows, their coats pulled up around their ears against the unseasonal wind.

She steps backwards until she can feel the wall against her spine. Why had she trusted this man? How could she have been so stupid? She is not aware that she is glaring at Monsieur Favre until he recoils from her expression.

'I have not selled tickets, Mademoiselle. I promise you this.'

'He'll probably auction your sheets as soon as you've left,' Byron says. 'The more stained the better.' His eyes are bright, the sneer on his lips slipping into badly concealed delight. This is all a performance and Byron is enjoying himself immensely. He seems not to care about Monsieur Favre's outrage or her own sense of betrayal.

The hotel owner had been so kind to her, just the day before.

'How *could* you?' she demands. Just as when she'd spoken out to Byron, she has a feeling of some weight shifting. Some scales within her are tipping. She feels lighter.

'Forgive me, Mademoiselle. People want to see Lord Byron and I must make money. Please understand.'

She turns away without saying anything, and allows her fury to propel her up the stairs. She can feel Monsieur Favre watching her, Byron too, but she will not turn back to offer them forgiveness or consolation.

On the landing, she has to step to one side to allow two local men to drag past four large dogs that strain at their leashes to sniff and lick her hands. Another man follows, holding two cages containing eagles, flapping their wings and shrieking.

She presses her back against the wall and tries to breathe through the sense that the place has gone a little mad.

The man bows apologetically and says, in blurred French, something about savage cats.

The door to their room is open and, even before she goes inside, she can hear Willmouse wailing. He is lying in the middle of a pile of clothes and shoes, trying to reach for a wooden rattle just beyond the stretch of his small arm. Every time he fails to grip it, he shrieks in frustration.

Claire, who usually dotes on the baby, is ignoring him. She stuffs clothes and books into cases, her expression grim. Shelley is lying on his back on the bed, reading aloud. He shifts to the left and right as Claire digs out clothes from underneath him but makes no effort to move. When Willmouse gives a high-pitched scream, Shelley raises his voice to be heard.

'We're leaving?' Mary scoops up Willmouse, with the rattle, and kisses his burning, tear-streaked cheeks. 'And so soon.' It is a struggle to keep her voice level. Slipping back into her usual role of being quietly practical, unprotestingly pleasant, is like stepping into a corset that is too small; it crushes the air from her lungs.

'Oh, so you've heard,' Shelley says, cheerfully.

'How was your walk?' Claire crumples a blue dress of Mary's and stuffs it viciously into the case. 'I am glad you are making *new friends*.'

'Claire, may I speak with you?'

'I don't see what you could possibly have to say.'

'I want to explain –'

'Well, *I* don't want to hear.' Claire balls up stockings and shoves them into the bag.

Mary tries to draw a slow, steadying breath. 'Please, Claire. It's not what you believe. You mustn't think –'

'I mustn't think anything except what *you* tell me. Because *you* are so clever and rational and *correct* that the truth must be whatever *you* think. Because *Mary* is always right. Isn't that so?'

A surge of irritation. 'That's not fair.'

'It's not fair on *me*, Mary.' Claire pulls her close, fingers digging into her arm. 'You *promised* you would help. You *left* me here and I thought –' She chokes on the words.

'I tried,' Mary whispers, glancing at Shelley, who is still reading, unconcerned. 'I tried but –'

'I don't believe you. I think you saw Byron pushing me away and you thought it was your chance at another famous poet.'

Claire's eyes shine with tears and, for a moment, Mary is speechless. A humming sets up in her skull. 'You can't think I *want* Byron . . .' She can feel, still, the pressure of his fingers on her wrist. But she had *wanted* to pull away.

'Stay away from him,' Claire hisses. 'If I see you flinging yourself at him, I will tell Shelley you plan to leave him. What do you think he will do *then*?'

'You're mad.' The words sound harsher than she'd intended; they feel like a punch to her sister's face – one of the most awful accusations. Men say it often, that women are *mad* or *crazed* or *hysterical*. Mary had never seen herself flinging the word at her sister, but some dark part of her enjoys saying it, enjoys how it silences Claire. She says it again, much louder: 'You're *mad*.'

Shelley finally puts down his book. 'Whatever's the matter?'

'I saw Mary out walking with Byron.' Claire crushes a corset of Mary's into a trunk. 'She was hanging off his arm. They were *gazing* at each other.' Claire's expression is bitter and triumphant. Mary imagines stepping forward and pushing her from the room, slamming the door behind her.

'I felt faint because I was hungry. Byron helped me. Nothing more.'

Shelley raises his eyebrows, amused. 'Why so fearful, Pecksie? You know such things don't trouble me. I don't believe in ownership. Love is not a prison.'

His words and his light tone knock the breath from her. Mary has always known that he doesn't believe in being possessive but surely he must be a *little* jealous. Surely she can't mean so little to him. Her throat is dry. 'It was nothing –'

'She's lying! I saw her. She *knows* how I feel about him and she still . . .' Claire's voice cracks.

'Hush now.' Shelley's hands move in small circles over Claire's back, rubbing away the tension. It is how he soothes Mary's distress; she swallows a sour taste.

Mary stacks books angrily in a trunk, trying not to listen to the whispered conversation from the bed. Claire has slumped backwards. Shelley lies next to her, stroking her hair. When she sobs, he pulls her close.

Mary's knuckles are white, her arms shaking with some tremor running through her – a shifting, bubbling force beneath her skin that she must hide, must breathe through, must pretend to smile through.

She tries to keep her attention on the packing, the folding, the stacking, the busy work of her hands, so that she doesn't look at the bed. When she glances up, Shelley is watching her, his gaze thoughtful. She catches his eye. The grin he gives is so wide and so natural that it takes Mary's breath.

He mouths, *I love you.* Somehow, this strange reaction to Claire's accusations feels worse, feels like a spiked nail being driven home.

They are soon packed and ready to leave. Claire has stopped crying, but she still won't talk directly to Mary. She gives instructions through Shelley instead: *Ask my sister to pass my handkerchief.*

The local men help the women with their cases, while Shelley reads Aristotle. Mary is about to step out of the hotel when Monsieur Favre appears from a side-room, pink-cheeked and wild-haired. He hurries up to Byron and the two men talk animatedly. Monsieur Favre's expression grows more and more horrified.

The wind whisks away their words as Byron points to his dogs and some of the caged animals, directing the men holding them back into the hotel.

Monsieur Favre wails, 'I cannot keep these rooms just for animals!'

'I don't see why not.' Byron gives a wicked grin. 'You said yourself that I have booked the rooms. And, as you've pointed out, they're already covered with shit.'

As Monsieur Favre hurries to Mary, she turns away, hoping he will walk past her.

'Mademoiselle Shelley, please.' The poor man is actually wringing his hands. He bobs in a little bow. 'I have a request.'

'I have no influence over Byron. And we can't stay. I'm sorry. Once Shelley has fixed his mind upon something, he is immovable. He wants . . . what he wants.'

'I see this. But I worry for your child. The weather is very strange this year. Too much darkness. Clouds are everywhere now. The fishermen, they think it will be worse soon. Storms for one week, maybe more. Floods and lightnings, thunders, cold. They say there is red snow falling in Italy still that may come here also. Very strange. I think you will be inside for many days. I think you should not be much near the Lord Byron. You and the baby must be away from them.'

Mary frowns, her patience worn thin from being told, again and again, what she should do, where she should go and how she should feel. What does this man understand of her life?

'I must go with Mr Shelley,' she says, aloof.

'I know this, Mademoiselle. But I fear for you, for your baby. These are not good men. It will end very bad, I think.'

When Mary hesitates, Monsieur Favre adds, 'My boy. He dies when we are not watching, my wife and me. You cannot watch your boy all the time. My wife, she dies two days later. Perhaps the infection takes her or perhaps her heart breaks. I cannot say.'

'I am sorry.' Mary turns to the mist hanging low over the lake so she doesn't have to see his grief – it is too painful.

'You are having two houses, yes? Perhaps the baby stays always in one house, where he can be safe. He will be happy.'

Mary wants to walk away from this interfering little man. But she knows he is right – Willmouse would be safer away from Byron's moods and drinks, medicines and animals – away from the chaos that the poet brings with him.

At the knowledge that she will have the freedom to think, the freedom to read and write, perhaps, the freedom to embrace a different life, Mary feels lighter, as if she should hold on to something to stop herself floating away.

Élise bounces Willmouse on her hip, then pretends to let him slip and catches him. He gives a squeal of delight. As Mary walks towards the cart, another woman holding her child, she feels equal amounts of liberation, guilt and envy.

She had planned to avoid Byron where possible, but he calls her over, smiling, his eyes bright. 'Mrs S! What do you say to this view?'

Claire shoots her a furious look, but Mary can't ignore the poet altogether. She is aware of his gaze on her, is aware of an energy that draws her to him, that throbs beneath her skin when he is near.

'Beautiful. Very inspiring.'

Byron surveys the lake, then yawns loudly, as if making an announcement – he performs every gesture as though he is the sole actor on the stage of a packed theatre: he laughs stridently, yawns demonstratively, sighs in a way that stops every other conversation. His sleeves are rolled back and, as he flexes his fingers, the muscles in his forearms ripple.

'Inspiring, I suppose, for old men who like writing about lakes and mountains. But don't you find Turdsworth a terrible bore?' There is a glint in his eye; his mouth tugs up at the corners.

She would have liked to ignore his childish bid for attention but, somehow, if she lets it pass she will feel he has scored a point against her. She forces herself to meet his gaze. 'Not at all. I rather like Turdsworth's daffodils.'

Byron starts in surprise, then gives a shout of laughter. 'She's wonderful, Shelley!' He slaps Shelley's shoulder.

Claire scowls.

'She is,' Shelley says. 'I set my life on fire for her, but I don't regret it.'

Mary doesn't return his smile. *I wish I didn't know you at all.* The words enter her mind clearly and completely, though she is sure she hasn't spoken aloud. Is it true? Does she wish she didn't know him, had never met him?

Because what has he lost, compared to her? If he left her, she would have nothing and no one.

Sometimes Mary thinks pityingly of his wife, Harriet, who is alone in the world with Shelley's other children. Then she remembers that Shelley must have told his family he still loves Harriet. Does he ever go back to his wife? Does he leave her waiting for him? Where does Harriet think he is now? Mary feels a wave of disgust – at herself and at Shelley.

If he left Mary, nothing of him would remain except private memories and public shame.

She forces herself to lean over and kiss his cheek. 'I love you,' she whispers. Which means, *I wish I didn't love you.* Which means, *I don't know how to leave you.*

He clasps her hand, only hearing the words she says. He doesn't listen to her tone. He doesn't try to read her body.

When she looks up, Byron is watching her again, his gaze intense. In this light, his blue-gold eyes are almost black. A shiver runs through her, as if he has reached out to lay cool fingers on the pulse at the base of her throat.

Polidori emerges from the hotel, puffing under the weight of two leather trunks, which he stows on the back of Byron's carriage. It is a magnificent, monstrous thing that Byron has had made, in the style of the coach owned by Napoleon: huge, dark blue, covered with ornate gold scrolls and with space inside for a writing desk, a large liquor case and a bed. Spectacular and ridiculous in equal measure, it makes the carriage that Mary and Shelley have hired look small and drab, though it is big enough to carry six people comfortably.

'It seems unfair to suggest a race.' Byron gazes at their carriage in amused disdain. 'But I know we are all eager to leave this strange little man's strange little carnival, so might I suggest that, as your . . . *cart* is in front, the women and children go first. Shelley, you come with me. I've a yearning to hear your thoughts on my latest work.'

Shelley doesn't hesitate or even glance at Mary before he climbs into Byron's luxurious carriage. She stands watching him, readying herself for the sting of abandonment.

It doesn't come. Instead she feels, in the space around her, the whisper of possibility.

She catches Claire's eye, sees the familiar mixture of rejection, dejection and resignation. Poor Claire, always hungry to be at the centre of things, always exiled to the edges. It takes Mary back to when they were children, longing to be close to the exciting party of poets and artists downstairs, but so often dragged from their hiding place behind the curtains and banished back to bed.

When she puts a hand on Claire's shoulder, Claire rubs her cheek against Mary's knuckles instead of shrugging her off.

'I tried to find a carriage for us to leave Geneva.' Mary keeps her voice low.

Claire's face goes very still. 'To leave Byron? And you'd *leave* Shelley?'

'I didn't have enough money.'

'How do you have *any* money?' Her expression is watchful.

Mary hesitates, before admitting, 'I've been . . . saving coins for some time.'

'I *thought* I heard you jangling this morning. I assumed you'd stolen from Shelley.' Claire's round-eyed expression looks forced and sly. 'Though *any* money you have is stolen from Shelley really, isn't it?'

'I . . .' *Oh, Lord.* Why had she said anything to Claire? Why on earth had she been so foolish as to share her plans so soon?

As if reading her thoughts, Claire says, 'Don't worry. You don't think I'd *tell* him, do you?'

Mary doesn't know how to answer this. Of course Claire would tell him if it suited her desire for drama, or if it advantaged her at all.

'You're my sister and my closest friend,' Claire says lightly. 'I wouldn't betray *you* any more than *you* would betray *me*.'

Mary feels the blood drain from her face. 'I've told you, nothing happened with Byron this morning. I didn't want to walk with him.'

'You keep saying that,' Claire says, in the same falsely bright tone. 'But you *did* walk with him. Didn't you?'

And before Mary can answer, her sister climbs into the carriage and sits next to Élise.

Mary is about to follow them when there is a light touch at her elbow and a man's voice says, 'Miss Godwin, can I help?'

Mary whirls around, ready to tell this stranger to take his hands off her. She comes face to face with Polidori. She must look fierce because he takes a step back, holding up his hands. 'Dr Polidori! I thought you would travel with Lord Byron.'

'No. They wish to talk of p-poetry and I will be in the way. "Off with the women, P-Polly."' His imitation of Byron's haughty drawl is surprisingly accurate. In spite of her dark mood, Mary laughs.

Polidori looks pleased. 'I must admit, I am happy to have the chance to s-spend more time talking to you, Miss Godwin.' Away from Byron, his stutter is less pronounced.

'And I you.' She likes this man's gentle manner and un-assuming presence. And it is a relief to be removed from the fraught and frayed back-and-forth between herself and Shelley, Claire and Byron.

As the carriage clatters around the lake, Polidori gazes at the water, which is blue-black and looks like ancient stone. With each gust and eddy, the gritty mist above the lake stirs and settles.

'I'm not one for superstition but the lake is certainly strange. You know the locals claim it is home to gigantic fish-like crea-tures, c-capable of eating a man whole?'

He is smiling but Mary shudders, remembering the poor dead man they'd seen.

'Of course,' he continues, 'there are bound to be legends about large bodies of water where p-people are liable to drown unexpectedly – am I upsetting you?'

'No,' Mary says, not quite truthfully. Then, because he looks so earnest and kind, she adds, 'It's a little unnerving.'

He speaks gently: 'In this odd weather, stories about the lake would unnerve anyone. But there are some charming myths too – an enchanted ship, for example, that rides upon the waters at dawn. Those who see it will live charmed lives.'

He is trying to comfort her, and she feels a little lighter. 'Thank you. You're very kind.'

He looks shyly pleased. 'You're welcome, Miss Godwin. There are plenty more delightful legends – you'll have heard of the strange magic that allows certain people to see things from the future in the far distance?'

'To see the future?' Mary thinks of the man she saw, walking alone above the water.

'Some locals believe they have seen things yet to come, or the future of their loved ones, suspended in the air above the lake. Future houses and future spouses.' Polidori smiles. 'Though it doesn't rhyme in French, of course.'

Mary tries to look amused to hide her discomfort: she'd thought that the figure she'd seen had just been some sort of echo in her own mind of the poor dead man. That she might be going mad. But what does it mean, if other people have seen these strange things above the lake, and have found them to be omens?

She shudders again, pulling her cloak more tightly around her shoulders.

The carriages slow outside a small villa, which is, Polidori tells her, Maison Chapuis, their rented house, very close to where Byron will be staying. But Byron has asked them to dine with him this evening at the Villa Diodati and has told them to meet him there.

'I, too, would be glad of your company, Miss Godwin,' Polidori says.

'It's not a suitable place for my son, William.'

Polidori stares at her, his expression startled, and she realizes how prim and spinsterly she must sound. But how can she explain the danger she feels around Byron? It is not only his drinking, his laudanum habit and the chaos he generates. It is something else – something in the way he looks at her. It makes her feel as though she is suspended above icy water.

She wants her child far away from it.

'Élise will stay here with Willmouse,' she says firmly.

'But you will come to Villa Diodati now?' he asks. When she hesitates, he adds, 'Please. I would be so delighted. Lord Byron, too, of course. And your hus– Mr Shelley will dine with us. It has already been arranged.'

His expression is so sweetly hopeful that she finds herself agreeing.

'You look worried, Miss Godwin. Your child will be safe, I am sure.'

'Mary is *always* worried,' Claire says. Mary had thought her asleep, but she must have been listening. 'She frets all the time – it's exhausting.'

Mary glares. How typical of Claire to try to ruin this new friendship, just because she feels bitter and hurt about Byron.

But Polidori gazes at Mary with even more admiration. 'So, you travelled in France aged just sixteen, away from your family, even though you were scared? You must be even braver than I'd thought!'

'*I* went with her around the Continent too, you know,' Claire says. 'I was only fifteen and I wasn't frightened at all.'

Mary rolls her eyes, suppresses a sigh.

'I would expect nothing else, Miss Clairmont. Your fearsome reputation travels before you.'

Mary feels a small stab of jealousy.

'Oh.' Claire smooths her hair. 'Pray, what reputation is that?'

'That you are determined and single-minded. That you have a habit of getting exactly what you want.'

Claire nods, pleased, though Mary doesn't think Polidori meant what he'd said as a compliment.

The driver helps Polidori unload Élise and Willmouse's trunks from the carriage. Mary kisses her baby all over his face, until he giggles.

Walking away from him will feel like splitting herself in two. She holds him tightly and makes a silent vow that she will find a way for both of them to be free and safe.

As she climbs back into the carriage, her heart clatters like a fractured rock.

Villa Diodati is a short way from their rented house. They round the corner, and the yellow sandstone villa stands at the end of a curved driveway, sheltered by sycamores and young plane trees. The new leaves, which should be a vibrant green, are the colour of cinders. With the pale sun sifting through dark clouds and the faint fug of smoke on the breeze, the villa seems shrouded in a tobacco-stained fog.

'Beautiful, isn't it?' Polidori says. 'Milton stayed here, you know.' His eyes twinkle. 'It's part of the appeal for Lord Byron – he thinks the walls will be imbued with genius.'

Mary hasn't met a man like the doctor before – he is so knowledgeable and clever but not at all superior. She thinks of how Shelley and Byron discuss things – lecturing each other and whoever else is listening, competing to appear the most erudite. Perhaps Polidori's gentleness will make their time here easier.

As they climb down from the carriages, the wind gusts gritty sediment into their mouths, noses and eyes; Mary shields her face with her sleeve, coughing. Shelley and Byron whoop and turn into the wind in what seems to be competition – they splutter and gasp as their eyes stream.

'I can escort you to see your child at any time,' Polidori says. 'If Mr Shelley is . . . indisposed.' He gives another of his shy smiles.

'Thank you. You're a very good man.' She wishes she could shake his hand, like men do to show their gratitude. She could curtsy, but that would feel stiff and formal, so, without thinking, she touches the sleeve of his coat.

He looks down at the pebbled driveway, clears his throat and scuffs at an invisible weed with his boot. Then he stares at her; he seems unable to speak. Mary is grateful when a blast of wind blows his hat from his head and he has to chase after it.

The sky is darker now, the first splashes of rain spattering down. Mary recalls Monsieur Favre's warnings about the bad weather. Storms and floods for a week in summer? Red snow in Italy? Surely not.

Another squall of cold rain hits her. The shock makes her gasp.

Polidori unlocks the door but the wood sticks – he kicks and shoves all his weight against it before it will open so he can light the lamps and fires.

Fletcher, Byron's stone-faced manservant, is hauling in cases and cages – though Mary knows at least some of the animals have been left at the hotel.

Mary turns to call Shelley in. He is standing next to Byron, both howling at the rain like wolves.

Claire watches them, then howls too. The men ignore her.

Do they even notice the desperation on her face, the brittleness of her delight? Do they see how she shivers, or how, when Byron turns his back on her, Claire's mouth tugs downwards briefly . . . in an effort not to weep?

Mary feels a flash of pity; she runs and flings her arms around her sister. Perhaps it is the rain, or because of her loneliness, but Claire hugs her back, her teeth chattering.

'I'll fetch you a cloak.' Mary rushes inside the house, where it is instantly quiet and still.

A single lamp lights the gloomy hallway, casting Mary's flickering shadow up the wall. Wind gusts in from outside and she pushes the door closed before the candle is blown out. She can't see Polidori – he must be lighting the fires.

Unease stirs in the pit of her stomach. 'Hello?' The walls fling the word back at her. *Hello?* The house is safe. No reason to be scared. She picks up the lamp. 'You're perfectly safe,' she whispers. Her voice sounds strange and hollow. She feels the hairs rise on her arms.

The wooden door is so thick that she cannot hear Shelley's voice from outside, Byron's shouts or Claire's simpering.

'Hello?' she calls again.

Hellohellohello.

Raised hairs again. She tries to mock her foolishness but can't quite shake the tightness in her chest.

The lamp swings in her hand; the rusty squeaking rebounds off the shadowed walls. No other noise, except her breathing.

Something brushes against her ankles. She yelps and recoils. A soft-bodied creature hisses and skitters off into the darkness. Mary leans against the wall. Was it one of Byron's cats? What else could it have been?

She has fallen into an unfamiliar world. She has crossed into some other life and is standing in a deserted house, alone in a storm, with only her own voice and these strange, shifting shadows for company.

A crash behind her. She whirls around in alarm to see Byron, Shelley and Claire standing in the doorway, all soaked to the skin and laughing.

'I've been baptized!' Byron pronounces. 'Listen here, Shelley, you can't go back to your villa. The weather's biblical. The whole place will be underwater if the rain carries on like this. You'll have to stay. I've had food and barrels of wine delivered.'

'An excellent idea! Bigger house, higher up, more to drink –'

'No,' Mary says. 'I can't stay.'

'Why on earth not, Pecksie?'

Because I don't want to be stuck in this place overnight. Don't you feel how strange it is here? To say it would be to sound mad. And she can't explain how Byron unnerves her. She can feel his gaze on her even now. She won't look at him.

'I'll have to return to feed Willmouse.' It sounds lame and unconvincing.

'Bring him here too!' Byron says. 'And the little nursemaid. What colour *is* her hair, exactly, under her . . . cap?'

'Élise will want to stay in our little house.' The last thing Mary needs is for Byron to start chasing the nursemaid. 'Willmouse will remain with her.' She turns to Shelley. 'Do you think that's best – to leave him? Won't he miss me?'

Shelley shrugs. 'He'll be well, I'm sure. No need to fuss, Pecksie.'

When he dismisses her fears like this, Mary feels a flash of disgust.

She thinks of the small coin purse in her trunk; she visualizes a map of Europe, with paths tracking over the mountains. Every time she conjures up the journey, the coins run out, leaving them stranded and alone.

Shelley takes her in his arms suddenly and kisses her. She closes her eyes and presses herself against him. When she opens them, Claire is watching them, her expression unreadable.

Behind her, leaning against one of the pillars, Byron, too, is staring at them. When Mary meets his gaze, he raises and lowers his chin, as if she has made an offer and he has accepted it immediately, without thought.

The gesture is so unnerving that Mary pushes Shelley from her and turns away, busying herself with hanging the cloaks on hooks by the door. A creeping unease tells her that Byron is still watching her. He is repellent, really – his arrogance, his insolence, his slow, self-assured smile. But even as she focuses on the reasons to dislike him, she can't help turning to meet his stare.

He continues gazing at Mary as he takes Claire's hand, kisses her palm, then bites it.

'Albe!' Her voice trembles with hope and – Mary sees – a little fear.

She can't look away.

'Miss Clairmont,' Byron's tone sounds resigned – almost bored, 'let's get you out of these wet clothes.'

Is it Mary's imagination or, as Byron turns to leave, does he raise his eyebrows at her and wink? The tiniest flutter of one eyelid yet it stops Mary's breath in her throat. Concern for Claire is making her nervous – she doesn't want her sister to be hurt, doesn't trust Byron not to be a brute. 'Should we stop them?' she whispers.

'Why would we do that?' Shelley murmurs. 'This is everything she wants.' There is something hungry in his expression, some longing that makes Mary look away.

As Byron leads her sister down the dark hallway, half carrying her, Mary can't help thinking of some huge creature bearing away its prey.

Shelley presses his lips to the back of Mary's neck. 'Let's find our bedroom.'

This is everything I want, Mary tells herself, as her lover kisses her.

Far away, from down some unknown hallway, Mary hears an echo of a cry and the boom of a door slamming.

PART THREE
Villa Diodati

I 2

It is true, we shall be monsters, cut off from all the world; but
on that account we shall be more attached to one another.

Villa Diodati squats on the hill overlooking the lake. Behind, it is half shrouded by enormous pines, which make a perpetual dusk, but the south side of the large garden is segmented by lines of smaller sycamores, which have been so aggressively pruned that they recall the gnarled hands of old men, swollen-knuckled and twisting skywards in silent supplication.

Returning from feeding Willmouse, Mary pauses at the gate, where a sign says *Villa Belle Rive*. The villa of beautiful dreams.

Strange. Mary worries that she has somehow become confused, that she has walked the wrong way, but this is the right house, with its many blank-eyed windows, shutters creaking in the breeze from the lake. It just has a different name from the one Byron has given it.

On the lintel above the front door is an engraving that says *1710*.

Stranger still: Byron has told them they are staying in an ancient villa, where Milton once wrote. But if this date is correct, the house is just over a century old – Milton can't possibly have stayed here. Had Byron been deceived about its name and age, or had he chosen to lie? How very like him to invent an elaborate fiction.

Everything Mary knows is being slowly eroded, as though

Byron's presence is slicing through the threads that hold her world together. Soon, nothing will make sense.

Even in daylight, there is something uncanny about the house. Standing out of sight of the windows, Mary has the same crawling sensation she had felt the day before, when Byron was observing her: she is being watched and measured. She thinks longingly of the butcher's cart, which might have taken her over the mountains, away from here.

A scuffling sound from above makes her jump.

'Hello!' a voice calls. Byron is leaning over the metal balcony. How long has he been staring at her?

She lifts her hand, attempts to cover her unease with a rigid smile.

'You've been gone too long, Mrs S.'

'I had to see William.' When he raises his eyebrows, she adds, 'My baby.'

'I thought you might be running away from us.' His expression is sardonic and her stomach drops. He is taunting her, but how much does he truly know? 'Not a grand escape, then?'

'No. I had to feed him.' She clamps her mouth shut around her desire to explain that she'd woken early, that she'd been worried about the baby, feels out of place in this strange house. How does he make her want to reveal so much of herself?

'Shame,' he drawls. 'I was looking forward to tracking you down. I do *so* enjoy an exciting pursuit.' As she walks inside, she hears Byron laughing to himself. 'Come up to the dining room,' he calls. 'We're having dinner.'

Mary hasn't even had breakfast. Perhaps, just as he renames houses and people, Byron simply rearranges the times and names of meals to suit his mood. Like a king, or a tyrant.

*

From the outside, the house looks like a solid square block, with traditional lines and the suggestion of logically placed rooms. Inside, it is a scrambled skein of hallways, staircases and landings. One room leads into another, then another two or even three rooms, with unpredictable stairs and passages between them.

The gloomy mist from outside presses against the windows, giving the damp, dimly lit halls the locked-up air of a shuttered vault. Though an iron-haired, scowling serving woman, Madame Müller, has lit gas lamps and beeswax candles, their flickering yellow glow only makes the shadowed corners seem darker. The heat heightens a stale smell, which had seemed at first like decay. Now, alone in the guttering gloom, it reminds Mary of a slick-bodied, sickroom sweat.

Trying to find the dining room, Mary walks up the main stairs and along a dim corridor, listening for the sound of voices or cutlery. The rumble of low, male amusement behind one door makes her push it open. No one is there: the furniture is covered with white sheets and a greyish film of dust.

The hairs rise on the back of Mary's neck. She pulls the door half closed again and stands listening.

Silence. A sweetish scent, like old roses rotting in green water. Perhaps Madame Müller has used rose-water to cover the smell of dust.

The next door is locked, though Mary can hear voices from behind it. Are they playing some trick on her? She tuts aloud to herself, and the sound of her irritation is soothing, somehow, an antidote to her rising fear, so she tuts again.

The noise vanishes into the dark corridor, rebounding in a faint echo, so it sounds as if some presence in the house disapproves of her.

'Hello?' she calls softly. 'Shelley? Shelley!'

Oh? the house whispers. *Sh . . .? Shhh!*

Her heart gutters. On the walls, the lamp flames flicker.

She feels the urge to turn and flee – but pictures herself running around and around the same dim rooms for hours, up and down the same staircases, in and out of the snarl of corridors, all tangled together like the contorted branches of the wind-warped trees outside. She thinks of Theseus in the labyrinth – some unknown, unseen monster stalking the twisted tunnels.

Be sensible, her father's voice says in her head. *Be logical.*

She will work her way along each corridor, opening every door in turn. There are no windows in this part, but a silver candelabrum rests on a table. She tries to lever a candle free and, when she can't without burning her fingers, she picks up the cumbersome metal holder, with all five candles, and carries the flickering lights ahead of her.

Like Prometheus. This time, her smile doesn't shake.

Something dark shifts in the shadows ahead. She blinks, waiting for the shape to disappear. Instead, it solidifies into something solid, creeping towards her. Its feet scratch the wooden floor. Horror freezes her to the spot as she hears a low growl.

Chest tight with fear, she lifts the candelabrum higher. In the dim light, she sees an animal face, yellow eyes fixed on her, teeth bared and gleaming.

Bear!

Her heart scrabbles in her chest. The creature cocks its head to one side.

Not a bear. A wolf!

Another guttural growl, lip curling. Its muzzle is too wide for a wolf, its shoulders too broad. She has never seen a dog of this size – its huge head comes up to her torso. If it stood on its hind legs, it would be far taller than she and must be twice her weight. With one snap of its jaws, it could rip out her throat.

She draws her arm back, ready to hurl the candelabrum at the creature – she will throw it and run back down the hall. But the enormous dog turns, as if it has heard a summons, and lumbers away, huge claws rattling against the floor.

Mary leans back against the wall, her heart still battering, her breath coming in gasps. Otherwise, silence. Had the dog truly been there, or had she conjured it? Was the huge beast a waking dream, brought on by her fear of these dark hallways?

She opens door after door, empty room after empty room, until, finally, she hears Claire's breathless voice, sees light under some double doors and pushes them open.

'Pecksie!' Shelley half rouses himself from the sofa where he's sprawled. His shirt is unbuttoned, his pale chest damp with sweat.

Mary stands in the firelight, fighting hot tears of relief, which she conceals by lifting the candelabrum higher. 'I found candles!' Her voice belongs to a woman who sounds calm and unafraid.

'I wondered where you'd gone,' Shelley says. 'We missed you.'

From a desk in the corner, Polidori raises a hand in greeting, his smile kind.

'*I* thought you might have left us,' Claire says archly.

Shelley takes another gulp from his glass and beckons Mary to him. His pupils are blown, his eyes feverish – what else has he had, besides the wine? Laudanum? She smooths her palm across his forehead. Hot and damp.

'Mrs Shelley!' Byron's shirt is half unbuttoned, exposing a triangle of sweat-sheened skin. His movements are loose; his speech is slurred. He presses a glass of wine into Mary's hand.

'Dinner, as promised!' he says. 'Now tell me something interesting.'

'Am I here for your entertainment?'

'What else?' He leans forward and drops his voice to a

confiding tone. 'Good *God*, your sister is boring! And so exhausting – not in a gratifying way, sadly.'

As he laughs, Mary watches him. After he has made one of his cruel jibes, his eyes slide left and right, as if he is keen to know he has amused the people around him.

He enjoys tearing others down and mocking them, yes, but there is more to it than that: he needs approval, just as much as Claire does, just as much as Shelley or as much as Mary. He is, she sees, like a small child flinging mud at windows and passing carts to raise a laugh from the other boys so that they will not see how scared he is that he may not matter.

No one mocks the limp he has had since childhood. When he walks, people adjust their stride to suit his, so subtly that he never notices, or at least never comments. And perhaps this is what it means to be a wealthy, handsome man with the gleam of glamour, the shine of fame and scandal to your name: it forms a transparent cocoon that you can't see but everybody senses. Nothing sticks to that glossy carapace. Mud slides off and disappears before it has ever really touched you.

Mary takes a gulp of the wine, then another. Byron watches her, his gaze too intense. She turns away and crouches next to Shelley. 'Perhaps we should stay in our little house after all,' she says. 'Willmouse misses us.'

'Nonsense! This house has food and *so* much wine – and Albe! Dear Albe.'

'You are the most delightful distractions. I won't allow you to leave. Although if you want to try, Mrs S, I shall enjoy chasing you.' He flashes large white teeth.

Shelley chuckles, giving him a look of such radiant adoration that Mary recoils. Even Shelley is in love with Byron.

She banishes the thought with another swig of wine, then drains the glass. Instantly, Byron is at her elbow, refilling it. Her head begins to swim, but the weight on her chest eases.

She perches on the end of the sofa where Shelley is loun-ging. He raises his eyebrows suggestively and squeezes her thigh. Mary's heart leaps – he's still so handsome, even drunk and dishevelled.

'Come here, my love.' He pulls her close, kissing her cheek, her nose, her mouth.

She returns the kisses, rests her body against his.

'I missed you.' His cheek feels rough against her ear. 'Will you hurry back, next time?'

'Yes.'

'This is wonderful, isn't it?' He strokes the hair away from her forehead – a gesture so tender it runs right through her – and her tension lifts.

'Yes.' This is the closest she has felt to Shelley in weeks, now Claire is distracted by Byron.

'You wouldn't think of leaving me, would you?'

It is as if she has swallowed a spiked bramble shoot. She can feel it working through her veins, into her lungs, into her heart. She shakes her head. She can't risk words.

'Good,' he whispers. His voice is still gentle. His breath, sweet with wine, brushes her neck. 'Of course you wouldn't – what sort of mother would risk leaving her child?'

Her blood hammers in her ears.

Shelley strokes the hair back from her forehead again. 'When mothers leave their children, they lose them for ever. A desperate situation.' He kisses her cheek again. 'You're a perfect mother.'

She nods.

'Are you happy, Mary?'

Her name sounds strange, coming from his mouth. It is too formal, too distant, almost as if he has called her *Miss Godwin*.

She nods again. It is as though a string is pulling her muscles. Shelley could say anything he wanted to her at this moment, could ask anything of her, and her body would respond. Her every bone, her every muscle, is moved by his thoughts, his wishes, his demands.

'Good. Now, drink.' He passes her his glass, which she drains, without tasting the wine.

'You love me, don't you, Mary?'

'Yes.'

'Tell me how much you love me.'

'Indescribably.' At this moment, that's the truth. How much does she love Shelley? How can she trace the snarled threads of memory and desire, obligation and need that stretch between them?

When she glances up, Byron is gazing at her, his dark eyes shadowed and unreadable, a faint smile playing across his lips.

Then she startles. The enormous dog, the giant, wolf-like creature she thought she'd imagined, is at his feet. Even half asleep, it looks terrifying.

He sees her staring. 'You've nothing to fear from Boatswain. He's friendly enough – to people I like, at least.'

The dog thumps its tail at the sound of its name, then gazes at Mary. Is there something menacing in its yellow eyes?

Claire lurches over, eyes bright with drink and excitement.

'Isn't Albe *wonderful*?' she slurs, too loudly, intending him to hear. 'I *told* everyone he was wonderful.' Her face is slack, her teeth stained reddish purple.

'I want to speak to you,' Mary says stiffly. 'In private.'

'And I want to be *in private* with Albe!' Claire titters, reaching out to pull him close.

Byron's mouth twists downward in distaste, but he grabs Claire's hair, then kisses her hard, before pushing her away.

She trips and falls back, crashing to the floor at his feet. She doesn't attempt to move, but lies there, gazing up at him.

He studies his glass of wine, as if Claire doesn't exist. For an unguarded moment, her expression is bleak and raw. Her chin trembles, her eyes glisten, and she looks much younger than her seventeen years.

'My God, Claire!' Mary takes her sister's arm and helps her to a chair. 'Are you hurt?'

'Of course not.' Claire's laughter is fragile. 'You're always *fussing*. You're so cheerless. Why do you have to be such a wet blanket all the time?'

Mary grabs her arm and grips it hard. Her sister's smile fades. Mary leans in close, so there is no chance the men will hear. 'Why did you tell Shelley I planned to leave him?'

'I didn't,' Claire says, too quickly. 'Why would I?'

'I know you're lying,' Mary says, very fast and very low. 'And I don't know *why* you've done it. But I want to tell you that if Willmouse is taken away from me I will *never* forgive you.'

The words feel like something from a bad dream – the child stolen, the mother left to drown in her own darkness. An empty room, the fire guttered to ash. A woman shivering, hopeless and alone.

'*Never*,' Mary says again.

Claire recoils from the savagery in her face. 'Why do you always think the worst of me, Mary? Haven't I always helped you? Though I think you're a fool.'

'*You* think I'm a fool?' Mary could almost laugh at this from her foolish sister, but she sees that Claire is serious.

'You might be clever, Mary, but you *are* a fool! Where on earth would you run to, if you managed to *escape*?'

'Hush!'

'Oh, they're not listening to us!' Claire waves her hand dismissively. 'They're far more interested in themselves.'

Still, Mary drops her voice to a whisper. 'I don't know where I would go. Back to England, I suppose.'

'And how would you live?'

Mary raises her chin. 'My mother survived by her writing, before she met Father. I wrote about our time in Europe, two years ago. Perhaps a publisher might take it.'

As she speaks, Mary feels lighter. Why has she only just thought of this? Her mother's books about her travels had earned her enough money to live. More than that: she'd had the freedom to speak.

'I thought you didn't want your journals read by anyone. Isn't that why you hide them or burn the pages? Oh, don't look at me like *that* – you can hardly think me oblivious, when you're always scribbling away.'

For a moment, Mary is too shaken to voice the indignation she feels at Claire snooping through her secret thoughts. 'Have you read them?' she asks.

Claire gives a wicked grin. 'Not for some time. I grew tired of reading about how *vain* and *petty* and *stupid* I am.'

Mary swallows. She thought she'd burned the most vicious parts about her sister. And perhaps she had, or Claire surely wouldn't be talking so cheerfully.

'You seem . . . different here, in this house. Brighter.'

'Byron makes me *very* happy.' Claire gives a lewd wink and laughs.

Mary leans in closer: her sister's pupils are huge, the whites of her eyes spidered with tiny veins. 'How much laudanum have you drunk?'

'Only a little. It makes me care less about everything. You should have some. It might make you less of a Cassandra.'

Mary lets the insult pass. 'I don't want my thoughts to be . . . clouded.'

'Why not? Élise is looking after Willmouse. You cannot begin to think about *escaping* anywhere while we are here and you have so little money. And I know you are furious about Harriet's new baby, but I promise even that will seem less –'

'Wait!' Mary's mind struggles to make sense of what she has just heard. 'Did you say *Harriet*'s new baby? Shelley's wife Harriet?'

'Oh, Lord.' Claire's eyes widen. She takes Mary's hand and grips it hard. 'I thought you knew. I thought he'd told you.'

'Told me what?' There is a buzzing in Mary's ears, as though some inner part of her is being shorn away. 'What did you think I knew?' Although she doesn't need to ask: Claire's expression tells her she'd heard correctly.

'Harriet is – She's pregnant again. It will arrive in December, they think.'

December. Mary does some quick calculations.

Those dark April nights spent crouching behind the sofa with Willmouse and Claire while the bailiffs hammered on the door of their rented rooms. Shelley had told her he'd been hiding with *friends*.

'Mary, I'm sorry. Truly, I thought he'd told you.'

Mary puts her hands behind her back so that Claire won't see them shaking. 'It isn't his child.' She speaks slowly and carefully, enunciating every word. 'It can't be.'

Claire gives the same half-shrug, something akin to pity in her expression. 'You always believe whatever you want, Mary. Whether it's true or not.' She pats Mary's shoulder, then goes to drape her arms around Byron.

When Mary looks down, her hands are numb and blood-less. She thinks of the hands of the man on the lakeshore, of Harriet in her London house, delicate hands cradling the swell of her belly.

The old scars on her arms burn, but when she runs her fingers over them, they, too, are numb. She doesn't know what she feels, doesn't know what to think, what to do.

There is not enough air in this room, in this house. She

can't stay here. She can't. She drains her glass, refills it from the decanter, drains it again.

If mothers leave their children, they lose them for ever.

Harriet is pregnant . . . I thought he'd told you.

Her knees are shaking too now, her whole body trembling as if she is sitting in the full force of an icy blast.

The rug by the fireplace has an intricate pattern of twisting stems and branches. She wonders if the weaver had meant it to look like a beautifully constructed cage.

She gives a snort, a single *ha!* that makes Shelley call, 'Are you well, Pecksie?'

She doesn't know what she replies but she turns and sits on the carpet, away from Claire, Shelley and Byron – away from Polidori, who is hunched in the far corner, writing notes in his journal. Distant from the others as he is, he still seems to Mary to belong to their group, part of whatever laughter and looseness they share.

She feels like a stranger in the foreign land of this room, unable to understand their bright chatter and loud laughter. She is floating on a woven cage of flowers and leaves. Every moment takes her further from these awful people, who carry on as if she isn't there at all.

Byron, Shelley and Claire are passing Byron's opium pipe between them. Byron takes long draws and exhales streams of smoke, while Shelley, who doesn't like smoking and would rather drink from his flask, takes small puffs and clears his throat, an anxious crease between his brows. Claire inhales deeply, then doubles over choking. Shelley claps her on the back, but Byron watches with detached disinterest as Claire wheezes, clutching her throat.

'Please don't die here. It'll be a terrible bother to drag you down to the lake.'

'I don't think the water will revive me,' Claire rasps. Even while coughing, she tries to make her expression sweet, her tone appealing.

'Exactly my thought,' Byron says. 'I can't have a corpse in the house – consider the rumours. *Byron the murderer! Byron the necrophiliac!* Though it would make you quieter in bed, which would be a boon to my ears.'

Claire's smile fades. 'Beast.' Her tone is hard; she takes another puff from the pipe and, still coughing, another. Shelley uncurls her fingers from around it, takes a draw himself, then sets it on the table and kisses her palm. On her carpet, Mary fights a queasy wave of wretchedness.

'Careful, dear Clairie,' Shelley says. 'He does not mean to hurt you, poor tender thing. He is only playing, aren't you, Albe? You would never want to wound this beautiful creature.' His speech is slurred.

Byron shrugs, watching with cool indifference as Shelley sleepily embraces Claire and strokes her hair. Mary contemplates slapping both of them, shaking them. She pictures Byron dragging Claire's body down to the lake.

Do it, she thinks. The sense of satisfaction is so awful that Mary suddenly can't bear to be in her own thoughts. Who is she, to have these monstrous feelings about her sister's corpse? What sort of person – what sort of *creature* would think like this?

She picks up the pipe from the table and takes a draw of the bitter smoke. Immediate lightness in her mind and heaviness in her limbs. She takes another draw, and another.

She sets the pipe down. The room is tilting now, so she walks slowly over to the desk, where Polidori is scribbling in his little notebook. He snaps it shut at her approach and looks up, his expression guilty.

'Didn't know you were a poet.' Her mouth feels rubbery; she isn't sure her words make complete sense.

'Not a p-poet.' Polidori reddens. 'This is a . . . journal of sorts.' He puts the book under a stack of others, as if tidying the desk.

'I keep a journal too. My reading. Books. Things.' Mary drops into the chair beside Polidori. Her movements feel loose. She is smiling but isn't sure why. She summons the memory of the pages of her journal that she has fed to the fire.

'I like to write what I observe,' Polidori says. 'P-p-people are so interesting.'

Even through the haze in her mind, Mary is struck by the strange expression on his face, by the way his eyes slide from hers. He is concealing something.

Through the fog, a thought arises. What if this near-stranger is observing *her*, writing about *her*? What if his friendliness has been to make her trust him, to tell him about her time with Shelley and Claire? The breath compresses in her chest. She can't bear to look at him any longer, can't bear to be here because she doesn't know what words will emerge from her mouth.

Does he know Harriet Shelley is pregnant? What had they all spoken of before she'd arrived in the room? Does Shelley truly love her? Should she leave him?

'I'm tired.' She sounds rude. It doesn't matter. She doesn't care.

Shelley, Claire and Byron are slumped on the chaise by the table. She picks up a leather-bound book of children's fairy tales. She will take it to read to little Willmouse tomorrow. He won't understand a word but he will gurgle and smile at the rhythm of her voice.

But as she bends down, she notices Shelley's cheek is pillowed on his silver opium flask. Has he drunk from it, as well as smoking? His breathing is laboured and irregular. She puts a hand on his shoulder and shakes him.

'Shelley! Shelley, wake up!' Her movements seem sluggish, as though she is reaching a hand through water, her fingers sliding over his sweat-slippery skin. 'Shelley!'

His eyes roll, bloodshot and unfocused. His fingers are unmoving, bluish at the tips.

'Shelley!'

Is he breathing? The fuzziness of her thoughts is chased away by sharp panic.

'Let me look,' Polidori says, behind her.

He picks up her lover's hand, presses his fingers gently to Shelley's throat.

'Is he all right?' *Is he alive?* 'Wake him, please!' Her mouth still feels rubbery, her speech too slow, even as her heart scrabbles in her chest.

She has dreamed about escaping, but not like this. Not for him to leave her alone for ever.

However furious she is with him, however much he has betrayed her, she doesn't want him to die. She loves him still. She loves him and she loathes him and, oh, God, she needs him to live.

'He usually drinks the stuff?'

She nods, unable to speak. Claire and Byron are sleeping peacefully, her head resting on his chest, all the disdain and flirtation gone from his relaxed features.

Shelley's face looks as if it has been carved from pale wax. And is there a bluish hue to his nose now? Are his lips darkening, from pink to purple, his fingertips too?

She clenches her hands so hard that her own fingers turn white. She will force him to live. He won't die. He can't.

Polidori draws a square of mirrored glass from his pocket and holds it under Shelley's nose. Nothing, no movement, no mist on the glass. Nothing except the dark, empty caverns of his nostrils.

The idea that he could move so seamlessly and silently from living, breathing man to a collection of cooling cavities turns Mary's stomach. Has she done this, somehow? Her angry thoughts, when she'd longed to hurt him, have they power in this awful house?

Has she *killed* him?

She wants to howl. She clamps her lips shut, clenching her teeth.

Polidori flicks Shelley's waxy cheek lightly. He doesn't stir.

Mary pushes him to one side. She pinches and twists Shelley's earlobe. She presses the mirrored glass closer to his nose. 'Wake up! Shelley? Shelley, wake *up!*'

She slaps his face. He doesn't stir. She slaps him again and screams, '*Shelley!*'

His eyes fly open. He gasps, wheezes, flails. 'Wha–?'

The glass fogs, clears, fogs again.

'Wha's hap'ning?' His eyes are glazed, his mouth slack. His chest rises and falls.

'You're alive!' Mary kisses his forehead, his cheeks, his lips with furious force, half relief, half anger.

'Good man.' Polidori pats Shelley's shoulder. 'Easy now. Breathe slowly. Good.'

'He'll be all right?' Mary asks. 'He's not . . .'

'Nothing to fret about, Miss Godwin.' Polidori sounds level and confident, a different man from five minutes ago, his stutter entirely gone. 'He'll be quite well. I'd wager he's not used to smoking so it took him hard, especially if he'd already drunk from his flask. Mixing the two is a fool's game.'

'He's always been reckless.' She exhales slowly, trying to shake off the remnants of her panic.

'You look a little unwell yourself. Perhaps you should lie down.' He indicates the end of the chaise where Byron and Claire are curled up like cats. 'I can keep watch over you.'

If Mary has a small sip of the liquid, she might be able to sleep. Or maybe if she has the tiniest puff of smoke from the pipe, she won't feel so desperate, as if one part of her mind is a caged animal and another the cruel captor holding the keys.

She sits on the end of the chaise and picks up the glass pipe. The brownish watery slick of tar in the bowl is still warm but she would need to light it again.

Polidori holds out one of the candles. As she leans forward, she looks up. Through the glass of the pipe, Polidori's face is suddenly bloated, his eyes bulbous, his mouth enormous, his teeth like tiny, misshapen fangs. She flinches and puts up her hands, warding off the pipe and the vision. 'I . . . I think I hear Willmouse crying,' she says, forgetting that her child is in a different house – a safe house, with Élise caring for him.

She is a terrible mother for forgetting her child. She is a terrible mother for using him as an excuse. She is a terrible lover for wanting to leave Shelley.

Is it like this for everyone – for all women, at least? Do they all feel as if they have ropes attached to each wrist and both ankles, and are being tugged in all directions at once, never satisfying anyone but with the constant sensation that, one day, they will be ripped in two? Then all the world will see that they are hollow inside, just stuffed dolls, pretending to be perfect mothers and wives.

Blindly, she pushes past Polidori. He pulls the candle flame back just in time to avoid burning her. She doesn't stop to apologize. On the dark landing, she pauses to lean against the walls and gaze into the blackness. Her breath comes in rattling gulps and she presses her hand to her chest. A hollow sense that she has lost or forgotten something.

Control yourself, Mary! She bites the inside of her cheek, digs her nails into the scarred, thickened skin on her arm. Gradually, her breathing slows. The hollow feeling remains.

From above her head, a rustling, like the shifting of a woman's skirts. She blinks up into the gloom, lifting her candle.

A tiny pair of black eyes gleams at her, unblinking.

Startled, she steps backwards and the creature – whatever it is – jumps too. There is a frantic fluttering, and the thing *launches* itself at her face.

Mary cries out, tries to bat it away.

Feathers brush her cheeks and the huge black bird gives a harsh shriek – is it a crow? A raven? It flutters down the corridor and disappears into the deeper darkness.

Mary stands for a minute, breathing hard. Twice now, she has been startled by one of Byron's creatures. They're just animals. She can't keep behaving like a timid girl. It's ridiculous.

Clenching her jaw to quiet the chattering of her teeth, she lifts her candle and walks, as steadily as she can, into the shadows.

It takes her some time of wandering down the dark hallways to find her bedchamber. She doesn't expect to see Shelley tonight, so she closes the heavy oak door and leans her head against the wood. Should she lock it?

The room is stark and white, built and decorated for long, bright summers. She tries to envisage Milton gazing at these walls, writing about hell and devils and judgement.

Then she remembers: Milton was never here. That is just another of Byron's fictions.

Mary pictures the cold marble floors glowing in the sunlight, sees the gauzy curtains shifting in a balmy breeze. The window rattles in its frame as rain pelts against it. The curtains gust into the room, then are sucked flat against the glass by the icy wind that whistles through unseen cracks in the woodwork.

The bed is hard, the mattress cold. When she gathers the

thin white sheets around her legs, they feel damp, as if the uncanny mist outside has somehow crept into the furniture. She doesn't change into her chemise but gathers her outdoor shawl around her shoulders and, shivering, lies down on the rigid mattress, squeezing her eyes shut.

Exhaustion is like a black pool but sleep slips away time and again: she is just beginning to drift when the wind thuds against the window, or the outdoor shutters bang against the wall, or the rain splatters against the glass. Once, she hears claws scratching at her door. She remembers the huge, wolf-like dog, its gleaming teeth. She rises, turns the key in the lock.

Why does she feel no safer?

Again and again, she jolts awake, heart thudding, only to reassure herself that she is not in danger. Nothing to fear. What was that? Just the wind. All is well.

At some time in the deepest dark – it must be three o'clock, or four – she sits up, certain that something is wrong. She has heard . . . *something.*

The maze of corridors is even more confusing in the darkness. Mary pats the walls and runs her hands over the tables and paintings, trying to keep track of her bearings. The air is heavy with the scent of aged oak and ancient dust and damp; each of her steps makes the floorboards creak. The haunting echo vibrates through the desolate rooms.

Ahead, movement: a figure in a white nightdress is moving towards her. She jumps.

The figure jumps too. She sees a woman flinging up her hands in terror, her face a twisted mask of panic.

Christ! Who is –? Oh!

Her reflection is wild-eyed in the antique mirror – pale, terrified, longing to find a way out. Strange to see her own fear-filled features twisted behind the cracked and fractured glass: it is as if her double has been trapped there for years, waiting for Mary to come and free her from beneath deep and lonely waters.

She avoids looking outside, where the rain is still lashing the trees. If she allows herself to think about what lurks in the darkness beyond the house, her mind will be dragged back into the shadows from her past. All of the things she never lets herself remember. All of the things she cannot forget.

She tries to ignore the eerie creaking of the wood beneath her feet, tries not to notice the dim shapes of statues, tries not to wonder who might be lurking around the next unknown corner.

Foolish woman, jumping at shadows.

It is the sort of thing her father used to say when she was small and scared of the dark, terrified of the creatures that waited in her dreams. *Don't be such a silly little girl. There's nothing there.* When that didn't work, he'd say, *Your mother would never have held with such nonsense. The daughter of Mary Wollstonecraft, frightened of the dark? Scared of nightmares? Preposterous!*

His scolding never made her feel any calmer, but it helped her to hide her fear, which was almost the same.

In the hallway of the Villa Diodati, Mary calls herself silly and foolish; she slaps her own wrist, her cheeks. She pinches the scarred flesh on the inside of her arm and twists it.

The sting drags her mind from the suffocating dark, helps her to breathe. Gradually, she calms and finds her bearings: look, there are the suits of armour in *this* corner; there's the heavy gilt frame on *that* wall. The drawing room must be close by.

Somewhere, in the depths of the house, she hears a howl. She startles, her heart hammering. But, of course, Byron's other animals are shut somewhere in the rooms below.

A light is burning still in the drawing room. She wants to run towards it, forces herself to walk.

The door opens soundlessly. None of the people on the chaise notice her.

It is hard, at first, for her brain to unpick what is happening – hard to tell Byron's body from Claire's, difficult to fathom where one ends and the other begins.

They are simply a moving collection of arms and legs, hands and mouths.

For a moment, Mary stands, transfixed, breathless.

Byron's chest is broad, his arms knotted with muscles that ripple beneath his skin as he pulls Claire on top of him.

Then she notices Shelley, on the other sofa, watching them.

Mary steps backwards out of the room, dragging away her gaze, though she can see them still, behind her closed eyelids. She feels as if a block of black ice has fallen from a great height and passed straight through her – as though she doesn't exist, apart from the tingling in her hands and her feet. She might just as well be a ghost, lurking in the doorway, trying not to see the slow-moving tangle of limbs.

Her mind shrinks as she stares at the half-open door.

Inhale. The whorls in the wooden door are animal faces, leering at her. A wolf. An eagle. A giant stag with shattered antlers. *Exhale.* The brass door handle is covered with a dark patina of fingerprints.

She begins to shut the door, as silently as she can. Before it closes, she sees Polidori, still sitting in the corner, watching everything and writing in his little notebook.

His eyes meet hers. His expression is not of embarrassment or arousal, but of unspeakable sadness.

Then the door clicks shut.

Mary turns and walks, as fast as she can, back to her lonely, draughty room and her hard, empty bed.

She can't make herself lie down.

She paces the six steps from one side of her room to the other.

She can't stay here. She can't stay in this house with these people.

Her journal is at the bottom of the trunk. She doesn't even write the date but scrawls, across the centre of the page, *I want to leave. I want to be away from him. I have to escape from here but how can I? I can't, I can't, but I want —*

The quill snaps in her shaking hand, spraying a column of ink across the page. The dark stain forks into two, then four, then eight. It tangles and flows, like entwined limbs.

Beneath, her words are nearly illegible. Still, too dangerous to keep.

There is no fire in the grate, so she rips out the page, screws it up and stuffs it beneath the mattress. Tomorrow she will burn it.

Her love for him sits alongside her hate, like a steel blade being dragged across a jagged flint, time and again. The sparks ignite and fly, gutter and fall. And if she stops loving him, she will have to pretend. She will have to drag her bruised heart back to him again and again, like the bloated, battered corpse of a drowned man, dredged up from the bottom of a foreign lake.

She tries to remember Shelley as she'd first seen him, as she'd first known him – the feeling that he understood her thoughts, her desires. She hadn't just felt her body light up around him: her mind had caught fire.

Now, when she tries to reignite that sensation, it is like trying to catch sight of a distant torch through a thick mist – the sort of false light that leads lost travellers to their doom.

Sometimes she sees a glimpse of it. More often, she wonders if it was ever truly there at all. She is lost in a foggy marsh, following a beacon she has conjured from her own imagination.

I love him. But I loathe him. I hate the person he has turned me into. I have made a life with a man who cannot love me – a man who has only ever been in love with the idea of love, with the illusion of grand, romantic poems and stories. He doesn't know me at all. I don't know myself any more.

How can she find a way out? How can she find a way back to herself?

The familiar fist of panic tightens around her chest, shortening her breath and –

No!

Terror will get her nowhere.

From somewhere within, a half-forgotten voice: *The beginning is always today.*

Feverishly, she digs through her trunk until she finds the book her mother wrote – the book that made her mother famous: it built her life, her reputation, her legacy. It spoke to her daughter after she was gone.

Mary knows every word of *A Vindication of the Rights of Women*. She could recite each sentence from memory. From beyond the grave, her mother had told her that women should not be men's servants. They should stand alongside men as intellectual equals. And yet, somehow, she has found herself in thrall to a man who reduces her. He encourages her to think and read and write, but only in a way that agrees with his thoughts, that doesn't question his ideas.

She searches through her mother's book, until she finds the line she needs: *Strengthen the female mind by enlarging it, and there will be an end to blind obedience.*

Suddenly, she sees it: Mary had thought she was forging her own path, but she was only ever following his.

Her mother had been free; her mother hadn't searched in the fog for a light to guide her: she had been her own torch.

And how had she done that? How had she supported

herself, as an unmarried mother to a young baby – Mary's half-sister, Fanny – travelling across Europe?

The answer rests in the pages in Mary's hands. It has been there all along.

She falls asleep, still clutching the book, still holding her mother's words.

Soft darkness. Water, closing over her face.

A woman's voice, whispering close to her ear.

She doesn't know the voice, has never heard it before. Yet she recognizes it instantly.

This is what you must do. This is how you will survive.

And then she is half awake in the darkness, but still inhabiting the world of her dream. And, in her half-conscious state, she is sure she can hear a throbbing thud, like the pounding of an enormous, inhuman heart.

There is something at work in me that I do not understand.

The words come, as if from outside her although they are also *within* her. There has always been something dark and terrible in her soul. A malevolent shadow, which has sent her into breathless panic time and again, as she has tried to hide her fury, to shut up her wrath.

Half asleep, floating, sinking, she knows she must let go of something. She has to find something.

Seek out the storm that stirs within you. Find your rage and let it roar.

She is blinded by white terror, paralysed by it, unable even to open her eyes. But she knows, somehow, that whatever this thing is, she must walk towards it.

However much it frightens her, this pulsing, seething darkness, she must embrace it.

13

The fallen angel becomes a malignant devil . . . I am
quite alone.

She gasps awake, as if surfacing from the bottom of the lake. Memories of last night return to her: the glow of candlelight on Byron's chest; the way the muscles flexed and hardened as he moved. Claire, with her head thrown back as she cried out.

Shelley, watching them both.

Outside, rain is still battering the windows.

I will leave this house today.

The thought of staying here, of being near Byron, makes Mary breathless. It is the same pulsing energy that had made her want to stay near the door last night, watching. Everyone is infatuated with Byron – wasn't that what Claire had said, laughingly, only a few days before?

And Mary *is* drawn to him – she can admit that to herself now, even as something in his magnetism unnerves her, makes her more determined to leave.

She will go to their smaller villa. She will begin to write – something that captures her confusion and hope and rage, something that would make her mother proud.

I do not wish women to have power over men; but over themselves.

This will be the starting point for Mary's own great work about women: their place in the world and how they should not allow their resolve to be curtailed.

Another howl from within the bowels of the house. A dog again? Or a human in pleasure or pain?

Her mother's voice comes back to her: *This is how you will survive.*

A jug of tepid water for washing has appeared in the corner of the room while she was asleep – unnerving to think of granite-faced Madame Müller creeping into her room. And who else could have come in during the night, without Mary knowing?

She visualizes Byron standing over her, watching her sleep. She would have woken and told him to leave, wouldn't she? She pictures his lazy, confident grin as he reaches out –

Enough!

Mary washes quickly – the water may be warm, but the room is shockingly cold. The chill has crept into her core, into her bones; she feels small and raw, like the tender flesh in the shell of a shattered oyster.

Outside her room, the landing is hushed and gloomy. The only noise is the whisper of the wind against the walls of the house, the spatter of rain against the windows. In the mountains, a far-off growl of thunder.

She shivers, tries to summon her father's commanding, practical voice, telling her she is a fool to be nervous of weather. But all she can hear is the storm, with its feeling of electricity and anticipation and, underneath it, a sensation of someone watching her, the same as she'd had in the woods outside and in the corridor last night.

A rustling behind her – not footsteps but a muffled movement, like someone shifting their clothing better to hide themselves.

She holds her breath.

Nothing. No movement. No noise but the weather.

Then a flicker in the shadows behind a pillar next to the wall.

Mary squints into the gloom. *Foolish girl, it's nothing.* 'You can stop hiding,' she calls. 'I'm not afraid of you.'

Silence. She stares at the pillar, at the darkness behind it, which starts to move and shift. Panic washes over her in a freezing flood. She wants to cry out, wants to run but she's fixed to the spot as a man emerges from the shadows.

'I am glad you are not afraid of me,' a voice says.

Words stick in her throat. Someone has been following her, watching her. And now he is walking towards her and she can't move and this is what it means to be frozen by terror.

The man steps forward and it is –

'Polidori!' she gasps, then says, more firmly, angrily, '*Polidori!* Why are you sneaking . . .? What are you *doing*?'

'Forgive me. I was looking at these p-p-p– the art, when I saw you coming out of your room.'

'You *hid*?' She is still breathless. Her voice sounds strange, strained.

'I didn't want to seem to be lurking, so I stayed behind the p-p-pillar.'

'Isn't hiding behind a pillar the very definition of lurking?'

'You're right. I'm so sorry.'

She gives a tight smile, tries to steady her breath, to distract herself from the still-panicked pounding of her heart. 'Which paintings were you looking at?'

His cheeks flush. 'Oh, I don't know the artist, but I think they depict some idea of Hell. Maybe someone was inspired by rumours of Milton staying in this house.'

Mary's footsteps echo as she walks over to the pictures. Perhaps they are indeed intended to suggest Hell: open mouths and outstretched arms and clutching hands and layers of legs and buttocks and torsos, all piled beneath the splayed legs of a screaming skeleton. She remembers last night: Claire and Byron. The slap of flesh on flesh. Shelley watching them. Polidori watching her.

Is that why he's shown her this painting – to see her reaction? He'd seemed so kind before now that she can't help feeling betrayed. And angry. Increasingly, she is *angry*, as if something in this house has woken a shadow of herself – a brooding, dreadful twin, which skulks in her wake.

'*Why* are you showing me this?'

'I'm sorry, Miss Godwin. I didn't realize that this p-painting was . . . I confess, I wasn't really looking at it –'

'I'm not interested in your excuses. Tell me.'

'Stop! Please.' He puts his hand lightly around her wrist and she recoils. He releases her. 'I haven't been honest with you, Miss Godwin. Forgive me.'

'What do you mean?'

'I wanted to s-speak to you this morning. I was, indeed . . . *lurking*, I'm afraid, not looking at the p-p-paintings. I would never have mentioned them if I had known . . . what they showed.'

He pauses. He must want her to ask *why* he was lurking. But, no, she won't make this easy for him – this strange man, whom she had thought might be a friend but instead had sat last night and watched while . . .

Sometimes the small piece of power she has is to be found in not speaking, in not moving, in not doing anything at all. She holds herself small and contained, like a creature inside a shell. Isn't that how pearls are made? Grit and friction turned to lustre.

'I was waiting for you,' he finally says, 'because I know you saw me when you came into the room last night. You must be shocked and disgusted by me.'

She stares at the pattern on the marble floor. Is it her imagination, or are there faces in it too? Does everything in this house contain a depiction of a face, crying out in pleasure or terror?

'I want to ex-explain myself. I want to apologize for any offence I might have caused.'

Another surge of irritation; she embraces it. Fury will help her to move, to speak.

People who don't know her assume she must be a loose slattern to be living with a married man and her sister. And people who *do* know her believe she is too strong to mind others' opinions. It is exhausting to be crammed constantly into the shape of other people's ideas.

'I was not shocked, Dr Polidori.' She hardens her voice, forces herself to meet his gaze. 'And I am not offended.'

His eyes are wide and brown and a little scared – he reminds her of a trapped wild animal. A rabbit, perhaps.

Good.

She leans her hand against the lewd painting, presses her palm to the splayed legs and gasping mouths. 'Do you really think that I understand nothing of the world?'

'Forgive me –'

'You make assumptions about who I am – about what might shock me and why.'

'I'm sorry. I didn't want you to judge me –'

It is liberating, this rage. An electric charge running through her limbs.

'I left my home when I was sixteen. I ran away with a man I knew to be married. Yet you think I would judge you. *You* are judging *me*. I see it in your face, and I will have none of it.'

She is able to move now. She strides swiftly down the hall-way towards the drawing room, with Polidori half running to keep pace, asking her to stop, to slow down, p-p-please, Miss Godwin.

Just before she reaches the doorway, he slips in front of her, blocking her path.

'I'm not judging you, Miss Godwin. But I'd like to explain why I was in the room last night watching –'

'Your pleasures are your own concern.'

'I took no p-pleasure in it!' Polidori snaps. He is sweating and looks suddenly older, angrier, the startled-rabbit expression gone. 'It was not for my p-p– I was not there out of desire.'

'I don't believe you.'

He rubs sweat from his forehead. 'Mr John Murray, Lord Byron's p-publisher, has offered me a large sum of money to write a . . . journal of my time with him.'

'You're . . . *spying* on us?'

'Not on *you*, Miss Godwin, and not s-spying. As I said, it's a journal. Byron is so infamous, you see, but p-people know so little of the real man – just the scandals.'

'So, you wrote about last night to *remove* the scandal around his name?' Mary snorts, then claps her hand over her mouth. 'How very *generous* of you.' She cackles. She can't prevent the sound spilling out.

'I'm sorry, Miss Godwin. I should have told you before. Please forgive me.'

He looks small and nervous again and she feels ashamed. She draws a slow, shuddering breath. What must he think of her – furious one moment, laughing uncontrollably the next? Does he believe her mad?

You fool.

She shouldn't have given in to her emotions, especially not near a doctor with connections to a publisher. Shelley and Byron can afford to be careless of what others think. To them, disapproval is an irritation, an inconvenience, a thorn in the side. Everything Mary is rests on what others think of her, no matter how she tries to pretend otherwise.

Breathing slowly, she waits for her fear and amusement and embarrassment to fade so that she can speak in the polite, level tone that everyone expects.

Her father had always told her that no one would listen to an angry woman. *If you have something to say, Mary, say it reasonably. Express your ideas clearly and calmly, like a philosopher.*

She waits for her usual mask of calm to return.

But instead of fading, her fury grows with every breath. 'I am so *tired* of being asked to grant forgiveness to men who are not in the least bit sorry.'

Polidori flinches as if she has slapped him. 'I –'

'If you plan to be sorry in the future, Dr Polidori, then you should change your behaviour in the present.'

As she stalks away, her anger feels like armour.

He calls her back; she ignores him, impervious, unreachable.

She wishes she could channel this rage more often. Why *shouldn't* women be angry? Why are men, who have so much already, allowed to rant and snap and take up all the space in every room, while women are expected to sit and listen, smile and nod? If they feel very strongly, women may cry, as long as they do so prettily and do not lapse into hysterics.

As she reaches the drawing room door, she still feels that she is being watched.

Good, she thinks again.

Let Polidori look. Let this awful house see a woman who is unafraid, who is furious, who may be half mad in this moment but does not care.

The door to the drawing room crashes open. Claire stumbles out and runs towards the bedrooms, sobbing.

'Claire, stop! What's happened?'

'Leave me alone!' Claire shoves past Mary, ignoring Polidori altogether.

In the drawing room, Byron is sprawled on the rug by the

fire with a sheet wrapped around him. He is unconcernedly leafing through a book but appears not to be reading. Mary catches a glimpse of his bare shoulder. His skin is darker and more muscled than Shelley's pale marble. It would be warm, she thinks. Byron glances up and sees her looking. She looks away, swallowing hard.

Shelley is slumped sulkily in a chair by the window.

'Whatever is the matter with Claire?' Mary asks, trying not to think of Byron's bare skin gleaming with sweat.

Shelley shrugs.

'Shelley, can I speak with you?' Mary gestures towards Byron. '*Alone.*'

'Must it be now, Pecksie? We can talk later, can we not?'

How easy it would be to say yes. Do other women feel this tug and pull and pressure of saying *yes* and *yes* and *of course*, while forcing themselves into whatever shape or mood is required?

She absorbs the pain it causes her, the exhaustion, the worry and fear. Those feelings are so familiar that she barely notices them. They are preferable to the guilt and condemnation if she speaks her mind. Everything she does is to please *someone*. Even her rebellion of running away from home, even *that* she had hoped would please her father in some way – he had brought her up, after all, to argue independently, to have her own ideas.

Through gritted teeth, she says to Shelley, 'I would like to talk *now*. About Claire.'

Shelley's eyes are closed.

Byron turns a page. 'Like most women, although not yourself, Mrs S, Claire has taken a dislike to the truth. Achilles! Achilles, here!'

Mary jumps as something scrabbles past her feet, then leaps onto the chaise behind Byron and squats next to his shoulder. A small grey monkey, no bigger than Byron's head. It stares at her with round, yellowish eyes.

'What on *earth* . . .?' Where had the monkey come from?

'Achilles. The most well-behaved of my children.' Byron holds out his hand. The little creature clasps his forefinger.

'Oh. But where is he –? Where are you keeping him?'

'He mostly stays in the cellars with the other animals. Madame M doesn't mind looking after him, do you, dear?'

Madame Müller, who is clearing plates from the table, grunts in what might be assent or disagreement.

'But Achilles misses me terribly. He's been quite mischievous, apparently.' Byron scratches under the monkey's chin. As he lifts his arm, the sheet falls back, revealing his bare chest and torso. Is he wearing any clothes at all? He grins at her, as if reading her mind.

Achilles bares tiny, sharp teeth.

Madame Müller clashes two of the plates together and mutters something that sounds like *merde*.

'You must admit that flinging shit is an excellent way of ensuring that you aren't forgotten. Isn't it, Achilles?'

The monkey leans forward and presses its mouth against Byron's eyes. The great poet laughs and pushes the monkey away.

'He's keen on licking eyeballs as a sign of affection. I try to discourage it, as the little blighter is also very enthusiastic about tonguing his own arsehole. Aren't you, Achilles, you little devil?'

A loud sob from along the hallway and Mary remembers Claire – Byron is so good at steering the conversation away from things he doesn't want to discuss. And, with Byron here, Mary can't ask Shelley about what she saw last night – or what she *thinks* she saw. More and more, the events are like something she dreamed.

'Is Claire unwell?'

'Oh, Claire is a damned nuisance,' Byron growls, and Achilles screeches his agreement. With his lips drawn back from his teeth and his little eyes stretched wide, the creature looks remarkably savage and disturbingly human.

Mary glances at the small brown bottle on the table. Part of her longs to drink and to lie down next to Shelley. Perhaps then she'd be able to forget the chaos, quell her growing anxiety.

Another sob from the hallway, the crash of shattering glass. Shelley reads his book. Byron strokes his monkey.

'I'm going to talk to Claire,' Mary decides. She will comfort her sister, and then they will leave Byron and his spy in this villa while they go to their own little house. Things will be more settled there. No dogs howling in the night, no monkeys licking eyeballs or flinging faeces. No Byron.

She walks past Polidori, avoiding his gaze, ignoring his whispered apology.

Claire's door is shut and, when Mary tries the handle, locked. But she can hear her sister weeping, even through the thick oak.

'Claire, open the door.'

The sobs grow louder.

Mary wants to kick the door, slap the wood with her fists, scream until she tastes blood. It is there in every breath – the strain, the injustice that people have always expected better of her, expect more from her. She wishes she could lie next to Claire on the floor, beat the boards with her fists and howl.

Mary presses her forehead against the wood. 'Please let me in, Clairie. I only want to help.'

The sound of feet scuffing the floor, then Claire opens the door. Her face is red, her eyelids swollen half shut. Raised red welts mark her neck, where she has scratched herself – another childhood habit that Mary hasn't known her to do in years.

'Oh, Claire!'

'He *hates* me!' Her sister sags into her arms and weeps noisily onto her shoulder.

'Christ!' Byron says from the drawing-room doorway. 'Does the woman ever stop performing?' With the sheet wrapped around his waist, he looks like a model for a Greek sculptor.

'I could ask the same question of you,' Mary snaps.

'At least I'm entertaining. Your sister's not in the least amusing and all her feelings are ridiculous melodrama.'

'Well, I don't think you're entertaining and I wonder whether you feel anything at all.'

Byron blinks. For a moment, she sees a flash of vulnerability. Then it is gone, replaced by his habitual sardonic grin.

'Why waste time on *feelings*, Mrs S, when I can spend it on wine and women and opium? *Santé!*' He raises his wine glass, then drains it in two gulps. But as he turns to go back into the drawing room, his face falls. A glimpse of some inner pain he conceals beneath his harsh humour. She stores it away to mull over later.

Mary ushers Claire back into her bedroom and makes her sit on the bed, which is pristine – she must have spent all night in the drawing room with Byron. Mary remembers the gleam of sweat on his chest, the muscles in his thighs . . .

Stop!

She fetches her sister a cup of water from the jug that Madame Müller has put on the dresser. Claire clasps the cup in both hands and shuts her eyes, as if she is praying, though she isn't religious.

'What happened?' Mary asks.

Claire shakes her head and gives another shuddering sob.

'We should leave,' Mary says. 'This place is a madhouse.'

There is a creak from outside the door, like a foot pressing against a floorboard. Claire's eyes widen and Mary thinks of

Polidori listening to their conversation, or – worse – Shelley. She flings back the door, ready to answer his furious questions about why she is planning to leave.

The landing is empty. Does she hear something skittering off into the darkness?

She slams the door.

Heart still hammering, Mary returns to the bed, squeezes Claire's arm, leans in close and says very softly, 'If I left this house today, would you come with me? We could go down to our little villa at first. Then, once the rain has stopped, we could find a way to get back to London. Somehow. Perhaps we could sell something or . . . And then, once we return, we could go to Skinner Street. I will apologize again. I will make Father see – I will make him see *me*.'

As she speaks, Mary envisages showing her work to her father – the piece she has written about their travels in France is good. It will remind him of her mother. She will beg his forgiveness. She sees him opening his door wide. There is tightness around her chest, like metal bands, but she ignores it.

She will show him that she can write a great work of philosophy, like her mother. She will show him she can be good again.

'We can't leave.' Claire's voice is strangled.

'We *can*, Claire. Byron is a monster. It will be better in our own house. Let's pack now.'

Claire shakes her head. 'You don't *understand*. We can't leave because the rain has washed out all the paths and roads to our house. There are mudslides everywhere. It's too dangerous to keep going back and forth. We have to stay here.' She gives another hiccuping sob.

A dark tunnel closes around Mary's thoughts, shrinking smaller and smaller. *Willmouse!* She cannot stay here. How will she reach him? She should never have left him. Her vision flares with spinning lights. 'Willmouse!' she gasps.

'He will be safe with Élise. No need always to fuss over him.'

When Mary stares at her, speechless, Claire glares back. 'What is it? Why are you looking at me like that?'

'I'm wondering how you manage to say exactly the wrong thing so often.'

'What have I said now?'

'If you were a mother, Claire, you wouldn't need to ask.'

Claire gives a bark of humourless laughter, then bursts into tears again. She presses her palms against her eyes, shaking. Her words are high-pitched, strangled. 'Well, Mary, *you* have a talent for saying exactly the wrong thing too.'

Mary waits, dread swelling in her chest, pulsing through her limbs. She wants to stop her sister speaking but it is too late – weeks too late – to stop any of this.

Claire draws a ragged breath and stares at Mary, her face swollen, tear-stained, devastated. 'I'm pregnant, Mary. I'm pregnant and Byron doesn't want anything to do with me. Or the baby.'

Claire's face crumples and she cries. Not prettily, as women are supposed to, but with the same howling, desperate anger that Mary feels towards Byron and Shelley. Towards her own father. Towards all the men who are happy to shut out the women who depend on them, happy to cast out into the cold the children they have made.

She holds her sister close and rocks back and forth, back and forth, as if clinging together and measuring time could change anything at all.

14

*Life, although it may only be an accumulation of anguish,
is dear to me, and I will defend it.*

In the past, when Mary was sad or anxious or angry, she would walk. The streets of London were no place for a woman or a young girl to be alone, but if she kept her head down and moved quickly with her hood up to avoid the notice of any men who might shout lewd comments or grab at her, she could reach the cemetery of St Pancras. There, she would pace in front of her mother's gravestone until the feeling of bleakness or fury faded. Faded enough, at least, for her to return to Skinner Street and slip back into her expected role of quiet girl, devoted listener, dutiful daughter.

In Geneva, the rain, wind and storms rage outside. Inside the villa, the rooms have the air of a street at night, just before a brawl. There is nowhere to walk, no way of avoiding the other people in the house, with all their fear and fury.

She has to leave this place. But how can she? Perhaps Madame Müller will be able to find her a way out – surely food and wine must be delivered.

The staircase down towards the kitchens is narrow and smells of ancient mould. Mary cups her hand around the flickering candle flame and mouths the words she has practised: 'I need to find a way home. I can pay you.'

A figure steps from the shadows. Mary jumps, heart thudding. 'Oh! Madame Müller! I wanted to find you.'

'*Que faites-vous ici?*' Her dark eyes are deep-set, her mouth crimped into a disapproving line.

Mary raises her chin. 'I need to leave this house. I want you to help me. I can pay you.'

'*Pas possible.*'

'Why not? I know the weather is bad, but a cart must deliver food.'

'*Déjà ici.*' She looks bored as she turns to walk back down the stairs.

'Please.' Mary touches the older woman's arm. Wool, rough and damp. 'Help me.'

Madame Müller looks down at Mary's hand. '*Comme on fait son lit, on se couche.*'

Mary shrinks. Mrs Godwin used to say this – *As we make our bed, so we must lie in it. There'll be no escaping your actions, young Mary. Sins have consequences.*

As Mary withdraws her hand, Madame Müller gives a satisfied nod and turns back towards the kitchen, leaving Mary standing alone in the faint glow of her flickering candle.

She cannot escape this place. No one will help her. She must find a way to help herself.

She shuts herself into her room and tries to write.

Women should not be subject to men, nor should their thoughts and ambitions be solely confined to the realm of the domestic.

Her breasts ache, heavy with milk. She rolls her shoulders to ease the pain. It doesn't help.

We must acknowledge that women have the capacity to match men's intellect.

A shriek from Claire's room, then a burst of male laughter.

Yet how can women realize their intellectual freedom when we remain dependent, both financially and socially? It is a great injustice that I have been raised and educated to strive for freedom in my thoughts and actions, only to find that I am confined by my gender, bound by the duties of motherhood and constrained by a lack of money or the means to earn it.

She writes faster and faster, her letters crowded, her fingers cramping.

When first I met Shelley, I believed him a fearless devotee of the Rights of Women. Now, I know that the high ideals he claimed were merely intellectual posturing. He wishes to believe himself good. He longs for others to praise his virtuous beliefs. It is all empty. All his words and all his vows and all his protestations amount to nothing.

Footsteps outside her door. Mary freezes, ready to hide her writing from Shelley. Beyond the door to the room, she can hear the men. She pauses, listening.

Byron's voice: 'But *this* is what I want to know, Shelley. Is the brat mine?'

Mary inhales sharply. No wonder Claire wept and screamed and has locked herself away.

He continues: 'She's hardly a model of chastity. Impossible to know the number of other men who have been grinding her corn.' A humourless laugh. 'I made her no promises, no protestations of love. I tried being cruel in the hope that she would leave me alone. And now *this.*'

Silence. Mary pictures Byron scowling, scrubbing his hand through his hair.

Finally, Shelley's tentative voice: 'If Claire says you're the father, Albe, I'm inclined to believe her.'

'But she flirts with everyone – with me, Polly, you. I wouldn't be surprised to find she'd ridden a whole troop of men bare-back from London to Geneva. The true father is probably some thick-thighed groom in Calais.'

'Not at all! Claire was with me and Mary the entire journey.' Shelley sounds indignant.

'You'll believe anything a pretty woman tells you.'

'I believe Claire.'

'You seem to forget that underneath that sweet face lurks a despicable person.'

'Albe! That's not fair –'

'Not *far* underneath, mind you – Claire doesn't have the requisite depth to contain layers.'

'Enough, Byron!' Shelley hates confrontation. Yet he's challenging Byron, whom he so idolizes. For Claire. He is confronting Byron for *Claire*.

'She doesn't deserve this,' Shelley says. 'Poor, dear Clairie. You must help her.'

Dark spots swim in Mary's vision. She knows that tone of Shelley's – she'd heard it two years ago, when he argued with Mary's father, defending their blossoming relationship before they finally ran away together.

Shelley loves Claire. Not as an idle, passing passion but a deep, unshakeable adoration – the sort of love that Mary used to think existed only once in people's lives.

'But how can I trust her?' Byron asks. 'I don't see why I should accept the word of a hysterical harlot who has already deceived all of us by claiming I invited her here –'

'She is *not* a harlot!'

There is silence. Mary's hands are trembling.

Rain batters against the windows. From along the hallway, Claire gives another howl.

'Listen to the woman,' Byron continues. 'She's been shriek-ing for hours. Entirely unstable. Who is to say she hasn't invented the pregnancy as a means of capturing me? She's been obsessed with me for months. Do you know, when we first met, she told me she was an *actress*?'

'She has aspirations to be on the stage.'

'Aspirations! She'd be better suited to back-alley entertainment. She could hold a show of her own and service half the audience afterwards.'

'I won't let you speak about her so –'

Mary throws down her quill. Claire is maddening but she doesn't deserve this cruelty and Mary will not listen to Byron's smug jibes or Shelley's lovelorn attempts to defend her.

'Enough!' She flings the door open. 'That is *enough*!'

Both men step backwards, startled.

Shelley recovers first. 'Pecksie! I didn't know you were there.'

'I gathered as much.' Her tone is acid. She will not let him see her pain.

He blinks rapidly, and she can see him trying to remember what he has said, what she might have heard. She can't bring herself to confront him – not here, not now. She turns all of her rage – with Shelley, with Claire, with herself – on Byron.

'*You!* How can you be such a brute?'

Byron's habitual mocking smile fades. 'I'm not a brute, Mrs S. I am merely wary of being manipulated by a woman who –'

'A woman who is pregnant with *your* child.'

'Pecksie!' Shelley says. 'Calm yourself, please.'

'I will *not* calm myself,' she snaps, feeling a sense of satisfaction when he flinches. She turns back to Byron, her teeth bared. 'You *are* a brute, abandoning your own child –'

'You cannot know –'

'Of course I know it's yours. *You* know it's yours. If you don't claim the child and support her, my sister will be ruined – you know that too. And I think *you* know something about ruined sisters, *Albe*.'

His expression darkens. She has gone too far. A muscle pulses in his jaw and she knows he is going to eject her from the house, this moment. He will shut her out in the wind and rain.

She doesn't care. She sees herself, slipping down the hillside towards the little house to see her child. Never mind the storm. Never mind the steep slope and the surging mud and the fallen trees.

Unbidden comes the image of her broken body, face-down and bloodied. The fear that her child will grow up motherless, as she grew up motherless.

Suddenly she wants to call her words back. The instinct to apologize for her outburst is almost overwhelming.

But *no*. She won't do it. She will not relent.

Still shaking, she stares at Byron and watches his expression shift as he looks her up and down. His shock turns into something that looks like a smile.

He looks . . . *impressed.*

'You're frightened,' he says softly.

'I'm *furious.*' Beneath her dress, her knees are trembling.

Without looking away from her, Byron says, 'Shelley! Go and tell *Miss Clairmont* that I am willing to discuss the future of her offspring *if* she will cease her hysterics.'

After Shelley has gone, Byron takes a step closer to Mary. Again, she feels the band of fear tighten around her chest. She raises her chin, tries not to let it show.

'Your allusion to my sister was vicious,' he says.

'Your comments about my own sister were hardly complimentary.'

She braces herself. He is so much bigger than her, so much broader. Next to him, she feels small and breakable . . . until she looks into his eyes.

There it is again – a flare of something that looks like . . . *admiration.*

He leans forward. She can feel his breath on her cheek. "'It is time to effect a revolution in female manners,'" he murmurs.

Her heart jolts – these are her mother's words, from her mother's book.

Byron's eyes are locked on hers. He speaks smoothly, without hesitation. "'It is time to restore to women their lost dignity, and, by reforming themselves to reform the world.'"

His face is very close to hers now – she can see the gold flecks that encircle his pupils, can smell wine, woodsmoke and the sweet tang of laudanum, though his gaze is steady and sober. 'I have been wrong,' he whispers. 'Forgive me.'

For a moment, she thinks he will lean forward further. She can almost feel him closing the electric hand span between their bodies and pressing his mouth to hers.

He takes a step back, concern creasing his brow. 'Do you forgive me?'

She draws an unsteady breath. 'I'll consider it.' Her voice wobbles. He must notice but he doesn't grin, doesn't mock her.

'I would not want to cause you pain.'

'Then don't.' She tries to make her voice light, but the words sound loaded, as though he has offered an invitation and she has accepted.

His eyes brighten. A small dimple appears on his cheek; she has never noticed it before. She wants to reach out to touch it.

When he turns to walk away, she sags against the doorframe as if she has been released, though she feels no relief.

She watches him retreat down the corridor, half hoping he will look back, half dreading that he will return to her. Is she being wistful or does he pause before he opens the door to the drawing room?

She leans her head back against the wall, exhaling slowly through pursed lips. Her hands are numb. She closes her eyes, listening to the faint murmurs from beyond Claire's door. At least she's stopped sobbing. Has she smothered her tears on Shelley's shoulder? Are his arms around her? Is her dress falling from her shoulders? Are his lips on her neck?

Stop it, Mary!

A cough and rustling from the shadows. Mary's eyes snap open.

'Who's there?' she hisses.

And when Polidori steps forward, his expression nervous, his notebook in one hand, all the fury of the past day – the past hour – surges through her.

'*You!*' she growls. 'Give me what you've written.'

His face whitens. He puts the notebook behind his back, like a child.

'Give it to me.' She holds out her hand.

'I'm not writing about you, Miss Godwin, I p-promise. It's about Byron.'

'Give me the pages.'

He takes a step back.

'If you don't give me the pages, I'll tell him you're writing about him.'

Polidori sighs and passes her two loose sheets of paper. His writing is so cramped – and it must have been written in the half-darkness – that she can't make out anything except the initials LB and PS. She finds CC and then, at the bottom of the page, she sees MG and a word she can't read.

'You said it wasn't about me.'

'I simply wrote – it's for myself only, Miss Godwin – I simply wrote that you are brave.'

Impossible to know if she can trust him. She should shred the paper, should burn the pages. She stares at him for two heartbeats, while the urge passes. Then she shoves it at him, into his chest. He staggers back.

'Don't write about me *at all*.' But even as she turns away

and walks back into her own room, slamming the door behind her, she understands that she can't control what he writes. She can't influence what he thinks, or the fictions that Claire and Shelley will spin between them. The only thing she can write, the only story she can craft, is her own.

15

Thus ended a day memorable to me; it decided
my future destiny.

Evening. Darkness. Golden candlelight flickering against the shadows on the walls.

In the drawing room, Mary has taken Polidori's usual place at the desk in the corner: if he is going to write about her, she will not sit and watch while he does it. When he'd come into the room and seen her sitting at the desk, arms folded, chin raised, he'd looked as if he might protest. His eyes had met hers and she'd watched him swallow, attempt a smile, then turn to sit on one of the chaises, near to where Byron has sprawled, a bottle of wine in one hand, a flask of laudanum in the other. By his side lolls the enormous dog, panting in the heat of the fire. Byron seems not to mind the animal's huge claws or its gleaming teeth – he rubs the creature's belly, lets it scratch at him and fix its jaws around his ankle in what must be some sort of game, though its savage undertones make Mary feel quesy.

The great poet's body seems relaxed, his long limbs loose, but Mary is aware of his every movement – each turn of his head or curve of his mouth. When he thinks her attention is elsewhere, she feels him studying her. Her skin hums beneath his gaze. She looks up. His eyes flick from hers to the dark, rain-spattered windows, to the shuddering candles, dripping wax from blackened sconces.

It had taken Shelley some time to coax Claire from her room. Her face is red, her eyelids swollen. Occasionally she casts mournful glances at Byron; he is studiously ignoring her.

Shelley and Claire are sharing a chaise. Shelley is reading and Claire's head is pillowed against his shoulder. Every time Mary looks at them, she tastes something acidic. She runs her fingers over the letter-opener in front of her, which is designed to look like a tiny sword.

Across the piece of paper in front of her, Mary writes, *She behaves like an overindulged child. And he tolerates her behaviour — encourages it!*

She starts to scribble out the words, then stops herself.

Let Claire see it. Let Shelley see it.

Along with the familiar sense of panic there is a reckless-ness that makes Mary feel, for a moment, as though she is falling. Instead of her usual, stifling terror, she feels a wild joy. She finds she is smiling. When she meets Byron's dark blue gaze, he smiles in return.

Wind and rain still batter the walls of the house, making the rooms feel smaller and darker, in spite of the candles. There is a feverish bite to the air, as though they are all trapped within the realms of a dream, where anything might happen. As another gust shudders against the walls, Claire gives a gulp of what Mary recognizes as feigned terror. Byron rolls his eyes. Shelley looks up from his book in concern. 'No fear, sweet Clairie. This house has stood through years of storms.'

'I know *that*,' Claire says, 'but it sounds so *loud*. And with the lamps so dim, it's like something from a ghost story in here. I expect I shan't sleep a wink tonight. *Ow!*' Something has hit her cheek. She turns to glare at Byron, who is balling up pieces from Madame Müller's dinner rolls. 'Did you just throw *bread* at me?'

'No. It materialized from the ether.' He stretches languidly and throws another ball of bread. It bounces off Claire's chest. 'See.'

'I think your behaviour is disgusting.'

'I think your dress is despicable.'

She scowls. He grins at Mary and she has to stop herself smiling in return.

How does he stir such contrary feelings? His goading of Claire is childish, yes, but it also eases some of the tension: angry, Claire stops sniffling. 'You're such a beast,' she snaps, and Mary can see she feels better for saying it.

Byron shrugs, unruffled. He must be aware that he manipulates the moods of those around him. His presence is like light in a darkened room: every face always turned to him, waiting for the next flash of illumination.

'I'm bored,' says Byron, swinging his leg over the arm of the chair. 'Bored, bored, *bored*.'

'I am too,' Claire says, picking bread from her hair.

'I'm bored because I lack intellectual stimulation. You're bored because you lack an intellect.'

'I saw a book of ghost stories in the library earlier,' Shelley interrupts, before Claire can react. '*Fantasmagoriana*.'

Byron flicks bread at him. 'Sounds dull.'

Shelley catches the little ball and pops it into his mouth. 'It's a collection of German ghost stories, translated into French –'

'I *love* ghost stories.' Claire angles her body towards Shelley's. 'I shall be terrified and in need of comfort.'

'Claire is such a sweet innocent.' Shelley strokes her hair.

Byron gives a bark of laughter. 'I've met more innocent whores and more honest thieves.'

'I *am* innocent!'

'Children should be innocent.' Mary fiddles with the sword-shaped letter-opener. 'In women it is a sign of weakness.'

'Your mother's wisdom again,' Byron says.

She feels a jolt of connection; they share another smile. Claire stares at them, her expression wary.

Shelley throws a cushion at Byron. 'How's your French, Albe?'

He catches it. 'Indifferent. A trifling language, spoken by trifling people.'

Mary laughs. 'How like *you* to dismiss an entire country because you don't speak the language.'

Byron looks amused rather than annoyed. 'I am not deriding the French people, merely those who try to conceal their lack of general intelligence by chattering in another language.'

'Claire's French is excellent,' Shelley says.

'You see my point, then.'

Claire's smile fades and Shelley rushes on. 'She could read to us. Honestly, Albe, you must see Claire's response to ghost stories. Sometimes she falls to the floor in terror.'

Claire pretends to cower into Shelley in mock-fear.

Mary presses her thumb against the tip of the little sword. 'She falls to the floor to gain attention.'

'You're being so *cruel*, Mary,' Claire says.

She is right, and part of Mary feels ashamed. The other part – some inner creature, crackling with years of silenced fury – feels no shame at all. She doesn't want Byron to abandon her sister's child, but she will not sit and watch Claire simpering and fawning over Shelley.

'I'm speaking the truth.' And though her voice is calm, that rage-filled inner creature bares its teeth. 'And I'm not being *nearly* as cruel as I could be.'

A moment of silence. Shelley stares at Mary as if he has never seen her before. Polidori writes something. She doesn't care. She has that sensation, once again, of falling from a great height – or as if, for the first time in her life, she has jumped.

Before Shelley or Claire can reply, Byron says, 'We should not expect the daughter of Mary Wollstonecraft to be quiet and biddable.' His eyes are fixed on her. Very softly – perhaps so only she can hear – he adds, 'We should not expect Hippolyta to play the part of Helen of Troy.'

'I'd rather not play any part except my own,' she says. And she watches the curve of his mouth, the intensity in his eyes.

Claire, eager to be the centre of attention again, has rushed to fetch the book – leather-bound, with an embossed cover. She runs her finger over the shapes. '*Fantasmagoriana* – it sounds like a story for children!'

They all laugh. Mary exhales. Perhaps these old stories will not be truly terrifying after all. Perhaps Claire will feel it is enough that everyone is listening to her read and she will not need to feign falling into unconsciousness to gain attention.

Achilles, the little monkey, sprints across the room and climbs the curtains, shrieking. Everyone jumps and there is more nervous laughter – even from Byron. It is comforting to Mary to see the cracks in his perfect sheen of handsome assurance.

The first story, 'Portraits de Famille' is a complicated tale involving a doomed family, a cursed portrait and a huge cast of characters, many of whom die or faint, or faint and then die, all after seeing the portrait of an unknown family member. It is tame and childish. Mary finds it hard to concentrate on the story. Instead, she finds herself staring at the way Byron's hair curls into his collar. When he leans forward, she can see the outline of the muscles across his back and shoulders.

On the piece of paper in front of her, she writes, *Does he know . . .*

She doesn't finish the sentence because she can't bring herself to write, *Does he know what he is doing? Does he know I am watching him?*

He stretches his arms up and she catches a glimpse of his stomach.

What does his skin taste like?

Claire turns back to the page of contents, her face and eyes bright. 'Ah! I've found the perfect story.' She drops her voice to a low whisper, filled with heavily dramatized menace.

'Are you ready? This story is called . . . "The Storm".' Claire draws out the long vowels.

Everyone gives an 'Ooooh!' of delighted mock-terror.

Byron throws back his head and lets out a howl, like a wolf's, then a genuine laugh. He glances at her and raises his eyebrows – the gesture is a little self-deprecating and Mary can see, all over again, why so many people are attracted by him, obsessed with him. It is not just that he is handsome and muscular and clever. She can see, now, the capacity for kindness that sits alongside his impatience. She sees the fierce, roving intellect that drives the great poet, the cruel intelligence that slices through foolishness. But she also sees how he uses his wit to ease the tension in the room, or to show that he understands someone – that he understands *her*.

We should not expect Hippolyta to play the part of Helen of Troy.

What must it be like to have such magnetism that your mood dictates the temperature of every place you enter? Would you even realize the power you had? Or would you simply assume that the world shaped itself to your moods, that other people mirrored your behaviour, felt your joy or pain as if it was their own? Would you believe everything revolved around your desires, that your dreams were those of a deity, your voice that of a tiny god?

Outside the lake flashes; lightning splits the sky. For a moment, everyone in the room is ablaze in white light, then plunged into half-darkness again. A grumble of thunder vibrates through the walls, through the floor, into their bones. The huge dog growls, a menacing rumble in the back of its throat.

A breath of silence. Mary feels everything inside her tremble.

Claire begins to read the story, which is about a group of people isolated in a large château in a fierce storm. Two friends, Isabella and Emily, are so frightened that they shut themselves away in a room together. The story ends with both women seeing something inexplicably terrible. They are stolen from the locked room. Their bodies are discovered weeks later. Their deaths remain unexplained.

Claire stops reading. Another silence.

Byron gives a snort of laughter. '*Terrible!* Why on earth aren't we told why the two women died or what they saw? And why did *both* women have to die in the first place?'

He chuckles again. Claire smiles along with him, tucking her hair behind her ears in a gesture Mary recognizes – her sister is anxious but pretending good humour.

Claire looks at her. Their eyes connect in one of those rare moments of perfect communication that used to happen all the time when they were children: Mrs Godwin would ask why on *earth* the girls were so unhappy and ungrateful. Mary and Claire's eyes would meet, each knowing what the other was thinking.

Now Mary and Claire know the answer to Byron's question but neither will say it: the women in the story both had to die because that is what women in stories are for. Like every object in the tale, they have their role. Food must be eaten, wine must be drunk, villains must be punished. Women must be obedient or be rescued or die.

'And why,' Byron continues, still mocking, 'aren't we ever told what on earth came to take them away?'

A man. Mary knows Claire is thinking the same. *A man or*

his ghost. Stories are full of monsters who kill women so that a hero can arrive and slay the villainous creature. The real world is full of men who would crush women or ignore them or trample them to get what they want.

Dimly, Mary is aware of Shelley making some comment about the villainous women in Greek tragedies. Claire gives a tinkling laugh.

Disappointing, Mary writes. And she doesn't mean only the ghost story. Her sister, with her constant need to please Shelley or Byron or both, is disappointing. Mary has been disappointing for so long – always striving for some idea of who her father thought she should be or who Shelley wanted her to become. All the while aware that, deep within her, a resounding roar was being crushed into silence.

Mary stares at the sheet of paper before her – how can she put her feelings into words?

No man has harmed my body, she writes, *yet I have been suffocated by my lover's cruelty. My former tenderness has turned to ash. I am waking from some terrible dream, when I had not even known that I was sleeping.*

'Fascinating!' Byron murmurs, from behind her. Mary jumps – she hadn't realized he'd moved from the sofa. He leans over, studying the paper. In his hand, the flask of laudanum.

Mary's instinct is to cover her words, but she stops herself. *Let him look. Let him see.*

His bright eyes travel over her words. Something in his expression changes. And when he looks at her, it is without any of his usual cynicism or scorn. 'Fascinating,' he says again, even more quietly. 'Everything about you is fascinating.'

He holds her gaze for a breathless moment. She knows he is truly looking at her. He *sees* something in her – not as he would like her to be but as she is.

'What's that, Albe?' Shelley calls from across the room, faint wariness in his tone.

Byron hesitates only a fraction of a moment, then claps his hands. 'I said, we should do something *fascinating*! More laudanum, Polly!'

He throws the flask to one side. It spins across the floor, drawing Shelley's gaze away from them. Byron flashes Mary a conspiratorial grin that sends a tremor through her chest.

While Polidori fetches more laudanum, Byron moves back to his couch and leans forward, a finger pressed to his lips. No one speaks. The thunder outside fades. Mary finds herself holding her breath. She is sure Claire and Shelley are doing the same. Even Polidori pauses in the middle of shutting his case.

It is as though they are the two women in the story, locked in the attic, waiting for whatever must happen, waiting for the footsteps on the stairs, the knock on the door.

'I have an idea,' says Byron.

Something is about to change.

'We will each write a ghost story. A tale to chill the blood. Let's see who can induce the most terror.'

'A competition?' Shelley asks.

'A challenge.' Byron looks across at Mary. Again, she feels he is gazing into her mind, that he sees her and she him. It is intoxicating.

She writes, *There is something at work in my soul that I do not understand.*

'A *ghost* story?' Shelley seems troubled and holds out his hand for the flask, which Polidori passes to him. 'I'm not sure I would be terribly good at writing a ghost story.'

'Oh, come, Shelley! You've enough despair in your soul to terrify anyone.' When Byron laughs, no one joins him. Mary had thought him eager for attention but had been wrong: he doesn't care, barely seems to notice what others think of him. She had thought it a kind of arrogance – another privilege reserved for men. And it *is*, but it is also, she sees, a choice. He says what he thinks and accepts the consequences.

'And you.' He looks at Mary with something that feels like hunger. 'Think what *you* could write. Something filled with darkness and terror.'

Mary feels her breath quicken. Everything she has tried to write before has been rational, reasonable – a philosophical argument to make her father proud, or a reasoned essay that her dead mother would have admired. Or a treatise to please Shelley.

All her darker thoughts, her bleaker imaginings, have been shut away in her journals, torn up or burned. Her most shocking ideas remain locked in her nightmares.

But even as she finds herself returning Byron's smile, even as she feels her body lit up by the excitement of writing something, her heart drops. She recognizes this fierce stirring of energy beneath her skin, this damp-palmed sense of anticipation and fear.

How has it taken her so long to realize? How has she blindly ignored this craving that makes her feel light-headed and damp-palmed and short of breath?

Desire.

She sees the word as if it has been scrawled across an unmarked page, or as if her flesh is a fresh sheet of paper and her longing is seared over every inch of her skin.

Damn, she thinks. She doesn't usually curse but the word feels good, feels right.

Damn, damn, damn!

Her eyes dart to Shelley. He seems oblivious – perhaps the wine and laudanum have dulled his senses. Or perhaps he knows and understands her even less than she had believed.

Byron's gaze on her is knowing, as if he can see her thoughts, can sense the way her body is responding to him.

Rain lashes the windows; the wind whistles down the chimney; lightning flickers across the surface of the lake. Dimly, Mary is aware of someone speaking but Claire has to call her name three times before Mary blinks and tears her gaze from Byron's.

'Yes?' She blinks dazedly at her sister.

'Never mind,' Claire says tightly. Without another word, she stands and stalks from the room.

She knows. The realization is a surge of icy alarm through her veins – if her sister has so quickly sensed the fierce energy between her and Byron, it must be clear to everyone. But Shelley is drowsing on the sofa now and Polidori is trying to peer out of the storm-battered window.

As the thunder rumbles overhead, Mary turns and follows her sister. She ignores the sensation of Byron's eyes on her. She ignores the feeling that she is being pulled back towards him.

Claire's door is locked. Mary hammers on the wood with her clenched fist. She will *not* let her sister say anything of her suspicions to Shelley. She will not allow Claire to twist and distort and manipulate her in the way that she has always done – as though Mary's feelings are pieces to be pushed about on a gaming board for Claire's amusement.

'Claire! I want to talk to you.'

'I *told* you to stay away from him. I told you what would happen if you didn't.'

Mary remembers her sister's warning: *I'll tell Shelley you plan to leave him.* At the time, the threat had filled Mary with terror – at the thought of losing Shelley, at the thought he might stop her seeing her son. Now she feels only rage, with a cold certainty: even without Shelley, she would find a way to survive. And *no one* will take away her child.

'Let me *in*,' she growls.

She slaps her palms against the wood, and, sure that Claire

will be leaning with her back against the door, she kicks it. 'Let me in, or I promise you'll regret it.'

Claire gives a hollow laugh. 'Empty words, Mary. How can you make me regret anything?'

'I'll make Shelley send *you* away,' Mary hisses. She is so angry she barely knows what she is saying. 'I'll tell him that I never want to see you again.' It is despicable to threaten to cast out her pregnant sister. And, as wicked as it is, the thought makes Mary feel powerful. 'You know I can do it, Claire. I asked him to send you away once before. I can make him do it again.'

A strange, strangled sound comes through the door. It takes Mary a moment to realize her sister is *laughing*.

'*You* made him send me away? Is that what you think?'

'It's . . . what happened.'

Mary remembers those months last year when Shelley had taken Claire to Dorset, then returned without her – so that he and Mary could have time alone together.

I know you have longed for it to be only the two of us, Pecksie.

'Oh *dear*, Mary,' Claire says, still laughing – a humourless, coughing bark. 'I never imagined you were so naïve. I thought you knew. We both thought you knew the truth, but that you were pretending to be ignorant to save your pride.'

'What are you talking about?' Mary's mouth is dry. She feels as if a dark, ragged space is being ripped open within her chest. '*What* did you think I knew?'

'You must have known.'

'Must have known *what*? Let me in, Claire. Let me in *now*! Now, or I swear I will break this door down.' Mary doesn't know how she would do such a thing, but the anger surging through her veins makes her voice savage as she kicks the door again and again, punctuating each kick with the words *Let. Me. In.*

Suddenly it opens, and her sister is standing in front of her, her face puffy, her eyes bloodshot, her cheeks tear-streaked.

There is an odd joy in her face, too, though, a small, smug smile, as she says very softly, 'I was pregnant.'

'You were . . .?' The dark space in Mary's chest opens further. Something awful is waiting within it.

'Pregnant. It was Shelley's. Obviously.'

'No.' The space in her chest feels huge now – an endless dark mouth that will swallow her whole.

'No,' she says again.

Claire gives a satisfied nod, a little shrug. 'We were sure you knew. How could you have been so oblivious? I've never thought of you as *stupid* before.'

Mary slaps her across the face. Claire's head whips to the side and she cries out. Mary's palm stings. Before Claire can protest, before she can say anything more, Mary slaps her again. Across the shoulders, then with both hands, as hard as she can, across the back of Claire's head.

She has never been violent, has never known this fierce cascade of power. She feels animal and brutal and immensely strong. It is as if her limbs are acting independently of her mind, as though her body is moving without her thought, without time for regret or remorse, striking and slapping until this strange and awful energy is spent.

With a cry, Claire shoves Mary backwards, out of her room, then shuts and locks the door. Mary is about to hurl her body against it, clawing at the wood like a wild beast, but she hears Shelley call from the drawing room, 'What on *earth* is happening?'

Mary doesn't answer him, doesn't stop when he calls to her. She runs to her own room and slams the door.

She sits at her desk and takes up her quill. Across the centre of the page, she writes, *I loathe him. I loathe him. I loathe her. I hate them both.*

The words are awful. The words are not enough. They are the protests of a wronged child. She wants something more – something darker and uglier – to scrawl across the white sheet of paper. *Damn him damn him damn him.*

Better, but still too feeble. She sees herself hiding the paper, as she always does, or burning it.

Or she pictures Shelley discovering it and reading the words, gazing at her, shocked.

She hears her future self: *Oh, I wasn't writing about you. Of course I'm not truly angry with you. Of course I forgive you.*

She sees herself apologizing, apologizing, apologizing.

No, no, no!

She feels a vicious contempt for the Mary who would pretend and fawn and placate. She will not be that woman any longer. She will not spend each day crushing her hopes and desires, her longing and her rage.

Pulling back her sleeve, she runs her fingers along the raised white lines on her forearm where, every time she has been furious, she has turned her rage inwards. Time and time again, she has tried to scratch the fury out of herself.

No more. No more.

She picks up her quill. Across her scars, she writes, *I hate him and I am not sorry.*

Then she gathers up her journals – the part she has always hidden from him, the part she has often considered burning. She lays them out on the desk, and she waits for Shelley.

Mary's Journal, 1815

23 February
Great agony. Anxious about labour pains, though it is two months before my time. Shelley in great distress. I had to console him.

*Birthed a baby girl just before midnight. So tiny. I do not
believe she will live. Thankfully, Claire away at Skinner Street
so none of her hysterics. I am very distressed, and Shelley is
little comfort. He says if this baby dies, we can have another.
I do not tell him what I think of this. My baby sleeps now
and so must I.*

24 February

*My little girl lives. I have called her Clara. I am able to nurse
her. She cries often. Weak mewlings. I think of my mother's
death. So frightened. Shelley no help at all. I wish I could return
to Skinner Street.*

28 February

*Baby has screamed all day. Shelley in town for hours, then
returned and complained at the noise. When I wept, he went out
again. I was in despair. Baby is sleeping now, though Shelley has
not returned. Father warned me that he was feckless and I fear
he may be right. I have always hated his wife Harriet. I think
differently of her now. Did Shelley neglect her too?*

1 March

*Baby Clara screams often still and is getting smaller, though
I nurse her constantly. Very painful and there is blood each
time. Shelley says this is normal and will improve. He doesn't
understand when I weep. Wait until Shelley leaves for town, then
I bundle my baby in a shawl and take her to Skinner Street.
Father will not open the door. I see his face at the window of
his study. I lift Clara up, to show him his granddaughter. He
pretends not to see us, then turns away. I return home and weep
all evening. Baby Clara cries very loudly. Shelley returns late, is
no help at all. I lie awake. I am desperate.*

3 March

We must move to different rooms because Shelley has not paid our rent. It is cold and both baby Clara and I catch a chill. She is very sickly. I stay awake all night nursing her. Shelley reads and sleeps. I cannot look at him.

5 March

Shelley has been away all day. I do not know where he has gone. Clara cries ceaselessly. I feel my head might explode with the noise, or my body might collapse – I am so exhausted. Shelley professes to love us. I do not know how to feel. Just before midnight, I wrap Clara in a blanket and lay her in her crib. When she finally sleeps, I go out in search of Shelley. He often walks along by the Thames or the Serpentine, only I do not find him. After half an hour I return home, bitterly cold. Clara is quiet so I sleep.

6 March

Shelley returns early in the morning. Our baby is still sleeping peacefully. I doze, then wake in the late morning because Clara has slept so long.

When I try to wake her, I find she is dead.

7 March

I must be cursed. She lived the same number of days that my mother survived my own birth.

Child of bones, mother of bones.

I will not tell Shelley I went out searching for him. He will say that I am a bad mother, that it is my fault she died.

Selfish, selfish. Hate. Hate. Hate.

8 March

I wish I could undo it all. I wish I had never known you.

*

She hears Shelley's footsteps along the hallway – tentative and uncertain – and she takes a steadying breath. He has spent nearly an hour in Claire's room and will come to Mary with apologies and excuses. She is ready to be strong and resolute.

On the desk are her journals; in her hand is a quill. These, she sees, are her shield, her armour, her bow and arrows. She will fight him with every part of her anxious, furious mind.

Shelley has always told her she should worry less, that she should remain calm and think sensibly. *You are too anxious.* Mary has berated herself for her fears, has seen them as a sign of weakness.

Now, for the first time, she understands they can be a source of strength. Her overwrought brain has always dreaded the worst in every circumstance. Now the worst circumstance has arrived, and Mary knows she can survive it. In fact, in some way, she has been planning for this worst moment from the first time she saw her lover smile at her sister.

As Shelley puts his head around the door, she sits up, arms folded across her chest. He expects her to speak, to berate him so he can *explain.* She will make him speak first.

He shuffles his feet. 'Well, Pecksie, I know you will be upset.'

'*Upset?* She had your *baby* and you didn't tell me.'

'We thought you knew –'

'Liar! You *hoped* I knew. You stayed silent because you are too much of a coward to talk to me.'

He flinches – she has never spoken to him with such fury before. She watches him try to calculate his response, which only stokes the fire within her: he is trying to find the right words to soothe her or quiet her.

'Now, my love, be reasonable. Even if you did not *know* – and you must have suspected, truly, Pecksie, because you are not a fool – we have discussed and agreed many times that our

275

love should be free and liberal. Love put under the confines of rules and laws is not truly love at all. It is passion reduced to servitude and obedience.'

'We did *not* agree!' she spits. '*I* did not agree. *You* forced me into obedience every time you told me I couldn't question your whereabouts or curtail your freedom. *You* reduced me to a state of servitude, then told me I was free to love whomever I chose. The only person I wanted, the only person I ever loved was *you*. Your ideas about *freedom* are simply a way of serving your own needs. Do not dare to pretend otherwise.' She is breathing hard now. There is the taste of blood in her mouth and at the back of her throat, as if she has been running hard, as if she has been screaming for hours.

'Now, my love –'

'Do *not* try to placate me. Do not pretend you have been honest. You have lied to me about Claire, just as you have lied to me about Harriet's baby. Yes, I *know* she is pregnant again. Don't try to deny it.'

Shelley stares at her, open-mouthed, as if he has never seen her before.

'Where is Claire's baby now?' she demands.

'It – She was stillborn. Unfortunate, but probably a blessing.'

Even through her fury, Mary feels a pang of pity for Claire. She keeps her face impassive.

'And Harriet's baby? What will you do?' She sees his throat move as he swallows.

'I will send her money. It may not even be mine.'

'Don't try to lie. You know it is.'

The wind slaps against the shutters. The house creaks and sighs. Shelley cannot meet her gaze.

She leans forward and speaks, slowly and clearly: '*You* have caused so much suffering. How could you be so selfish? I have tried hard to be the woman you said you wanted –'

'You *are* the woman I want, Pecksie. You are my sweet love. I know you are angry with me now. Can you not find it in your heart, in your soul to forgive me? You have always had the perfect soul of a saint –'

'I do not! I am no saint and I do not belong to you.'

She watches his face, waiting for her words to reach him, but he is still shaking his head, still trying to half smile at her, as though he can coax her from a momentary bad mood, or cajole her from a tantrum.

'Here!' She holds out her secret journal, open to the pages where she had written about baby Clara's death. 'I have *dreaded* you finding this. I have fretted and hidden it from you for more than a year. I would have burned it, only it contains memories of our baby. I was so desperate and frightened that you would think me a poor mother and a monster. I don't care now. Read it.'

He steps forward, picks up the book as though it might burn him, then reads quickly. She watches him blink and recoil. When he sets the book down, his eyes shine with unshed tears.

She waits for him finally to apologize, to beg her forgiveness.

She will refuse. She will throw his apology back in his face. Let him see how it feels to be shut out and cut off.

Finally, in a very quiet voice, he says, 'Sweet Pecksie, you needn't berate yourself. Poor baby Clara was born so early. It was not your fault.'

It takes her a moment to understand that, even having read of her fury, even having read how he neglected her, how he left her alone and desperate, he believes himself innocent. He thinks that her loathing and her rage is still for herself.

A little of it had been – at times she still believes herself a terrible mother for leaving her baby alone.

'Poor Pecksie.' Shelley reaches for her. 'I don't blame you.'

She slaps his hand away. 'I blame *you*! You left me and your infant daughter and disappeared into town day after day. I was alone. Both of us were sickly and exhausted. We had to move lodgings in the rain because of your debts. It's your fault – all of it. Our baby died and you are to blame and I loathe you for it. Damn you, Shelley, it's all your fault, *damn* you!'

'Stop, Mary! This isn't you. You're not seeing clearly – you're not yourself.'

'I *am* myself! I am myself and I see you clearly, Shelley.'

She is trembling, but her mind is clear. The crushing compression in her chest has gone. She draws one ragged, clean breath after another. He doesn't understand her at all. She sees it now: he has never understood her, has never truly wanted *her*.

He fell in love with an idea of who he wanted her to be. He fell in love with the perfect version of Mary Wollstonecraft Shelley that he had made in his own mind. She has spent years trying to contort herself into the shape of a woman who didn't exist.

'What do you see?' His voice is barely a whisper. His eyes flick to the words she has scrawled across her scarred arm, then flinch away again.

'You are a coward.' She says each word clearly and carefully, as if her heart is not hammering in her chest, as if speaking the truth doesn't terrify her. 'You are a coward, Shelley. You are weak and petty and selfish, and I wish I didn't know you.'

He has gone very still. There is no half-smile in his eyes, no soft affection in his expression. He has the blank, inward look of a condemned man.

He says nothing. She wonders if perhaps he is still waiting for her to apologize – if he is so used to her anxious soothing that he doesn't know what to do without it.

'Anything else?' he finally asks.

'Go away, Shelley,' she says wearily. 'Go and cry on Claire, if you must, but leave me alone.'

16

Have a care: I will work at your destruction,
nor finish until I desolate your heart.

After Shelley has left, Mary forces herself to sit very still.

Follow him, sighs an old, familiar voice. *Call him back.*

'No!' she growls, through gritted teeth. If she goes after him, there is a risk she will apologize again – even though she knows she is not to blame. As he takes her in his arms and smiles and kisses her, she will feel small and sad and alone.

A gust of wind rattles the window. The candle flickers, gutters, recovers. Somewhere, deep in the belly of the house, an animal shrieks. And all the while, within her, something is spinning, turning in on itself, building.

She is alone now, too, but at least she has chosen it.

Another blast of wind flings rain against the walls, blustering against the glass.

That's where you will find yourself, whispers the voice. *If you don't apologize, you will be out in the darkness and the rain. You will starve and die on the streets. You will never see Willmouse again –*

'Stop!' she chokes. Is she losing her grip on her sanity? 'Stop!' she says, loudly, firmly, but it is still not enough to prevent her from going to the door.

What will you do? Will you crawl after him yet again?

If she does, he will crush her beneath his needs, his desires, his endless edicts. He will confound her with his *reasonable arguments*, which only ever benefit him.

She goes to the window and throws it open. A freezing wind whips into the room, hurling icy rain against her skin, snuffing the candle, extinguishing the fire. She gasps, then closes her eyes, her hands stretched in front of her, palms up, as if she is drawing something from the storm or offering something up. She is not sure which. She knows only that the water feels searingly cold, burning through her clothes, her skin, her bones. Everything she has tried to be is being scorched away: all the layers of politeness and pretence, all the years of feigned coolness and calm. The storm devours it all.

It whisks the papers into the air, hurls them at the walls, at the floor, under the bed. The ink on the pages bleeds and blurs. The words *I wish I had never met you* dissolve into a far-off thunderhead – the sort of cloud Mary could watch from a distance, with the knowledge that it needn't touch her or that, if it does, she will find a way to be safe and dry again.

By the time she pulls the window shut, Mary feels frozen down to her bones and the whole room is soaked. She pulls off her wet dress and smooths her damp shift over her icy skin, her teeth chattering. She wraps the half-sodden blankets from the bed around her, then goes out into the hallway in search of a fire.

Moonlight casts strange shapes of bleached white and pitch black on the walls. Her own shadow is unrecognizable. Who is this woman walking with purpose towards the drawing room? Who is this woman walking past Claire's door, who pauses to listen for the sound of two voices, two sets of laughter, two sighs?

The sensation is hot pain, not yet. It is like the shock of a burn, when the skin is smoothed by heat: though agony is waiting beneath that oddly shiny flesh, it does not yet hurt.

I will not let it, she thinks. *If it does hurt, I will keep on anyway, because the change will be worth the pain.*

It is a new voice. Unfamiliar, yet closer than her skin. She recognizes it instantly as her own.

Byron is in the drawing room, as if he is waiting for her, as if he knew she was coming for him. She stands in the shadows of the doorway, watching him.

He is reading and doesn't look up. Candlelight burnishes his cheekbones, his nose, his lips, his chin. She wonders how his mouth would feel against hers, and her neck grows warm, though her body is still frozen and damp.

She should leave. She should turn and walk away. Go back to her cold and lonely room.

But she can no longer hear the anxious voice, which, for so many years, has made her obey her father's wishes, her mother's expectations or Shelley's demands.

Go on, says her new voice.

The beginning is always today.

She takes a breath, then steps into the heat and the light of the room.

Though he doesn't look at her, she sees his awareness change, sees some tension creep in around his mouth, in his hands, which hold the book a little more tightly.

From behind Claire's closed door, a cry, quickly smothered. Mary wants to cover her ears. Instead, she steps fully into the room and sits on a velvet armchair in the darkness, across from Byron's chaise.

He turns a page. 'Laudanum helps, I find.'

'Will it change the past?' Her tone is spiked, abrasive.

He smiles. 'It's excellent if you can't sleep. Or if there's something you don't want to hear. Or don't want to think about. As for changing the past – if only it could.' He laughs without humour, then picks up the silver laudanum bottle and brings it to her.

She takes it but doesn't drink. For a moment, she thinks he will press his body next to hers on the armchair. He sits on the floor at her feet. She can feel his gaze on her face, can feel the blood rising across her chest and neck, though it is cold away from the fire; she has to tense her muscles to stop herself shivering.

'Such strange weather,' she says. 'Do you believe it is the end of the world? That we are all doomed?'

'Why are you here?' His voice is soft.

'You have been writing.' She stands and walks away from him to the desk, where piles of papers are covered with his distinctive looping hand.

'Is that why you're here? To talk about my writing?' He rises, picks up the laudanum again and holds it out to her. It sits like a gift, a proposition in silver on his open palm.

She takes it.

A thump from Claire's room, then low laughter.

Mary swigs the bitter liquid and passes it to Byron. He drinks, smacking his lips in exaggerated satisfaction. She smiles, wondering where he learned to ease others' anxiety, and why, so often, he chooses to add to it instead.

Outside, the wind hushes. In the grate, the fire shivers. The candle glimmers. On the walls, the portraits of long-dead men and their wives loom, lurk, leer . . .

Mary can feel her thoughts peeling, moving away from her. The laudanum spreads a thin gauze between herself and her mind.

Strange – she has never before considered that her body might be separate from her thoughts. Without them, she feels freer, lighter – a heavy rope has dropped from her shoulders. This is different from drinking laudanum with Shelley. Then, she is always intensely aware of him, of where he is, of what he is doing.

Now she is more aware of herself.

When she raises her arms and smiles, she is conscious of the movement, of the breath in her lungs, the laughter in her mouth.

She stumbles and Byron helps her to sit on the chaise. She lies back and closes her eyes, her body heavy and light, close and distant.

'Come here,' she murmurs.

'Are you sure?' There is a rasp in his voice, a hesitation she hasn't heard before.

It only makes her more certain that she wants him close to her. This distance between them, this agonizing tension: she wants it gone.

When he lies down with her, the length of his body presses her against the side of the chaise.

She feels enclosed but not trapped. If she wanted to, she could leave.

She doesn't want to leave.

Next to her, the bulk of him, so hard and muscled – so different from Shelley.

No, she won't think of Shelley now.

She can feel the rise and fall of Byron's chest. She counts how many breaths it takes before they are inhaling and exhaling in unison. Three. That is all. And she couldn't say which of them has changed to fall in with the other.

She opens her eyes. His face is a hand's width from hers.

He lays his palm on her chest, just beneath her throat. He must be able to feel the rising rhythm of her heart.

She wants to put her arms around him.

She wants to push him away.

She is cold, still, her body warm only where he is touching her.

And he must feel her hesitation because he studies her

face, his dark blue eyes searching. In this dim light, she cannot make out the gold flecks that encircle his pupils with light.

She is reminded of the first time she saw the lake, which shifts and sighs outside the window; the thought of the secrets concealed beneath its dark, fathomless depths had stolen the air from her lungs.

If she makes this choice, it could change everything, could end her life as she knows it.

'You want me to stop?' he asks.

She feels him start to pull back, feels a breath of icy air where his body moves away from hers. The sight of the sea had terrified her, two years ago, but she had sailed upon it anyway, had let it carry her far away from everything safe and familiar. The storms outside this house scare her. Byron scares her. Yet she is still here.

Fear is not the end.

Now, she twines her arms around his neck, pulls him in close, and kisses him.

She feels him freeze, feels his hesitation, the last shreds of his uncertainty.

Then his mouth is on hers, feverish. He rolls on top of her. She arches against him, pushing her hips against his, drawing him closer still. She has never felt this before: this urgency, this frenzy, this ravenous ache in the base of her belly.

Shelley used to like her to stay still while he stripped her and kissed her – pausing to describe her body, to declare her beauty. She had felt, sometimes, as if he was writing her: her desire only existed because he was calling it into life with his words. She was a blank page, powerless beneath his hands. He'd remained, somehow, outside it all, observing, and so had she.

Byron's need matches her own: he encircles her wrists with one hand, lifts her arms above her head, then pulls off her shift. He doesn't pause, doesn't want to observe or examine her, but tugs off his shirt. In the firelight, his bronze skin gleams. She runs her fingers over the muscles of his chest, presses her lips to the corded tendon that runs from his shoulder to his neck.

And then there is only her mouth, his mouth. He moves, she moves. Their matched breath, building, travelling towards something together.

Outside, the storm. Inside, the storm.

At the last, he says her name, his lips against her ear, and for the space of three heartbeats, they are like two halves of a struck tuning fork, sounding a single perfect note.

She dozes with her head on his chest, the sweat cooling on their skin. She shivers and he wakes, kisses her forehead. Then, finding that the covers she'd brought from her room are damp, he pulls down a thick, velvet curtain and lays it gently across her.

She hadn't known he could be so tender.

He curls his body around hers, pulling her close. For the rest of the night, whenever she stirs, he presses his lips to the back of her neck.

Once, the sound of the storm and the darkness of the room fill her dream and she finds herself underwater, struggling to emerge, breath burning in her lungs.

'Wake up,' he whispers, stroking the hair from her damp forehead.

She startles awake, drawing a panicked gasp, then remembers where she is. Byron is holding her hand, his fingers intertwined with hers.

'What was it?' he asks softly.

'Water,' she says, and is grateful when he nods, when he doesn't ask for more. But it is strange: she feels so safe with him, so utterly bare and uninhibited, as if she could tell him anything. Her voice barely audible above the wind, she adds, 'Usually, it's bodies.'

He kisses her shoulder. 'Mine's fire. Always fire. But,' he presses his lips to her cheek, 'I haven't dreamed tonight at all. You're good for me, clearly.'

And he compresses his twined fingers around hers and holds her close, kissing the back of her neck, her shoulder, her breasts, then back up to her jaw until they are breathless and laughing softly. As they fall asleep again, she floats on the feeling of his hand in hers, his body next to hers. She is drifting in a vast, featureless sea and she is not afraid.

17

I have longed for a friend; I have sought one who
would sympathize with and love me.

Mary wakes in her own room. For a moment, in the grey light,
she thinks it was all a dream: the muscled weight of his body
on hers, the dark intensity of his eyes as he kissed her, the
soft hum of his groan against her neck as he moved inside
her, the salt taste of his skin.

She sits up, feels the ache between her legs, the pleasant
burn in every limb as she stretches, and she knows: it was real.
Perhaps somewhere, within the house, he will be waiting for
her. The thought sends tension skittering over her skin: she
wants to go to him, but it is impossible to know how he will
be with her. She thinks of his cruelty towards Claire. What
will Mary do if Byron turns that sneering contempt on her?

Now, she can remember returning to her own room,
just before dawn. He had been sleeping on the chaise, still,
but as she'd risen to leave, he'd reached out and looped his
fingers around her wrist. He'd pulled her close and kissed
her, sleepily, affectionately, then released her. The laudanum
blur had faded by then, but her head still swam with a giddy
euphoria – the glow of desire, yes, but also the hope that
Byron might . . . *feel* something for her, something more
than lust.

What will it mean for her, if he does? And what does she
feel for him?

The wind whips the shutters back and forth – smack of wood on stone. Something outside shatters.

In the dining room, Byron is sitting opposite Shelley and Claire, his expression bleak as he stabs at his eggs. Mary's stomach sinks and she readies herself for his cruel jibes.

When he sees her, his face brightens. 'Ah! Mrs S!' He rises and pulls out a chair next to his. 'Did you sleep well?'

'I did,' she says, as smoothly as she can. His hair has flopped over his forehead, and she feels an urge to brush it aside. Instead, she sits, lets him push her chair in.

'The storms didn't wake you?'

'Not the storms, no.' She smiles, enjoying the subterfuge. It feels like a thin filament of connection to last night – Byron is reaching out to her still.

'Very chivalrous, Albe.' Shelley bites into his bread. He says nothing to Mary, doesn't even look at her. Yesterday his rejection would have felt sharp as a slap. Today she notes the sting of it, but she also has a sense of power as she sits down without trying to meet his gaze, without showing that she even knows he exists.

She will not apologize for raging at him yesterday. She will not apologize for anything.

As Mary sits, Claire reaches out and takes her hand. She clasps Mary's fingers; her skin is icy and pale, her nails gnawed to the quick.

Mary knows her sister is seeking forgiveness. She forces herself to meet Claire's gaze and readies the words, *How dare you? How dare you take so much from me, then expect absolution?*

But as she looks at her sister's greyish complexion and bloodshot eyes – at the raw patches on her lips where she has chewed at the skin – Mary sees the desperate, vulnerable girl she grew up with. The sharp edges of her anger dull to a weary sort of pity. She pulls her hand away, but gently.

From above their heads, a shriek – Mary startles.

Perched on the curtain rail, a large black raven is staring at her, head cocked to one side. Its black eyes are sharp with a watchful intelligence. Mary thinks of Odin's messenger ravens, which surveyed battlefields with impassive disdain because they already knew who would live and who would bleed out onto the indifferent ground.

'Miss Godwin,' a voice says from behind her – too close to her ear. She jumps again and turns.

Polidori is soaked, hair plastered to his head. He gives a damp smile. With one wet hand, he proffers a plate of toast and eggs. On the side of the plate, a single white rose. 'The garden is flooded. It's the last one. I wanted you to have it.'

'Polly, you sly devil!' Byron says. 'Are you attempting a seduction?' His tone is as mocking as ever, but there is a new sharpness to it.

'You might have *asked*, Polidori.' Shelley's gaze is suddenly hard. 'I might have wanted to give a rose to my wife.'

'Your *wife* is in London, Shelley. Besides, I thought I was free to love whomever I please,' Mary says. 'You don't believe in ownership, remember?' She looks directly at him and watches his expression change as he sees her – truly *recognizes* something of who she is, for the first time, rather than only ever perceiving the woman he wanted her to be – the woman he'd held captive on a pedestal built of his own desires.

Here I am, she thinks. *Furious and flawed. I am not your soulmate or your muse.*

She takes the plate from Polidori. 'It's a beautiful rose. And *I* know you intend friendship, not seduction.'

He swallows and nods. Too late she sees her mistake. She sees the affection in his eyes. His longing.

'Of course . . .' Polidori flushes. 'Friendship, Miss Godwin.'

'For Heaven's sake, Polly, stop fawning over her,' Byron says. 'You look like a simpleton child who's been scolded by Nanny.'

Claire and Shelley join in Byron's savage laughter. Polidori looks away, crushed, and suddenly Mary cannot endure any of it – the mockery, the pretence, the snarled yearnings and the way the others are all gazing at her, wanting something from her. Love or sex or penance or forgiveness.

She doesn't want to give any of it. At this moment, she doesn't want to give any more of herself to any of them.

On the curtain rail above, the raven shrieks again, its black eyes watchful.

'Excuse me.' She stands. And she walks out.

Behind her, she hears Shelley and Claire calling her back but she continues down the hallway, towards her own room. Somewhere, in her body, is the growing feeling that she could keep walking if she wanted to. Out, into the thunder and the floods, beneath the electric sky. She could fetch her child and return to London, and she would find a way for them to live.

When she pauses at the window, the garden is like a lake, its dark skin punctured by slicing rain. Above, the sky boils with grey-black clouds.

The dark menace of it fixes her here, even as it calls to her. The desire to walk out into the water seethes in her limbs, yet she is repelled and frightened by the urge. Just as she is repelled and frightened by the need she has to return to Byron, to wrap her arms around him, to look into his eyes, to ask him, *Was it real, what I felt last night? Did you feel it too?*

She is unmoored by her desire to stay in the dining room with Byron – she hates that her heart had raced when he'd moved the chair for her, that her mood had plummeted when he'd reverted to his usual callous jokes. In her body, still, the memory of his kisses on her skin, the echo of his ragged breath against her ear as he lost himself in her – or so she'd thought.

She doesn't want to feel so much and so quickly for another man who will slowly, lovingly, tenderly twist her into the shape of his will.

'Mary!' She turns at Byron's voice, her stupid heart lifting in her chest at the sound of him speaking her name. Still, she won't smile and simper at him, as Claire does.

'I wish you wouldn't be so –'

He pulls her towards him, crushing his mouth to hers. While he is kissing her, he runs his fingertips very gently down her neck. The sensation flames through her; she presses against him.

He draws away, breathing heavily, and leans his forehead against hers.

His dark blue eyes are serious. 'I was an ass.' That is all he says. There is no explanation, no excuse, no expectation that she should absolve him. He is still gazing at her. 'I haven't stopped thinking about you, about last night. But this morning I was an ass.'

She can feel her mouth curving up in a small smile. 'You were.'

Still, he doesn't apologize. It is strange and wonderful to be with a man who asks nothing of her, expects nothing of her, except what she wants to give.

She kisses him, wrapping her arms around his neck and pressing her whole body against his. His breath quickens and she remembers how, the night before, even as she'd felt terrified, she had known that every moment with him was a choice she was making.

She feels the same apprehension now, the same power. As if she is standing with her toes curled over the edge of an ice sheet, preparing to jump. Ready to fall.

'I will not start batting my eyelids and chasing after you,' she says against his lips.

She feels him grin against her mouth. 'Good. Because I am happy to bat my eyelids at you. And I am the one in pursuit – if you want to be caught.'

He takes her hand and leads her towards his room. Then he shuts and locks the door and kneels in front of her.

She is aware of the rain lashing the windows, the rumbling of yet another storm in the distance, lightning licking the mountaintops. She is aware of the power within her limbs, in her core, beneath her skin, the electricity that stems from seizing this moment. In the cold sobriety of daylight, she is choosing this, is choosing him.

'Tell me what you want me to do,' he says.

And she does.

She wakes in the middle of the night, his arm heavy across her chest. She sits up, breathless.

In her dream, she was watching the executions at Newgate, seeing necks snapped. As the bodies fell to the ground, they broke into pieces, arms falling away from ribcages, legs parting from torsos. Everything tumbled into an enormous pit, the body parts indistinguishable from each other. Mary looked down at her own body and watched herself fall apart. Her own arms and legs fell from her, the separation of each limb was a rending – as though some unseen force was ripping at her flesh.

She must write this in her journal. As she stands, Byron reaches out and clasps her arm.

'Come back to bed.' His voice is blurred with sleep.

'I need to write something.' She tries to pull away. He clasps her tightly. Those strong rower's hands, which he'd used to hold her hips, to pull her closer –

Not now!

'I need to write.'

'You can write in the morning.'

'Let me go!' A flash of the rage, which sits so close to the surface always now. She slaps his hand away.

He draws a sharp breath. In the gloom she sees him sit up. His eyes glint as he stares at her.

'I *need* to write.' She will not explain any more than that. She will not tell him that he can't hold her like that, can't make her his captive – even if only briefly.

She shuts the door quietly and leaves him alone, in the dark.

Mary's Journal, 1816

18 June

My life may appear an accumulation of anguish, but I will defend it.

I feel, sometimes, a half-formed creature. The power rests within me to become whole.

20 June

When we are alone, he is tender. In his room, in his bed, we exist only for each other. In front of the others, it is different – he is different.

I try not to watch him but he draws back my gaze again and again.

My foolish, treacherous heart was fashioned for love and sympathy. When wrenched by misery to vice and hatred, I cannot endure the violence of the change.

S seems not to notice but I feel C watching us. She fawns over S and makes jealous comments towards B. Earlier, she found me alone. She said, 'It's just companionship between me and Shelley. We are only friends.'

And P watches too. He watches everything and gazes at me with such devotion. I do not think he truly sees me. He sees part of me, or what he would want me to be. Like S.

Sometimes I wish to shake off all thought and feeling.

21 June

I must write a terrifying ghost story but all I can compose is this journal.

I feel no regret, no remorse. My mind is my own, my will is my own. I will do whatever I must to retain it. I will make my own way in the world. I will find a way to keep my child.

The beginning is always today.

As she writes, Mary feels nauseated with fear. It is like the times when she has stood on the banks of the Serpentine river, half longing to throw herself into the flow but too fearful to move. Only this time, somehow, some unseen force has grabbed hold of her and hurled her into the flood. She is flailing and gulping, consumed by the terror that she might be swallowed by this crushing darkness.

But as she floats from one word to the next, one sentence to the next, along with the fear there is a sense of exhilaration, of being borne along and upwards by some force that she doesn't understand and cannot control.

There is a freedom in this movement of my quill across the page. Making and unmaking, creating and destroying. There is a darkness in my soul which I can neither control nor understand. I can hide it no longer. I do not want to flee from it.

I have been trying to find a way to escape but I cannot flee from myself.

I will not hide from the thing I might become.

Thunder gives way to more torrential rain, reducing the world outside the windows to a shuttering grey. Mary longs for a glimpse of sky, or the distant mountains. Instead, she feels they will all be trapped here for ever in this house, with their rage and their longing.

All the words they write. All the words they cannot say.

Byron seems oblivious to Claire's moods and manipulations. He sits with a quill and paper, writing furiously, then crossing out and growling to himself. It is a comfort for Mary to see that Byron doesn't simply summon poems as he might order food for a banquet, then have it set before him, gleaming and delicious.

Sometimes he looks up from his paper and gazes at her thoughtfully, before asking, 'Have you written a story yet?'

The question makes her feel a fury she cannot fully understand or explain. She wants to write something *more*, something greater and better, but her story exists, for the moment, as a churning mass of feeling for which there is no language.

How can she put her anger into words? Her grief, her love, her desire for revenge. Words feel hollow, insufficient to capture the emotions they contain. Outside, the slate surface of the lake is wind-battered and looks empty of all life.

'I have no story,' she says quietly. Her cheeks flame. The admission is mortifying.

Everything with Byron is different from how it has been with Shelley. Yet she feels the same sense of expectation. The same rage-inducing thought: that she is not quite *enough*.

She cannot bear to be in the drawing room with the others all day, so she sits alone in her room, listening to the push and rush of wind along the walls of the villa, feeling the thrum of thunder in her bones, the flicker of lightning across her closed eyelids.

Difficult to know if the moans and murmurs are made by the weather, or the house, or if she is hearing Claire and Shelley, some ghost of their past encounters that has spread sighing tendrils in her mind. Or it might be Byron's animals, howling and mewing and screeching at the storm.

Write something, she thinks. *Write something terrifying.*

The world is a secret I long to discover. And yet I remain here, shrouded in the fears. I try to cast them off. They stick like cobwebs. It will not be good enough. I will not be good enough –

She presses the nib of the quill to the paper; it snaps and ink spills across the page.

Closing her eyes, she listens to the groaning of the house and the moaning of the wind. That is all it is.

Claire says it is just friendship between her and Shelley now. And yet – these noises!

She reaches for another blank piece of paper, picks up the quill that leaks ink onto her hand and stains her skin. She traces the pattern of the veins on her scarred arm, thinks of the blood beating frantically beneath the calm surface.

What force is it that keeps her going? What is it that has put the spark of life into her, the need to endure? If Shelley left her, would she feel as her mother had felt when she was a deserted young woman with a baby? Would she be ruining Willmouse's chance of happiness? Mary's older half-sister, Fanny, still mourned the loss of her mother, still grieved for her father, who had wanted nothing to do with her. Would Mary, like her mother, find herself compelled to continue, in spite of despair and long-ing, in spite of all emptiness? Is that, perhaps, what a ghost is, after all? A spirit that has continued in the living person's mind?

And if this is true, might her mother exist somewhere, somehow, in her?

Mother, she thinks.

No reply except the wind.

When she was young, she heard stories about men who prowled through graveyards at night, digging up bodies and selling them to doctors or medical schools for research and experiments. She has a nightmare, sometimes, of her mother's body being stolen and disassembled, sawn apart and stitched back together. Again and again, she has dreamed of her mother brought back to life, but as someone else. Her mother reanimated, turning away, as though Mary is a stranger.

A howling and shouting from somewhere in the house. It builds to a crescendo, then cuts off suddenly. What was that? Did she imagine it?

Silence yawns. The walls shift and pulse in time to her breath.

She falls asleep with her face on the blank page. When she wakes, long after midday, she looks in the mirror. Along with the dark shadows under her red-rimmed eyes, a line of ink slashes from her lips to her jawbone. It is as if she has been slit open and sewn up, like those bodies dug up from the ground.

The thought is so awful that it is almost funny. When she smiles at her reflection, the movement is as smooth and real as if she is a whole person, not a woman frightened that she is coming apart at the seams.

She touches a finger to the cool glass. *Who are you?*

Outside the window a dim light, the colour of sulphur. Where the sun should be behind the clouds, it is a faint, whitish circle, like bone so bleached it will crumble under a strong breeze.

Even before they had left England, before these storms, the newspapers had been full of gloom: this is the beginning of the end. Everything is coming apart. The sunless starvation and tempests of this summer are only the start.

She thinks of the preacher she had seen on Threadneedle

Street, weeks ago now, though it feels like a lifetime. *Your Father sees you. He judges you.*

'No, he doesn't,' she says to her face in the mirror. 'He doesn't see you at all.'

What are you? Who are you? Are you a monster, a blot upon the earth?

No! I am a creature of fine sensations – a creature poorly fashioned for this brutal world. I feel too much. When I look around, I see no other like me. Still, there is power in me I barely understand.

The thought makes her feel stronger. She stands up straighter.

Splashing water onto her face, she resolves to go into the drawing room today. She cannot keep avoiding Shelley and Claire, Byron and Polidori. She cannot keep avoiding herself.

Byron's eyes light when he sees her – a flash of genuine joy, before he remembers to shift into the habitual acerbic sneer he adopts in front of others. 'Ink-stained fingers, I see. And paper! Have you been writing late into the night? Are you ready to terrify us all?'

Mary can feel Shelley's eyes on her, can sense his hope. How odd that he needs this extra reason to love her again, or to prove to a man he met barely a week ago that she is a worthy prize.

She is suddenly tired of, exhausted by always straining for excellence in everything. Why must she be the best mother, the best lover, the kindest sister, the most intelligent woman in the room?

Why must she rise to every expectation? Why must she write something brilliant to impress Byron and win Shelley's adoration? If she is to write anything, it will be for herself.

She slaps the blank sheet of paper onto the table.

'I haven't written a word,' she says. 'And you?'

Byron doesn't shrink from her irritation, as Shelley would: he understands it, allows it. It is one of the things she likes about him.

Byron shrugs and takes a mouthful of egg. 'Started a story about some bloodsucking creature who feeds off those around him. Then, I'm afraid to say, it felt a little too autobiographical for comfort.' He flicks a piece of toast into the air, catches it in his mouth and grins.

She laughs, in spite of her frustration. He has this knack, Byron, of mocking himself just enough. It is hard to remain angry, but it is also impossible to be close to him. Only when they are alone together does she feel she might know him. When he is touching her, his eyes are full of naked need. In those first moments when he moves inside her, she sees a glimpse of vulnerability, which exists alongside his strength. She truly sees him – she knows it. *Stay!* she thinks.

He whispers her name in her ear, like a prayer or incantation. He gazes at her as if she is the only thing that matters in his world.

But almost as soon as it is over the shutters descend again.

Byron flicks a toast crust to the floor; the dog snaps it up. 'Shelley tried to write a horror story about his childhood too but is instead writing a love poem to the imagination.'

'"Hymn to Intellectual Beauty",' Shelley says brightly, gazing at Mary. Again, that pressure from him to be something more than she is. He has always said he finds her mind beautiful, her thoughts sublime, as if that is somehow nobler than valuing her for her face, her shoulders, her breasts and waist.

His love of her mind is just as much a prison as his love of Claire's body, if not more so: Claire must primp and preen, rub oils into her skin and lacquers into her hair, for fear that people will be repelled by seeing her as she truly is. Mary, though never slovenly, is not as vain about her appearance, but feels the constant need to be fascinating and original, as well as mild and kind, loving and caring.

Shelley fell in love with her intellect, he has always told her. She used to find the thought enchanting. Now, she realizes, he wants her to keep her mind as smooth and flawless and beautiful as Claire's gleaming skin and hair. If she rages and accuses and shows the darkness of her fury, the demon that squats in her thoughts, Shelley will grow tired of her mind, just as he will one day become bored with Claire's body.

Even as she tells herself she doesn't care how he feels, she knows that her life is still so deeply entwined with his that leaving him would be almost impossible.

On the paper in front of her, she scrawls, *Shall I not then hate them that abhor me? I will keep no terms with my enemies.*

When she looks up, Byron is staring at her with the same burning intensity as when he tells her to strip, then kneels in front of her. He wants to know what she has written. She folds the paper in half, then again and again, until it is a damp wad. She crushes it in her fist.

Polidori hasn't even sat at the table but is standing in the corner, like a scolded dog. He is holding a scrap of uneaten toast; his seat, which is next to Byron's, is empty and his blue china plate is smashed into five pieces, as if something has been dropped onto it from a great height. In its shattered centre, there is a rust-coloured smear.

She picks up a knife from her plate, tilts it towards her face, trying to catch her reflection. It is clean but its surface is too tarnished for her to make out anything other than a dark blur where her features should be. She could be any woman – faceless, replaceable.

She unfolds the piece of paper and writes, *Invention does not consist in creating out of the void, but out of chaos.*

Again, Byron gazes at her expectantly, eyebrows raised.

The look she gives him is glassy, implacable. He can touch her body, but she will not give her mind to him, or to anyone.

'Well,' Byron wipes his mouth on a napkin and drops it onto his lap, 'as it is not even midday and we already have need of candles and lamps, I think we should hear a ghost story. Shelley and I have been working on our poetry and Mrs S has already told us that she hasn't written a word, though I'm sure I have seen her write twice this morning. I expect Claire has been too consumed by the stories manufactured about her own life to write anything, even if she were able. Hmm?'

Claire picks at the skin around her fingernails, her soft mouth pressed into a thin line.

'Actually,' Mary says grudgingly, 'Claire's letters are wonderful.'

This is true. Nearly every time they have been separated, Claire has written bright, amusing letters to Mary. This was the case, Mary remembers, even when Claire was in Dorset, giving birth to Shelley's baby, who died. In spite of her grief, Claire had still taken the time to write letters to Mary, trying to lift her spirits.

Let me tell you, dear sister, of the curious little woman who rooms in the house across the street: she is always scowling at me and, as she has a face like an old apple, you can imagine that her features are not made more pleasant by her frowns. I can't see why she should dislike me so, but this is often the way with women – do you not agree? How sad that we are always sniping at one another and criticizing, as though we were all competing for some great prize.

Perhaps Father and Mother made us believe that too – do you not think so?

In our family, unless you can compose an epic poem before breakfast, or write a great novel, you must be a despicable creature.

Now Claire gives Mary a grateful and surprised smile. Mary isn't sure why she had said anything at all to defend her sister, except that she'd wanted to say something that was true.

'I have a thought!' Byron says, raising one finger in a stagey gesture that must surely have been rehearsed. 'How about a little tale from our very own P-P-Polly?'

A jagged bloody slash runs along the meat of Byron's palm, from little finger to wrist bone, but no one has mentioned it. The stain on the smashed plate makes sudden sense.

In the corner, Polidori is still nibbling at the same piece of toast. He points at his mouth, indicating that he can't talk while eating.

'Ah, you agree!' Byron smiles broadly. 'Jolly good. No need to rush your food – we'll wait.'

Polidori's eyes are wide and panicked. Mary can't help but feel sorry for the stuttering young doctor, who will be forced to read aloud his words in front of two of the most esteemed poets of his generation. His throat bobs as he tries to swallow, fails, then tries again. Massaging his neck, he says, 'It's not really finished . . .'

'No matter! Nor is mine and I am happy to tell you more of it. It is about a young acolyte, a sycophant, who follows a mysterious and wealthy lord on his travels. He finds himself entirely in thrall to the rich lord's dying requests. The wealthy lord is, of course, the bloodsucking creature I mentioned earlier. Now, the acolyte must bury the man, then dig him up at midnight. I suppose you can predict the hapless young fool's fate . . . But, still, I think something worse than death would have befallen him, had he disobeyed his superior's wishes.'

Byron grins wickedly. Again, Mary wonders what it must be like, to be able to say and do whatever you please, to push and mock and bully with no thought of reprisal.

'So,' Byron says to Polidori, 'I've told you mine. Now you show me yours.'

'I've mislaid the p-p-paper.'

'Not a p-p-problem. I recounted the main points of mine from memory. That's all we need, Polly – a flavour of your masterpiece.'

Polidori's chin trembles. He casts Mary a desperate glance, as if she might save him.

'Perhaps,' she says, 'Dr Polidori needn't tell us about his story until it is finished.'

'Nonsense! I expect to be trembling in my seat. Shelley is always ready to be rigid – with fear, of course! And you, Claire, if you are sure you are not too *fragile* in your *delicate* condition?'

Both Shelley and Claire nod wordlessly, as if their heads are attached by fine threads to Byron's bloodied hand.

A clacking from above. Mary looks up. The raven on the curtain rail is watching, always watching.

Silence, apart from the dim roll of distant thunder over the mountains beyond the lake. Mary has become used to judging the sounds of the storms: this one will arrive later tonight, in the full darkness of evening.

She keeps her gaze fixed on the window and the dim world outside as Polidori shifts, fidgets and clears his throat. 'It's . . . it's about a man,' he says. 'Or . . . p-p-perhaps a lady, a skull-headed lady.'

Byron sloshes more wine into his glass. 'Sounds *gripping*. Go on.'

'She is alone in . . . a dark house when she hears a . . . a noise from the room above her.'

'Fascinating. Do continue,' Byron says, leaning forward with what might now be genuine interest but Mary suspects is still mockery.

'And,' Polidori swallows, 'she reaches a door and looks through a keyhole and sees . . . Well, I haven't decided what she sees. But it is something so awful that she is rendered blind.'

'Blinded by a distressing sight!' Byron gasps. 'Might she have been peering through *your* keyhole, Polly, then been so disgusted that she plucked out her own eyeballs?'

Polidori turns away from Byron and looks directly at Mary – she can feel his eyes on her, though she doesn't stop gazing at the dark shadows of the wind-blown pines outside the window.

'It's about the dangers of spying, you see,' Polidori says more quietly, 'and how p-p-people might be p-punished for . . . for trying to trick others.'

'Ah!' Byron crows. 'Claire should pay careful note to that advice.'

Polidori looks defeated. His body is hunched, as if he is bracing himself for a physical blow. Slowly, Mary grasps that he doesn't care what Byron thinks, that he is ignoring Byron's crowing and teasing. He is looking only at her, waiting only for her. He is desperate for a sign that she has forgiven him for spying on her, for writing about her.

What can she say? His story sounds like a hackneyed, moralizing children's tale, aimed at teaching them not to pry or stare through keyholes. But Polidori has so clearly written it as an apology to her: *he* is the skull-faced woman, blinded as punishment for his trickery.

'It sounds like a dreadful retribution for spying,' Mary says. 'Especially when we don't know what the skull-headed lady actually saw.'

'Well,' Polidori says, 'she will never tell anyone.'

Byron drains his wine and claps slowly. '*That*, ladies and gentlemen, is an excellent example of a story in which the reader learns *less* by reading it. Bravo, Polly! The critics will love it. And I'm positively trembling with fear. Terrifying stuff!'

Polidori is still ignoring Byron, his gaze fixed on Mary. She inclines her head in a gesture that might not quite be forgiveness but must feel something like it to him, because he smiles. His whole face is transformed. 'Well,' he sighs, 'I feel quite relieved. I shall probably write something else, of course . . .'

'Oh, you *should*!' Byron exclaims. 'Take it up as a vocation! You'll wake up famous and rich beyond your wildest dreams, Polly.'

Again, Polidori doesn't react to Byron's ironic jibes but continues talking to Mary. 'As I was telling my tale, I felt that p-perhaps I needed to think more about my character. A skull-headed lady with no explanation isn't perhaps very frightening, but p-p-possibly if I wrote about someone who was cursed somehow, and they were able to p-pass on that curse to others . . . that might be more disturbing, don't you agree?'

Mary nods, thinking, dry-mouthed, about the curse she sometimes feels she's inherited – motherless daughter, daughterless mother, doomed for all around her to love her only half as much as they might.

'Now,' Byron says, 'you must have *some* idea of your story, Mrs S. I see you there, deep in thought.'

Clearly Polidori registers the alarm on her face because he takes a pipe from his pocket. 'You said you had planned an afternoon of smoking and dreaming, Byron. We are due an enormous storm later – those clouds over the mountains are spectacular.'

'A grand, theatrical performance,' Byron says. 'We should watch it in here together.'

Polidori lights the pipe and passes it to him. Byron inhales deeply, then coughs and laughs as he exhales and offers it to Shelley.

'I have my flask. But Mary might want . . .'

She reaches out, then pauses, remembering the night when she and Byron had drunk laudanum. He is thinking the same: something flares behind his eyes. He leans in close to her and whispers, his breath caressing her cheek. 'The only way you can escape this place,' Byron indicates the room and Shelley and Claire, who are huddled in the corner, his hand on her leg, 'the only way to get out of any place is to go *in*.' He points at his own temple, then at hers.

When she says she wants to go to her room to write, Byron follows her. She can feel him walking close behind; her nerves hum at the sensation of his eyes upon her and then, as she turns into his room, his hands around her waist.

He shuts the door, pushes her up against it, kissing her face, her mouth, her neck, her chest. And she kisses him back, as though by kissing his smooth skin, by stripping off his shirt and her dress and pressing her body to his, she might find a way to know him, to understand him, to understand herself.

Afterwards, he falls asleep. The far-off rumble of thunder keeps her awake and restless. She goes to his desk and, listening to his steady sleeping breaths, leafs through his papers.

> *as lovers who have parted*
> *In hate,*   *though broken-hearted:*
> *Though in their souls,*
>   *Love was the very root of the fond rage*
> *Which blighted their life's bloom, —war within themselves to wage . . .*

Her heart gallops. No reason to expect that he has written these lines about her – they have not parted in rage. And yet, if not about her, these fragments are about some other woman. She is *not* jealous. There was never any reason to think she had a claim on Byron's heart. What she is feeling is *not* jealousy. And yet . . .

And yet, *damn him*, he had made her feel possessed, hopeful, aching, *consumed* with desire for him, with hope for him. Damn him.

She picks up the piece of paper and its scraps of poetry, already folding it to slip beneath her dress, next to her skin. Then she sees the paper beneath.

~~My dearest Augusta =~~
~~Augusta, my love =~~
~~My heart – I was and am yours entirely =~~

A high-pitched note in her ears, her breath rough in her throat. She closes her eyes, her pulse thundering, bile rising and –

No.

She will not give him her fury. He never belonged to her. She could never have made a life with him. He is heartless and cruel. She does not love him, barely even likes him. The hollowness in her chest is nothing at all. She has lost nothing because how could she lose something she never had?

Her fingers do not itch with the urge to rip the page in half, to hurl it into the fire, to screw it into a tight ball and shove it into Byron's open mouth while he sleeps.

Hands shaking, she takes the aborted letter, lays it on his chest and walks unsteadily from the room.

Her own bedchamber is empty, her sheets still crumpled from last night's dreams, the desk still littered with open books and ink-stained paper, covered with mostly incoherent scrawl.

Deformity . . . a demon . . . a hideous wretch.

307

She picks up a crumpled page.

All men hate the wretched . . . followed by some other words she has scribbled out.

The torn-out leaves of her journal are stuffed back beneath her mattress. She kneels to pull them out. She will write about Byron – her rage, her betrayal, her envy. Then she will burn the page. As she watches his name flame to ash, she will try to forget she ever looked at him with longing.

She feels like a book written in a language that no one understands – a language she has long-since forgotten and must learn how to speak again.

'You truly haven't written anything of note,' a voice says behind her. She jumps and turns. Shelley is sitting on the floor behind the door, his knees pulled up to his chin, his gaze distant, his eyes red-rimmed. In his hands, more sheets of paper from the desk, crosshatched with discarded words.

'What are you doing in here?' Her heart is a trapped animal, battering the bars of its cage. What has he read? Is Byron's name on the papers? She can't remember. 'You scared me.'

He holds up a piece of paper. 'I thought you might have written *something.*'

'I said I hadn't thought of a story.'

'I know.' He runs his finger along the edge of the paper, then folds it carefully, neatly down the middle once, then again. 'But I hoped you might have written something about me. About us.'

So he'd been looking for her journal or a letter.

'Were you searching for a description of collapsed ruins then? A shipwreck, perhaps?'

'You're unhappy with me.'

'Ha!' The harsh burst of laughter surprises her. '*Unhappy* with you! I would not describe it so mildly.'

'How would you describe it?'

This is dangerous territory. He *knows* she is furious; he loathed her telling him so; perhaps he is hoping for forgiveness this time. At the thought of him asking for it, her rage boils higher.

A thin veneer of restraint stops her flying at him: part of her wants to claw through it. Part of her is terrified of what she will say, what she might do.

'How would *you* describe it, Shelley? You are bedding my sister. And you think I am *unhappy*?' She fights to keep her tone controlled but the rage licks dangerously around the edges of her bitten-off words. On the desk is a glass inkpot. She clutches it so hard her hand aches.

'I took Claire to bed *once*, Mary. And I have apologized for that –'

'You have not apologized! And *once*? I don't believe you.'

'Believe whatever you please. I haven't bedded her for years.'

'Not at *all* here?' she says, disbelieving. 'Not *once* in this house?'

He shakes his head. 'I have been giving her comfort – that is all.'

'And where was the *comfort* you gave me after baby Clara died? Where was the comfort when my father had cast me out of the house? You were away for *days*.'

'I was trying to resolve my debts.'

'You were running from the bailiffs and pursuing your own pleasure, while I was wretched and alone, with no one in the world to rely on for *comfort* – or food – except you.'

She is close to him now, close enough to see the flicker of guilt in his eyes. But just as soon as it appears, it fades.

'Pecksie.' His voice is soothing, placatory. 'This is all behind us now.'

'It is not behind me.'

'You must know how sorry I am.'

'You have not shown it.'

'I hate to see you so embittered by the past.'

'It is not the past! You spend all your time with her . . .'

'I want you to be happy, Pecksie.'

She laughs, incredulous. 'Why won't you listen to me? Do you hear a single word I say, Shelley? Do you hear *anything* but your own voice?'

'It is not like you at all, my sweet Pecksie, to be so full of rancour.'

'It *is* like me. This *is* me. You do not see it because you do not see me.'

'I do see you!' He rakes a hand through his hair in frustration. 'I understand.'

'Oh, *do* you? Do you think you understand?'

'Be calm.' His tone is more severe now.

'Do *not* tell me to be calm.'

'This is too much, Pecksie. I will not listen to such rancour from –'

'Shut up, shut *up*, Shelley!'

She flings the glass inkpot at his head. He doesn't have time to dodge or duck. It strikes his cheekbone, then shatters against the wall.

'Christ, Mary!' Shelley clutches his cheek, then looks at his fingers. 'Am I bleeding? Christ!'

Part of her is shaken by the rising bruise on Shelley's face, the black spatter of ink running down the wall, the shards of glass at their feet.

A larger part of her is awed by the awfulness of what she has done and wants more. An itch builds in her hands to tear down the curtains and smash the windows. She wants to upend her trunk of books and hurl every one of them at Shelley's face.

'I think I'm bleeding! What the bloody hell have you done, Pecksie?'

'You're not bleeding.'

Her voice sounds as though it is coming from a long way off – or perhaps from some deep darkness inside her.

The beginning is always today.

'I don't understand. Are you mad? This isn't like you.'

'It *is* like me,' she hisses, the fury still surging through her. 'This *is* me. You don't understand me.'

'I do! You are my sweet and kind and adoring Pecksie.'

'Stop calling me *Pecksie.*'

Silence. His face, watchful. Her fists, clenched.

'I don't understand,' he says again. 'What has happened to make you like this, my angel? You've changed so.'

'I haven't changed. You've never truly looked at me. You don't *know* me, Shelley. You've never even tried to know me.'

'I know you entirely.'

'No. You don't. You fell in love with the daughter of Godwin and Wollstonecraft – you told me so! You *told* me you fell in love with my genius, but you only ever wanted me to fawn on you and repeat your own thoughts back to you.'

'That's not true, my angel.'

'You *invented* a woman, and you called her Pecksie. My name is Mary Wollstonecraft Godwin, and I am *no one*'s angel.'

She watches her words sink in, watches his confusion turn to dread. *Good. Let him be afraid. Let him feel the agony of losing me.*

'And I did the same, Shelley. I fell in love with your clever ideas and your mind. But it's all hollow. It's a pretence. Just stories we told ourselves. Not a person to love.'

His face is rigid. She doesn't care. The satisfaction she is taking in his pain is wicked. She does not care. She revels in it. This is who she is. Perhaps it is who she has always been, or perhaps he made her this way, when he tried to turn her into a sweet, flawless idol. But within her, always, this shadow. She will not conceal it any longer.

Growl of thunder overhead: something in the shrouded skull of the world is shifting.

Shelley sinks onto the floor, as if his legs can no longer support him. When he leans against the wall, ink smears across his shoulders and through his hair. He seems not to notice.

'Is it this house?' he asks quietly. 'Is it . . . Byron?' His eyes flick up to hers, then away.

Terror lurks in the question – she can see what it has cost him to ask. For all his talk about *free love*, he has never truly wanted her to be with another man. He offered her freedom because he never believed her capable of taking it. Now he looks at her warily, as if she is a savage beast.

'Is it Byron?' he asks again.

Another snarl of thunder. A monstrous storm is building.

Almost, she tells him. The words sit on her tongue – loaded, waiting, like hot metal.

It is not fear that stops her, or pity – though she notes the tremor in his jaw, the shaking of his clasped hands, the way he looks smaller than he had an hour ago.

If she tells him about Byron, he will turn it into something about himself. He'll make it into an act of deception or betrayal – he will flaunt the *honesty* he has always claimed to show her, the *freedom* he has always pretended to grant her. He will say something like *If you had just told me, Pecksie, I might have given you my blessing.*

He will remind her that he never truly attempted to hide his relationship with Claire. He will say, again, that Mary had known all along. She must have.

Mary doesn't want to talk about her sister.

What Mary has with Byron – the way she feels about him, with all its knots and fractures and splintered longing – belongs to her. The secret of it exists between them and within her body. It is a cascade of sparks that fires her veins, flowing through her limbs. The illumination of it sits alongside the darkness inside her. Together they are power.

There will be a time to tell Shelley. But not yet. He is staring at her as if he has never seen her before – and he hasn't. Not truly.

'It's not Byron.' She'd always thought that lying about such a betrayal would be impossible. The words slide easily from her tongue.

Relief floods Shelley's face; the pressure in the room eases. 'I am sorry,' he says softly.

She takes a breath to say that his apology changes nothing – it's only a word, after all – but he speaks again.

'I didn't intend to hurt you, Peck— *Mary*. I'm sorry.' He pauses. 'I . . . I fetched Willmouse and Élise from the little Maison Chapuis earlier. I thought they would be safer here. I thought you would want to see him but would be too nervous of the storm to go out yourself.' Clutching his reddened cheek still, he looks pitiful.

But it is the tiny correction in her name, and that he has thought to fetch their child, that softens her a little, makes her believe him.

A crack of thunder overhead. A flash of white light scours the room and makes them jump. They share a nervous smile.

'I see you can't forgive me now, but perhaps in time, I can hope . . .?'

He wants to hear her say she *does* forgive him, or that she is sorry too. And she understands: perhaps everyone feels this desperate desire to know they are not alone.

You have been heard and understood. You are still loved.

But it is too early for absolution. Too soon to know what she feels for him. And she will not pretend. Not any more. Instead, she says, 'Will you come and watch the lightning over the lake?' She can give him this – a tiny glimmer of connection.

His tentative smile broadens. He follows her from the room.

18

If I cannot inspire love, I will cause fear.

Back in the drawing room, everyone is more sober. Mary has been to see Willmouse, who is sleeping in one of the small rooms, alongside Élise. She was glad when he didn't wake to greet her – she doesn't know how to reconcile the person she is becoming with the mother she has been. There will be time for that, time in the weeks ahead for her to find a way to be free and fierce, and also a tender mother.

The drawing room is almost entirely dark, lit only by candles, which flicker as the wind pulses against the windows and whines down the chimney. In the air, a metallic smell warns of the coming storm and also reminds her of Skinner Street: the carcasses on the butcher's block, or swinging in the breeze, dripping thick blood onto wet cobbles.

Shelley is sitting by the window, with Polidori and Byron. Mary wonders if they will notice his bruised cheek, if he will tell them what she did.

And what if he does? whispers the new voice inside her – which is also an old voice, the voice that has always belonged to her, though she has ignored it and smothered it.

Even as she realizes that the dim candlelight hides his pain and conceals the bruise, she knows that it doesn't matter: some actions change everything. In the past, this thought has frozen her, silenced and stilled her. Now she is ready for the consequences, whatever they may be.

'Come, sit here with us,' Byron calls. At his feet, as so often, the enormous dog. In his lap, a black cat Mary hasn't seen before. It gazes at her with bright green eyes, then blinks, implacable. Byron scratches behind its ears. 'No need to squat with the riffraff.'

It is then that Mary notices Claire, alone on the opposite side of the room, huddled in the corner of the sofa, as though she has been banished. Near the window, a fourth seat is ready for Mary, positioned between Shelley and Byron. 'Join us. We're having a fascinating discussion about the creative spark within storms.'

For a moment, she imagines sitting alongside Byron, imagines forgetting about his letters to Augusta. She can make herself ignore the truth, if she tries. His body in the seat next to hers, his leg inches from hers – the energy that flows between them, without words. The constant undertow of desire.

But then she sees the anticipation on their faces – Byron, Shelley and Polidori, all gazing at her expectantly, all longing to show off their ideas, all waiting to be impressed by her *genius*.

She doesn't want to do it, doesn't want to be the rational intellectual, stating theories about the storm. The dark presence she has felt stirring in her since she entered this house does not want to sit and listen to the men, while she waits her turn to display her intelligence.

She wants to sit within the shadow of the storm outside and the storm within her. She wants to feel its rage stirring like fire within her veins, flickering like lightning across her skin.

'I'll stay here.' Mary takes a seat on the sofa in the centre of the room. As she sits, she surprises herself by beckoning to her sister. 'Come – sit with me.'

Claire hesitates, her expression wary.

Between them lurks the memory of one sister's betrayal and the other's attack. Between them, twin spectres of retribution and revenge.

Claire uncurls from her own sofa and perches awkwardly, nervously on Mary's.

For a moment, Mary feels the words gathering, *I've been to bed with Byron*. She pictures the shock on her sister's face, the hurt, the despair, feels her own sense of satisfaction. Is this why she has called her over?

The men are watching, waiting, as if the two sisters are part of the spectacle, part of the storm to be viewed and unpicked and understood. As if love, anger and pain can be tallied, like beads on an abacus.

When she looks at her sister, Mary sees Claire's pain afresh. Not the screams that the family have always dismissed as tantrums, not her petty accusations or the barbed remarks that stem from her jealousy. Claire's anger, like Mary's, is an outcast beast, a shadow born of her need to be seen and loved, her need to belong.

Deliberately, Mary turns her face so that the men can't see what she is saying, pitches her voice low so they can't hear. 'You needn't allow yourself to be cut off from everybody.'

'That's not what I'm doing,' Claire snaps. She swallows and, looking at Mary's ink-stained hands, says, more softly, 'You've been writing. Is it your story?'

'My journal. I can't write the story. My words come out an ugly mess.'

Claire rolls her eyes. 'Not everything has to be *poetry*, Mary.'

It is something she would never dare say to Shelley or Byron and the disdain is so typical, so very *Claire* that Mary can't help smiling. She lays her head on her sister's shoulder and puts her hand, gently, on the barely perceptible swell of Claire's stomach.

'I'll look after you,' she says. Because even if she can't forgive her sister, not fully, or trust her, Mary knows her desperation. She has felt the dark, smothering weight of it so many times herself.

'Thank you.' Claire puts her arm around Mary's shoulders. They lean against each other, perfectly still as the storm begins.

Thunder rolls over the mountains and lightning sketches across the sky. It pulses and flares in electric flashes, flickering in jagged single lines from the dark clouds to the lake, or forking into a web of light that could be the branches of a tree or its pattern of reaching roots. A monstrous bellow reverberates through the vault of the sky like the anguished howl of a primal being – some creature that is impossibly old and yet startlingly new as it roars into life.

No one in the room says a word, their faces illuminated by the constant blue-white bursts of energy. Mary can feel the crackle of it, can feel the hairs on her arms and scalp rising, as if whatever force is in the sky is reaching out to pluck at every nerve in her body. Her heartbeat feels hollow, fragile – a tiny animal barely daring to move in the presence of its god.

The wind gusts and gulps around the house, around the trees in the waterlogged garden, whipping the branches into a demented gavotte. They thrash and contort, bending at impossible angles before snapping and being hauled high into the air, then crashing down.

Something heavy smashes onto the roof. Everyone starts – even Byron looks unnerved.

'The house is safe, is it not, Albe?' There is a telltale tremor in Shelley's voice.

'It has stood for the past hundred years. I am sure we have nothing to fear.' He doesn't sound sure.

The next gust sends a loose branch thudding into the wall beside the window. The cat startles awake, hissing.

Claire gives a strangled cry. 'Come away from the glass,' she begs.

The men ignore her, staring in rapture at the darkening chaos.

'It makes you wonder at the force behind all of this, doesn't it?' Even Byron cannot keep the awe from his voice. 'Not God, of course – something else. Whatever impulse it is that gives everything life. How could we harness that?'

Another crash.

'*Please* come away from the window,' Claire begs.

The cat bolts from Byron's lap with another hiss and dives behind the curtains.

Mary presses her hand against her chest. It isn't her will alone that keeps her heart thudding onwards. If anyone could harness the power of life, then surely a grief-racked mother, cradling the body of her dead child by the fire, could channel a spark like the lightning overhead.

She remembers Robert Crosse's lectures on electricity. He talked of how he'd directed lightning through copper wire. Mary had sat next to her father, her mouth open in wonder that energy could be drawn from the sky and used.

'It's magnificent,' Byron says. 'Of course, you've heard of Dr Darwin's experiments to give life to dead *vorticellae*?'

Shelley nods.

The dog rises from next to Byron's feet, a growl rumbling in its chest.

'And you've been to Galvani's nephew's lectures?' Byron asks.

'Aldini and his frogs? Of course.'

Nearly everyone Mary knew had attended Aldini's talks – had watched him touch wires to a frog's severed legs and then, through means of an electrical spark, make them twitch and jump, as though the creature were still alive.

'Ah, but did you hear about his experiments on that hanged convict? Apparently, he made the dead fellow blink and grimace and move his arms and legs about. He said that, with enough electricity, he could bring a man back to life.'

'Perhaps,' Shelley says doubtfully.

The dog snarls, hackles on its back rising. It is staring out of the window, as if it senses something lurking in the storm – the same presence that lifts the hairs on Mary's arms and on the back of her neck.

'Well, look at the power of this storm,' Byron says. 'Aldini used metals and rods to produce just a small spark and that was enough to make a man's leg move. Surely with something like this lightning, a dead man could be reanimated.'

Something else must be involved, Mary thinks, not just electricity. If a bolt of lightning hits a man, it will surely kill him. How, then, could a huge storm like this give life back to a man, without snuffing him out?

Again, she remembers baby Clara. How cold and still and final death had felt in her hands. 'I don't think it would work,' she says. 'There must be something more to it.'

The men ignore her and talk on. How can Shelley have these arguments about death without thinking of Clara?

The memory is so overwhelming that she is unable to join in with the rest of the conversation, while wind and rain still batter against the glass and the dog whines and growls, the rumble of its discontent blurring with the roar of the storm.

Byron, Shelley and Polidori argue about how a corpse could possibly be made to walk, move and speak – whether it would have to learn language again, whether it would retain the memories of the dead man or have to forge new ones.

How would it learn morality? Would it have a sense of beauty? Would it feel love, hatred or fury?

Mary wants them to stop, wants space for her own thoughts, but the men's words are like the wind and the rain, whirling and crashing and re-forming the world.

The thunder is directly overhead now. Flashes of lightning web the sky with skeins of electric veins. Mary feels every reverberation echoing through her bones, her blood. She feels both impossibly small and inconceivably powerful – as if she is part of the storm. Or as if, for a short time on this electric night, her fragile body has ceased to matter. Something larger is surging through her – some inarticulate roar, like the anguished howl of a primitive creature, desperate for life.

A crash. The dog barks, lips pulled back from its huge teeth.

She cries out. At the same time, the wind hurls a huge black branch at one of the windows. Someone screams – perhaps it is Claire or perhaps the sound is coming from Mary's own mouth.

Another branch hits the window. The glass shatters.

Byron shouts. Claire shrieks. Mary throws herself to the floor. Wind blasts into the room, flinging shards of glass and chunks of wood over the furniture, against the walls. From deep within the house, there is an animal screech. The dog roars, then whimpers and cowers.

Willmouse! Mary wills him to be safe, every part of her being begging the bellowing world, and whatever monstrous spirit breathes within it, to let her child live.

Mary hears Polidori yell. He has dragged open a door into the study and is beckoning everyone towards it. They crouch and creep forward, shielding their faces with up-flung arms. Claire crawls on her hands and knees. But to reach the door, Mary would have to stand, would have to dash around the sofa and the chair to the other side of the room. She is closer to the door that would lead back to her own room, would lead her to the room where Élise is, with her child. But she would have to go alone.

'Mary!' Byron shouts, waving her towards the study. And she is about to do it, about to stand, when the other window smashes. Glass scythes through the air and shatters against the far wall. If Mary had been standing at that moment, the shards of glass would have embedded in her face, her neck, her chest.

She isn't aware of deciding to crawl towards the closer door, leading to her room, but suddenly she is there, she is through it, in the corridor, alone. She slams the door on the maelstrom, leaning against the wood, gasping as if she has been running.

Her left hand throbs; she lifts it to look. A bloodied sliver of glass is embedded in her skin. She pulls it out and puts her mouth to her palm, driven by some ancient atavistic instinct that doesn't flinch from the sour metallic heat of blood and tells her to rip the sleeve from her dress to bind it tightly. There is no pain, not yet.

She runs along the hallway until she reaches the room where Willmouse should be safely with Élise. Outside the door, she pauses, remembering Clara. That poor, cold little body. What will she do if the storm has harmed her child? She couldn't go on.

And yet she would, just as she had after Clara's death. Her stubborn heart would drive her onwards, one broken beat at a time.

The beginning is always today.

She pushes open the door, preparing herself. Élise sits up in her bed.

Next to her, Willmouse stirs and grizzles.

'Madame?' Élise's face is shocked. Mary catches a glimpse of a wild-haired stranger in the mirror: her dress is soaked, her skin slick with rain.

'Is he safe? Is he well?'

'He is. But you are bleeding!' Élise exclaims.

'It's nothing.' The wound has started to ache. 'Stay in this room, please, where it's sheltered. Promise you won't come out.'

She kisses her sleeping child's forehead, smearing crimson blood and dirt across his skin. Élise recoils.

How monstrous I must look.

Nothing like a good, caring mother. Nothing like Élise, who brushes the dirt from Willmouse's forehead with her smooth, clean hands.

Mary stumbles back to her room, the shock of the storm still pulsing through her. Byron, Shelley, Claire and Polidori must be safely in the study.

No way for her to reach them. No way she could help them in any case.

Her room will be storm-wrecked. She prepares herself for the mess of glass and rain-drenched papers, the mass of broken wood and scattered leaves across her bed.

When she finds her room exactly as she had left it, untouched by the storm, she has the uncanny feeling that she is dreaming. A mad thought: she has been killed by the flying glass. She is a ghost, doomed to haunt this house for ever.

The wound in her hand throbs with every beat of her living heart.

This room must be sheltered by its position: the sounds of the storm are less brutal here. The roaring, howling beast that had raged around the drawing room has become a high-pitched keening spirit, which batters grubby fists against her small window, rattling it in its frame.

Trembling, she lies on the bed. She feels raw, every nerve exposed. Each time a pulse of lightning flashes across the sky, she startles.

Promethean fire.

She puts her hands over her eyes and presses her thumbs to her ears, trying to block out the storm. Across the darkness of her eyelids, she sees the rivers and branches of her veins.

When she removes her hands and opens her eyes, the same pattern is stamped across the sky: streak after luminescent streak of electrical webbing scudding across the heavens, its rhythm pounding and growling as though it truly has a life force of its own.

She is at the centre of an enormous heart, the grey clouds of its flesh lighting up with each beat, its veins and arteries scratched out in fierce light.

Half awake, she counts her breaths, places one hand on her chest, the other on her forehead. She is holding life. There is some force beneath her hands that she doesn't understand.

She isn't dreaming. Her eyes are shut, she is sure of it, yet she sees a pale stranger in her room. How has he appeared here?

Leave, she says, but no word emerges.

The pale man kneels at her writing table. The paper has gone. The table has become an altar. There is something huge upon it, something half covered with a sheet.

The pale man, she knows suddenly, as if she has been introduced to him, is a student. A scientist by training, he has become more and more enamoured of the dark arts, the occult secrets of the universe. He has been feverishly working on a creation for months. Now he waits, breathless, to see the result of his labours.

Not here, she thinks. *I don't want to see.*

He pulls the sheet to one side. Mary wants to look away but cannot.

Stretched out on the table, like some hideous half man, half beast, is an enormous body. Perhaps a collection of bodies. The huge form is covered with welts and gashes. The scientist has stolen creatures from charnel houses and bodies from a graveyard and – *oh, God* – he has stitched them together.

He has made an enormous body from corpses.

He kneels before his grisly creation in an act of devout worship.

As Mary continues to stare, transfixed, some strange force works upon the creature on the table. It is almost as if a powerful engine has gripped its limbs. The awful thing begins to stir in an uneasy, jolting motion. It lifts first one arm, then the other. It flexes great, misshapen fingers.

As it moves, its joints – so recently dead – crackle and grate, bone on bone.

Its creator recoils in horror – in revulsion at the thing he has brought forth. He is filled with sudden fear at the terrible implications of his act. He has twisted death upon itself, has hunted it down to its source and killed it. He has not only created life, he has murdered death, has unravelled the fabric of nature.

The pale young man backs away from the creature. Left to itself, it must die. The spark of life he has ignited will be quenched. The cold silence of the grave will creep back into those heavy limbs. Death will still that great skull. Silence will crawl inside that beating brain.

Behind her own closed eyelids, Mary watches. The young scientist who has devoted himself to dismantling the mystery of life, lies down upon his curtained bed and sleeps.

A sudden thud shocks him awake.

His eyes open. Alert and fearful, he searches for the source of the sound. Nothing.

Only the stillness of the tightly drawn curtains around his bed.

He sits up but can see nothing, hear nothing, except the ragged gasp of his own breath.

A rustling behind him.

He turns and howls in panic. The terrible, monstrous *thing* he has created is looming over his bed. It holds back his curtain and stares at him with rheumy, brooding, yellowish eyes. It reaches out with enormous fingers, grasping for his face –

'No!'

Mary jolts upright, scrabbling back so that she is sitting up, staring at her unmoving bed curtains.

Her breath is tight in her chest, as though a huge hand is compressing her ribcage, squeezing her struggling heart.

Oh, God, it is the monstrous hand she'd seen in her dream. But it had not been a dream: she had been wide awake, she knows it. The grotesque creature is alive. It has a mind and will of its own. It will crush the spirit out of any man, woman or child.

It is watching her. If she tries to move, it will smash her brittle body into the wall.

Mary presses shaking hands to her eyes, hoping to erase the horrid image. Outside, the thunder roils and rolls. Her mouth is dry, her mind whirling. She will not sleep again.

Gingerly, fearfully, she pulls back the curtain from around her bed.

The flickering light from the pulsing sky illuminates her small room. Though she barely dares to look at her desk, there is no hideous body upon it – no dreadful creature, mis-shapen, misbegotten. Only her quill and a pile of paper wait, ink-smudged and crumpled.

She eases out of bed, shivering when her feet touch the

marble, and pads her way to the desk. Still glancing over her shoulder, she sits in the chair and finds the least creased piece of paper.

Trembling, teeth chattering, she begins to write:

It was on a dreary night of November that I beheld ~~the fiend on which~~ my man completed. ~~and.~~ With an anxiety that almost amounted to agony, I collected instruments of life around me and endeavoured to ~~that I might~~ infuse a spark of being into the lifeless thing that lay at my feet . . .

19

What can stop the determined heart and resolved will of man?

All that night and into the next morning, Mary writes. She wraps the sheets around her but still she shivers. Her toes are numb, her hand cramps. Beneath the ragged makeshift bandage, the wound on her palm throbs.

Occasionally she pauses to blow on the fingers of her writing hand, her breath ghosting in the chilled air. Even in these moments when she has laid down her quill, her mind is still working, circling around the story of the creature and its creator.

What awful, selfish ambition would drive a man to create a living being? What sort of calculating arrogance would lead an intelligent man to try to craft something perfect and beautiful, without ever acknowledging that his own concept of beauty and perfection was flawed? And what kind of brutality would lead him to shun the thing he had made?

How would it ever be possible to abandon the being you have created?

She thinks of Shelley's disappointment in her. She thinks of her father, shutting the door in her face as she wept. She pictures the pitiful, rejected creature, longing for affection, yearning for understanding. The roar of the storm raging outside becomes its desperate, aching howl. Still, the poor wretch's creator does not hear it.

When Mary imagines that barred threshold, closing her

eyes, it is the slammed door of Skinner Street she sees. The key rasps as it turns. The lock *thunks*, like a nail in a coffin. She presses her hands against the dead wood. On the other side is her living, breathing father.

Strange to know that the safety of an embrace is less than a finger's width away, yet also beyond reach, unless she crawls on hands and knees repenting. Unless she denies everything she is – everything her father has made her.

He had raised her to think for herself, to speak her mind, to question and to analyse. Yet once she embodied this spirit of independence, he found her hideous and shameful.

As she writes, it becomes easier to place herself inside the poor creature's skin, deep within the longing of his tortured mind. The thing labelled *fiend* and *devil* by his creator will love beauty and poetry and nature. Alone and abandoned, he will teach himself to read. He will long for the company of humans. Unseen and unthanked, he will plough their fields, clear their weeds and carry their logs. They will fear him; they will be repulsed by the sight of him. They will cast him out into the wilderness.

When he speaks, it will be with anguish for the way he is loathed. *All men hate the wretched; how, then, must I be hated, who am miserable beyond all living things!*

Her fiend, her monster, will use the language of poets – the language of Milton, whose shadow haunts this very house. Mary's creature will have all the capacity for kindness and generosity that may reside in the human soul. Human rejection and hatred will twist his gentle spirit until he becomes a vengeful demon.

As the candle gutters, Mary's eyes itch and burn with exhaustion; her head begins to droop. Every time her thoughts drift into sleep, she sees the wide, watery eyes of the creature, hears his desolate cry.

Shocked back to wakefulness, she writes on.

At some point, she must have fallen into a deeper sleep, still at her desk, her head pillowed on her hand, because she wakes to Shelley embracing her in the light of dawn.

'My love!' he says. 'Were you injured? I've been so worried, but it was too dangerous to come to you. My God, your hand!'

'I'm well,' she says. 'Are you hurt? Or anyone else? Oh! I must see Willmouse again.'

'He is still asleep.'

'You went to him?'

'You sound surprised.'

'I am.' Even two days ago, she might have denied it, but she will not pretend any more. 'And is Byron –?'

'He is well.' Shelley's expression shifts. There is something frightened behind his eyes.

'Shelley, I must tell you something.'

'Have you been writing?' His gaze is that of a drowning man.

'I must tell you that Byron –'

'Oh, is it your ghost story?' His voice is desperate. He looks from her face to the papers on the desk. 'May I read it?'

'It's not finished. It's barely started.'

'No matter. I'm sure you will have written something wonderful.'

He reaches for the papers; she grasps his hand between her ink-stained fingers and her bloodstained bandage. A bolt of pain shoots up her arm. She ignores it.

'Listen to me, Shelley. I want to tell you –'

'I do not want to know.' He speaks so fast and so low that she thinks she might have misheard him. 'I do not want to hear it. I have been a fool, Mary. A damned fool. I thought I didn't believe in ownership. But thinking about you and –'

Mary realizes he can't even bring himself to say Byron's name. 'You are *jealous*,' she says wonderingly. And the jolt of surprised pleasure this gives her is strange. She'd convinced herself that she no longer cared what he thought. But he is jealous and wounded, rather than angry.

He loves me still.

'Can I see your story? Please.'

Silence. She could say no. She could demand that they talk about Byron this minute. He waits, eyes wide with entreaty.

Drawing a deep, unsteady breath, she leafs through the papers and gives him the first page.

Letting go of it feels, briefly, like letting him rip apart the cut on her hand. Or as if she were to slice herself open, from collarbone to navel, and allow him to pluck out her bloodied heart to weigh it.

While he reads, she walks over to the bed and lies face down, breathing into the pillows. The idea is so fragile – she can still feel the faint glint of its gossamer thread at the edge of her exhausted mind. If Shelley criticizes or questions it, the gleaming filament might dissolve.

She hears him lay down the papers, hears him clear his throat and braces herself for his criticism. The work is good, she thinks, she hopes . . . She feels the power of the creature she is creating – physically *feels*, deep in her belly, the electricity of his fury, his longing, his loneliness.

'It's *magnificent*,' Shelley breathes.

'Really?' Her heart lifts.

'Truly.' He picks up her quill. 'Although I do think that *here*, you could describe the vile creature in more passionate terms. You call him *wretch*. I think *devil* has more power.'

'But don't you see? The poor creature is *not* a devil. He is misunderstood and abused.'

She moves from the bed to read over his shoulder. Standing

behind him, she is acutely aware of her thighs against his back. He doesn't turn but leans against her, puts his hand on her leg. She feels, very faintly, the stirrings of desire.

It exists between them still, she sees, the intellectual sparring that she thought had faded, the excitement at challenging each other.

'Here,' Shelley says, pointing to a separate note at the bottom of the page, 'where you have written, *I do not wish to hate you*, should Dr Frankenstein not say, *I will not be tempted to set myself in opposition to thee?*'

Mary laughs. 'No!'

'Why? What is it?'

'I didn't write that for Dr Frankenstein.'

'For the creature, then?'

'Very likely, now. But actually . . . I wrote it about you.'

He blinks, and she glimpses his hurt outrage, as when she had flung the ink bottle at his head. Then she sees him take a breath. Something passes over his face – a wonder and delight she hasn't seen in his eyes for years.

'About me?'

She nods. And then she says it. 'I do not wish to hate you.'

His mouth lifts. He smiles, starts to chuckle. Then they are leaning against one another, laughing as if they will never stop, just as they used to.

Can it truly be so simple to recapture everything she thought was lost?

'Is something wrong, Mary? You look –'

'Nothing is wrong. Well, nothing *new*.'

'Then what is it?' he asks, gazing intently at her face, his expression worried.

'This,' she says, smiling.

'What about it?'

'It feels . . . hopeful.'

Without waiting for his response, she picks up her quill and begins to write.

When she next becomes aware of her surroundings, it is later in the day and Shelley has gone. She has been writing for hours. The room is full of the dull grey light that has punctuated their time in this house.

She stands and stretches – she feels drained but lighter than she has in years, or perhaps ever. Washing herself in front of the small mirror, she peers at her hollow face, the shadows like bruises beneath her eyes, the tracks of dried ink across her cheeks. Her hair is wild. She laughs. It is a little like looking at her face after she has had too much wine, or after she has drunk laudanum: the features are familiar yet strange.

Her dress from yesterday is still where she left it, draped over the bed, the material a little creased from Shelley's embrace.

She pulls it on, immersed in thoughts of the creature in her story. It is only as she goes to leave the room that she remembers to put on stockings and shoes and that the reason her dress doesn't quite fit her is that it is on back to front. Straightening her clothes, she laughs again. She feels buoyant, giddy, euphoric.

The door to the drawing room is shut and she doesn't want to peer into it and see the devastation wrought by the storm.

Voices from the dining room. Though she is reluctant to be drawn from her reverie, she can't avoid all company for the rest of their time here. Before she has reached the room, she sees Polidori, who is leaning against the door frame, watching the hallway. His face lights up at the sight of her. 'Miss Godwin! Let me help you. I heard you injured your hand in the storm.'

Polidori rushes forward, arm held out ready to support her.

As he steps through the door, the rug slips from under his foot. He stumbles, then falls, rolling down the stairs. His ankle gives an awful *crack*. He lands in a tangle of limbs at Mary's feet.

'Oh, forgive me, I –' He tries to stand but his ankle gives way. He groans in pain.

'Mr Polidori, let me help *you*. Here.' She holds out her un-injured hand. He hesitates, then accepts it, heaving himself to his feet. His face is grey as he leans against the wall in the hallway.

A chuckle from the door. Mary looks up to see Byron watching. In spite of his laughter, his expression is grim.

'Poor Polly! Good job you have a lady to rush to your aid.'

'I thought you didn't *want* to behave like an ass,' Mary snaps. 'And my hand has stopped bleeding – how kind of you to ask.' The words are out before she has thought them. She doesn't wait to see Byron's response.

'Here, sit.' Mary guides Polidori away from the dining room, helping him to an oak chest.

Wincing, he pulls up his trouser leg and examines his ankle, which is already bluish and puffy. The breath hisses from between his teeth as he prods at it and, gingerly, rotates the joint.

'A sprain, I think, not a break. At least, I hope not. Still, I will need to bandage it. My case is in my room.'

He starts to rise. Mary stops him. 'I'll fetch it.'

'I would rather – if you wouldn't mind. Could you help me to my room?'

She can see the strain of Byron's mockery in the tension around Polidori's eyes and she understands his need to be away from judgement.

His room, next to Byron's, is far smaller than any of the other bedrooms. It is also meticulously tidy: were it not for

Polidori's trunk and medical case in the corner, Mary would think it unoccupied. What has happened to this kind, clever man to make him take up so little space in the world?

He sits on the single chair next to the bed. Mary finds the bandages in his medical case, then stands, watching awkwardly, as he binds his ankle. His pained expression and strangled gasps seem, in this room, too intimate.

So that she doesn't have to look at him, she pours a glass of water.

While he is drinking, she can feel his gaze on her face.

'I do not know if we will be alone again, Miss Godwin, and while p-propriety tells me that I should stay silent, my soul commands me to speak.'

She feels a sense of dread at what he will say. She wants him to stop talking but can't find the words to silence him without being brutal.

As he continues, his speech sounds smoothly rehearsed – he barely stumbles or stutters but he also cannot meet her gaze. 'I know your – attachment – with Mr Shelley is unusual in that it grants both of you some . . . freedom. Though I dare not hope that you recip-reciprocate my feelings, I must take this opportunity to tell you that, since our first introduc tion, I have no longer been master of my own heart. Your wit, your fearless nature and your beauty have enslaved it. I have never encountered a woman such as you and I do not believe another exists in this world. I am, Miss Godwin, most tenderly devoted to you. While I dare not consider my own merits anything against yours, p-please trust that I offer you my hand and my heart, my hopes and my future. All that I am, all that I can ever be, is yours.'

When he first started speaking, Mary's embarrassment and sense of pity for the poor man had been agonizing. Now, seeing the adoration in his earnest brown eyes, she feels only admiration for the bravery it has taken to bare his heart to her. She draws a slow breath. 'I think you very courageous, Mr Polidori, but –'

'Ah! I will beg you not to continue. I fear one more word from you will shatter my hopes for ever.'

'I wish I could return your feelings.' As she speaks, she realizes it is true. Her life with this sweet, kind, gentle man would be quiet and contented. She would know that he loved her entirely, without reservation or restraint. And she would feel just as confined as she has done with Shelley. The bars of her prison would be the soft trappings of wealthy domesticity. Mary would want for nothing, save the freedom of her heart – the freedom to be, sometimes, her darkest self.

She continues: 'You are a good, kind man. I wish I could return your love, truly.'

'You cannot? Even in time? I would leave Lord Byron, of course – or not, if you wanted to stay, if you still wanted to . . . *see* him or Shelley.' His mouth trembles and she sees the force of his longing: he would do anything for her, would permit her anything.

'The attachment I feel for you is that of friendship,' she says gently.

She watches her words sink in, watches him blink.

'Do you think it could become something more? Do not answer me now. Only p-promise me that you will think upon it. P-please?'

She nods.

'You've started writing your story.' It's not a question. He has been watching her so closely. He is so attentive.

'I have.' She isn't ready to talk about it.

He must sense this, because he rushes on: 'I have started mine too. It is about a rich lord who seduces those around him, then feeds upon them, sucking the blood from their bodies. I am sure you can deduce my inspiration. I am calling it *The Vampyre*.'

'It sounds terrifying.' They share a smile.

As he passes her the opening pages to read, he says very quietly, 'I will not stop hoping for your heart to change.'

She doesn't look up from his story. 'Neither will I.'

As she walks from Polidori's room, Byron's door opens. Before she can react, he takes her wrist and pulls her inside.

'You're becoming harder to catch.' He runs tender fingers over her bandaged hand. 'Does it hurt?'

'Not too much. I thought it best to avoid being alone with you.'

'Because of my letter to Augusta.' There is none of the usual irony in his tone, no trace of his smooth social nonchalance or the feigned mockery he puts on in front of others. His eyes are large and troubled. He looks . . . *pained.*

'You're in love with her.' She is not being fair. They have made no promises to each other. She doesn't want to feel anything for him except the hum of desire, the longing for his body, yet she feels so betrayed by his letter, by his scraps of bitter poetry about doomed love.

'My feelings for her are none of your concern.'

'I see that.'

'Is it that she is my sister? Or that I have feelings for her at all?'

Both, Mary thinks.

'She's my half-sister and we didn't meet until we were adults. Does that console you?'

'But the date on the letter. You wrote it after we . . .'

'Christ, Mary, what do you want me to say? Would it please you to hear me confess that I wanted to write to her *about* you but could not summon the language to describe it? *I have no*

338

words, Mary. I cannot say what you are, what you have meant to me. Would you rather I renounced her entirely? Would you like me to say that I long for her death, to claim that I wish I had never met her?'

'Don't mock me. There's no need for you to be melodramatic and cruel.'

'I am not mocking you! I have thought *all* these things, Mary, devil that I am. I have sometimes wished my own sister dead because I cannot help but love her. She is the only woman in the world who has ever come close to understanding me. Until you. Until this.'

Mary tries to speak. No sound emerges. She tries to swallow but her mouth is dry.

He steps close enough for her to touch him. It is suddenly harder to breathe, harder to meet his gaze, the longing in his eyes, which makes her think of his hands upon her, but also of the flames that could rise up and scorch everything to dead ash.

He presses himself to her and she to him. No darkness between them, no shadows, no secrets. She sees what he might be to her now: he summons a desire and a love in her so consuming that it erases everything else. It is intoxicating and terrifying. Briefly, she is his and his alone.

Later, she is watching him sleep, the gentle rise and fall of his chest, when he speaks: 'My father used to throw things at me. He'd chase me around, try to catch me and then beat me. I hated him, of course. But I loved him too.'

His eyes are closed. His voice is soft, almost a whisper, as if he is speaking to himself. She holds her breath and listens.

'Mad Jack, they called him. I was glad when he tried to cut his throat, then died in an asylum. My mother was just as bad in her way. Violence, madness, death haunted me. Or

I thought so for a long time. I was frightened of how their shadow hung over me. You understand?'

She nods, and although he still hasn't opened his eyes, he must know that she understands. She thinks of the hard slap of Mrs Godwin's hand; her father's expectations and disappointment. The scars on her arm; her banishment. Mary thought she'd hidden her pain so well, but Byron must have seen it, must recognize the shadow of fear in her: the broken, beaten child in him reaching out to the small, furious child in her.

He continues: 'I was frightened and angry for a long time, drowning in a pit, I thought.' He opens his eyes, stares at her. His expression is vulnerable and exposed, as though he is letting her see him, as though he sees her.

'But you must understand this, Mary. Fear is a horse you can hitch a cart to. You can put a bridle on terror, clamp its jaws around the bit and drive that panicked creature over land you would have never travelled, had you always felt safe and loved. Do you see? This pain you feel,' he places his warm hand above her heart, 'you can use it.'

She nods and kisses him. She does see. And as her lips travel down his chest, over his belly, she thinks of the fear and anger that brought her to him. She wouldn't change any of it.

Afterwards she sleeps curled into him. When she wakes from the grip of another nightmare, faces twisting in the dark, she sits up, heart thumping.

You can use it.

She kisses his shoulder, inhales the scent of his skin and returns to her room, to her quill, to the monster in her mind.

20

I was benevolent and good; misery made me a fiend.
Make me happy and I shall again be virtuous.

The way her story grips her is unlike anything else: it wakes her in the grainy dawn light to hunch over the little desk in her room, fingers ink-blackened, hand aching. It pulls her from the heat of Byron's bed, from the comforting weight of his strong arms, wrapped around her while he sleeps, into the frozen isolation of her own room, into page after blank page, which she must fill with the creature's terror, his fury, his loneliness.

It is late afternoon by the time she comes back to herself, by the time her stomach growls because she hasn't eaten all day. More importantly, she hasn't fed Willmouse. Her breasts ache; she regrets letting Élise give him so much goat's milk.

Guiltily, she hurries along the hallway to his room but finds him perfectly content, beaming gummily at Élise. Mary expects her to be sullen because she's been ignored but the girl smiles and says that she has fetched food for herself and milk for Willmouse from Madame Müller in the kitchen. When she picks him up, her child stares at her, saucer-eyed. Does he still recognize her? But that's silly. Of course he does. She passes him back to Élise and he smiles again. Her arms feel so light they could float up above her head.

Mary finds the drawing room empty of people but filled with a strange, yellowish sunlight and the devastated aftermath of the violent tempest. Someone has tried to tidy the mess of soaked papers and smashed glass into piles. All of it glistens and gleams, broken and beautiful in the eerie, dusty glow.

The storms have faded. The wind has dropped to a dull moan, which seeps through the shattered window and under the door. The wordless sigh of the dying breeze seems to come from everywhere and nowhere, from the house itself.

'Shelley? Byron?'

Mary runs her fingers over the damp velvet of the sofa, the silk of the curtains, which, only a few days before, had appeared so fine. By candlelight, by firelight, in the darkness of the storm, the rich wood and fabric had glinted with some inner opulence. Now, in the broken ochre light, she can see the ruin that must have been there even before the storm swept into the room: the sad, bald patches on the sofa, the weeping of damp on the faded wallpaper, the greyish mould, creeping into the corners where ancient cobwebs gather dust.

It is as though she has stepped into a slightly skewed version of the world she has known and understood, or as if the world itself has ended and Mary is the only person left in it.

But wait. She listens intently. She can still hear Élise talking to Willmouse. Beyond, another voice, singing softly and sweetly.

Mary traces the sound back along the hallway. All the bedrooms are empty and have the dark, dank feel of rooms long left unoccupied.

'*Suivez moi,*' sings the voice, from somewhere in the house. *Follow me.*

Mary's chest tightens. Her breath quickens. She will return to her room. Or, if everyone has gone somewhere without her, she could take Willmouse and leave this house and these noises behind her. She could steal whatever money Shelley, Byron and Polidori have in their cases. It would be enough, surely, to pay for her passage across France and over the Channel.

And yet she doesn't begin packing, doesn't start riffling through the men's belongings in search of coins and jewels. Instead, when she thinks of escape, her thoughts go to her room, to the pile of paper that tells the story of an abandoned creature and his hopeless search for a home, for love, for belonging.

She had come to Geneva hoping to find escape from her loneliness.

Instead, she has found herself.

The singing draws Mary onwards, up the winding staircase and to the dining room. It, too, seems deserted – the table littered with food-crusted plates and wine-stained glasses. It looks frozen in time, as if the house might have been abandoned years ago and Mary is a wraith, haunting these hallways.

'*Suivez moi, tuez moi*,' the voice sings, from behind her. *Follow me, kill me.*

Mary whirls around and sees Claire sitting in a corner of the room, a book open in her lap. She must know that Mary is there but doesn't look at her, just stares down at the book and sings again.

'*Suivez moi, tuez moi, vengez moi.*' *Follow me, kill me, avenge me.*

'What are you doing in here alone?' Mary asks sharply.

'Singing.' She doesn't look up from her book.

Why does Claire have to be so *difficult*?

'I can hear *that*. Why are you sitting by yourself singing? Where is everybody else?'

'It's a song from the Revolution. It means –'

'I know what it means.'

'And you must know why I'm singing it. The man who

composed it was betrayed by his friends. Then he was beheaded.'

'My God, Claire. Why must you always try to cause turmoil?'

'Why must *I* try to cause turmoil?' Anger and disbelief twist Claire's features. She lifts the top page free from the book she is reading, which is, Mary sees, not a book at all, but a collection of loose papers.

She recognizes Byron's writing immediately.

Although she doesn't want to reach for the paper, doesn't want to read another love letter to Augusta, Mary takes it anyway.

If we two part
In silence and tears,
Half broken of heart
To sever for years,
Pale grows my cheek and cold,
Colder thy kiss;
All our sweet joy foretold
The sorrow of this.

In secret we met —
In silence I grieve,
My heart cannot forget,
Nor my spirit deceive.
If I should meet thee
After long years,
How should I greet thee? —
With silence and tears.

L.B. for M.W.G.

Mary runs her finger lightly over where Byron has scratched her initials and his.

She hears his voice saying *Mrs S*. The mocking tone he uses to conceal his feelings in public. The heat of his breath against her ear as he sighs *Mary*, then kisses her.

'You're *smiling*!' Claire hisses. 'Do you truly have no heart? Do you not care how this makes me feel?'

A vicious energy surges through Mary. What was it Claire had said when Mary had confronted her about Shelley, about their baby?

'But we thought you knew,' she says. 'You *must* have known.'

She hears the crowing victory in her voice, the vengeful shadow she has concealed for so long. She is *glad* to see her sister's face crumple, is *glad* to see Claire suffer a fraction of the pain she has felt.

'I don't understand you,' Claire's eyes gleam. 'Why must you be so vindictive and bitter? You have stolen or spoiled *everything* I have ever loved.'

'I've stolen from *you*?'

'Ever since we were children, from the first moment I met you, you were determined to take everything from me. *Perfect Mary* had to have everything her own way.'

'You're delusional!' Mary hears a strangled laugh come from her mouth. 'How can you say that I spoiled or took things from you? It's absurd! *You* have always stolen from me, Claire. You came into our house like a demon. You shouted and screamed and raged. Your tantrums were unbearable.'

Claire shakes her head. 'That was *you*, Mary.'

'Don't be ridiculous.'

'It was. You *know* that was you. You have not always been *Saint Mary*, so you needn't feign patience and sweetness around me. It is all an act and both of us know it.'

'What do you mean?' Something in her is shaking loose – part of her mind flapping in a biting wind that won't let her go. Claire is lying. She's always lied.

'Stop pretending, Mary – you can't have forgotten. *You* were the child who was so full of rage. Do you truly think I would have dared scream at my mother? She would have knocked me into the middle of next week! But when we came to live with you, your father had coddled and indulged you so that you ruled the house. He taught you to argue like the devil. Then, if that didn't work, you raged and tore at your skin until you had your own way.'

'It's not true.' Mary's thoughts whirl. It can't be true.

'It's *there* on your *arm*!' Claire points at Mary's scars – the scars that had made Mrs Godwin persuade her father to send her to *recover* with friends in Scotland.

'It's not true,' Mary repeats, but even as she says it, a string of memories begins to unravel: she remembers screaming outside her father's study. She remembers shrieking until he opened the door and told her he would listen to her, if only she would be logical and rational.

She remembers howling to come downstairs to her father's evenings with Wordsworth and Coleridge and being told she could hide beneath the sofa and listen quietly. If she was noticed, she was to smile sweetly and say something clever.

She remembers the burning, metallic taste of anger and how, no matter how much she raged, it was never enough.

Her mother had left her all alone. Except she hadn't left. She'd been killed. She had died and it was all Mary's fault. That small, squalling baby was a murderer and Mary *loathed* her. However loudly she screamed, the void of loneliness within her would gulp it down, ready to spew it into the world: her endless, furious longing. Her fear of abandonment. Her terror of rejection.

She swallows. 'But . . . Shelley. I have never shouted at Shelley before . . .'

Before these last few days. She remembers the glancing blow

346

of the ink bottle against his cheek, her surge of exultation as it shattered against the wall. *Shut up, Shelley!*

'Only because I *told* you he would never stand for it,' Claire says. 'I said if you screamed at him, he would not want you.'

Mary's teeth are chattering. Dread runs through her, like the slow calving of a glacier, cutting a path through the rock that had seemed solid.

'You *stole* him from me.' The words are distorted by the clattering of Mary's teeth but, still, her sister hears.

Now Claire gives her own bark of humourless laughter. 'I stole him from *you*?'

'You did it intentionally – maliciously. Sometimes I think you took him just to hurt me, just because you have always wanted what was mine.'

'Mary, he was *mine* to begin with. I met him while you were in Scotland. I fell in love with him and he with me.'

'No!'

'And then *you* appeared and you took him from me.'

'No.'

'You *cannot* pretend you didn't know. I told you how much I loved him.'

'You said you *admired* him, perhaps. But we were already in love by then.'

'How can you believe that, Mary? You cannot simply change the past to suit what you want to think.' Claire's face is wild, her voice raw. 'That has always been your way but I'm tired of it. I won't endure it any longer. And now you *have* screamed at Shelley – don't think I haven't heard you! Don't think I haven't seen that bruise on his cheek – he won't endure you either.'

Mary feels something dark in her uncoil. She feels the urge to howl at her sister, to hurl something at her, to tear, to claw, to bite . . .

But some tiny part of her, the small-voiced, half-forgotten child within her, knows that her sister is right.

'Where is he?' Mary chokes. It is hard to draw a full breath. Fury and confusion make her voice shake. 'I need to talk to Shelley.'

'He's out on the lake with Byron. I told them the water was too rough. They wouldn't listen, of course . . .'

Claire's last words are lost as Mary runs back down the stairs and into her room. Even as she finds her outdoor clothes, she can hear the words from her past journals, as though she is whispering them aloud to herself. As though the pages hadn't been torn up or burned or lost. As though they have been with her, all along, seared into the very fabric of her vengeful soul.

Many times I have considered Satan as an emblem of my condition.

Should I feel kindness towards my enemies? No! I declare everlasting war against the species.

I loathe those that formed me and who have sent me forth into this insupportable misery.

Breathing hard, she closes her eyes and presses her fingers to the lids, until all she can see is a hard, white light, like the relentless glare of a snowy landscape, empty of life.

The ground outside is strewn with leaves and branches, shattered roof tiles and shards of glass. A felled tree blocks the path to the lake.

Every time Mary considers turning back, the memory of Claire's words drives her onwards.

He was mine to begin with. I was in love with him and he with me.

The storms have died but the wind still blusters and gusts around her. Overhead, the branches creak unnervingly. She squints across the squall-slapped lake. White-tipped waves rise from the surface. It reminds her of the Channel during a storm. The water roils, as if some shifting creature lurks beneath the surface.

She can see no boat. Claire must have been mistaken about them going out on the water – just as she is mistaken about everything else.

Then Mary sees two loose ropes, where a boat has been untied from its moorings. And at the end of the dock, the green wool of Shelley's scarf. With a stirring of dread, she walks closer to the lake, scanning the white-peaked water for a dark shape beneath the surface. Even with these waves, surely, he could not have drowned – not so close to the shore.

Alongside the ropes, the dead body of a swan floats in the wind-whipped water. Further out on the lake, its mate circles, calling out its fury and its grief. Mary tries not to believe in omens, but it is impossible to escape the feeling of foreboding she has, watching the slack body of the dead swan among the reeds.

She remembers the drowned man who had washed up on the shore when they first arrived here. All those stories about the dangers of this lake, the menace that people believe lives beneath the dark waters . . .

Shelley cannot swim.

He has no hope of floating on this rough water. Byron was a rower at Cambridge: Mary can conceive of him swimming to safety. But when she visualizes Shelley in the lake, she sees the water closing over his face, the thread of his last breath bubbling through the darkness, emerging into nothing.

Even as the thought scrapes through her veins in a scrabbling panic, part of her mind remains calculating and detached. She has tried to imagine her life without Shelley so often. Her choices have always felt desperate: begging forgiveness from her father, or throwing herself upon the mercy of Shelley's family, who loathe her.

Now, when she pictures her life without Shelley, she is not alone. She has Willmouse, his small hand in hers. And the creature she has created stands beside her; he has always been with her. The wrath-filled monster, who has survived every trial, has been rejected and cast out and ignored, has emerged from the wilderness of her mind time and time again. His story of ferocious survival, of fighting to be heard and understood, will be her lodestone and her solace.

She will not crawl back to her father, full of regrets and apologies. Instead, she will present him with a manuscript to show to his publishers.

Here, she will say. *Look at what I have created. Look at the monstrous loneliness that breathes inside me. Look at its strength, its power. Ugly it may be, but it is also magnificent.*

She feels *relief*, as though the whole of her life, which was being pushed along a tight, dark tunnel, has suddenly emerged into a blank, white space.

It is terrifying. It is electrifying. And she will find her way through it, with the ugliest part of her, the fiercest most brutal part of her.

She has spent so long trying to escape, trying to find some way out of her father's house, or away from Claire, or from the bailiffs or from Shelley, whom she has adored and hated and contorted herself to please. All the time, the escape she needed was the part of herself she had squashed and ignored. The shadow has always been at her side: there is no escaping it. And now the vicious brutal beauty of the storm within her is the only way she will survive.

The wind surges across the steel surface of the lake from every direction, stealing Mary's breath. The waves surge higher.

She closes her eyes, feeling grief for her son: he will be a fatherless boy, just as she was a motherless girl. But she will be everything to him. She will keep him safe. He will be loved, always.

She pictures Shelley's face as she'd first seen him, standing in her father's dining room – the words of his poetry had woken something in her soul. Even without him that fire will continue. And she thinks of Byron – the bark of his laughter, his sarcastic drawl, the unexpected tenderness in his eyes when he kissed her, when he made love to her.

When she opens her eyes again, a dark smudge is moving across the surface of the lake.

She squints, watching as the boat, tiny in the distance, rises on each wave, then plummets into the troughs.

It must be them. Who else would be reckless enough, careless enough to venture into such dangerous waters?

Dread rises like vomit: her punishment for being so callous at the thought of Shelley's death is that she will be forced to watch him drown.

Is the boat moving away from her, closer to the centre of the lake? She shields her eyes and peers out into the roiling grey. Impossible to know where anything is, to know how close or how far. Impossible to unpick the tangle of panic and anger, guilt and relief that constrict her chest and throat.

She blinks out at the surging grey mass.

She can't watch him die. She doesn't *want* him to die. She only wants to be entirely free of the constant sense of expectation that she should batter and bludgeon her every thought and feeling to please Shelley – or to please anyone.

To the left of her foot, a rock pokes out of the water. Stepping onto it will give her a better view of the lake, but it will mean she is no longer standing on dry land – she will have to half jump, half scramble onto it.

She takes a breath.

She can't do it.

She can't.

She is too frightened.

She jumps and lands hard on the rock, slipping down, her hands scrabbling for purchase; one foot splashes into the icy water. A sharp edge slices into her palm on the hand that had been cut open by the glass in the storm. For a lurching moment, she thinks she will lose her grip, thinks she will fall.

She sees herself slipping into the lake, her skull smacking against the stone, dark blood blooming in a cloud around her hair.

Nothing knows loneliness like a lakebed, a riverbed, the bed at the bottom of an ocean. Except, perhaps, the abandoned lover, their own bed cold and empty.

She grips the rock and hauls herself upright, ignoring the searing pain. She wipes the blood on her skirt and looks out across the water again. It is only a metre or so higher here, but she is sure she can make out the boat, closer than before.

She cups her hands around her mouth and shouts Shelley's name. No response. She steps forward and down, onto the other side of the rock, her feet in the water now. She ignores the cold.

The boat moves nearer still. She can make out the shapes of two figures.

I do not want to watch you die.

She remembers Shelley's tenderness when they first met, the feeling of his arms around her, the sound of his voice, his laughter. The light in his eyes when he gazed at her – it is there, still. It was there when he read about her creature, about its anger and its despair. Even after she had hurled the inkpot at him and cursed him, he had forgiven her.

Perhaps he loves her still, will love her still, in all her fear and rage and brokenness.

Perhaps she loves him, in all his thoughtlessness.

Perhaps they can learn each other all over again.

She wills them closer, keeping her gaze fixed upon them, as if she could draw them back through the force of her hope.

She can't explain the feeling. It must be the same hope that people cling to when they pray to a God they cannot see. The same hope that thousands of people all across the Continent must feel as they kneel on indifferent stone and beg for sunlight.

What else is there to do but hold on to the unknown, the unproven, the unreal?

The boat is closer still. She can make out the figures clinging on tightly as the wind slaps it from side to side: Shelley's thin frame, half standing, and Byron pulling at the oars.

'Shelley!' Mary calls, her throat aching.

Her voice must be swept out to him because he looks towards her, then stands fully and lifts his arms, waving.

She hears Byron's shout, just before the boat tips and flips, just before both men vanish beneath the surface.

'Shelley!' She shouts his name again and again.

She watches the water, the upturned boat, her eyes burning.

Movement! A man – someone is in the water, his arms beating a steady rhythm. It must be Byron. Her relief that he is alive only increases her desperation to see Shelley.

Come back! she thinks. *I will find a way to forgive you. Please come back.*

She sees Byron put his arms together, then dive beneath the water. She waits, holding her breath. He emerges moments later, alone.

Again, he dives, and again. Each time he comes up without Shelley.

She thinks of the uncanny image of the man she had seen when she was in the boat all those weeks ago. Polidori had said that people saw visions of the future above the lake. Is this what she saw? A foreshadowing of her lover being carried off alone?

Byron dives again. She counts to thirty, sixty, ninety. The water grey and storm-boiled. They are both gone, the men she has longed for, the men she still loves.

Her heart is a panicked bird, battering hopeless wings against the bars of its cage.

Byron surfaces with a shout. There is another shape next to him.

'Shelley!' Her voice raw, ragged.

He doesn't move. He has been under too long.

She sees Byron's arm rising and falling, slapping Shelley, beating on his back and chest.

Then there is a cry. Does Shelley stir?

She calls his name again. This time, she is sure of it: he lifts his hand.

Byron clings to Shelley with one arm and swims on his back, making slow but sure progress towards her.

When they are closer, Mary steps down from the rock, into the dark water, heedless of its icy, sucking clutches, or her skirt billowing around her legs, threatening to trip her on every unsteady step.

She wades out until the cold water slaps at her thighs. Byron and Shelley are there, grey-skinned and shivering, stumbling against one another and splashing shakily towards Mary.

'Did you see . . . Mary?' Shelley croaks. 'I sank to . . . the bottom.' He coughs. 'Like a stone.' He coughs again. 'I held the air . . . in my lungs.' He wheezes; he smiles. 'I knew Byron would rescue me. I was . . . a merman waiting for him!'

'He was!' Byron laughs shakily. 'He was sitting on the bottom of the lake, holding his hands up. I caught hold of him.'

She embraces her lover, clings to him, presses her lips to the wet skin of his cheek. He is grey and stone-cold, as though he is still at the bottom of the lake, waiting to be dragged to the surface.

Over Shelley's shoulder, she sees Byron watching. As he turns away, something like pain twists his expression. He doesn't try to meet her gaze.

'I took a mouthful of water,' Shelley says. 'On the way up . . . I thought I would die. I was ready to die. Think of the stories . . . they would have told about me . . . drowning in a storm . . . in the middle of summer.'

Byron steps onto the bank and climbs from the lake, then leans down to haul Shelley up beside him. They clap each other on the back, like returning heroes, recounting their deeds again and again.

As she lifts her skirt above her knees so she can scramble out, Mary slips on the mud; a rock smashes into her shin. Immediate pain, a purpling bruise and a shallow, bloodied gash. The men don't notice, don't turn, don't check to see if she is following them.

She drags herself from the lake on battered, bloody legs.

When she stands upright, she feels a heady euphoria. It is as if she has spent half her life sitting on the muddy obscurity of the bottom of some shadowy lake inside herself, waiting to be rescued. Now, she has swum upwards, has hauled herself out of the water, out of the darkness. And from now on, everything will be different.

The men walk past the dead swan, seeming not to notice it.

She hears Byron say, 'Christ, I'm tired! Give me a bottle of brandy and a fire.' He still hasn't looked at her. How can she tell him what she feels for him? She doesn't fully know how to explain it herself.

He'd foreseen their parting. He'd written it into his poem, as though it had already happened.

Mary pauses next to the swan, no longer trying to read its body for meaning.

There is no omen in its passing. There is no divine balance in the world, making sure that the measure of pleasure and pain is dealt out fairly. The only strength she has exists in her own scraped hands and bruised legs. Her will to survive beats in her own blood, in her own mind.

There is no oracle; there is no force of right and wrong that she must obey. There are no messages from beyond. Only this: a mass of weighted feathers, with no explanation, and her will to survive. The stubborn and bloody determination that drives her onward.

She follows the men back up to the house, her legs shaking.

Across the water, the swan's mate circles. Her calls ring out, unanswered in the gathering dark.

2 1

We are unfashioned creatures, but half made up.

Mary helps to settle Shelley in the dining room, under blankets, close to the fire. Claire rushes to him, her expression stricken. Then she sees Mary and stops, her hands half lifted, as if to show that she carries no weapon, that she means no harm. She has rarely meant to cause true pain: she is lively and pretty, and longs for love. She may be selfish and petty but she is incapable of true malice or real viciousness.

He was mine to begin with, Claire had said.

Perhaps, Mary thinks, *but he is mine now.* And he is, she sees it clearly – the way his eyes search for hers, even while Claire is stroking the hair back from his forehead.

The gesture doesn't make her angry. So much of her exists beyond Shelley – parts that belong to her alone.

She loves him but she doesn't exist for him, not any more.

If he deserted her, or disappeared, or died, she would find a way to survive.

Along the hallway, Byron's door is half open. He is lying on his bed, fully clothed, staring up at the ceiling.

She closes the door and lies down beside him, her head on his chest. His skin is damp from the lake, still, and a slight shiver runs through his limbs. Pressing her body close to his, Mary pulls the blanket across them.

They lie in the quiet of their shared breath. Mary wants

to find the words to tell him that she cannot split herself like this again, that she will not spend her days devoted to another man who may not always want her in the same way as she wants him.

Before she can speak, Byron says, very quietly, 'I wanted to let him drown.'

Mary lies still, barely breathing.

'I saw him, below me in the water, and I thought, *If I let you die, everything will be simpler.*'

'Do you believe that?' Mary whispers.

Byron blinks, then kisses her forehead. 'Sadly not.'

She waits. His heart pounds a steady, ceaseless rhythm.

Finally, he says, 'For brief periods of my life, I have been faithful. It does not come easily. And it does not last. Even when my heart is fixed and devoted, my body is fickle. *I* am fickle. I would betray you, Mary. I would hurt you and you would loathe me for it. I would loathe myself.'

Along with the loss, there is a sense of relief: they will give each other up, however unwillingly.

They will never have to lose each other.

'I would hate to loathe you,' she says, and presses her lips to his.

'*Remember me as one who loves not wisely but too well.*' His mouth curls into a smile. He leans his forehead against hers.

Love. Had he truly said love?

So close, his eyes are large and fathomless, their blue-gold depths impenetrable. However honest he might want to be, there is part of himself he holds back.

And perhaps that is what he senses in her too – the part of herself that she keeps hidden, that she pours onto the page when she is alone, as though spilling her own blood.

She had once believed him shallow, had thought he wanted love and adoration, while giving nothing of himself, so that he could feel powerful. Now she understands that, however much he might love, he cannot vow devotion and he will not make false promises.

He will not offer her his heart because he cannot.

'Are you angry with me?' he asks. It is such an unexpected question, coming from him, that she sits up and stares at him – at the vulnerable hope in his large eyes, at the fear that presses his full lips into a tense line.

She shakes her head. 'Everything ends,' she says softly.

As she kisses him, as she peels off his shirt and presses her mouth to his chest and belly, feeling him harden beneath her, she thinks that, yes, everything ends. Every moment passes.

But perhaps the ending isn't as important as everything that follows. Perhaps the ending is only the start.

Shelley recovers slowly from his near-drowning. He sleeps more. He tells the story again and again, with more excitement and exaggeration each time, but when he thinks no one is watching him, Mary sees him staring blankly at a wall or a piece of furniture, his skin pale, his expression haunted.

Whenever she passes him, Shelley grabs her hand and pulls her close, kissing her neck. As he bends forward, she hears the slight wheeze in his lungs. Sometimes he coughs and complains that his chest hurts. It is strange how the texture of her love for him has changed. By the lake, when she'd thought him dead, along with her grief, she'd felt free. Yes, she'd wondered how she and Willmouse would survive without him. But she'd known she could do it – she *would* do it, just as her mother had. She will write and be published. She will make her voice heard.

They haven't talked about what Claire told her. They haven't spoken about the flung inkpot, the shouts of fury. They haven't spoken about Byron.

Mary knows they must. Otherwise all of it will sit in the dark space that exists between them – a fracture thin as a spider's web, deep as an abyss.

In her room, they try to make love. Shelley kisses her stomach, her hips, the tops of her thighs, then pulls her onto him.

His touch on her breasts feels nauseating; he presses his fingers between her legs, and she flinches. It is difficult to fit her body to his. His kisses are awkward, as though there is some hard carapace between them. She wants to feel as she had when they first met – as she feels with Byron: consumed by the passion, devoured and devouring.

She stops, pushes Shelley away. His expression is glazed, and he blinks at her, confused.

How can she begin to say what she feels? The words will stay lodged in her throat as they have so many times before.

For goodness' sake, Mary! You're a grown woman, not a child. You have a voice: use it.

His expression is attentive. He is waiting, listening.

She says, 'Claire told me you loved her first – is that true?'

A flash of panic in his eyes, then he reaches out and puts his hand on her knee. 'I love you best. You are the one great love of my life. Don't you feel that?'

In the past, she would have lied. She would have said *yes* because once, long ago, it had felt like that. She had fallen in love with the Shelley of her mind, just as he had fallen in love with the Mary of his, both creating the other.

I cannot heave my heart into my mouth, she thinks.

Not because she cannot describe how much she loves him, but because, if he doesn't understand why she has felt such hollow despair, she may never be able to love him again.

Now she will not lie.

She says, 'I don't know.'

'You don't *know?*' His voice fractures on the final word; his expression is as shocked as when the inkpot had hit his face.

'I don't know . . . *you*, Shelley. And you don't know me either – not truly.'

'I don't understand.' He clenches his hands together, his knuckles whitening.

'I am not trying to be cruel, but you must see –'

'I have hurt you. I know that, Mary. Can you forgive me? Can we return to how things were at the beginning? I love you so dearly.'

It is not enough, not nearly enough. 'I don't want to go back to that. I wasn't myself then. I was trying to be some other woman. I wanted to be whoever you wanted me to be. I can't do that again. I won't.'

Apologies are too easy: he has begged her forgiveness before; it has changed nothing.

He touches the fading bruise where the inkpot had struck his cheek and speaks quietly, haltingly, in a tone she has never heard him use before. 'I understand . . . why you were so . . . furious with me. I know you will be angry for . . . a long time. You have every right to be so. I have not deserved you, Mary. But if I try to change – if I can be better, more worthy of you – do you think you can ever forgive me?'

It is this acknowledgement that cracks something within her: not that he is apologizing, but that he has recognized her rage, is trying to understand why she feels it.

He has seen and heard her fury. He is still here, still holding her hand.

'I want to try,' she says very quietly.

The words sound like a weak promise, but they are stitched from the threads of her own desire, her own choice, her own free will. She is not trying to crush and smother her feelings; she is not attempting to hide. She is not looking for an escape. She wants to find a path to the people they might be. Within her now, an understanding that, if she were to run from Shelley, she would be trying to run from herself.

Escape can't allay her rage and there is no freedom that could quench it. The anger is an old wound, ragged at the edges where it has split again and again, though no one else sees the depth of it, the pain. The only way to make others understand – the only way to understand herself – is to live alongside her fury, to sit with it and learn the shape of it. To write it.

Day after day and late into the night, she sits at her desk and writes out her wrath, though it feels as if she is breaking open the wound, as if she is scrawling in her own blood.

The beast inside her is full of fury. The beast inside her is tired of being shut away and ignored. He will roar across the blank page; he will kill men and women; he will murder innocent children. He will be vengeful and remorseless. Rejected as he is, he will have nothing left to lose so he will fear nothing.

She is horrified by the creature she has created. And yet she loves him.

Monstrous and murderous as he is, he is part of her.

I love you, she says aloud. Not to Shelley, not to Byron, but to the small, furious, grubby-fisted girl who still lives in her mind, though she has been ignored for so many years – though Mary has cast that little girl out into the wilderness, calling her evil, vicious, monstrous. She has told that little girl time and again that no one could possibly want her.

Now she says, *Come here. Come sit with me. I love you.*

She writes as she used to write when she was a child – with a fierce energy that sears itself onto the page, without her thought or control. The creature's story is life and death to her now.

She writes as though electricity is running through her limbs, every fibre of her being poured into her words. And with every sentence comes the knowledge that this ferocious power has always been hers. The scratching of the quill across the paper is the ticking of her blood through her veins, the whisper of air into her lungs. This is her voice, and she must use it.

She falls asleep at her desk, wakes and writes again.

One morning she looks out of her little window and sees the rising sun shading the snow-capped mountains in the most delicate pink and apricot. The beauty and brutality of the lonely, savage peaks are breathtaking. Suddenly she sees what her creature must do, where he must go.

Poor, outcast wretch, he will hide himself in the ice-crusted mountains. He will find solace in nature; even as his solitude brings him despair, it will give him joy. And if Mary is to understand what he suffers, what he will endure and what he will sacrifice, she must go into the mountains herself.

Her eyes burn with exhaustion and, as she stands from her desk, stretching her arms, a wave of dizziness passes over her. When had she last eaten or drunk? Is it days or weeks that have passed, with her hunched over the desk, hoarding the light from a single candle, her hand aching and cramping, her mind a furnace?

The hallway is silent and still. A distant murmur of voices and clatter of cutlery from the dining room.

All four are seated at the table, the remains of a meal in front of them – breakfast? Supper? Before they can speak, she rips a chunk of bread from the loaf in the centre and takes an enormous bite, then washes it down with a gulp of wine, directly from the flagon.

'Are you well, Pecksie?' Shelley's expression is apprehensive.

'I need to go into the mountains. There's a huge ice lake – Mer de Glace.'

He blinks, startled. 'I don't think that's a good idea.'

'I want to go. I want to see it.' It feels good to say *I want*. She rips another handful of bread, stuffs it into her mouth. Polidori, Shelley and Claire watch her, slack-jawed. Byron is grinning.

'All right.' Shelley's voice is uncertain. 'We could go next week.'

'I'll leave tomorrow.'

'It's not – it wouldn't be safe for you to go alone. I'll come with you . . . if I may?'

'If you like,' she says, her thoughts still fixed on her creature. He is more real to her now than any of them. The fierce energy of his desire burns through her.

She can feel them staring at her with some expression she can't decipher or can't find the will to care about. They seem distant from her, as though they exist in a different time from the one she now inhabits.

'Will you read it to us?' Byron says, next to her. She hadn't noticed him moving and she jumps. Almost, she bares her teeth, but she turns the expression into a smile.

'Yes, read it, please, Miss Godwin,' Polidori says. 'I'm sure it is wonderful.'

'He – It isn't ready.' She has a sudden dread of bringing the monster into the room, of revealing him in all his brokenness and rage. What if they are disgusted by him? What if they find him too awful or even ridiculous?

'It will never feel ready,' Byron says.

'You don't understand.'

She imagines them laughing, pictures her creature reduced by their mockery into a character from a melodrama. Some longing deep within her heart would shrink and die, or some furious hope, hidden in her mind, would explode into violent life.

Byron's expression softens. 'I understand better than you can know,' he whispers. 'Don't become lost in there.'

'I have seen parts of the story. It's an excellent piece,' Shelley says. 'Aren't you proud of it?'

Proud of it? She couldn't say. It fills her thoughts and her dreams; she feels compelled to write it. When she sits down with her quill, it is as though the ink is spilling straight from her split skull. Afterwards, she feels exhausted, unnerved and dazed, like the drawings she has seen of women who believe they have had spirits cast out of them.

But is she *proud* of it?

'Read it,' Claire says. 'You like it. I can tell.' She has had a lifetime of deciphering Mary's expressions and is surprisingly perceptive when her interest is piqued. 'And you're a genius, so it will be brilliant.'

Surprised by this compliment, Mary stutters, 'I – I don't have it. It's in my room.'

'I have the first part,' Shelley says and, walking over to the bookshelf, pulls out a sheaf of papers. When had he taken them?

She has a feeling that she is standing outside herself, watching some other woman's mouth open and shut, some other woman shake her head. 'Don't . . . It's not finished. It's not good enough.'

She means that the creature terrifies her and is part of her. She means that bringing him into this room to be judged and assessed will feel like peeling off her own skin and allowing these people to run their hands over the exposed nerves beneath.

Shelley passes the papers to Byron. He scans the first page, then raises his eyebrows and looks at her, some indecipherable expression in his eyes.

Then he begins to read aloud: '*It was on a dreary night of November that I beheld my man completed . . .*'

'Please stop,' Mary says. 'It's not ready.'

Byron slaps the papers onto the table next to him and glares at her.

It is the first time he has looked at her with anything like real anger. She freezes.

'Stop protesting and *whining*, Mary!' he snaps. 'You wanted to write a story. Now we want to read it. Your task, like ours, is to sit and listen. Of *course* it isn't ready – it will *never* feel ready. It will *never* feel finished. It will *never* feel good enough to you. But I assume you didn't write this just for yourself?'

She doesn't know how to answer: in a way, she *had* written it just for herself, pulling the monster from her mind, piece by painful piece. It belongs to the darkest part of her. She wants to hide it.

But now that Byron has started reading, a small part of her wants other people to look at it, to examine it and to tell her if these bleak and savage parts, these twisted and violent emotions are understandable, are acceptable. Are they forgivable? Is *she* forgivable?

The torturous wrench of being caught between two feelings is familiar. It is like her affection for Claire, which sits alongside her anger and loathing. Or it is like her love for Shelley, her need for him, with her fury at his selfishness, her longing to be free of the turmoil he brings. It is like each moment with Byron, in which she desires him and wants to be possessed by him, but knows they would burn each other until nothing remained but bitter ash.

'Writing is difficult.' Byron's smile is kind. There is no flattery or flirtation in his voice. He is talking to her as he might address an equal. As he might talk to another man, another writer. 'Nobody tells you how hard it is, putting your thoughts down – finding something to say and the words to say it. But letting people *read* your work is agony. The exposure

366

is excruciating. You will have to make armour from your own skin.'

She swallows and nods. Her mouth tastes of old pennies.

Byron picks up the papers and continues: '*With an anxiety that almost amounted to agony, I collected the instruments of life around me.*'

She closes her eyes as Byron reads the moment when the ambitious young scientist first truly sees what he has created.

'*His limbs were in proportion, and I had selected his features as beautiful. Beautiful! Great God! His yellow skin scarcely covered the work of muscles and arteries beneath; his hair was of a lustrous black, and flowing; his teeth of a pearly whiteness; but these luxuriances only formed a more horrid contrast with his watery eyes, that seemed almost of the same colour as the dun-white sockets in which they were set, his shrivelled complexion and straight black lips . . .*'

Oh, God, it is too gruesome.

The creature is too repellent, too furious, while also being too sensitive.

There is an excess of emotion in the tale. Also, it is too confusing – should our loyalties lie with Dr Frankenstein or with his misbegotten creation?

Mary clasps her hands together and digs her nails into her skin, as she had done at the start of the labour of bringing her children into the world, when the agony that racked her body had still felt like something she could control, or distract her mind from, by inflicting other pains upon herself.

And yet, as Byron reads on, page after page, she risks looking at the faces of her companions.

Shelley has his eyes closed and is nodding, as if listening to a rapturous piece of music; Claire is staring into the fire, but Mary can tell her attention is on Byron's voice. Polidori gazes at Mary with an expression of such adoration that she can't bear to meet his eyes.

Between chapters, Byron glances up at her, his handsome face full of wonder.

When he reaches the end of what she has written so far, there is silence in the room, apart from the crackling of the fire and the faint shudder of the wind against the windows.

Mary's hands ache. Her knuckles are punctured with purple half-moons from the pressure of her nails.

'It's . . . *remarkable*,' Byron says. 'Unlike anything I've read before. The rawness, the savagery – it's terrifying and wonderful.'

Mary feels her cheeks flush. She can't speak.

'Truly, the way you weave in all these voices, the way you allow the monster to *rage*. It's beautiful and brave, Mary, and it could only have come from you. I hear your voice through the creature.'

She nods, unable to speak, waiting.

She doesn't want to look at Shelley in case she reads some hesitation in his face. Finally, he says, 'There is so much in it. I don't know where to begin.'

Shelley hears her voice in it too – she knows he does. He hears her anger now – the scope of it, the horror. She can see a new fear in his wary expression. She can see alarm.

She feels stripped and skinless. She feels numb.

Then the thought comes, clear as a single thread of lightning that stitches together earth and sky: *I do not care if he is horrified. I do not care if he is disgusted.*

Part of her still cares desperately; part of her wishes she didn't have to care at all.

How can I hate you?

Mary remembers the moment when she'd flung the inkpot at his head. Shelley had looked shocked and horrified. Then he had told her he loved her. He had called her his angel.

It is possible to be disgusted by someone's behaviour while still loving them.

And it is impossible to truly loathe the thing you have created, the thing that has made you.

All this time she had believed her own feelings to be a snarled and knotted mass of rope, tying her to Shelley. Now she knows: the rope is his too. They have both shaped this tangled mess.

The wind sighs around the walls.

Flames flicker and lick at the soot-stained grate.

Finally, Shelley says, 'Why must the creature be *so* awful and brutish? If Dr Frankenstein is playing God and creating life, should not the man he makes surpass him in every way?'

'I . . .' What can she say?

That the story is not just about man's capacity to create but also about his desire to control, his aptitude for neglect. That it is about his inability to take responsibility, even as the world around him crumbles and his actions bring distress and death to those he loves. Can she explain to her lover that her story is not just about creating something wonderful? It is also about man's arrogant belief that the act of creation is itself an achievement, because it brings glory without demanding any sacrifice.

The hardest thing is not the creation, but loving and teaching the thing that has been created, even though it may be monstrous.

The grind of nurture, love and commitment brings no accolades but that is the real work.

Daily love, in spite of everything, is the true miracle.

'It felt more believable to me,' Mary says carefully, 'that the doctor would be horrified by his creation and would reject it.'

'More dramatic, certainly – but not more believable. Think how much I care about my poems when they are released into the world. I would never disown or abandon something I had crafted with such love and care, even if all of society rejected it.'

Mary braces, waiting for Shelley to consider his children. She waits for him to acknowledge the connection between the rage he has brought out in her, and the furious abandoned beast in her story. Shelley is surely too clever not to see his selfishness reflected in Dr Frankenstein – his obsessions, his conviction that he alone is right, his disregard for others in the pursuit of his goals. Is he pretending ignorance, then? Or is he truly too blinkered to see how he must appear?

'I just don't find the ambiguity credible,' Shelley says. 'Either the doctor should create a perfect being, then feel himself to be inadequate in its presence . . . Or else the creature should be entirely monstrous, and the scientist should feel no affection for it at all.'

Mary says nothing, not because she agrees with him but because disagreeing with him would be like shouting into the wind. And, truly, she realizes, it doesn't matter that he doesn't agree with her. She knows that every gateway she will have to pass through to have her work accepted, for it to be read and sold and reviewed, will have a man standing in front of it. And they will all want to shout their opinions. They will tell her she is wrong, or that the work is too dark, too fierce, too full of madness. They will say that a woman couldn't possibly have written something so horrific.

They will be mistaken, just as Shelley is mistaken now.

'You're wrong,' Mary says to him. And she doesn't care if he has listened, barely cares if he has heard. She turns and walks from the room, half expecting him to follow, though she doesn't look back.

'Mary, wait!'

It is Claire, not Shelley, hurrying breathlessly after her.

'I wanted to say . . . I liked your story. Well. I *loved* it. I did. It's . . . That poor abandoned creature! How have you been able to bear writing about such loneliness?'

'It has been . . .' How can she convey what it has been like? That it has felt like opening her veins and bleeding onto the page? That she has felt compelled to write, drawn to her desk, chained to her story, but that the world it has cracked open in her mind has freed something within her? That she feels she now understands herself, even as she knows that the people who read her story will misunderstand her?

She can anticipate the reviews: *unnatural, grotesque, the product of a diseased imagination.* People will say that a woman could not possibly have written it. They will say it disgusts them.

You will have to make armour of your own skin.

Mary says to Claire, 'It has been difficult.'

'Yes – your desperate creature is so sad and so far from any home. He is a pitiful thing and wants only to be loved.'

Mary sees it then. She had thought she was writing about herself, about her own rage, but perhaps other people feel something of it also, see something of themselves in the abandoned monster.

Claire, too, had been plucked from her home by Shelley. She has been changed and shaped by him, has spent most of her days trying to please him, or Byron, while feeling utterly abandoned. Claire, too, is a furious, desolate creature, who depends on the whims and desires of men for survival.

'Thank you,' Mary says quietly, meaning it.

Now, Claire reaches out with her toe and taps it lightly against Mary's shin, not gently enough to be affectionate, not hard enough to hurt. 'Anyway, your story is brilliant and terrifying. You're a genius, just like Father always said you would be.' She looks sad for a moment, then brightens. 'Will you really leave tomorrow for the Mer de Glace?'

Mary nods. Her creature is calling her to walk with him through the brutal desolation of the mountains. Once she has placed him there, in the lonely desolation of the jagged, snow-swept peaks, she will be able to finish her story.

'Can I come with you?' Claire asks.

'You're asking *me*?'

'I won't come, if you don't want me to.' In the past, Claire and Shelley have always decided where they would go and Mary has followed, without question. Even their escape to France two years ago had been Claire and Shelley's idea.

'Why do you want to come?' Mary asks warily.

'I'd like to see where your poor creature goes. And I thought it could be . . . something new. For us.' Claire's expression is open and hopeful.

For the first time in weeks, perhaps in years, Mary has a genuine urge to embrace her sister. As if a slammed door inside her is slowly opening. As if some betrayed creature, still bloody and broken, can finally be welcomed home.

22

Beware, for I am fearless and therefore powerful.

That night, she dreams of the creature again. She is on the mountain, staring over the vast desolation of ice and snow, when she sees a movement from the corner of her eye. Turning, she finds her creature looming over her. She wants to run but her feet are frozen into the snow.

'There will be death,' the creature says. 'I feel it approaching.'

She struggles again; her feet do not move.

The creature says, 'You can't run – remember?' And the voice he speaks with is her own.

Trembling, she reaches out to run her fingers over the pitted, stitched seams that mar the pale face. His skin is smooth, like wax beneath her palm, as she cups the huge jawbone.

'See there,' the creature says. She looks back to the icy lake, where other creatures are emerging. Their battered bodies are scarred and misshapen as they lumber free of the frozen surface. They shake themselves, like dogs shedding water; shards of ice whistle through the air.

'There will be death,' her creature says again. 'You have always known this.'

The creatures in the ice begin to drag themselves up the rocky slope. Mary's scream freezes in her throat. When she turns to her own creature, his face is impassive. Beyond him, she sees everyone she loves or has ever loved: her mother, her father, Shelley, Byron, Claire.

None of them move as the monsters lurch towards them. One of the great creatures stops in front of Shelley – the monster is fawning, rubbing its scarred head against Shelley's hand, then Claire's, then Mary's, like a cat in search of affection. Its skin feels like slick scales under her fingers, but it soon turns away from her, searching for someone else to stroke its badly stitched skull.

Finally, it returns to Shelley. When he ignores it, the creature reaches out with both its huge hands and rips Shelley's head from his shoulders.

She gasps awake, her feet twisted in the sheets, her chemise damp with sweat. The creature's words echo in her mind – in her own voice. *There will be death.*

She tells herself she doesn't believe in omens.

Each time she closes her eyes, she sees the shattered ice, the lumbering creatures. It takes her a long time to fall back to sleep.

Just before dawn, Byron creeps into Mary's room. She wakes to him kissing the back of her neck. She rolls over, drawing him closer, drawing him into her. As they move together, she tries to imprint it all on her memory – the salt taste of his skin, the woodsmoke smell of his hair, the rasp of his stubble against her cheek, then against her breasts, between her legs.

The hum of connection, which goes beyond the pleasure of their bodies. His eyes, in the darkness, afterwards. The luminosity she can see there.

Love is a light you can see only when you reach for it. You hold it in your hand and, for as long as the flame glows, it warms you.

Mary reaches for it. She holds it.

'I don't usually enjoy farewells,' he murmurs.

'Nor I.' She tries to remember saying goodbye to someone she has truly loved but cannot. She left her father's house in the middle of the night. Her mother left before Mary could know her.

'I won't share you.' His voice rumbles through her. 'And I won't force you to share me. But you must know, Mary Wollstonecraft Godwin, you carry with you as much of my heart as I am able to give. I would say that I will miss you. But I think the Greeks say it better. Μου λείπεις.'

Mary knows the words. Now, for the first time, she feels their meaning. 'You are missing from me.'

'Yes,' he whispers. 'You are missing from me.'

She falls asleep with her head on his chest, listening to the thud of his heart. When she wakes, the room is filled with a watery yellow sunlight.

Byron is gone.

Claire is too sick to travel with them in the end, so Mary and Shelley leave her in the villa with Byron, Polidori, Willmouse and Élise.

The carriage is lighter and faster than the one that had brought them to the house. Mary's plan is to travel up into the mountains around Chamonix, which they should reach by nightfall, if they are lucky. The sky above, like clean pages ruffled by a pale blue hand, promises better weather.

She feels a tug in her chest at leaving her child, but tells herself they will return within a week. She tries not to think of Byron at all. He has not come out to wave them off – only Polidori stands on the steps, as if he has been plucked out of time and frozen there: a statue of himself, his expression pained, forever saying farewell.

As the carriage rolls down the driveway, swerving to avoid the fallen roof tiles and scattered branches, Mary promises herself that she won't look back, but as they turn the corner, she pulls the latch on the window and turns to catch a last glimpse of the house. Sharp wind snaps her hair across her face, pricks tears from her eyes, but through the blur she sees him.

Byron is standing at the broken window in the drawing room, his face framed by the hole in the shattered glass.

Some thread of longing in Mary reaches out for him, but it is not enough to call her back, not enough to make her want to stay.

In the mountains ahead, her creature calls. He is part of her, but he is also part of this wild and ruthless landscape, these raw-toothed mountains, this dark force and longing for life. He is waiting for her there, waiting for her to come and continue his story, which is also her story – the story of who she will become. The story of the woman she has always been.

So many times, Mary has been left or abandoned or cast out. She has hidden from bailiffs and run from her father and fled from a locked room in the middle of the night. Each time, her escape has been tinged with a sour tang of terror; her hope has been coloured by fear.

This is the first time she has left of her own volition. She is not running because she has no alternative: she has chosen to travel into the mountains. The power of acting of her own free will feels at once dizzying and sobering – as though she has inhaled lungful after lungful of opium and, instead of a blurred heaviness, she feels lighter and sharper than ever before.

A sound swells in her throat – something like a laugh or a shout. Once, she might have ignored the sensation, stifled it, stuffed it deep within herself, where it would have wrapped itself like a fist around her chest, around her heart.

Now, she puts her head out of the window and yells. Uninhibited, unrestrained, it is like the raw, ferocious cries she gave in childbirth, only this comes not from pain but from a wild and indescribable joy.

'Pecksie,' Shelley says, putting his hand on her arm.

She jumps – she'd lost all sense of him, sitting opposite her in the carriage, staring at her, slack-jawed.

'I'm well.' Mary laughs, in answer to the question in his eyes. 'Truly, I'm well.'

He nods uncertainly, and looks as though he might say more. Before he can, Mary puts her face out of the open window again. His words are drowned in the clatter of hoofs, the grind of the wheels, the rush of cold, clean air against her face.

Closer to the lake, the path is littered with branches and scarred by deep gashes, where rushing water has carved out gullies. At one point, their way is blocked by a fallen pine. The *voiturier* stops the carriage and indicates that they should climb out, while he leads the horses around the tree, through the shallow water at the lake's edge.

'Perhaps we should turn back,' Shelley frets.

'You can leave, if you like.' Mary steps out of the carriage.

She doesn't hear Shelley's reply. Something about this part of the shore is familiar. The water is higher but, still, she recognizes the curve of the bank, the way the soil transitions to stones and sand, making a natural bay – a beach for things from the lake to wash up.

The place where the man's body had lain is ankle-deep in water and covered with scattered leaves and broken branches. Among the wreckage, a lump of waterlogged wood, perfectly spherical, about the size of her fist. She plunges her hand into the frigid water, palms it, then examines it. The head of a child's carved toy, carefully shaped by some loving hand. Swollen as it is, she can still make out where the chisel has cut the lips, the eyes, the triangle of a nose.

'What's that?' Shelley asks.

For a moment, she is taken back to her dream – to the creature that came out of the ice and lurched towards Shelley before tearing off his head.

'Nothing.' She tosses the head back into the water, where it floats, then bobs further out into the lake, swallowed by stillness and silence. She can feel its shape still, in her palm. And beneath the water too, she can feel the presence of the drowned man, as if he'd left part of himself in the lake.

Suicide, people had whispered, as if speaking too loudly of such pain would cast some pall over those who heard it – as if by silencing the word they could mute the anguish it contained.

But, standing in the spot where the man was found, Mary feels a sense of the shifting distress she had stifled for so long. And she knows, she is *certain*, that the thing that led the poor man out onto the lonely water was the rage and isolation of the neglected creature inside him.

The desperate, unloved, darkest side of himself: ignored and silenced, it would have dragged him down to the coldest depths. Ignored and silenced, Mary's creature would have done the same to her. But she will not spurn and reject it again. She will take its rough-palmed hand in her own and she will drag it into her arms.

'Are you thinking about your story?' Shelley asks her.

Again, she'd half forgotten he was there. As she turns to him, she sees that new wariness in his eyes, as if he doesn't truly know her, or what to expect from her, now that he has seen her darkness, her ugliness, her fury.

'I'm thinking about the creature.' She pauses. '*My* creature.'

'Will you tell me about him?' He holds out his own hand, his expression hopeful.

She hesitates, then places her palm in his. His hand is strong, his smooth skin familiar. As he pulls her close and begins to walk back to the carriage, he waits for her to speak.

She takes a breath, aware that, perhaps for the first time, he is truly ready to listen.

He holds her hand while they walk by the storm-battered shore. Though she has spoken very little, she has the feeling that she could say anything she wanted. The sensation carries a pleasant vertigo.

Back in the carriage, they pass fishermen repairing their nets, the weak sunlight retreating behind a cloudy haze as wind gusts in from the east. Everything is thrown into shadow – the frost that silvers the trees, the dark water of the lake, rumpled fabric in the wind. The rust on the fishermen's blunted knives, like old blood.

A distant stag booms, belling a warning through the valley, its antique antlers, ancient spires, or like the raised hands of kneeling worshippers in a church.

Ahead, the signature of the rocks and mountains, scrawled against the sky in a child's unsteady, heavy-handed scratches. For the first time today, Mary feels apprehension. The peaks don't look real. They are too distant and too huge, forgotten gods, hewn from something that is too vast and elemental for Mary ever to comprehend. She feels dwarfed and insignificant. And yet, at the same time, the awe that raises the hairs on the back of her neck seems to be reaching for the great unknown authority that rests within those jagged peaks. Some inner part of her has been waiting for these mountains, just as she feels that some part of them is waiting for her.

At first, as the carriage travels higher, she thinks of Dr

Frankenstein and of what it would feel like to be an intelligent man, wealthy and beloved, who has the arrogance to think he can create life and is then appalled by the thing he has fashioned.

It shouldn't just be the creature's appearance that horrifies him, Mary decides. Frankenstein will be furious that his creation has its own free will, that this hideous wretch reasons and argues like a lawyer, while containing all the rage and violence of a rejected child.

As they clatter ever higher, over the untrodden black and seedless rock, Mary thinks of her mother's diaries about her journeys through Norway and Sweden, where she had described the mountains as *the bones of the world, waiting to be clothed with everything necessary to give life and beauty.*

Strange: when she was a child, she used to long for her mother to hold her, to carry her. More and more now, she thinks of how much she would have loved to meet Mary Wollstonecraft as a grown woman. Her mother must have loved her, must have carried her carefully in the swell of her belly, spoken to her and sung to her before Mary knew what life was. How terrified her mother must have been as she fought, in agony and exhaustion, spilled blood and split flesh, to bring her daughter through her bewildered body into the world.

Mary, who is half the age her mother was when she died, would still be old enough now to comfort that labouring woman in her pain. She would be able to hold her, to tell her that she was doing so well, so well.

With her own hands, which she has been told are so like her mother's, Mary would have held a glass of water to that pained woman's lips, cradling her head as she drank; she would have wiped the hair back from her damp forehead and gazed into her frightened eyes.

She would have told the dying woman, *She's alive, your daughter. She's going to live.*

And more quietly, against the curled shell of the woman's ear, she would have whispered, *She will create something astonishing.*

Because this is how her story feels to her now: not *excellent* or *very good* or any of the words that Shelley and the others have used to describe it.

Her story feels astonishing and new and unlike anything she has seen before, in the same way that a newborn baby, laid on its mother's chest, is the most miraculous creature she has ever seen.

Late afternoon, and the sun drops behind the mountains, casting them into instant shadow and cold. The lake is behind and below them now – the menacing peaks of the mountains are far closer, far bigger. Above and ahead, the crags tower in huge walls of ice, though it is July and the snow should long since have melted, the ice receded.

There is a thundering, like the approach of hundreds of hoofs. When they round the corner, Mary sees that their way is blocked by a stream of water, which gushes from the mountain, across the path and flings itself over the rock into some unseen dark crevasse below.

The *voiturier* stops the carriage next to two small ramshackle huts and a low-roofed barn, all so covered with moss that Mary would have thought them part of the mountain.

'No further,' the *voiturier* calls. 'I go back now.'

Before Shelley can answer, Mary climbs from the carriage. 'You said you'd take us to Chamonix.'

The *voiturier* scowls. 'Too much ice melt. Too dangerous. You stay here.'

He indicates the huts, where Mary can see, in the window, a dim candle burning, a shadow moving.

'Perhaps we should turn back, Mary,' Shelley says.

She waves away his comment and addresses the *voiturier*. 'How will we continue our journey tomorrow?'

'Tomorrow?' He gives a bark of humourless laughter. Then he must see something fierce in Mary's face because his expression grows serious. 'Very dangerous. Strange weather. Too much ice falls.'

He looks up at the mountain, crosses himself. 'The man who live here, very experience in snow. He has mules. Better for the path.'

Before he leaves, he knocks on the door of one of the huts and talks in rapid French to a broad-shouldered, craggy-faced man, who stares at them, in apparent disbelief.

As the two men talk, Mary hears the words *fou* and *mort*.

Madness and death. Yet she has never felt clearer, has never felt more alive.

For an exorbitant fee, the craggy-faced man, who introduces himself as Monsieur Moritz, lets them sleep in his tiny hut, in chairs pulled close to the fire. A frigid wind gusts around her ankles and the cramped room is full of choking smoke, so they barely sleep. Still, Mary can't help the joy that rises through her.

She feels as she had felt when she and Shelley first escaped to France: as though she has forced a different, secret part of a map to open up before her. The future stretches out, obscure in the mists of the unknown, but the thought of everything it might contain fills her with a thrumming energy.

Perhaps Shelley feels the same, because he reaches out in the night and takes her hand, threading his fingers through hers. In the cold and the darkness, he squeezes her palm. She squeezes back.

*

Before the sun has fully risen the next morning, Monsieur Moritz rouses them from the chairs next to his fire and takes them out to where he has saddled two mules. He will guide them as long as it is safe. If they still want to go on, he will leave them to continue alone.

Even with the mules, it is a hard climb through thick fog and Mary fears that the *voiturier* was right – there is a storm coming and they are foolish, risking their lives. But when they reach the end of the path overlooking the frozen lake, they stop and stare.

The sky is a scouring blue. A few leafless trees are sketched across the slopes, like the scattered bleached bones from long-dead hands.

Beyond, fangs of snow bite skyward. At the base of the mountains, a frayed white lace of ice spreads across the darkness of a vast, frozen lake. In the distance, the white-peaked summit of Mont Blanc disappears into dark clouds.

Even Shelley is speechless. It is a place of wonder: mountains like an unopened letter, their solitude absolute. Though the snow on them must one day thaw and melt into streams, something about it looks eternal and untouched. It is as if she and Shelley have entered another age, another time. Or as if they have stepped out of time altogether.

They scramble down from the mules and into the valley, picking their way over hummocks of ice and around deep crevasses.

Shelley's mood has lifted again: he talks excitedly about the beauty of the place, his face alight with awe, desperate for Mary to share his delight – desperate, she sees, for her admiration, her love.

Perhaps the thinner mountain air is unravelling her thoughts, but suddenly, it seems simple: in this moment, he wants her to be happy and, in this moment, she is.

And, for this moment, that is enough.

Splinters of ice on her skin make her gasp, almost comically, and all at once she and Shelley are laughing as he balls up snow and hurls it into the hood of her cloak.

She feels again the old delight in his childlike impetuousness, his impulsivity, which had seemed so charming at first but had gradually become wearing, exhausting – just as the snow itself, so enchanting now, would become tedious if she had to live in it every day. She would grow weary of the frost seeping into her bones, slush slipping into her boots, the immaculate drifts sagging into soot-stained mush.

She slips and nearly falls into the snow. Shelley reaches out and pulls her upright.

'I'm sorry I left you,' he says.

'You came back.'

'I did. But sometimes, even when I was there, I left you all alone. I'm sorry.'

In the past, she'd have told him she forgave him. She'd have said it didn't matter when it did. It does.

'I love you very much,' he says. 'I'm so glad I found you.'

'I know.' She smiles, then kisses his chin. He wants more from her, but she will not say what she does not feel. Not any more.

In time, her love for him will return, growing back slowly, painfully, like a wind-blasted tree, its roots meshed improbably into the side of a mountain.

He gazes at her. 'Do you ever regret escaping with me to France?'

'Sometimes,' she says. And she can see that her honesty hurts him, but their lies and secrets have hurt them both.

'I never regret it, Mary. Not for an instant. I'll never regret rescuing you from your father's house.'

'Is that what you believe happened?'

'Well, isn't it?'

'You didn't rescue me.' She smooths his windblown hair and, before he can object, before he can ask what she means, she turns and climbs on, scrambling up the mountain.

'Wait for me.' He follows.

When the blizzard comes in, it throws them to their knees.

Mary is alone suddenly in a blank space that is otherworldly and strange.

Lost in thought and amazement, neither of them has paid attention to the storm sweeping in. The clouds above are black, the wind picks up. Without warning the air is thick with stinging snow; it is impossible to see, impossible to move.

Mary stops and falls to a crouch, afraid that if she takes another step, she will plummet into a crevasse.

She calls, but the snow fills her mouth. The wind throws her voice back into her face.

The snow stings her eyes, clings to her lashes. She dashes her hands across her face and blinks into the shifting white void ahead of her.

Is that someone moving up ahead? A huge, grey shape, lurching through the snow – too big to be Shelley, too fast and sure-footed to be a man at all.

It is here. Her heart alarms with the sudden knowledge of it, the certainty that drops through her body, like a sharpened stone.

Somehow the creature has found her. The awful, beautiful, brutal thing she has created has crawled out of her nightmares, slipped from beneath her skin, and now it is roaming the frozen, snow-swamped mountain.

She wants to remain huddled on the ground, wants to curl into a tight ball and wait for the blizzard to pass but she knows she must not, she cannot.

To stop is to die; to lie down is to die. She forces herself to her feet and walks, though every step feels like wading against an icy torrent. Each movement burns, as though her muscles are being torn from her bones, but still she walks.

She will not lie down. She will not die.

The whiteness closes in around her, like the jaws of some malicious, predatory being, but she pushes forward. With every step, she wipes her hands across her eyes and sees, ahead of her, the shadowy figure of the creature.

It is drawing her onwards.

It is leading her.

Her mind reduces to a frantic, animal thing: follow; move; survive.

One step after another, she moves closer to the creature, closer to its huge, muscular bulk, which is inhuman, but is also the most human thing she can imagine – lonely, filled with a desperate desire to be seen and known and understood. To be loved.

She is almost within arm's reach, close enough to hear its gasping breath. She stretches out and touches – nothing. It is lost in darkness and distance.

A gust of wind and the snow flurries around her.

'Where are you?' she cries.

Where are you? the creature shouts.

'Come back!' she roars.

Come back!

It is when the roar returns her own voice to her that she understands.

The creature was never here.

The creature is always here.

The creature is her own ferocious, indefatigable will: her hunger to survive; her determination to be heard; her yearning to be understood. It has been with her from her first furious, motherless howl and it will stay with her until her last letting go.

She hears another cry, another voice in the snow, which fractures her reverie.

'Mary!' Faint but clear, ahead of her. 'Mary!'

'Shelley!'

A brief burst of sunlight through a break in the clouds and the snow and she sees him.

This is the moment that she will recall in dreams for years to come: the shape of him, outlined against the polished sheen of the frozen world. The shadow of a man, hand up to his face to shield his eyes from the blinding illumination – straining to see her.

She thinks he spots her. He lifts his hand higher, waving, as if he is sinking beneath vast waves, but is still struggling, still reaching out to touch her.

She lifts her own hand in return, stretching across the distance to find him.

Acknowledgements

I am so grateful to all those who have cheered on the writing of this book over the last four years. It's been a labour of love and I know all those involved in supporting the delivery of this novel have noted, along with me, the (wonderful, meta) irony of me struggling to write a novel about a writer struggling to write a novel. At four in the morning, when I was woken yet again by the need, desire and drive to write, I felt very close to Mary Godwin. Thanks must go to her for writing such an incredible novel. Since it was first published, *Frankenstein* has never been out of print. It has consumed readers and viewers and the social consciousness, in much the same way that it must have consumed its writer, more than two hundred years ago.

To my fierce, brilliant, brutally honest agent Nelle Andrew, for all your support and faith in me and my work, thank you. I am so very lucky to have you in my corner, along with all the lovely team at RML.

Thank you so much to my wonderful, insightful editor, Jill Taylor, for your patience, enthusiasm and cheerful belief in my writing. I'm so grateful for the ways in which you push me to make every book better than the last. Every time I write, I have your voice in my head, demanding more pace, more plot, more . . . everything!

It's such a privilege to be published by Penguin, Michael Joseph. Thank you to Sriya Varadharajan, Paula Flanagan, Jessie Beswick for all your brilliance in bringing this book into the world. The cover is a work of genius! Hazel Orme, copyeditor extraordinaire, thank you for your eagle eye: your sharp instincts and perception are so humbling. I'm so grateful, also, to the brilliant Bea McIntyre – you and your wonderful team of proofreaders have saved me from my missteps countless times. Thank you also to Sarah Scarlett and the MJ Rights team, who have pitched this novel so wonderfully to editors in Europe and the US – knowing that my work will be published in other countries and other languages is such an honour.

To all the booksellers at Waterstones and at independent bookshops (particularly Mog and Pauline at Warwick Books and Judy and Charlotte at Kenilworth Books), I cannot thank you enough. Knowing that you recommend my books to customers time and again is mind-blowing and I'm so grateful. Huge thanks, also, to all the wonderful book bloggers, BookTokers, Bookstagrammers and other book enthusiasts who have championed my work.

Thank you so much to my early readers, Elizabeth Schächter and Claire Williams; you were so very generous with your time and comments. And to Luisa Cheshire, most wonderful of friends, thank you for your lovely comments about the other book, which I drafted before this one! I also want to thank Bill and Nettie Gurney, who are so fantastic and insightful about, well, everything, but especially books.

Enormous thanks to Jonathan Davidson at Writing West Midlands and to Angela Hicken at the West Midlands Readers' Network.

Thanks must go to all the friends who have supported me over the years of writing this book and listened patiently to my doubts and fears and endless quibbles and wobbles: Laura Baxter, Sachin Choithramani, Penny Clarke, Andrea Docherty, Harriet Gott, Jane Guest, Alison Hall, Elodie Harper, Bansi Kara, Adele Kenny, Sarah Kenrick, Pamela Lyddon, Anna

Mazzola, Jenny Mitchell-Hilton, Ritch Partridge, Claire Revell, Emma Ritson, Cathy Thompson, Phil Tuck, Bert Ward-Penny.

To my Mum, Sue Lea, and my sisters, Annabelle Flambard, Sophie Pooler, Penny Mourant and Chris Beresford – thanks and so much love.

To Jinny Sumner, who helped me more than I can ever articulate and to whom I owe more thanks than I can ever express. I couldn't have written this book without the insight you helped me to find.

Thank you, dear reader, for your dedication in getting this far . . . and for recommending this book to all your friends. Or your enemies. I'm not fussy.

Lastly, as always and with *so* much love, to my boys, Arthur and Rupert, whom I adore an unreasonable amount. I love talking about stories with you. I love talking about everything with you. And to Roger, you lovely, funny, clever dickhead. Thank you for being the opposite of Byron and Shelley in all the ways that count.